DEATHWING

It was impossible to tell where the man had ended and the machine began.

Its entire body was soaked in blood, gobbets of torn flesh still hanging from its claws and teeth. But the final horror, the most sickening thing of all was that where the metal of the dreadnought's hide was still visible, it was coloured an all too familiar shade of dark green.

And upon its shoulder was the symbol of the Dark Angels.

Whatever this creature was, it had once been a brother Space Marine.

Now it was the Angel of Blades and as the Space Marines recoiled in horror, the monster howled in mad triumph and stamped forwards on its scythe legs.

More Warhammer 40,000 from the Black Library

• GAUNT'S GHOSTS •

FIRST & ONLY by Dan Abnett

GHOSTMAKER by Dan Abnett

NECROPOLIS by Dan Abnett

HONOUR GUARD by Dan Abnett

• SPACE WOLF •

SPACE WOLF by William King

RAGNAR'S CLAW by William King

• LAST CHANCERS •

13TH LEGION by Gav Thorpe

KILL TEAM by Gav Thorpe

• EISENHORN •

XENOS by Dan Abnett

• OTHER WARHAMMER 40,000 TITLES •

EXECUTION HOUR by Gordon Rennie

PAWNS OF CHAOS by Brian Craig

EYE OF TERROR by Barrington J. Bayley

INTO THE MAELSTROM
eds. Marc Gascoigne & Andy Jones

STATUS: DEADZONE
eds. Marc Gascoigne & Andy Jones

DARK IMPERIUM
eds. Marc Gascoigne & Andy Jones

DEATHWING

Edited by
Neil Jones & David Pringle

A BLACK LIBRARY PUBLICATION

First published in Great Britain in 1990 by
GW Books, a division of Games Workshop Ltd., UK.
This edition comprised the following stories:
Deathwing, Devil's Marauders, Lacrymata, The Alien Beast Within,
Seed of Doubt, Warped Stars and Monastery of Death.

This edition published in Great Britain in 2001 by
Games Workshop Publishing,
Willow Road, Lenton, Nottingham, NG7 2WS, UK.
Pestilence, Suffer Not the Unclean to Live and Unforgiven first published
in *Inferno* magazine, copyright © Games Workshop Ltd, 2001.

First US edition, November 2001

10 9 8 7 6 5 4 3 2 1

Distributed by Simon & Schuster
1230 Avenue of the Americas
New York, NY 10020

Cover illustration by Paul Dainton

ISBN 0-7434-1171-4

Set in ITC Giovanni

Printed and bound in Great Britain by
Cox & Wyman Ltd, Cardiff Rd, Reading, Berkshire RG1 8EX, UK

See the Black Library on the Internet at
www.blacklibrary.co.uk

Find out more about Games Workshop
and the world of Warhammer 40,000 at
www.games-workshop.com

CONTENTS

DEATHWING

Bryan Ansell & William King

*T*HE PASSAGE OF time *is ineluctable, irresistible. It touches everything, and its touch is change. All living beings are doomed to a mayfly existence, their brief efflorescence largely unnoticed among so many millions, billions of others. Only the undying Emperor endures, humanity's light in the darkness. Like the sea beating against a cliff, time wears away all that has been built, all that has been created, all that has been dreamed. History turns into legend, and even legends are slowly changed, finally forgotten.*

What follows is just one of the legends of the Deathwing, the First Company of the Dark Angels chapter. Like all legends, it changes with the telling, so that every one who hears it and retells it perpetuates the process of change. Who can now say what the truth of the matter ever was?

CLOUD RUNNER GAZED on the wreckage of his home and felt like weeping. He closed his eyes and took three breaths, but when he looked again, nothing had changed. He turned back towards the dropship *Deathwing*.

Weasel-Fierce had just descended from the ramp. He gazed round ferally at what once had been Cloud Runner's village and brought his storm bolter into attack position. A grin split his skull-like face.

'Dark Angels, be wary. Death has walked here,' he said. The sun glistened off Weasel-Fierce's black Terminator armour. With his white hair and Y-shaped scar-tattoos, he looked like the Eater of Bones come back to claim the world.

Cloud Runner shook his head in disbelief. For two hundred years he had held the memory of this place in his mind. Although the chapter was his home and the battle brothers were his family, he had always felt his spirit would return here when the Emperor granted him rest.

He glanced in the direction of the burial mounds. They had been broken open.

Cloud Runner made his way to the entrance. He could see that the bones had been broken and mingled. It was a blasphemy that only the bitterest of foes would perform. It marked the ending of his clan.

'The ghosts of my ancestors wander homeless,' he said. 'They will become drinkers of blood and eaters of excrement. My clan is dishonoured.'

He felt a heavy, gauntleted hand on his shoulder and turned to see Lame Bear gazing down on him. Two centuries ago, Cloud Runner and he had belonged to enemy clans. Now the clansmen who they had fought alongside were dead, and the old rivalry had long ago become fast friendship.

'The Dark Angels are your people now,' Lame Bear said in his soft voice. 'If necessary we will avenge this dishonour.'

Cloud Runner shook his head. 'That is not the way. The warriors from the sky are above the squabblings of the clans. We choose only the bravest of the plains people. We take no sides.'

'Your words do honour to the chapter, brother-captain,' Lame Bear said, stooping to pick up something that lay in the grass. Cloud Runner saw that it was a metal axe-head. Sorrow warred with curiosity and won.

'This was not the homecoming I had imagined,' Cloud Runner said softly. 'Where are children gathering flowers for the autumn feast? Where are the young bucks racing out to count coup on our armour? Where are the spirit-talkers who wish to commune with us? Dead. All dead.'

Lame Bear limped away, leaving Cloud Runner alone with his grief.

TWO HEADS TALKING studied the desiccated bodies within the lodge. One had been an old warrior. His shrivelled hand still clutched a stone axe inscribed with the thunderbird rune. The other had been a squaw. Between her skeletal fingers was the neck of an infant.

'She strangled the child rather than let it fall into the hands of the enemy,' Bloody Moon said. The librarian noticed the undercurrent of horror in the Marine's voice. He took a deep breath, trying to ignore the musty stench that filled the long house.

'Something evil happened here, but it happened decades ago,' Two Heads Talking replied, seeking to relieve Bloody Moon's superstitious fear. He wanted time to consider, to probe the events of the past. The aura of old terror almost smothered him. Shadows lay over this lodge. Something was ominously familiar about the psychic aura of the area.

'Lord-shaman...' Bloody Moon began.

The librarian almost smiled. The habits of their ancient former lives had returned in strength now that they once more walked the soil of their homeworld.

'Brother-librarian is my title, Bloody Moon. You are no longer my honour guard. We are both Marines.'

'Lord– brother-shaman,' Bloody Moon continued. 'No warriors of the plains would have wrought such havoc. Do you think–'

'We shall have to investigate, old friend. We must visit the other lodgetowns and speak with their chieftains. If someone has returned to the customs of the reaving time, we will put an end to it.'

It was rumoured that some of the hill clans still kept to the old daemon-worshipping practices from the time before the Emperor's people came. If that were true, it was up to the Space Marines to take action. Somehow Two Heads Talking did not think it would come to that. This did not have the feel of daemon worshippers, although there was a taint in the air that was akin to it. An almost recognisable horror clawed at his mind. He fought it down and hoped that his suspicions were not true.

THE CITY REARED above the plain like a soot-grimed leviathan. Cloud Runner spotted it before the others and ordered Lame Bear to land the dropship in a valley, out of sight of its walls.

From the brow of the hill, he studied it through magnoculars. It was an ugly place that reminded him of the hiveworlds he had visited. It covered many miles and was enclosed by monolithic walls. Great smokestacks loomed in the distance, belching acrid chemical clouds into the greyish sky.

Outside the walls, the river ran black with poisons. As Cloud Runner watched, he saw herd elk being driven squealing from barges towards great abattoirs within the walls. From huge stone barracks, people swarmed through the streets towards enormous, brick factories.

Smog drifted everywhere, occasionally obscuring the grimy city and its teeming inhabitants.

'That is where Lame Bear's metal axe came from,' Two Heads Talking said, lowering himself to the ground beside Cloud Runner. 'I wonder who built it?'

'It's a nightmare,' murmured Cloud Runner. 'We return home to find our lodges ravaged and this… abomination in its place.'

'That city could hold all the clans of all the peoples of the plains and ten times more besides. Could our folk have been enslaved and taken there, brother-captain?'

Cloud Runner remained silent, considering. 'If they have been, then we will go down with flamer and storm bolter and free them.'

'We must know more before we act. We could be outnumbered and trapped,' replied the shaman.

'I say we go in with weapons armed,' said Weasel-Fierce from behind them. 'If we find foes, we burn them.'

'Suppose they think the same? The soot and filth give the place an orkish look,' said Lame Bear. He had been scouting further along the crest.

'No ork ever put stone on stone like that,' countered Two Heads Talking. 'That is human workmanship.'

'It is not the work of the people,' said Cloud Runner. 'Those barracks are a hundred times the size of a lodgehouse and built of brick.'

'There is only one way to find out anything,' said Two Heads Talking. 'One of us must visit the city.'

The warriors nodded assent. Each tapped a scar-tattoo to indicate that he volunteered.

Two Heads Talking shook his head. 'I must go. The spirits will shield me.'

Cloud Runner saw the rest of the warriors look at him to see what his decision would be. As captain, he could overrule the librarian. He looked at the city, then at the shaman standing quiet and proud before him.

A sensation of emptiness, of futility came over him. His people, his village had gone.

'As you wish, lord-shaman. Speak to the spirits and seek their aid,' he said, giving the ancient ritual answer. 'Bloody Moon's squad will remain here to watch over you. The rest of us will take *Deathwing* and seek out any surviving lodgetowns.'

NIGHT FELL AS Two Heads Talking completed his preparations. He laid the four rune-etched skulls of his predecessors on the ground about him. Each faced one of the cardinal points of the compass and watched over an approach from the spirit realm.

He lit a small bonfire in the deep hollow, cast a handful of herbs on the fire and breathed in deeply. He touched the ceremonial winged skull on his chest-piece and then the death's head inlaid on his belt. Lastly, he prayed to the Emperor, tamer of thunderbirds and beacon of the soul path, to watch over him as he made magic. Then he began to chant.

The fumes from the herbs filled his lungs. He seemed to rise above his body and look down upon it. The other Terminators backed away from the spirit circle. A chill stole over him, and life leeched away until he was close to the edge of death. Great sobs wracked his body, but he mastered himself and continued with the ritual.

He stood in a cold shadowy place. He sensed chill white presences at the edge of his perception, clammy as mist and cold as the gravemound. Above him he could hear the beating of mighty pinions from where Deathwing, the Emperor's steed and bearer of the souls of the slain, hovered.

The shaman talked with the presences, made pacts that bound them to his service and rewarded them with a portion of his strength. He sensed the hungry spirits surge around him, ready to shield him from sight, to cloud the eyes of any who might look upon him, causing them to see only a friendly being.

He walked from the circle, past the watching Marines. As he crested the brow of the hill, he saw the distant city. Even at night, its fires burned, lighting the sky and turning the metropolis into a giant shadow cast upon the land.

ABOVE THEM, THROUGH the gloom, loomed the Mountains of Storm. Cloud Runner wondered how Lame Bear was taking it. The big man's face was a blank mask. He was not allowing himself to think about what might have happened to his people.

The Hunting Bear village was the last they had visited: the most remote, built in caves beneath Cloud-Girt Peak. Lame Bear limped up the narrow pathway in the cliff-face.

Cloud Runner tried not to think of the other lodgetowns they had seen. They had found nothing but desolation and desecrated graves. No living soul except the Marines walked among the fallen totems. They had buried the bodies they had found and offered prayers to the Emperor for the safety of their slain kin.

Cloud Runner could see Weasel-Fierce pause. The gaunt man's hand played with the feathered hilt of his ceremonial dagger. He studied the ledges above the paths and seemed to sniff the air.

'No sentries,' he said. 'As a buck, I raided these mountains. The Hunting Bears always had the keenest watchers. If anyone was alive, we would have been challenged by now.'

'No!' Lame Bear shouted and ran across the lodgetown's threshold and into the caverns.

'Squad Paulo, overwatch!' Cloud Runner ordered. Five Terminators froze in position, guarding the entrance.

'The rest of you, follow me. Helmets on. Keep your eyes peeled. Weasel-Fierce, establish a fix on Lame Bear. Don't lose him.'

Night-lights cut in as they entered the cave mouth. Dozens of tunnels led from the place. Chittering things flapped away from their lights. For a moment, Cloud Runner allowed himself to feel hopeful. If they were to find any survivors of the plains people, it would be here. In this huge night-black maze Lame Bear's people could have hidden out for years, dodging any pursuit.

As they followed Lame Bear's locator signal through the warren of tunnels, despair filled Cloud Runner. They passed hallways where the dead lay. Sometimes the bodies were marred by the mark of spear and axe; sometimes they were crushed and mangled by inhuman force. Some had been ripped asunder. Cloud Runner had seen bodies butchered like that before but told himself that it was not possible here. Such a thing could not happen on his homeworld – in vast hulks that lay cold in space, perhaps, but not here.

They found Lame Bear standing in the largest cave of all. Bones littered the floor. Scuttlers fled from their lights. Lame Bear sobbed and pointed to the walls. Paintings dating from the earliest times covered the caveside, but it was the last and highest-situated representation that drew Cloud Runner's attention. There was no mistaking the four-armed, malevolent form. Hatred and fear chased each other through his mind.

'Genestealers,' he spat. Behind him, Lame Bear moaned. Weasel-Fierce gave his short, barking laugh. The sound chilled Cloud Runner to the bone.

TWO HEADS TALKING stalked past the city's open gates. The stench assailed his nostrils. His concentration faltered, and he could feel the spirits struggling to escape. He exerted his iron will, and the spell of protection fell into place.

Studying his surroundings, he realised that he had no need to worry. There were no guards, only a toll-house where a pasty-faced clerk sat, ticking off accounts. In its own way this was ominous: the city's builders obviously did not feel threatened enough to post sentries.

Two Heads Talking studied the scribe. He sat at a little window, poring over a ledger. In his hand was a quill pen. He was writing by the light of a small lantern. Momentarily, he seemed to sense the librarian's presence and looked up. He had the high cheek-bones and ruddy skin of the plains people, but there the resemblance ended.

His limbs seemed stunted and weak. His features had an unhealthy pallor. He gave a hacking cough and returned to his work. His face showed no sign of manhood scars. His clothes were made of some coarse-woven cloth, not elk leather. No weapon sat near at hand, and he showed no resentment at being cooped up in the tiny office rather than being under the open sky. Two Heads Talking found it hard to believe that this was a descendant of his warrior culture.

He pushed on into the city, picking his way fastidiously through the narrow, dirty streets that ran between the enormous buildings. The place was laid out with no rhyme or reason. Vast squares lay between the great factories, but there was no apparent plan. The city had grown uncontrolled, like a cancer.

There were no sewers, and the roads were full of filth. The smell of human waste mingled with the odour of frying food and the sharp tang of cheap alcohol. Low shadowy doors of inns and food booths rimmed each square.

Unwashed children scuttled everywhere. Now and again, huge, well-fed men in long, blue coats pushed their way through the throng. They had facial scar-tattoos and they walked with an air of swaggering pride. If anyone got in their way, they lashed out at them with wooden batons. To Two Heads Talking's surprise, no one hit back. They seemed too weak-spirited to fight.

As he wandered, the librarian noticed something even more horrible. All the members of the crowd, except the urchins and the bluecoats, were maimed. Men and women both had mangled limbs or scorched faces. Some hobbled on wooden crutches, swinging the stumps of legs before them. Others were blind and were led about by children. A dwarf with no legs waddled past, using his arms for motion, walking on the palms of his hands.

They all seemed to be the accidental victims of some huge, industrial process.

In the darkness, by the light dancing from the hellish chimneys, they moved like shadows, scrabbling about crying for alms, for succour, for deliverance. They called on the heavenly father, the four-armed Emperor, to save them. They cursed and raved and pleaded under a polluted sky. Two Heads Talking watched the poor steal from the poor and wondered how his people had come to be laid so low.

He remembered the tall, strong warriors who had dwelled in the lodgetowns and asked nothing of any man. What malign magic could have transformed the people of the plains into these pathetic creatures?

He felt a shock as a child tugged at his arm. 'Tokens, elder. Tokens for food.'

Two Heads Talking sighed with relief. His spell still held. The child saw only a safe, unobtrusive figure. He could feel the strain of binding the spirits gnawing away at him subconsciously, but they had not yet slipped his grasp.

'I have nothing for you, boy,' he said.

The urchin ran off, mouthing obscenities.

DEPRESSED AND ANGRY, the Space Marines left the cave village. Cloud Runner noticed that Lame Bear's face was white. He gestured for the big man and Weasel-Fierce to follow him. The two squad leaders fell in beside him. They marched up to a great spur of rock and looked down into a long valley.

'Stealers,' he said. 'We must inform the Imperium.'

Weasel-fierce spat over the edge of the cliff.

'The dark city is theirs,' Lame Bear said. There was a depth of hatred in his quiet voice that Cloud Runner understood. 'They must have conquered the people and herded them within.'

'Some clans resisted,' Cloud Runner said. He was proud of that. The fact that his clan had chosen to continue a hopeless struggle rather than surrender gave him some comfort.

'Our world is ended; our time is done,' said Weasel-Fierce. His words tolled like great, sad bells within Cloud Runner's skull. Weasel-Fierce was right. Their entire culture had been exterminated.

The only ones who could remember the world of the plains people were the Space Marines of the Dark Angels. When they died the clans would live only in the chapter fleet's records. Unless the Dark Angels broke with tradition and recruited from other worlds, the chapter would end with the death of the present generation of Space Marines.

Cloud Runner felt hollow. He had returned home with such high hopes. He was going to walk once more among his people, see again his village before old age took him. Now he found his world was dead, had been for a long time.

'And we never knew,' he said softly. 'Our clans have been dead for years, and we never knew. It was a cursed day when we rode the *Deathwing* back to our homeworld.'

The squad leaders stood silent. The moon broke through the clouds. Below them, in the valley, they saw the faded outline of a giant winged skull cut into the earth.

'What is that?' asked Weasel-Fierce. 'It was not here when last I stalked in the valley.'

Lame Bear gave him an odd look. Cloud Runner knew that his old friend had never pictured the brave of an enemy clan walking in his people's sacred valley.

Even after a century, the taciturn, skeletal man could still surprise them.

'It was where our spirit talkers made magic,' answered Lame Bear. 'They must have tried to summon Deathwing, the bearer of the warriors from the sky. They must have been desperate to attempt such a summons. They trusted us to protect them. We never came.'

Cloud Runner heard Weasel-Fierce growl. 'We will avenge them,' he said.

Lame Bear nodded agreement. 'We will go in and scour the city.'

'We number only thirty, against possibly an entire city of stealers. The codex is quite clear on situations like this. We should virus bomb the planet from orbit,' Cloud Runner said, listening to the silence settle. Lame Bear and Weasel-Fierce looked at him, appalled.

'But what of our people? They may still survive,' Lame Bear said, like a man without much hope. 'We must at least consider that possibility before we cleanse our homeworld of life.'

Weasel-Fierce had gone pale. Cloud Runner had never seen him look so dismayed.

'I cannot do it,' he said softly. 'Can you, brother captain? Can you give the order that will destroy our world – and our people – forever?'

Cloud Runner felt the weight of terrible responsibility settle on him. His duty was clear. Here on this world was a great threat to the Imperium. His word would condemn his entire people to oblivion. He tried not to consider that Lame Bear might be right, that the people might not yet be totally enslaved by the genestealer horde. But the thought nagged at him most of all because he hoped it was true.

He stood frozen for a moment, paralysed by the enormity of the decision.

'The choice is not yours alone, Cloud Runner,' said Weasel-Fierce. 'It is a matter for all the warriors of the people.'

Cloud Runner looked into his burning eyes. Weasel-Fierce had invoked the ancient ritual; by rights, it should be answered. The Terminator captain looked at Lame Bear. The giant's face was grim.

Cloud Runner nodded. 'There must be a gathering,' he said.

TWO HEADS TALKING saw a commotion break out across the square. A squad of bluecoats forced the maimed beggars to one side. People were crushed underfoot as they pushed through the throng like a blade through flesh.

The librarian dropped back toward the entrance of a tavern. A surly bravo with fresh-scarred cheeks came too close. He raised his truncheon to strike Two Heads Talking, obviously perceiving him as one of the throng. It bounced off the carapace of his Terminator armour. The bluecoat squinted in astonishment at him, and then backed away.

A palanquin borne by two squat, shaven-headed men in brown uniforms moved through the path cleared by the bully-boys. Two Heads Talking looked at the sign of a four-armed man on its side and a thrill of fear passed through him. His worst suspicions were justified.

'Alms, elder, give us alms,' the crowd pleaded, voices merging into one mighty roar. Many had abased themselves and kneeled, stumps and grasping hands outstretched in supplication towards the palanquin.

A curtain in its side was pulled back, and a short, fat man stepped out. His pale skin had a bluish tint, and he was wearing a rich suit of black cloth, a white waistcoat and high, black leather boots. A four-armed pendant dangled from a chain hanging around his neck. His head was totally hairless, and he had piercing black eyes. He gazed out at the crowd and smiled gloatingly, great jowls rippling backward to give him a dozen small chins.

He reached down and found a purse. The crowd held its breath expectantly. For a second, his gaze fell on the librarian, and he looked puzzled. A frown crossed his face. Two Heads Talking felt a tug on his leg and fell to one knee, although it went against the grain to kneel to anything except the image of the Emperor. He felt that malign glance linger upon him and

wondered whether the fat man had somehow penetrated his
bound spirits' disguise.

ALL THE SQUADS gathered around the fire. The great logs smouldered in the dark, underlighting the faces of the Marines, making
them look daemonic. Behind them, *Deathwing* sat on its landing
claws, a bulwark against the darkness. He knew that beyond it
lay the city of their enemy, where dwelled abomination.

Nearest the fires squatted the squad leaders, faces impassive.
Behind them were their men, in full battle regalia, storm
bolters and flamers near at hand. Firelight glittered on the
winged swords painted on their shoulder pieces. Their garb was
Imperial, but the scarred faces that showed in the firelight
belonged to the plains people.

He had known these men for so long that not even Two
Heads Talking could have done a better job of reading their
mood. In each stern visage, he saw a thirst for vengeance and a
desire for death. The warriors wished to join their clansmen in
the spirit realm. Cloud Runner, too, felt the tug of his ancestral
spirits, their clamour to be avenged. He tried to ignore their
voices. He was a soldier of the Emperor. He had other duties
than to his people.

'We must fight,' said Weasel-Fierce. 'The dead demand it. Our
clans need to be avenged. If any of our people survive, they
must be liberated. Our honour must be reclaimed.'

'There are many kinds of honour,' responded Bloody Moon.
'We honour the Emperor. Our Terminator suits are the badge of
that honour. They are signs of the honour our chapter does us.
Can we risk losing all traces of our chapter's ancient heritage to
the stealers?'

'For a hundred centuries, the armour we wear has borne
Marines safely through battle. The suits will not fail us now,'
replied Weasel-Fierce hotly. 'We can only add to their honour
by slaughtering our foe.'

'Brother Marius, Brother Paulo, pray silence,' Cloud Runner
said, invoking formality by the use of chapter ritual and calling
Weasel-Fierce and Bloody Moon by the names they had taken
on when they had become Marines. The two Terminators
bowed their heads, acknowledging the gravity of the moment.

'Forgive us, brother-captain, and name penance. We are at
your service. Semper fideles,' they replied.

'No penance is necessary.' Cloud Runner looked around the fire. All eyes were upon him. He weighed his words carefully before he spoke again.

'We are gathered tonight, not as soldiers of the Emperor, but by ancient custom, as warriors of the people. To this, I give my blessing as captain and warchief. We are here as speakers for our clans, joined in brotherhood so that we might speak with one voice, think as one mind and discern the correct path for all our peoples.'

Cloud Runner knew his words rang false. Those present were not speakers for their clans. They were their clans – all that was left.

Still, the ritual had been invoked and must be kept to.

'Within this circle there will be no violence. Till the ending of this gathering, we will be as one clan.'

It was strange to speak those words to warriors who had fought together in a thousand battles under a hundred suns. Yet it was the ancient rite of meeting, meant to ensure peaceful discourse among the warriors of rival tribes. He saw some Marines nod.

Suddenly, it felt right. The ways of their people had been born on this world, and while they were here, they would keep to them. In this time and space, they were bound by the ties of their common heritage. Each needed the reassurance after the trials of the day.

'We must speak concerning the fate of our world and our honour as warriors. This is a matter of life and death. Let us speak honestly, according to the manner of our people.'

THE ELDER FONDLED his chain of office and continued to stare at Two Heads Talking. A frown creased his high, bulbous forehead. Abruptly, he looked away and fumbled in his purse.

A ragged cheer went up from the crowd as he threw handfuls of gleaming iron tokens out to them, then withdrew into his palanquin to witness the scramble. The Space Marine watched people grovel in the dust, scrabbling for coins. He shook his head in disgust as he entered the tavern. Even the most debased hive world dweller would have shown more dignity than the rabble outside.

The place was nearly empty. Two Heads Talking looked around at the packed earth floor and the crudely made tables over which slouched a few ragged, unwashed drunks. The walls were covered in rough hangings which repeated a stylised four-armed pattern made to look like a crude star. Outside, in the distance, he heard the long, lonely wail of a steam whistle.

The innkeeper leaned forward against the counter, gut straining against the bar-top. Two Heads Talking walked over to him. As he reached the counter, he realised that he had no tokens. The innkeeper stared at him coldly, rubbing one stubbled, broken-veined cheek with a meaty paw.

'Well,' he demanded peremptorily. 'What do you want?'

Two Heads Talking was surprised by the man's rudeness. The people had always been a polite folk. It paid to show courtesy when an offended party might hit you with a stone axe. He met the man's gaze levelly and exerted a portion of his will. He met no resistance from the man's weak spirit, but even so, the effort was fatiguing.

The innkeeper turned away, eyes downcast, and poured a drink from a clay bottle, without being asked.

Outside the doorway came the sound of footsteps. The doors burst open, and a crowd of workers flooded in, bellowing orders for drink.

Both men and women had gaunt, tired faces. Their hands and bare feet were as grimy as their clothing. Two Heads Talking guessed that a shift had just ended. He took his drink and sat down in a corner, watching the workers slump down in the chairs, listening to them listlessly curse their overseers and their lack of tokens. A group set up a dice game in the corner and gambled indifferently.

After a while, Two Heads Talking noticed that people were drifting through a doorway in the back of the tavern. He rose and followed them. No one seemed to object.

The room he entered was dark and smelled of animal fat. In its centre was a pit surrounded by cheering, cursing workers. Two Heads Talking made his way forward, and the crowd melted away about him. He stood at the edge of the pit and saw the object of everyone's attention.

Down below, two great plains weasels were fighting, ripping long strips of flesh from each other while the audience roared and betted. Each was the size of a grown man and wore a spiked metal collar. One had lost an eye. Both were bleeding from dozens of cuts.

Two Heads Talking was disgusted. As a youth, he had hunted weasels, matching stone axe against ferocious cunning. It had been a challenge in which the warrior gambled his life against a fierce and deadly adversary. There was no challenge to this cruel sport. It was simply a safe outlet for the bloodlust of these weary, hungry workers.

The librarian departed from the pit, leaving the workers to their sport. As he left, he noticed that a bluecoat had entered the bar and was talking to the bartender. As he stepped outside, he saw that they were looking in his direction. He hurried into the smoggy night, thinking that he felt inhuman eyes watching him.

CLOUD RUNNER LOOKED at the faces round the fire. They were waiting for him to begin. He took three deep breaths. By long tradition, he must be the first to speak. A gathering of warriors was not an argument in the formal sense, where words were used as weapons to count coup on the enemy. It was a pooling of experience, a telling of stories. Words must have no sharp edges on which to snag anger. He chose his carefully.

'When I was twelve summers old,' he began, 'I dwelled in the yellow lodge among the young bucks. It was my last summer there, for I was pledged to marry Running Deer, who was the fairest maiden of my clan.

'Often, the bucks would talk of the warriors from the sky. A hundred years had passed since their last visit, and the red star was visible in the sky. The time was near for their return.

'Hawk Talon, my grandfather's grandfather, had been chosen and taken to the spirit realm to serve the Great Chief Beyond the Sky. My bloodline had acquired much honour because of it, although he had left his son fatherless and needing to found a new lodge.

'Silver Elk was a buck with whom I had vied for Running Deer's hand. Because she had chosen me, he hated me. He boasted of how he would be chosen. His words were a taunt, aimed at belittling my kinsman's honour. Silver Elk's own line had no spirits who had ridden Deathwing and ventured beyond the sky.

'I was stung and responded to his taunt. I said that, if that were so, he wouldn't mind climbing Ghost Mountain and visiting the Abode of the Ancestors.'

Cloud Runner paused to let his words sink in, to let the warriors imagine the scene. The memory seemed fresh and clear in his own mind. He could almost smell the acrid wood smoke filling the young men's lodge and see the furs hanging from its ceiling.

'That was what Silver Elk had wanted me to say. He sneered and replied that he would go to the mountain if someone would accompany him as a witness. He looked straight at me.

'So I was trapped. I could not back out without dishonour. I had to go, or he would have counted coup on me.

'When she heard, Running Deer begged me not to go, fearing that the spirits would take me. She was a shaman's daughter and had the witching sight. But I was young, with a young man's pride and folly, so I refused her. Seeing that I could not be swayed, she cut a braid from her hair and wove it about with spells, making it a charm to return me safely home.

'It was a three-day trip at hunter's walk to Ghost Mountain. Fear was our constant companion. What had seemed possible in the warmth of the lodge seemed dreadful in the cold autumn nights when the moon was full and spirits flitted from tree to tree. I believe that if either of us had been alone, we would have turned back, for it is a terrible thing to approach the places of the restless dead at night as winter approaches.

'But we could show no fear, for the other was witness, and our rivalry drove us forward. Neither wanted to be the first to turn back.

'On the evening of the third day, we met the first warning totems, covered by the skulls of those the sky warriors had judged and found wanting. I felt like running then, but pride kept me moving on.

'We began to climb. The night was still and cold. Things rustled in the undergrowth, and the moon leered down like a witching spirit. Stunted trees hunched over the pathway like malign ghosts. We climbed until we came to the vast empty plateau marked by the sign of the winged skull.

'We were filled with a sense of achievement and our enmity was, for the moment, buried. We stood in a place few men had ever seen. We had defied the spirits and lived. Still, we were on edge.

'I don't know what I thought when Silver Elk pointed upward. There came a howling as of a thousand roused ghosts, and fire lit the sky. Perhaps I thought the spirits had chosen to strike me down for my presumption. Perhaps I was so filled with terror that I thought of nothing. I know that I was frozen in place, while Silver Elk turned and ran.

'If I had been afraid before, imagine how I felt when I saw that great, winged shape in the distance and heard the roar of the approaching thunderbird. Picture my horror when I saw it was Deathwing itself, steed of the Emperor, chooser of the slain, Winged Hunting Skeleton.

'I bitterly regretted my folly. I could not move to save myself, and waited for Deathwing to strike me with its claws and release my spirit.

'I was surprised when the thunderbird stooped to earth in front of me and ceased its angry roaring. Still, I could not run. Its beak gaped, disgorging the massive, black-armoured forms of the chosen dead. On each shoulder, they bore the sign of the winged blade.

'I knew then that I was in the realm of spirits, for Hawk Talon, my grandfather's grandfather, stood among them. I had seen his face carved on the roof pole of our family lodge. He looked old and grey and tired, but there was still a family resemblance.

'To see a face so familiar and so strange in that dreadful place was somehow reassuring. It enabled me to overcome my fear. Filled with wonder, I walked forward till I stood before him: that terrible, grizzled old man whose face was so like my own.

'For a long time, he simply stared at me. Then he smiled and started to laugh. He clasped me to his armoured breast and shouted that it was a fortunate homecoming. He seemed just as pleased to see me as I was to see him.'

Cloud Runner paused, comparing his ancestor's return to his own. There was no laughter here as there had been among those Marines long ago. He understood now how glad the old man had been to see a familiar face. He was glad that Hawk Talon wasn't here now to see the destruction of their people.

'Of course, I was overwhelmed, standing among these legendary warriors, speaking with my ancient blood-relative. I knew they had returned to choose their successors in the Emperor's service, and forgetting everything else, I begged to be allowed to join them.

'The old man looked at me and asked me whether I had any reason to stay or any reason to regret going. I thought of

Running Deer, and I hesitated, but I was a callow youth.
Visions of glory and the wonders beyond the sky filled me.
What did I truly know of life? I was being called on to make a
choice that I would have to live with for centuries, although I
did not know it.

'My ancestor did. He saw my hesitation and told me better to
stay in that case. I would have nothing of it, and insisted that
they put me to the test.

'They strapped me to a steel table and opened my flesh with
metal knives. I had endured the weasel claw ritual to prove my
bravery, but the pain was as nothing to what I then endured.
When they opened my flesh, they implanted things which they
said would bond with my flesh and grant me spirit power.

'For weeks, I lay in feverish agony while my body changed.
The walls danced, and my spirit fled to the edge of the cold
place. While I wandered lost and alone, one of the brothers
stood beside me reciting the Imperial litanies.

'In a vision, the Emperor came to me, riding Deathwing,
mightiest of thunderbirds. It was different from that which had
borne the sky warriors home. It was a beast of spirit; the other
had been a bird of metal, a totem cast in its image.

'The Emperor spoke to me, telling me of the great struggle
being waged on a thousand thousand worlds. He showed me
the races other than man and the secret heart of the universe,
which is Chaos. He showed me the powers that lurked in the
warp and exposed me to their temptations. He watched as I
resisted. I knew that, if I had given in, he would have struck me
down. Eventually, I awoke, and I knew then that my spirit
belonged to the Emperor. I had chosen to abandon my people,
my world and my bride for his service. I knew I had made the
correct choice.'

Cloud Runner glanced around at the other Terminators. He
hoped he had told the story well enough to catch his listeners'
minds and remind them of their duty to the Emperor. He
hoped he had reminded them that they had all made the same
decision as he had and that they would once more make the
correct choice.

He shook his head and touched the charm of braided hair
that he still wore round his throat. He wondered if he had
made the correct choice all those years ago, if he would have
been happier staying with Running Deer. The bright, bold

vision he had possessed in his youth had faded and lost its glamour over the years of endless warfare. I never even said goodbye to her, he thought, and that somehow was the saddest thought of all.

He judged that he had swayed many of the Marines, but when Lame Bear leaned forward to speak, he knew the struggle had only begun.

'I would speak of genestealers,' the big man said quietly. 'I would speak of genestealers, their terror and their cruelty...'

TWO HEADS TALKING wandered the nighted streets. They seemed empty now that the workers had returned to their barracks. A slight breeze had sprung up, blowing flecks of ash through the streets, clearing the smog slightly. A bitter ash-taste filled his mouth.

He passed by the factories where giant steam engines stood, still working. Their din filled the air. Their pistons went up and down like the nodding heads of maddened dinosaurs. He knew they never rested.

He strode down a street of rich mansions, driven by morbid curiosity. He felt as though he had been shown the pieces of a vast puzzle, and if he could only locate the last piece, it would all fall into place.

Each mansion he passed had wrought-iron gates which bore the signs of the night-owl, the puma and the rat. These were the totem animals of the hill clans. Two Heads Talking wondered whether the chieftains of these people dwelled within. He could well believe that they might make pacts with whoever had done this. Those people had dark reputations.

He felt anger grow within him, driving out the sense of bewilderment. His life had been rendered meaningless. His people had been betrayed. His world had been stolen. Even the Dark Angels had been destroyed. Ten thousand years of tradition ended here. There were no more bold huntsmen of the plains for the sky warriors to recruit.

The chapter might continue, but its heritage had been destroyed – it would never be the same again. Two Heads Talking was of the last generation of Space Marines recruited from the plains people. There would be no more.

As he moved beyond the mansions, toward the polluted river, his spirit senses warned him he was being followed. Part of him did not care, would welcome confrontation with whatever watchers shadowed him. From up ahead, he heard a groan of pain.

'WE DO NOT know where they come from,' said Lame Bear. 'Not even the curators of the Administratum know that. They appear without warning, carried in the mighty space hulks which drift on the tides of warp space.'

A shiver passed through even these hardened Terminators. Cloud Runner saw the gaze of those who had faced the genestealers turn inward. Their faces reflected the grim memories of the encounters.

Unconsciously, they sat up straighter and looked around nervously. For the first time, it was brought home to the captain that they really did face the genestealers once more. They faced a threat that could kill them.

'They are dreadful foes: ferocious, relentless, knowing neither pity nor fear. They do not use weapons, perhaps because they do not need them. Their claws are capable of tearing adamantium like paper. They do not use armour; their hides are so tough that they can survive, for a time, unsuited in vacuum. They have the aspect of a beast, yet they are intelligent and organised. They are the most terrible enemies any Space Marine has faced since the time of the Horus Heresy.

'How do I know this? I have faced them, as have others here.'

Cloud Runner shivered, recalling the times he had faced the stealers. He remembered their chitinous visage, their gaping jaws and four rending claws. He tried not to recall their blinding, insect-like speed.

'It is not their fearsome battle prowess that makes the stealers such dreadful opponents. It is something else. I will tell you of it.

'One hundred and twenty years ago, before ever I donned Terminator armour, I was sent with the fleet that investigated the strange silence of the hive world Thranx.

'The Imperial governor had not paid tribute for twenty years, and the Adeptus Terra had decided that perhaps a gentle reminder of his sworn duties was in order.

'The fleet arrived bearing sections from the Dark Angels, the Space Wolves, the Ultramarines and an Imperial Guard regiment from Necromunda. As the fleet moved into drop position, we expected resistance, rebellion. But the orbital monitors did not fire at us, and the governor spoke fairly to us on the comm-link.

'He claimed that the world had been cut off by warp storms and ork raids. He apologised for the non-payment of tribute and offered immediate reparations. He suggested that Inquisitor van Dam, who was in charge of the punitive expedition, descend and accept his obeisance.

'We were naturally suspicious, but van Dam suggested that any chance to take a world back into the Imperial fold without the expense of military action should at least be investigated. He requested that the Dark Angels provide an honour guard. We set our locators and teleported down into the governor's reception hall.

'Thranx was a world encased in steel. Its natives never saw the sky. The governor's hall was so vast, though, that clouds formed under its ceiling and rain fell on the trees that surrounded the ruler's pavilion.

'It was a sight to stir the blood. Long ranks of guardsmen flanked the curving metal road that led to the pavilion. The pavilion itself floated on suspensors above an artificial lake. The governor sat on a throne carved from a single industrially cultured pearl, flanked by two beautiful blind maidens who were his court telepaths. He bade us welcome and showed us the tribute.

'It was brought from vaults by specially bred slaves, grey-skinned eunuchs with muscles like an ogryn's. Even so, they could barely carry the chests. They paraded past us in a seemingly endless procession, carrying industrial diamonds, gold-inlaid bolters, suits of armoured ceramite and jade.

'All the time the governor, Huac, kept up an endless, amiable chatter. We watched, dazzled and beguiled by his smooth voice and affable manner. As the long day wore on, we began to accept that there was no need to fight, that we should simply take the tribute and go home.

'Our minds were pleasantly befuddled, and we were prepared to agree to anything our gracious host suggested when the great cryogenic coffins were brought forth. Huac claimed they carried his greatest treasures. It is a measure of how under his sway we were that we almost took them, without thinking.

'It was Two Heads Talking who said no. He stood there, for a moment, like a man bemused, and then he began to chant. It was as if cobwebs had been lifted from our eyes and we saw the snare that had been so subtly set for us.

'The spell of the magus, for such was Huac, was lifted, and we saw to our horror that we had almost taken two genestealer coffins back to our fleet. All that afternoon, as our minds had been lulled by the long, slow march, Huac had been inserting subtle, mystical tendrils into our minds.

'Still, so near to being enthralled were we that we almost protested when Two Heads Talking riddled Huac and his two apprentices with bolter fire. Only the living dreadnought Hawk Talon joined in the firing. We reacted slowly when he warned us to defend ourselves. Huac's guardsmen almost had us.

'But we were Space Marines. No sooner had they opened up with their lasrifles than we returned fire with our bolters, cutting them down. Van Dam tried to contact the fleet but our comm-links were being jammed, and we could not teleport out. There was nothing for it. We had to fight our way to the planet's surface and hope that a dropship could reach us.

'It seemed as if the whole planet had turned against us, and that was more or less what had happened. Two hundred of us fought our way out of the audience room. We were met by armed men, unarmed children and their mothers. All threw themselves against us with insane ferocity. As we cut them down, they showed no fear – only a strange, unholy joy. The whole world had been infected.

'Our trip to the surface was a nightmare. We battled along dark corridors, crawled up access ladders and through narrow hatches never meant for Marines. I saw Steel Fist tumble back headless from one hatchway. Van Dam lobbed a handful of crack grenades through and we were spattered with the remains of a full-grown stealer.

'My brother Red Sky was pulled down by a wave of feral children with explosives in their hands. They detonated them as they crawled over his body. He did not live.

'Twice in the endless corridors, we were almost overrun. It came to hand-to-hand combat with purestrain stealers.

'Twenty of our brothers were cut down before Two Heads Talking's force axe and Cloud Runner's power sword carried us clear.

'It was while guarding the final hatchway that I lost the use of my leg. A stealer cut right through the floor and grabbed me, trying to pull me down. I blasted frantically at it. The last thing I remember was its horrid, leering face as it pulled me down toward it. Around it was a group of Thranxians who stroked and pushed against it fondly.

'The others told me what had happened when I woke up in the medical bay of the ship with a new bionic leg. Two Heads Talking and Cloud Runner had pulled me clear and carried me to the roof of the world, where the dropship waited.

'There was only one thing to do: order the Exterminatus. The whole place was sterilised from orbit with virus bombs. Later, inquisitorial investigators ascertained that the whole business had begun only sixty years before, when an unrecorded space hulk had swung through the system.

'It had taken only three generations for the stealers to infect a whole world. For that is how they reproduce – by turning people into hosts for their offspring. Their victims endure this willingly, due to the stealers' hypnotic powers.

'Many nights I have lain awake wondering whether we could have saved the world if only we had arrived sooner. Perhaps if we had been able to eliminate the stealers before the cancer had spread, we would not have had to order the Exterminatus.'

Cloud Runner could see that the warriors had been swayed and angered by Lame Bear's tale.

He could tell that they were considering the assimilation of the people as breeding stock and the possibility that, by swift action, they might prevent it.

'Let us go,' said Weasel-Fierce, leaping to his feet. 'Let us enter the city and kill the stealers' spawn.'

Several other warriors made to accompany him.

'Wait,' said Bloody Moon. 'The gathering is not over and I would speak...'

ANGER AND IMPATIENCE drove Two Heads Talking toward the sound of pain. By the bank of the river, in the shadow of a monstrous factory, he saw that a group of bluecoats had pinned an old man against the wall and were slowly and surely beating him to death with their truncheons. One of their number held a lantern, occasionally giving a calm, precise order.

'Talk seditious nonsense, would you?' said one bravo. His stroke ended with the crack of breaking ribs. The old man groaned and fell to his knees. The other bluecoats laughed.

'Preach heresy against the Imperial cult and the warriors from the sky, eh? What makes you old fools do it? By the Emperor, I thought we had got the last of you.'

Their victim looked up at them. 'You are deluded. The warriors from the sky would not have built this place and herded us here the way elks are herded to the slaughter. Nor would they have broken the burial mounds of our people. Your masters are evil spirits summoned by the hill clans, not true sky warriors. Deathwing will return and rend them asunder.'

'Silence, blaspheming no-name,' said the leader of the bluecoats. 'You wish to prove your courage, do you? Perhaps we should return to the old ways, drunkard, and practise the weasel claw ritual on you.'

The old man coughed blood. 'Do what you will. I am Morning Star of the line of Running Deer and Silver Elk. I have the witching sight. I tell you that the spirits walk. Ancient powers stalk the land. The red star burns bright in the sky. A time of trouble is coming.'

'Is that why you chose to start ranting this night? I had thought the only spirits that talked to you came from a bottle,' said another bluecoat, kicking Morning Star in the ribs. The old man groaned. Two Heads Talking made his way forward through the mist, till he emerged into the lantern light.

The bluecoat leader spoke to him. 'Go away, buck. This is warrior lodge business. If you don't want to join this drunkard in the river, you'll leave now.'

'You dishonour the idea of the warrior lodge,' said Two Heads Talking quietly. 'Depart now, and I will spare you. Remain a heartbeat longer, and I will surely grant you death.'

The old man looked up at him, awestruck. Two Heads Talking could see the winged skull tattoo of a shaman on his forehead. A few bravos laughed. Some, the wiser ones, heard the soft menace in the Marine's voice and backed away.

The leader gestured for the bluecoats to attack. 'Take him!'

Two Heads Talking parried the swipe of a truncheon with his forearm. There was a metallic ring as the bludgeon snapped. He broke the bravo's nose against the butt of his force axe then lashed out with his foot, driving it into another bluecoat's stomach with inhuman force. As the man bent double the librarian chopped down on his neck, breaking it.

The bluecoats swarmed over him now. Their truncheons were as ineffective as twigs against a bear. A few tried to grab his arms and immobilise him. He shrugged them off easily, swinging killing blows with weapon and elbow. Where he struck, men died.

As the battlelust swept over him, he felt the bound spirits slip away. He knew that he stood revealed in his true form. The last of the bluecoats turned to run. Two Heads Talking hooked an arm around his neck and twisted. There was a crunch of shattering vertebrae.

The old man gazed on him with religious intensity. 'The spirits spoke truthfully,' he said, as if he did not quite believe it. He reached out and touched him, making sure he was real.

'You have come at last to free the people from their bondage to the false Emperor and lead them back to the plains. What is your name, sky warrior?'

'In my youth, it was Two Heads Talking, apprentice to Spirit Hawk. When I entered the service of the true Emperor, I took the name Lucian.' He could see tears running down the old man's scarred cheeks.

'Tell me, old man, what has happened to our folk? How did they come to fall so low?'

'It began when I was a buck,' said Morning Star, wiping his face. 'One summer night, the sky burned, and there was a great roaring. A trail of fire raced across the sky, and there was an explosion. Where we are now was a vast crater, and in the centre, where the temple of the four-armed Emperor stands, was a great, red-hot pile of metal.

'Some people thought the sky warriors had returned, that the roaring was the voice of their thunderbird. The shamans knew that this could not be so, for Deathwing returns only once every hundred years, in autumn, and it had been only fifty years since the red star was last visible. We were pleased because we thought that we might ride Deathwing. Most of us had reckoned on being old men when the sky warriors came again.

'Our visitors were not the armoured warriors of legend. They were feeble, pale-skinned men who claimed that they had come from the Emperor to show us the way to build an earthly paradise. They preached the virtues of tolerance and brotherly love and an end to warfare. The chiefs sent them packing, which was a mistake, for when honeyed words did not succeed, they tried force of arms. They allied with the hill clans and gave them metal blades which our weapons could not withstand.

'Eventually, clans were forced to trade for the new weapons in order to withstand their enemies. Tales were told of how witching spirits with four arms and terrible claws destroyed our warriors. Soon, the pretenders ruled the plains, taking slaves and destroying utterly those who opposed them.

'Then came the building of this great city, using slave labour and paying the freemen in trade tokens.'

Suddenly, the old man's eyes went wide with horror. He was looking past Two Heads Talking and into the night. The librarian turned, and from the mist, shapes emerged.

One was the fat man who earlier had been riding in the palanquin. Flanking him were two huge four-armed figures. Their carapaces glistened like oil. They raised large claws which glittered in the moonlight.

'We would have told you all this if only you had asked,' said the fat man, gazing at Two Heads Talking with his dark, magnetic eyes.

The librarian flexed his fingers, and his force axe hummed a song of death in his hand.

'IT WAS IN the time of Commander Aradiel, a hundred summers gone,' said Bloody Moon. 'We were aboard the battle barge *Angelus Morte* on sector edge patrol when the alarms went off. Sensor probes indicated that a space hulk had dropped from warp space near us. Deep scanning revealed nothing. We were ordered to investigate.

'We crouched within the boarding torpedoes and were fired at the hulk. It was unpowered and dark when we disembarked, so helmet lights on, we moved to secure the perimeter. We met no resistance, but as per standard operational procedures, we proceeded with extreme caution.

'We identified the hulk as *Prison of Lost Souls*, an appropriate name as it turned out. We moved nervously through the shadowy corridors, for the taint of the warp still hung about the craft. It made us uneasy.

'At first, there was no sign of danger. Then we came across the bodies of some Space Wolves. They had been riddled with bolter fire. We could not guess how long they had lain there – perhaps since the hulk had last entered normal space. It might have been ten years or ten thousand – we did not know. The tides of warp space are unpredictable, and time flows strangely there.

'Brother Sergeant Conrad ordered us to be wary. Then a terrible thing occurred. A Space Wolf's corpse sat upright, its eyes glowing crimson. "You are doomed," it told us. "Every one of you will die as I have."

'We riddled it with fire from our weapons, but still its horrible whispers echoed in our minds.

'We began to fall back. All around us, blips suddenly appeared on our sensors. They were running parallel to us, trying to cut us off from the boarding torpedo.

'At corridor intersections, we caught sight of armoured figures. We exchanged a few shots with them. I hit one and heard its scream over the comm-link. They were using the same frequencies as we were. When we realised that, our blood ran cold. We asked ourselves: could these be Space Marines?

'We did not have long to wait for an answer. They swarmed down the corridor toward us in a vast wave. They were garbed in the armour of Marines, but they were horribly mutated. Some clutched rusty bolters in tentacles instead of hands. Some had faces that were moist and green and slimy like toads. Some had claws and extra limbs. Some dragged themselves along, leaving a trail of mucus behind them.

'The mark of Chaos was upon them. They called on Horus and those powers that are better not named. And we knew them – they were renegades, survivors from the Age of Heresy who had pacted with Chaos in exchange for eternal life. The fighting became close and heavy. They had the weight of numbers, but we had our Terminator armour and the strength of righteousness.

'For a moment, it looked as though they might overwhelm us, but then our thunder hammers and lightning claws came into play, and we cut through them inexorably. They fought like daemons, and they had the strength of the damned, but eventually we won.

'I stood looking down at the body of my last foe, and a thought occurred to me: this man had once been a Marine like myself. He had undergone the same training and indoctrination as I had. He had sworn to serve the Emperor. And yet he had betrayed humanity. How could this be?

'How could a true Marine become forsworn? It seemed unlikely that he would suddenly turn his back on the pattern of a lifetime and pact with the darkness. What had Chaos to offer him? Wealth? We have no use for the baubles that other men covet; we already have the finest of everything that a man could wish for. Sensual gratification? We are taught its transitory nature. Power? We know true power, which is the will of the Emperor. Who among us could equal his sacrifice?

'No – as I stood over his body I came to understand. He had deviated not in one leap but in small steps, by increments.

'First he had come to place trust in the Warmaster. An easy step, for was not Horus the chief champion of the Emperor?

'Then he had come to follow the Warmaster. Who would not? A soldier follows his commander.

'Then he had come to believe Horus divine. An easy mistake. Was not the great heretic one of the primarchs of the first founding, gifted with god-like powers second only to the Emperor himself?

'Thus did he stray from the path of truth, till eventually he lost both his life and soul. It is a way that is open to anyone, one small mistake leading to another until at last the great error is reached. This I came to realise as I studied the body of the renegade on *Prison of Lost Souls*. I resolved then and there to submit myself to the Emperor's will. I knew that all our regulations and our codes have a purpose, and it is not for us to question them, for they keep us from the path of the deviant.'

Around the fire, there was silence. Cloud Runner could tell that Bloody Moon's words had touched a chord within the Marines. He found himself examining his own conscience for signs of heresy. The implication of Bloody Moon's tale was quite clear: if they lapsed from the service of the Emperor, they were taking the first step down the road to damnation. He had also reminded them that they were Marines, the chosen of the Emperor. If they did not keep the faith, who would?

For a long time, all was quiet. Then Weasel-Fierce indicated his wish to talk.

'I will speak of death,' he said, 'the death of men and worlds...'

* * *

Two Heads Talking felt the impact of the fat magus's will like a physical blow. The great, dark eyes seemed to swell, to become bottomless pits into which the librarian fell. At his feet, Morning Star whimpered.

With a wrench, the Marine broke the mental contact, thankful that his librarian's armour was equipped with a psychic hood. The magus was strong, and Two Heads Talking was already tired.

The stealers raced toward him. The librarian raised his storm bolter and sent a hail of shells blazing out. Tracer fire ripped the night apart. The leading genestealer was shredded by the heavy bullets. The other dodged with inhuman speed.

Morning Star leapt between the librarian and his assailant. A claw flickered, and the old man's body was torn in half. Two Heads Talking lashed out with his axe, willing it to strike hard, and its blade burned coldly as it passed through the stealer's neck. He leapt back to avoid its reflexive death-strike.

The magus laughed. 'You cannot escape. Why struggle?'

The fat man concentrated, and a halo of power played around his head.

The librarian hosed him down with fire, but some force intercepted the shells, causing them to explode harmlessly a few feet from their target.

Two Heads Talking strode forward, swinging the axe. He felt his own power build within him as the blade arced toward his target. Something stopped it a handsbreadth away from the magus's head. Great muscles bulged under his armour as he forced it forward. Servo-motors whined as they added their strength to his. Slowly, inexorably, the Marine forced the blade toward his enemy. Sweat ran down the fat man's brow as he concentrated. A look of fear passed across his face. He could not save himself, and he knew it.

He gave a single shriek as his concentration lapsed. The force axe sheared through him from head to groin. Two Heads Talking felt the magus's psychic death scream echo through the night. He sensed hundreds of minds answer it. In the distance, through the deadening curtain of mist, he heard the sound of scuttling, coming ever closer.

Knowing his only chance of survival lay in swift flight, Two Heads Talking turned and ran.

* * *

'OUR WORLD IS dead,' said Weasel-Fierce. Some Marines muttered about the fact that he was addressing them directly, rather than keeping to the ritual. He silenced them with a short, chopping gesture of his right hand. When he spoke again, his tone was scathing and savage. 'This ritual is a sham. It comes from a time that is ended. Why pretend otherwise? You may wish to delude yourselves by keeping with the old ways, but I do not.

'You can speak in parables about our oaths to the Emperor, the horror of the stealers or the nature of damnation. I choose to speak the truth.

'Our people are dead or enslaved, and we sit here like old women, asking ourselves what to do. Have we been put under a spell? When were we ever so indecisive? A true warrior has no choice in this matter. We must avenge our people. Our weapons must taste enemy blood. It would be the coward's way not to face them.'

'But if we fail–' began Bloody Moon.

'If we fail, so be it. What have we to live for? How many summers have we left before we die of old age or are encased in the cold, metal body of a dreadnought?'

He fell silent and glared around the fire. To Cloud Runner's surprise, he looked down, and the fury seeped out of him.

'I am old,' he said softly. 'Old and tired. I have seen more than two hundred summers. In a few more, I will be dead, anyway. I had hoped to gaze again on my kin before then, but it is not to be. This is my only regret.'

Cloud Runner could see the weariness in him, felt its echo in his own mind. Every man about the fire had served the Emperor for centuries, their lifespans increased by the process that turned them into Marines.

'If I had remained among the people,' Weasel-Fierce said, 'I would be dead by now. I chose another path and I have lived long – longer perhaps than any mortal should.

'It is time for an ending. Where better than here, on our homeworld, among the bones of our kin? The day of the plains people is done. We can avenge them, and we can join them. If we fall in combat, we shall have had warriors' deaths. I wish to die as I have lived: weapon in hand, foes before me.

'I believe that this is what we all want. Let us do it.'

All was quiet except the crackling of the fire. Cloud Runner looked from face to face and saw death was written in each of them. Weasel-Fierce had voiced what they had all felt since first seeing the shattered lodges. They had become wraiths, walking in the ruins of elder days.

There was nothing left here for them, except memories. If they departed now, all that loomed before them was old age and inevitable death. This way, at least, their ending would have a meaning.

'I say we go in. If the contamination has not spread too far, we can free any survivors,' said Lame Bear. Cloud Runner looked at Bloody Moon.

'Providing we command *Deathwing* to virus bomb the planet if we fail,' he said. The rest of the warriors put their right fists forward, signifying assent. They all looked at him, waiting to see what he had to say. He felt once more the pressure of command fall on him. He considered the destroyed lodges and his own loss and weighed them against his Imperial duty. Nothing could bring back the plains people, but perhaps he could save their descendants.

But that was not all there was to it, he realised. He wanted the satisfaction of meeting his foes, face to face. He was angry. He wanted to make the stealers suffer for what they had done, and he wanted to be there when they did. He wanted vengeance for himself and for his people. It was as simple as that. Such a decision was not the correct one for an Imperial officer, but it was the way of his clan.

In the end, to his surprise, he found out where his true loyalty lay.

'I say we fight,' he said at last. 'But we fight as warriors of the people. This battle is not for the Emperor. It is for our murdered clans. Our last battle shall be fought in accordance with our ancient ways. Let us perform the rite of Deathwing.'

Two Heads Talking ran for his life. Through the darkened streets, genestealers pursued, loping along, swift and deadly. He sensed their presence all around.

He leapt over a pile of rubbish which lay in his path and swept round a corner into a main road. Two workers poked their heads through a doorway to see what was going on. They swiftly withdrew.

Two Heads Talking ran wearily. His heart was pounding, and his breathing was ragged. The strain of maintaining the spell of concealment for so long had sapped his strength. He wondered how long he could keep up this pace.

He risked a swift glance over his shoulder. A genestealer had just rounded the corner. He fired his storm bolter at it, but his shot was inaccurate, and the stealer lurched back into cover.

Sensing danger in front of him, he turned. From out of a shadowy doorway, a stealer uncoiled. He had just enough time to raise his force axe before it sprang. He thrust the blade out before him, chopping into the monster's chest. The momentum of the thing's charge knocked him over. A claw cut into his arm, searing it with pain.

If his blow had not landed cleanly, he realised, he would have been dead.

Ignoring the pain, he rolled onto his belly, catching a clear glimpse of his pursuers as they charged. He squeezed the trigger of his bolter and stitched a line of fire across their chests. The strength of the armour allowed him to hurl off the ambusher's carcass with ease. He continued on his way.

Not much further, he thought, forcing himself to reel onward. He could see the huge walls jutting upward above nearby buildings.

He recited a spell to free his mind of pain and made for the gates.

His heart sank when he saw what awaited him – a mass of hunched, evil-faced men with dark, piercing eyes. Some held ancient-looking energy weapons. Some gripped blades in their three hands. Towering over them were purestrain genestealers, flexing their claws menacingly. Two Heads Talking came to a halt, facing his foes.

For a moment, they eyed each other in respectful silence. The librarian commended his spirit to the Emperor. Soon Deathwing would be carrying him off. His bolter was almost empty. With only his force axe, he knew he could not withstand so many.

As if at an unspoken signal, the genestealers and their brood surged forward. A bolt from an energy weapon burned into his armour, melting one of the skulls on his chest plate. He gritted his teeth and returned fire, cutting a great swathe of death. There was a loud click as his bolter jammed. He did not have the time to clear it, so he charged to meet his foes, chanting his death-chant.

He rushed into a sea of bodies that pressed against him, hitting him with blades and rending claws. He summoned the last dregs of his strength to power his force axe and swung it in a great double arc. He lopped off heads and limbs with a will, but for every foe who fell, another stepped into place. He could not guard himself against all their blows, and soon he bled from scores of great wounds.

Life fled from him, and overhead he thought he heard the beating of mighty pinions. Deathwing has come, he thought, just before a blow smashed into his head and all consciousness departed.

CLOUD RUNNER PAUSED briefly before he painted out his personal cloud-and-thunderbolt insignia on his armour's right shoulder. He felt changed. By blanking out his Imperial insignia, he had blanked out part of himself, cut himself off from part of his history.

Slowly he began to etch in new totem signs on the armour, the marks of vengeance and death. As he did so, he felt the powers of the totem spirits begin to enter him.

He looked at Weasel-Fierce. The gaunt man had finished painting out all the icons on his armour. It was now white, the colour of death, except on its left shoulder, where the skull had been left unchanged. It seemed somehow appropriate.

They performed a rite that dated back to ancient times, before the Emperor had come to tame the thunderbirds. Only once before had Cloud Runner seen it performed. As a boy, he had watched a party of old warriors, sworn to vengeance, paint their bodies white and go after a horde of hill clan raiders that had killed a small child. They had painted their bodies the funeral colour because they did not expect to return from facing so overwhelming a foe.

Bloody Moon looked over from beside the fire and gave him a weak grin. Cloud Runner walked over to him.

'Ready, old friend?' he asked. Bloody Moon nodded. Cloud Runner bent over the fire and put his hands into the ash. He pressed his palms, fingers together, flat against his face, making the sign of Deathwing on each cheek.

'I wish Two Heads Talking would return,' said Bloody Moon, repeating Cloud Runner's gesture.

'He may yet surprise you.'

Bloody Moon looked doubtful. Cloud Runner gestured for the warriors to assemble. They formed into a circle around the dead fire. One by one, they began to chant their death-songs.

EVEN AS THEY carried him through the long steel corridors, Two Heads Talking knew he was dying. Life leaked from his wounds. With every drop of blood that dribbled over his bearers, he became weaker.

It felt like some evil dream, being borne down dimly lit tunnels by the hunched, daemonic figures of the genestealer brood. The librarian watched these events through a fog of pain, wondering why he was still alive. Part of his mind realised that he was within whatever vessel had carried the brood to his homeworld.

Agony lanced through him as one of his bearers jolted him slightly. It took all his will power not to scream. They entered a long hall in which a hunched, dreadful figure waited. He was placed on the floor in front of it. It cocked its head to one side side, studying him.

Tears ran down the librarian's face from the pain as he forced himself to his feet. Genestealer guards raced towards him, but the huge creature glanced at them, and they froze in position.

Two Heads Talking stood unsteadily, knowing he faced a genestealer patriarch. He had heard dim legends of such things, the progenitors of entire broods, the most ancient of their lines.

He looked into his enemy's eyes. He felt an almost electric shock pass through his body as their minds made contact. The librarian found himself confronted by a foe that was ancient, implacable, deadly. His mind reeled under the assault of its ferocious will. He felt an urge to kneel, to do homage to this ancient being. He knew that it was worthy of his respect.

With an effort, he managed to restrain himself. He reminded himself that this was the being that had destroyed his people. He made to throw himself at it, to aim a killing blow with his good arm. He sprang, but his legs gave way underneath him, and the patriarch caught him easily, almost gently, and held him at bay with its claws. The long ovipositor on its tongue flickered out, but did not touch him.

Suddenly, he found himself engaged in a bitter, psychic struggle. Tendrils of alien thought insinuated themselves into his mind. He blocked them, chopping them off with the blades of his hatred. He countered with a psychic bolt of his own, but it was stopped by an ancient will that seemed impervious to outside influence.

The patriarch exerted his full power, and Two Heads Talking felt his defences begin to buckle under the terrible pressure. The cold, focused power of the genestealer was enormous. Even fresh, Two Heads Talking doubted he could have matched it. Now, strength fading because of his wounds, exhausted because of his earlier struggles, he could offer no contest at all.

His outer screen fell, and the patriarch was within his mind, sorting through his memories, absorbing them into itself. For a second, while it was disoriented, he tried a psychic thrust. The stealer countered easily, but for a moment, they met mind to mind.

Strange alien memories and emotions washed over the librarian, threatening to drown him. He saw the patriarch's past spread out before him. He saw the long trail that led through despoiled worlds and past many children. He saw the hive world it had fled from in a fast ship, just before the virus bombs fell. With a shock, he realised that he had been there himself – on Thranx – and that the creature had recognised his aura from then. He saw the ship crippled by an Imperial battle barge and barely able to make the jump into warp space.

He experienced the long struggle to return to normal space and the frozen eternities it took to escape and crash-land the crippled ship on a new, virgin world. He saw the pitifully few survivors emerge; only a few purestrains and three hybrid techs. He saw them make axes from the wreckage of the ship for trade with the tribesmen, and he watched them start the long struggle to establish themselves in a hostile world.

He was gratified as the web of psychic contact expanded with each new brood member. He felt cold satisfaction at the destruction of the tribes and the knowledge that soon a new industrial base would be built. The ship would be repaired. New worlds to conquer would be within reach.

For a bleak moment, despair filled Two Heads Talking. He saw the stealers planning to spread to and infect new worlds. And he could do nothing to stop this old, invincible entity. He almost gave in. He could see no way out. Death loomed, and

that thought gave him pause. He knew what he must do. Part
of him gave way before the patriarch's assault; another part
willed his spirit towards oblivion.

He stood once more in the cold place, sensed far-off the
spirit of the Emperor, bright and shining as a star. Near at hand
were the angry ghosts. The patriarch was a hungry, ominous
presence, determined to enslave him. Somewhere in the distance, he could hear the thunderous pinions of Deathwing
coming to claim him.

Too late, the patriarch realised what he was doing and tried
to break the link. Two Heads Talking focused all his hatred,
anger and fear and held the link open, a task made easier by
their earlier intimate contact. The patriarch struggled frantically, but could not free himself.

The wingbeats came closer, drowning the librarian in a roar
that might have been a hurricane or his own last breath. From
the middle of a vortex of agony, he was borne up into darkness.
The maelstrom sucked in the patriarch. It died, slain by the
librarian's death agony.

Briefly, Two Heads Talking felt his foe vanish, felt the sense
of loss from its brood. As the librarian's spirit rose higher, he
reached out and touched the minds of his comrades, bidding
them farewell, telling them what they must do. Then Two
Heads Talking knew no more.

CLOUD RUNNER FELT the presence as he stared into the fire. He
looked up and saw Two Heads Talking standing before him.
The librarian looked pale. His face was distorted by agony, his
body gashed by dreadful wounds. He knew that this was a
spirit vision, that the old shaman was dead.

For a moment, he thought he heard the sound of titanic
wingbeats and saw the mightiest of thunderbirds soaring
toward the moon. The presence vanished, leaving Cloud
Runner feeling cold and alone. He shivered in the sudden chill.
He knew he had been touched by Deathwing's passing.

He looked toward the others and knew that they had seen
the same thing. He raised a hand in a gesture of farewell and
then swept it down as a signal for the Marines to advance.

Filled with determination, the white-armoured Terminators
marched toward the distant city.

* * *

CLOUD RUNNER SAT enthroned and looked down upon his visitors. His people were drawn up in long ranks, forming a corridor along which the Marines advanced warily. They were led by a captain and a librarian. From the doorway, the huge armoured form of a dreadnought performed overwatch. Cloud Runner found the sight of that old, familiar form comforting.

He saw the uneasy, worshipful faces of his people look to him for reassurance. He kept his face grim and calm. He sensed the battle brothers' unease at the strangeness of the folk within the great lodgehouse. They held their bolters ready, as if expecting violence to erupt at any moment.

Cloud Runner was glad to see them. Since Lame Bear's death, he had felt very alone. He spotted several familiar faces among the oncoming Imperial warriors. Memories of the old days in the chapter house flooded back. He took three deep breaths, touched the ancient, white-painted suit beside him, for luck, and then spoke.

'Greetings, brother sky warriors,' he said.

'Greetings, Brother Ezekiel,' said the Marine leader suspiciously.

Cloud Runner rubbed his facial scar-tattoos with one gnarled hand, then grinned. 'So they made you a captain, eh, Broken Knife?'

'Yes, Brother Ezekiel. They made me a captain when you failed to return.' He paused, obviously waiting for an explanation.

'It took you ten years to come looking for the Dark Angels' honour suits?' the old man asked with a hint of mockery.

'There has been war: a great migration of orks through the Segmentum Obscura. The chapter was called to serve. During that time the absence of our Terminators was felt grievously. You have an explanation for this, of course.'

The Marines stared at Cloud Runner coldly. It was as if he was a stranger to these grim youths, or worse, a traitor. He remembered the first time he had stood among Marines and, for the first time in long years, became aware of their uncanny quality. He felt isolated and uneasy.

'These are not our people, Cloud Runner. What happened here?' asked a deep rolling voice. He recognised it as the dreadnought's. Suddenly, he did not feel so alone. Hawk Talon was there, hooked into the life-support systems of the dreadnought. There was at least one person present who was on his side, who was old enough to understand. It was like their first meeting under the shadow of deathwing, when he had sighted that one familiar face among strangers.

'No, honoured forefather, they are not. They are the untainted survivors of the genestealer conquest.'

He heard the shocked murmur of the Marines, saw the way that they instinctively brought their weapons to bear on the lodge people.

'You had better explain, Brother Ezekiel,' said Broken Knife.

CLOUD RUNNER FOUND himself telling his tale to the astonished Marines. He told them of the Terminator company's landing and of their discovery of the devastation that had been wrought by the genestealers. He told them of the gathering and of the choice the warriors had made – of Two Heads Talking's spirit walk and the Terminators' final march on the city. He spoke to them in the intricate syntax of the Imperial tongue, not the language of the plains people.

'We marched through the black gates and were assaulted by stealers. At first they seemed confused, as if they had suffered a great shock. They attacked in small groups with no pattern and no guiding intelligence, and we cut them down.

'We pushed through crowds of screaming people as we followed our librarian's locator beacon toward the city centre. Huge purestrain stealers erupted from buildings as we advanced. They attacked with insane fury, but without thought, and so we bested them easily.

'In the centre of the city we found a temple – a building that obscenely parodied the Imperial cult, dominated by a huge four-armed statue of what was intended to be the Emperor. We toppled it into the street and beneath it found an entrance into the underworld.

'Down we went into the cold, metal corridors. We passed through airlocks and bulkheads. It was like a buried spacecraft. We still followed the locator fix, determined to reclaim Two Heads Talking's armour and avenge his death.

'At first we made easy progress against isolated stealer attacks, but then a change occurred. For a while, there was peace.

'We exchanged wary looks. Bloody Moon asked if we could possibly have killed them all. I can even now picture the puzzled look on his face. It was still there when a stealer dropped through an air vent and took his head off. I blasted the thing with bolter fire, reducing it to bloody mush.

'Now the stealers began to attack again. But this time their attacks were co-ordinated, guided by some malign intelligence. It was as if they had been leaderless for a time, but a new fiend had now taken charge.

'They flanked us through parallel corridors, dropped through vents in the ceiling. Hordes of stealers and their human brood attacked from all sides. Waves of them scuttled forward with blinding speed, threatening to overwhelm us with sheer numbers. It was a horrible sight, watching those great armoured beasts race closer, ignoring their kin as they were cut down.

'Still they came. Our point men and rearguard were ambushed and killed. The threats came so fast, we almost didn't have time to respond.

'I saw a score of them slain by flamer fire, and the stench that filled the air was indescribable. They spent their lives recklessly in their blind lust to kill us. There was a sense of terrible, oppressive anger in the air. It was as if they had a personal score with us and were all prepared to die to settle it.

'Any other squad, even other Terminators, would have been beaten back by the sheer, fury of their attack, but we wore the mark of deathwing. Our funeral dirges had been sung – fear was not in us, and we had our own scores to settle. We pushed forward, inch by tortuous inch.

'Blood washed the corridors as we fought our way into a great central chamber. There we found the body of Two Heads Talking. He was dead, his body rent by great wounds. Nearby lay the body of the patriarch, not a mark upon him.

'The hall was full of foes, purestrain and brood. A handful of us had fought our way into the throne-room. We faced many times our number. For a moment, we stood exchanging glares. I think both sides sensed that they faced their ultimate enemy – that the outcome of that fight would decide the fate of this world. There was quiet in the hall, silence except for the cycling of our breathers. I could hear my heart beating. My mouth felt dry. But I was strangely calm, sure that soon I would be greeting the spirits of my ancestors. The stealers formed up, and we raised our bolters to the firing position.

'At an unspoken signal, they charged, mouths open but making no sound. A few of the brood fired ancient energy weapons.

Beside me, a battle brother fell. We laid down a barrage of fire that tore the first wave to pieces. Nothing could have lived through it. Everything we fired at died. But there were just too many of them. They swarmed over us, and the final conflict began in earnest.

'I saw Weasel-Fierce go down beneath a pile of stealers. His bolter had jammed, but he fought on, screaming taunts and insults at his foes. The last I saw of him, he was tearing the head from a stealer, even as it punched a claw through his chest. Thus passed the greatest warrior of our generation.

'Lame Bear and I fought back to back, circled about by our enemies. Power glove and power sword smote the stealers as we cut them down. If there had been only a few more purestrain, things would have gone differently that day, but most of them seemed to have died in the initial futile attacks.

'As it was, things were close. Lame Bear fell, wounded, and I found myself breast to breast with a huge, armoured horror. The leader knocked my sword from my hand with a sweep of a mighty claw. I thanked the Emperor for the digital weapons in my power glove and sprayed the monstrosity's eyes with poisoned needles, blinding it. In the brief respite, I found time to bring my storm bolter to bear and slay it.

'I looked around: only Terminators stood in the hall. We whooped with joy to find ourselves still alive, but then the number of our fallen struck us, and we stood in appalled silence. Only six of us survived. We did not count the number of the stealers fallen.

'In the world above, the children of the plains people waited. A huge crowd had gathered outside the temple to see the outcome of our battle. They looked at us, awe-struck. We had destroyed their temple and killed their gods. They did not know whether we were daemons or redeemers.

'We looked on the weary creatures who were the only remnants of our former clans. We had won, and we had reclaimed our world. Still, our victory seemed hollow. We had saved our descendants from the stealers, but our way of life was gone.

'As we stood before the assembled throng, it struck me what we must do. The Emperor himself provided inspiration in that moment. I explained my plan to the others.

'We drove the crowds from the city and assembled them on the plain outside. We searched for traces of the brood among them, but there were none. The stealer taint seemed to have been destroyed in our vengeance war.

'I walked through the factories and past the toppled chimneys. Then we took our flamers and burned the city to the ground. We divided the people up into six new tribes and said our good-byes to each other, for we knew we would likely never meet again. Then we led our descendants away from the still-blazing city. Lame Bear took his folk to the mountains. I brought my people to my old village, and we rebuilt it. I do not know what became of the others.

'I have told these people that I was sent by the Emperor to lead them back to the old ways. I have taught them how to hunt and fish and shoot in the old manner. We do battle with the other tribes. One day they will again be worthy of becoming sky warriors.'

Cloud Runner fell silent. He could see the battle brothers had been moved by his tale. Broken Knife turned to the librarian. Cloud Runner felt the pressure of mind-to-mind contact.

'Brother Ezekiel speaks the truth, Brother-Captain Gabriel,' said the librarian. Broken Knife looked up at the old Marine.

'Forgive me, brother, I have misjudged you. It seems the chapter and the plain's people owe you and your warriors a great debt.'

'Semper fideles,' said Cloud Runner. 'You must take back the suits. They belong to the chapter.'

Broken Knife nodded.

'Perhaps a favour. In honour of our dead, leave the suits the colour of Deathwing. The deeds of our brothers should be remembered.'

'It will be so,' replied Broken Knife. 'Deathwing will be remembered.'

The Marines turned and filed out past the dreadnought. The mighty being stood there, watching Cloud Runner with inhuman eyes.

The Terminator's departure left Cloud Runner suddenly tired. He felt the weight of his years heavily.

He sensed the dreadnought gazing at him and looked up.

'Yes, honoured ancestor?' he asked in the tongue of the plains people.

'You could go back with us. You are worthy of becoming a living dreadnought,' it said.

He wished he could return and spend his last years with his chapter, but he knew that he could not. His duty was to his people now. He must return them to the Emperor's way. He shook his head.

'I thought not. You are a worthy chieftain of the people, Cloud Runner.'

'Any sky warrior would be, ancestor. Few are given the chance. Before you depart, there is something I must know. When first we met, you told me I should not become a sky warrior if there was anyone I would regret leaving behind. Did you have any regrets about becoming a Marine?'

The dreadnought regarded him. 'Sometimes I still do. It is a sad thing to leave people you care about behind, knowing they will be lost to you forever.

'Goodbye, Cloud Runner. We will not meet again.'

The dreadnought turned and departed, leaving Cloud Runner enthroned among his people, his hands toying with a braid of ancient hair.

DEVIL'S MARAUDERS

William King

'THEY'RE COMING,' SAID Nipper, peering out into the jungle. Even
with his nightsight goggles set to max he couldn't really see
anything, but he could tell something was wrong. The jungle
was too still, everything was too calm. He had a crawling feeling between his shoulder blades. That feeling had kept him
alive for nearly six months in the steaming arboreal wastes of
H'thra. He respected his intuition.

'I can't see anything,' Borski said. Nipper turned to look at
him. In the moonlight filtering down from topside the commissar looked even more skeletal than usual. Amazing how he
manages to keep that uniform so clean, Nipper thought.
Everyone else looks like they've been swimming in a pool of
sweat, but not Borski.

His trenchcoat was immaculate, his silver skull buttons
gleamed. His youthful fanatic face gazed out from beneath his
peaked cap through a transparent spore mask. 'If Nipper says
there's something out there then I believe him, sir,' Sergeant
Krask said, hesitantly. Borski glanced over at the sergeant as if
he could measure Krask's devotion to the Emperor at a glance.

'Very well, soldiers, lock and load. Ogryn – the Emperor
wants you to ready the grenade launcher.'

49

'Sure thing, sir,' Truk said worshipfully. 'Truk is ready to dine.'

Nipper watched the huge ogryn raise the heavy weapon like a toy. Truk grinned at him. He looked as if he were enjoying himself. It was hard to believe he was the last survivor of the company's ogryn section. Nipper considered the comrades he had lost in the previous three nights' fighting, and was anything but cheerful.

He turned his attention back to the jungle, trying to ignore the pain-filled moan of Lieutenant Mikals. A small suckerleech crawled across Nipper's combat jacket and he swatted it with one heavy gauntleted hand. He wiped his palm on his thigh before adjusting his spore mask left-handed.

Need to change the filter as soon as possible, he thought. It was only a temporary distraction. What's wrong, he wondered? Why am I so uneasy?

'No tree-swingers,' Sal said. Nipper looked at the little sanctioned psyker. She had crawled over to where he was and lay on her stomach beside him. He noted her lovely face on top of her thin twisted body. He saw eyes and teeth discoloured by the crimson stain of witch-spore addiction. She has a strange beauty, he thought.

'Thank you,' Sal said. Nipper felt his face flush. Sal's talent was intermittent but her mind-reading ability was at peak tonight. She had been taking huge doses of witch-spore to enable her to track the rebels. It had amplified her powers greatly. Suddenly what she said sank in.

'Hey, sergeant, no fuzzymonkeys.' He pointed upwards to topside, straining to make out movement through the clouds of spores that drifted in the moonlight.

'That's it,' Borski said, drawing his pistol. 'Prepare to hold your positions, men. For the Emperor!'

'Commissar, I can feel mindforms moving about half a click east. Human but strangely distorted. Feels like rebels.' Sal looked deeply disturbed. She said there was something about the minds of their foe that made her uneasy. Nipper thought he understood. Delving into the minds of heretics must be upsetting.

The thirty or so survivors of A Company were taking up their prepared positions. Everyone was tired after three days of daytime sniping and night-time warfare. They had been ordered to hold this position for as long as possible before falling back. So far they had blocked the rebel offensive but tonight Nipper did not doubt that the heretics would break through.

All around him he could see the green ready lights of weapons wink as their owners made final checks. The familiar litany of the Weaponers' chant filled his ears.

'Emperor save us,' muttered Nipper worriedly, his nerves frayed by the three long days of combat. He was singled out for Borski's special attention.

'The Emperor will aid you if, and only if, you fight bravely,' the commissar thundered. 'And the daemons of hell will take all cowards. I personally will see to that.'

The religious intensity in Borski's voice made Nipper shiver. The commissar had risen in full view of his men, eschewing cover. Nipper had to admire his courage. If the Emperor protects the brave he will certainly watch over Borski, Nipper admitted.

Some of the commissar's unshakeable certainty in his own righteousness transmitted itself to Nipper. He prayed silently to the Emperor. The rest of the company seemed similarly enthused. The whining and quiet chatter had stopped.

'Our faith is our shield,' said Borski. 'We are weapons in the fist of the Emperor and we will be worthy. We will smite the unrighteous.'

Nipper turned to see movement among the distant branches of the nation-trees.

'Tea's out,' said Truk.

All around him the jungle seemed to burn. From overhead came blinding laser flashes as rebel jetbikes swooped insanely under topside. Nipper raised his laser and snapped off a quick shot. He hit a bike-pilot in the face. The wounded man leaned forward on the controls. The bike nose-dived. Nipper could see his gunner trying to jump clear.

Nipper tracked its fall, ready to shoot any survivors. The jet-cycle hit a weak patch in the carpet moss and vanished from view. Nipper heard a long scream followed by a splash. Involuntarily he shuddered. The things that lived below, in the eternal wet darkness beneath the nation-tree's roots, were things he had nightmares about.

'Nipper, down!' he heard Borski shout.

Without thinking he threw himself flat on the greenside floor. A stream of bolt pistol fire passed through where he had

just been standing. Nipper looked at the point of impact and
saw a tall, thin warrior in the camouflage uniform of the rebels
fall. He turned to thank the commissar but he had already
moved on, rushing towards the cover of a muck-fungus tree.
Laser fire withered the carpet moss behind his feet.

Nipper rolled over and searched for the firer. He saw a huge
dark figure moving among the shadows of nearby tree boles.
He brought his lasrifle up to the fire position and sent a full-
intensity burst towards his target. Brilliant white fire played
over it. Burn, heretic, thought Nipper.

He felt a thrill of fear as the figure refused to fall. His finger
slackened on the trigger. He could make out details as the rebel
advanced towards him. His heart sank. It was a killer robot,
obviously modified to find its way through the greenside. One
hand was a chainsword, the other had a heavy bolter which it
was laboriously bringing to bear on Nipper.

He could hear the whine of servo-motors as the arm moved.
The heavy plasteel of its carapace had melted and ran where
Nipper's laser had struck. It was painted with several strange
and disturbing runes. Nipper leapt back as it opened fire.

Explosive bullets churned the carpet moss where he had
been. He cast a glance towards the nearest cover. Too far, he
thought, I'll never make it. He grinned, as adrenaline raced
through his body. His circle of awareness seemed to expand as
he waited for bullets to rip through him. He turned and he
could make out the tiny webwork of engraving on the robot's
carapace, hear the crack of small arms fire and the screams of
the dying. Everything seemed discrete and distinct. He could
hear his breath rumble within his chest and feel the individual
movement of every muscle. He stared down the barrel of that
huge gun.

Facing death, he felt totally alive.

He rolled to one side and the robot's arm seemed to track as
if in slow motion. He raised his own weapon and reached for
the action of the grenade launcher. Only one chance, he
thought. Better get it right.

He came to rest and fired the grenade. It arced towards the
robot's feet and detonated. Nipper felt the force of the explosion ripple the carpet moss.

He looked back at the robot. It still stood. I'm dead, thought
Nipper.

Then the robot seemed to slowly disappear. It vanished from view and fell. As Nipper had intended, the grenade had weakened the moss beneath it. He let out a long breath. It felt good to be alive. He noticed more rebels advancing among the trees. Their full-face spore-masks and bulging goggles made them look like horrible insects. He saw that they too had strange runes on their chests where badges of battle honour should have been.

'Fall back,' he heard Borski shout. There was a note of bitterness in the commissar's voice. He did not relish sounding the retreat.

Nipper ran back towards his own lines. Each step took forever. He felt light, as if he were walking on the moon. Laser beams blurred past his head, almost blinding him. Miraculously none hit him. Under the shadow of swooping jetbikes he reached the cover of a snapwort bush. A familiar figure huddled behind it, laspistol in hand.

'LEAVE ME,' SAL said. 'Save yourself.'

Her wounds looked worse than they were. The long sticky leaves of the vampire plant fondled them obscenely, looking for blood. Nipper looked out from cover.

Flitting from bole to bole were hundreds of rebel troopers. From above, a dozen heavily modified jetbikes gave covering fire. The enemy had broken through.

Nipper checked Sal's filter mask. It was still completely in place. Good. He unclipped some med-plas from his belt and sprayed the wounded area.

'That should kill any spores,' he muttered, watching the plasti-flesh congeal. He hoped the disinfectant and fungicide worked better than the last lot or Sal was in for a painful death.

'I mean it, Nipper. Go! If you're still here when the rebels come, they'll–'

'No can do, Sal,' he said. 'You know the code.'

She looked up at him and smiled in spite of her pain. 'The Marauders look after their own. Nipper, we're not back on Thranx and this isn't a streetfight.'

He shrugged. 'Hey… If we don't look after each other no one else will.'

Suddenly Sal's face went slack. He knew she was in listening trance. A moment later intelligence flooded back into her face.

'Borski and Krask have the rest of them about two hundred metres back. They're heading for the old comms hutch. Go the way I tell you. I think we'll have a clear path.'

Nipper nodded. 'Can you run, Sal?'

'I'll have to.'

Just before they made the break she turned and looked back towards the oncoming enemy. An expression of fear passed across her face.

'By the Emperor, they hate us so,' she said. She and Nipper ran. From behind came the sounds of sporadic firing as the rebels mopped up the last of the opposition.

'WE'RE ON OUR own,' Borski said, with a certain grim satisfaction. He looked like a man who had just found a big enough challenge to measure his faith against. He cut the comm-link with HQ. Lieutenant Mikals cried out in agony.

Wonderful, Nipper thought, looking around the old Harvesters' cabin that some dead tech-adept had converted into a communications nexus. It had a familiar homey look. He had grown up surrounded by machinery, not giant plants. For a moment he felt home-sick for a place far beyond his ability to measure distance.

He slumped wearily down on the hard bench. He was tired, as much from the brief firefight as the night of marching that had followed.

He didn't want to think about that nightmarish journey through the green. He had had to partially carry Sal while keeping alert for any threats from the surrounding forest. Once he had almost been ensnared by a dreamspider's web. Several times he had nearly fallen through the carpet moss to swampside thirty metres below. Twice he had to hide, frozen with fear, while rebel scouts filtered by. It had taken them what felt like forever to reach the comms hutch.

He looked around at the few survivors of A Company. He saw Borski, the sarge, Lieutenant Mikals, Truk. There were few familiar faces from the old days when the Devil's Marauders had been a streetgang in the worldcity of Thranx. That had been before the Raising when they had been fierce and desperate enough to be inducted into the Imperial Guard.

By the Emperor, there had been nearly a hundred of them then. Now there was only himself and Sal, Hunt, Glyn, Mak and Colquan. His friends had changed. They still wore their gang colours but they had been incorporated into the uniform of the guard. The only real sign of their former allegiance was the huge devil head on the backs of their combat jackets. They still had the old face tattoos but the faces themselves were thinner, gaunt and haunted, patched with scars. Hunt had a bionic eye visible under his face mask. Mak had an arm of plasteel and servomotors.

A palpable air of demoralization had fallen over the room. All the others are dead or in the hands of rebels, Nipper thought. He didn't know which was worse. Mikals whimpered in agony.

'No chance of any support?' Krask asked. The sarge looked more tired than any man had a right to be and still be alive, Nipper thought. He had carried the terribly wounded Mikals all night on his own.

'None,' Borski said sternly. 'The heretics have begun a massive offensive right across Blue Zone. Still, the righteous will prevail. Within one standard day *Divine Retribution* will cleanse this whole zone with an orbital bombardment. We have been ordered to fall back.'

'What?' Krask was both frightened and bewildered. Nipper broke from his reverie. Anything that scared Krask terrified Nipper. He had never seen the sergeant display anything but laconic cool.

'That's madness,' Krask muttered. 'The whole reason for sending us into the jungle in the first place was to drive Governor Damian's rebels out without damaging the witch-spore crop.'

'That was before the full scale of the insurrection was realized,' Borski said, almost gently. 'We did not realize the cancer of heresy had spread so deep. We are not facing simply a rebel garrison but many of the native tribes of the interior. They're armed and they're allied with something dark and terrible. They bear its mark.'

For the first time Nipper thought that he detected a trace of what might have been fear in the commissar's voice. He thought back to the strange runes he had seen on the robot. He had heard stories, muttered tales, of daemons who existed in the dark between worlds and sought to undermine the works of the righteous. He had always dismissed them as stories to frighten children.

Beside him Sal muttered. 'It makes sense. Where better for them to strike than on the world where witch-spore comes from? Many latents would have their powers brought to the fore.'

Nipper wondered what she was talking about. He knew that psykers were dangerous. The priests of the Imperial cult told everyone so. Only ones who had been bonded to the Emperor or who had undergone the terrible training to become sanctioned could be allowed to live. Could those who had not been bonded provide some sort of gateway for enemies of the Emperor?

Nipper felt Sal nudge him in the ribs. She gave him a warning look. 'You are on dangerous ground,' she whispered. 'Best to not even think of such mysteries.'

Another more pressing problem struck Nipper. He addressed Borski. 'Sir, if they are going to cleanse this place in twenty-four hours what will happen to us?'

'We are ordered to fall back to Zone Amber.'

Mikals reached out imploringly, eyes filled with pain. 'Commissar, I am wounded. I will only slow you on the march. I have failed the Emperor. I seek atonement.'

Borski looked down at him, cold eyes hooded. He nodded. 'Very well. Soldiers outside, prepare to depart.'

The guards left the hut. From within came the sound of a single shot. Borski emerged alone. 'Now we must go,' he said.

'Zone Amber is fifty kilometres away. We'll never get there before the bombardment starts,' Nipper said.

Borski showed his chilling smile. 'Then we will die joyous in the knowledge that we have served our Emperor well,' he said.

WEARILY THE SURVIVORS pushed on through the nation-forest. Dawn had come, bringing a wash of green light down through topside. Nipper watched the endless tide of airborne spores rise on convection currents. Dazzling dragon-moths, long as a man's arm, pursued shoals of glitterflies. Sometimes puff-balls would roll out onto the main branches they followed and Truk would kick them, laughing moronically as they exploded.

Only Truk did not seem oppressed by their surroundings and the fact that they were twenty hours from being reduced to plasma by the orbital bombardment. Nipper wondered how he could ever have liked this place.

It had all seemed so fresh and amazing to him six months ago: a riot of green life erupting across a continent. From the two hundred metre high banyan-like nation-trees to the triple-tiered ecology they supported, it had all been wonderful to a boy from the steel corridors of the hive-world of Thranx.

He had marvelled at the differences between the layers. It had delighted him that topside, with its swinging monkeys and bright sunlight, was as different from greenside as that was from the devil-python-infested swamps below.

He could well remember his first sight of topside: an endless garden of flowers visible from the armoured aircar's glassteel windows. He could remember the terror of his first patrol, hunting raiders in the eternal darkness of the humus swamps at the nation-trees' roots. Even that had held a strange kind of wonder, as they had walked across the rippling surface on pontoon shoes while pale beasts scuttled from the light of their torches.

But it had been greenside he had loved best. He had marvelled at the way branches of the great trees had intermeshed so tightly that carpet moss could grow between them to form a near solid surface which could, mostly, support a man's weight. It had seemed miraculous that it was all supported underneath by the steel-hard cablewebs of the weavers.

It was so perfect that it could almost have been designed by a god. Even now that the initial glamour had faded it still seemed slightly blasphemous to him that it was about to be vaped from orbit.

He looked up at the cathedral-like arches of the trunks rising above him and shook his head, as if he could shake off his feelings of reverence as easily as a dog shaking off water. He couldn't. The place dwarfed him, as it dwarfed the straggling line of his companions, even mighty Truk.

'You're right,' Sal said from beside him. She was looking up at him with a strange expression on her face, as if seeing him for the first time. 'We don't belong here.'

'We don't fit, do we?' he said. 'Everything else here has symmetry, contributes something to the pattern about us. Even the rebels have learned to blend in, in a weird sort of way. That's why they are beating us.'

Sal smiled. 'Symmetry – it's because this world was designed by bio-adepts during the Dark Age of Technology. That's what records say. I was in the mind of the clerk who was transcribing the report back at Dropsite.'

Sal fell silent. Nipper looked down at her. She was pale and drawn. Already lines of pain and fatigue were etched into her face. She stumbled and almost fell but Nipper supported her. She did not ask to rest. Nipper guessed that, like the rest of them, she knew she would be left behind.

SIX HOURS INTO their march they found the body. It was that of a man. He had been left stretched out in the glistening coils of a dreamspider's web. His mask had been torn away and fungus emerged through his mouth, nostrils and other orifices. Nipper thought it was a ghastly way to die – lungs filled and insides eaten away by parasitic fungus. Yet the man was smiling. The narcotic strands of the web had done their work. He could see the dreamspider retreating from its decomposing prey as they approached.

Krask looked at the body, a haunted look on his face.

'What's wrong?' Borski asked.

'Look at the man's clothing, sir. He's wearing green bark-cloth and carrying a spore-harvesting pouch. He's one of our loyalist scouts.'

'So?' Borski said.

Nipper understood. 'A man like that knows the forest. He wouldn't blunder into a dreamspider web.'

'Someone put him there?' Borski looked thoughtful.

'Rebel woodsrunners. The natives believe that the web of a dreamspider ensnares the soul. It's the worst form of death in their book. We lost a man up near Spook Mountain last spring. They'd done the same thing.'

'This means rebels had already passed our outpost line before their big push,' Borski snapped. 'Weapons at the ready. Be wary of ambush!'

Without any great enthusiasm the guards began to check their weapons. Gingerly they passed the web.

For some time afterwards, as he and Sal limped down the trail, Nipper could feel the dead man's calm, ecstatic eyes staring at his back.

NIPPER SURVEYED THE surrounding woods fearfully, looking for signs of the rebel woodsrunners. He knew that if they were

concealed his chances were slim. The natives wore chameleo-
line suits and were expert at blending in with the terrain. He
paused for a minute and placed the stimm injector into the
conduit on his filter mask.

There was a hiss of gas and he breathed deep. Artificial
energy surged through him and he felt suddenly strong and
alert, as if he could count the leaves on all the nearby trees. He
knew the feeling would not last and in the end would leave
him feeling worse, but at the moment he needed some encour-
agement to trudge on.

He offered the injector to Sal but she shook her head.
Perhaps it interferes with her powers, he thought.

'That's right,' she said. 'I'd go bug-crazy if I mixed that stuff
with witch-spore. It's bad enough having to try and tune everybody out all the time but when you're on stimm it's like
everything is so loud it hurts.'

Nipper looked at her. For the first time he considered that her
gift might also be a curse. He had always imagined what fun it
would be to be able to listen in on other people's thoughts,
what advantages he could gain from it, how god-like it must
feel to have that power. He had never considered that it might
have disadvantages as well.

Sal smiled knowingly at him. He felt a brief flash of resentment. Damned spy, he thought. She shook her head and
looked away.

Almost at once he was sorry. She had been a good friend to
him. It was just that he had never seen her power so active
before. She seemed to be reading him all the time. It was as if
the proximity of death had tripped a switch within her, turning
her power up to full. It was disturbing for him but he decided
he could live with it. He squeezed her shoulder.

'Sorry,' he said but she did not reply. He noticed that her eyes
were closed and she was once more in trance. Her eyes snapped
open. Nipper could see panic in them.

'They're out there,' she said. 'East and west, about twenty of
them. They're running parallel to us.'

Overhead the restless movement of branches had stopped.
The tree-swingers were gone.

'COMMISSAR, SHOULD WE stop?' enquired Krask. 'We could make
a stand.'

Borski turned and glared into the jungle, keen fanatic eyes searching. 'What are they waiting for?'

Krask shrugged. 'Maybe for us to tire or make camp. Maybe there's something ahead that we don't know about. Best be wary.'

'I doubt if we could surprise them,' Borski said. 'Best that we continue southward as swiftly as possible. We have our orders.'

'Commissar, Truk would like to fight. Truk will wait for enemy. Cover others.'

Borski looked at him. 'The Emperor appreciates your bravery, ogryn. But that will not be necessary.'

'We'll see action soon enough,' Mak muttered.

Nipper examined the nearby trees carefully but could see no sign of the enemy. He was not reassured. He had known men to pass within two metres of rebel scouts who had killed them and they had never noticed their killers. He cast an uneasy glance at the sky. Up there was another invisible threat that was just as deadly.

By now the *Divine Retribution* would be in position, awaiting merely the command to fire. He checked his wrist chrono. Ten hours to go.

GLYN DIED FIRST. A hail of magnetically accelerated shuriken ripped through his body.

Nipper saw a dozen cuts appear on Truk. The ogryn looked around bemused, as if he did not really feel any pain. He was searching for the source of the attack.

Nipper flung Sal to one side, then threw himself flat into the hollow of the mainbranch they had been following. He peered around but could see no sign of the enemy.

He knew shuriken catapults were perfect for jungle warfare. They accelerated their razor-edged weapons to a speed where they could penetrate body-armour. They were rapid-firing and silent. All rebel scouts carried them.

Nipper lay quiet, feeling his flesh crawl, expecting at any minute to be shredded by their hidden assailants.

'Nipper,' Sal said. 'That tree fork fifty metres south-west, about five metres up.'

He stared at where she directed. He thought he saw some-thing just as he heard Hunt scream. The cry was cut off by a horrid gurgling sound, as if blood clogged Hunt's throat.

Now Nipper could just make out the outlines of a humanoid form. It was almost invisible, so perfectly did its cham-cloth suit blend into the surrounding green.

Sweat rolled down Nipper's face. He made himself take careful aim at the target, all the time fighting to hold down the fear that the rebel was drawing a bead on him.

He opened fire, praying to the Emperor that his aim was true. He saw a line of fire blacken the branches he had aimed at. He heard a scream of intolerable pain and it seemed for one obscene moment as if the tree was screaming. Then something fell from the bole onto the carpet moss below. For a second it was conspicuous, a green body on the brown forest floor, but then it seemed to vanish as its suit did its work.

Nipper looked at Sal. 'Where are the rest?'

She concentrated. 'They seem to have pulled back out of range. I think it was a lone sniper. Hunt and Glyn are dead. I felt them die.'

Her face was white and she seemed close to tears. Nipper was truly glad that he was not a psyker. It's bad enough watching comrades die but feeling it from the inside must be dreadful, he thought. There was a void inside him, a vacuum. He had known the two men for most of his life. Now they were gone. He shook his head.

He noticed how drawn Sal looked. A tick twitched far back in her jaw. Her eyes were wild and staring. He wondered how much more of this she could take. Wearily he checked his chrono. Eight and a half hours left.

'Don't worry,' he told her. 'We'll make it.'

He wished he sounded more convincing.

ONE FOOT IN front of the other, Nipper thought. And again. And again. It was physically painful for him to move now. It was as if a great weight had been attached to each foot and he had to swing it to move. He no longer watched the forest for rebel scouts. He was past caring. There were times when he would have welcomed being cut down by enemy fire. It would have put him out of his misery.

The forest had become a green hell. His companions were damned souls on their way to purgatory. The light hurt his eyes and made the trees seem like looming gigantic daemons. It was if the forest had taken on a malevolent sentience and mocked them. It sneered at the tiny people who crawled across its body like ants.

Well, you'll get yours, Nipper thought feverishly. You won't laugh at us when the *Divine Retribution* blasts you right out of existence.

Beside him Sal was a constant drag, pulling at him like the gravity of a black hole, slowing his steps, draining his energy. Her eyes were half closed and her movements were stiff. Nipper felt that if she had not been leaning against him she would have fallen right off the main branch. By the Emperor, he would probably fall over himself if she had not been there.

From behind him he could hear Truk singing in a deep tuneless bass. He seemed to be repeating the same words over and over again, occasionally changing the order in which they came. The monotony worked on Nipper's frayed psyche. It was exquisite torture. Ahead of them Mak and Colquan bickered like two drunk men. Their arguments had the relentless circularity of people too weary to think. They were reduced to making statements that they had said before. Their words had become mantras as leeched of meaning as Truk's song.

'We should wait and ambush those daemon-loving scum-suckers,' said Mak, flexing his metallic fingers.

'Naw, we should push on back to Zone Amber before the bombardment, otherwise we'll all fry.'

'Look, if Damian's little buddies get us, we won't care about the bombardment. We'll all be dead anyway.'

There was an edge of hysteria to Colquan's voice. 'We've got to move. That way we can keep ahead of them.'

'They know the terrain. They're natives. We'll never outrun them.'

They seemed to be about to come to blows.

'Silence,' said Borski in a hoarse rasping whisper that cut through all the other noise. 'Such bickering is unseemly among the Emperor's chosen troops. You are a disgrace to the uniform.'

Both Mak and Colquan stiffened and pulled themselves up straight. They said nothing but nodded shamefaced and began to march with renewed vigour.

Six hours, thought Nipper. Let them pass quickly. All I want is an end to this. He stumbled and both he and Sal fell. It was nearly a minute before they could get up again.

* * *

THEY CAME TO a vast open space between the nation-trees. All around the forest was burnt. Nipper looked down. For a moment his curiosity overcame his weariness.

Already weavers were throwing their silk cables across the gap. He could see a huge web, brilliant in the green light. It was anchored against the boles of the nearer trees. Strands of carpet moss were starting to fill in the gaps. He could see the dull lumps that were the weavers continue their work. It was hard to believe that the mindless dog-size arachnids could build such a perfect structure.

'What caused this?' Borski asked.

Krask looked up and then moved ahead to the edge of the webbing. 'Crash,' he said.

Nipper saw that above them a huge swathe of topside had been cleared away. In the clear sky above he could see hive balloons floating, their long stinger lines dangling.

Nipper moved to the edge of the burned-out area and looked down. He peered into the gloom. Something was half-buried in the humus-swamp below. He upped the magnification of his goggles and saw that it was an armoured transport flyer. It looked like a gigantic beetle.

'Side's been torn out of it,' Krask said. 'Somebody must have hit it with a rocket-launcher. It's no use to us.'

Nipper shook his head. He wondered who had been on the flyer, whether he had known any of the people for whom the vehicle was a coffin. It all seemed so futile.

What are we doing here, he asked himself; walking the surface of a world so far from home that the distance is incomprehensible. Fighting people I don't even know, against whom I have no quarrel. In this jungle thousands of people are dying, and for what? The glory of the Emperor? The megalomaniac dreams of an insane governor?

He was shocked to find himself thinking such thoughts. They ran totally against his training, his indoctrination. What had happened to him? Once he had been proud to be an Imperial guardsman, to fight for the safety of the Empire. Now he just felt hollow. He was thinking like a heretic.

He was suddenly ashamed of himself. He was staining the honour of the regiment for which many of his comrades had died. He looked over at Borski and envied him his faith. Nipper had reached the limits of his. He felt an overwhelming urge to go to the commissar and confess his failure, to say that he was unworthy to be a soldier of the Emperor, to beg for the release from the endless fear that the commissar's gun would bring him.

He was afflicted by a weariness not only of the body but of the spirit. It seemed pointless to go on. Even if, by some miracle, he escaped the bombardment he would just be sent back into the jungle to fight again. He did not want that. He had failed. The only thing left to do was atone.

He began to move towards the commissar. He felt Sal clutch at his hand with desperate strength.

'No, Nipper, don't,' she said. 'We can do it. If only you can make yourself go on.'

He tried to shake her off.

'I can't make it without your help,' she said imploringly. He looked at her. She seemed desperate. He could not let her down. He did not feel capable of living up to the Imperial tradition of discipline and self-sacrifice but this was personal. The Marauders looked after their own.

They trudged on, a step at a time, away from the abyss. Behind them the weavers continued to work mindlessly, unaware of the passing of men or the imminence of their own doom.

Only three more hours, Nipper thought. And it will be over one way or another. I can put off death for that long.

'I THINK THEY'RE getting ready to attack,' Sal said. Nipper had thought he was too tired to be afraid but found he wasn't.

'You sure?' he asked.

She nodded. 'They've been following us all this time. They thought we might lead them to a hidden base. Now they're getting impatient. Something seems to be affecting their minds. They want to kill.'

'You hear that, sergeant?' Nipper asked.

Krask nodded and muttered something to Borski. The commissar straightened up and brushed spores from the cuff of his uniform.

'Break out what's left of your stimm. We are going to kill some heretics.'

Nipper emptied the inhaler and felt a trickle of nervous energy pass through him. It was enough to make him alert. He saw Mak and Colquan looking at him. I wonder, he thought, do I look like that?

There was a jerky quality to the other guards' movements and their eyes seemed dead beneath their bubble goggles. They cocked their heads like caricatures of people listening, assumed postures of exaggerated wariness. They looked so ridiculous that Nipper almost laughed, but he recognized that as a side-effect of the drug and fought to bring the mad hilarity under control.

'It's going to be dark soon,' Krask said. 'That's when they'll attack.'

'This looks like as good a position as any to defend,' Borski said crisply. 'Krask, use your chainsword to cut down those fungus trees. They will give us some cover.'

A feeling almost of relief swept over the other Marauders. They seemed happy. It was as if they were tired of running, as if they had already given up on their lives and relished the chance of some action, Nipper thought. At least it would be a break from the monotony of the march, he found himself thinking crazily. Still he was full of fear.

'COME ON,' COLQUAN muttered.

They had been waiting twenty minutes and there was still no sign of the enemy. Their drug-induced energy was starting to fade. Lying behind their fungal barricades reminded them of how tired they were. Darkness swept over the dense forest like a wave.

'Truk is feeling peckish,' the ogryn said.

Borski glared at Sal. 'Are you sure they are going to attack, psyker?'

'Yes, commissar,' she said. She had drawn her laspistol and was inspecting it carefully. 'They are out there now. About two hundred metres and closing. They're advancing warily. They wonder what we are up to.'

'Keep your eyes peeled, soldiers,' said Borski. Nipper sighted in the direction Sal had indicated. He ventured a quick glance at the sky, visible through a gap in the foliage. Was that rapidly-moving star the *Divine Retribution*, he wondered, or just the nearest planet, Ka'ana? He checked the time. Under an hour till the bombardment starts, he thought. How far had they come? He felt sure it wasn't far enough.

It was strange. Earlier, filled with shame at his own weakness, he had wanted to die. Now when death seemed imminent he found that he desperately wanted to live. He was filled with disgust. Truly I am a spineless creature, he thought.

Was that movement he saw? He felt a thrill of fear pass through him. He stared at a patch of shadow suspiciously. No, he thought, just jumpy. Adrenalin was pumping through his system and weariness had begun to recede.

Was that shadow lengthening? It was, and in no natural way. Emperor guide my hand, he prayed, and squeezed the trigger of his lasrifle. There was a hum as the weapons generator kicked in. A perfectly straight beam of light crackled though the night and hit the shadow, illuminating the figure of a man. Nipper heard a scream. In the torchlight of the burning figure other rebels were revealed.

All of a sudden everyone was firing. Nipper saw the flash of las-fire out of the corner of his eye, partially dampened by his protective goggles. He heard the strange coughing sound of the grenade launcher as Truk fired it. A brilliant explosion shattered the night. Nipper saw rebel bodies tumble through the air away from the point of impact. He felt vibration ripple through the carpet moss.

Mist rose from the fungus tree trunk. For a second he wondered what was happening, then he realized that shuriken darts were hitting it.

Nipper took a wild guess at where they were coming from and fired a burst in that direction. He was rewarded with a shout of pain. He dropped flat just as a hail of shuriken hissed through the air where he had been. Pure terror surged through him. That had been too close.

Once more the ground trembled, once more he heard the sound of an explosion. He fought the urge to remain still, to huddle up in a ball and beg for mercy. He remained frozen in place. He could not move. Tears streamed down his face.

Suddenly a shadow passed over him. He cringed with fear, forced himself to look up. It was Borski. He looked calm and unafraid.

'Get up, soldier,' he said, ignoring the hail of darts which blurred by him. Nipper shook his head. Borski raised his pistol and snapped a shot off into the distance. Nipper heard a ricochet, saw Borski grimace with annoyance, like a man who had just missed a target on a practice range. He fired again and something close by groaned.

'You can die like a cringing dog or like a soldier of the Imperium,' Borski said. His calm voice carried clearly over the noise of battle. He fired again. The noise of his pistol seemed impossibly loud. 'Be quick, your soul is in peril.'

Momentarily the noise of battle seemed to recede. Nipper looked up at the face of the commissar. Borski was strong and certain. His faith seemed to shield him as he stood amid the hail of enemy fire. Nipper knew his own hopelessness and lack of faith and felt diminished. He was filled with terror at the certainty of his own death. It turned his limbs to liquid.

He tried to make himself move. We all die in the end, he told himself. It is the manner of our dying that counts. Insight filled him. He knew as Borski knew that they were going to die here. That being the case, he had nothing to fear. His fate was already sealed. There was nothing he could do to alter it. His only choice was the way in which he met his end. Borski was setting him an example of how to do it. He smiled up at the commissar and rose to his feet.

Borski nodded, satisfied. 'The correct decision,' he said. 'You are a true guardsman.'

Then his face was blown away by a hail of shuriken. Nipper looked at him and screamed.

A red haze fell over Nipper and he twisted, firing insanely into the oncoming rebels. He vaulted on to the top of the tree stump he had been cowering behind and set his lasrifle for full coverage. Howling with rage, he sprayed the enemy. He clicked the single-shot grenade launcher and fired again. An explosion racked the air. He continued to fire until his rifle powered down.

His terror had been transmuted to berserk fury. Filled with rage, he charged towards the enemy, miraculously avoiding being shot. The Emperor protects me, he thought crazily. He began laying about him with the butt of his rifle, crunching into the rebels with insane strength.

'Follow me, Marauders,' he yelled. 'For the Emperor, for Borski, for our dead!'

Suddenly he was the centre of a swirling melee. He could hear the crack of small-arms fire and the gleeful shouts of Truk as he went hand-to-hand with the foe. Nipper picked up a chainsword from the hands of a dead rebel NCO and began to lay about him. Everywhere he struck a man died. The Emperor guides my hand and fills my heart with fury, he thought. The others emerged to join him in the fight.

Soon the enemy were routed, unable to face Nipper's insane anger. As he watched them depart Nipper did not think they would return. He fell on his knees and wept.

'HALT! IDENTIFY YOURSELVES!' said a harsh voice in Imperial Gothic.

'A company of the Fifth Thranxian Regiment, the Devil's Marauders,' replied Krask.

'Pretty small company,' replied the sentry. Nipper agreed. Only Mak, Krask, Sal, Truk and himself were left of all the people who had set out. The ogryn carried the body of Commissar Borski under one arm.

'Any more disrespect and I'll have you shot,' Krask said in his best imitation of Borski's tone. 'Where are we anyway?'

Nipper heard the sentry gulp. 'Pretty far south, sir. Perimeter station Amber Twelve.'

'We're inside Zone Amber then?'

'Yes, sir. Five kilometres.'

Nipper felt relief flood through him. He looked forward to getting some sleep in a relatively secure camp.

The sentry spoke again. 'You just made it in time.'

'I know,' Krask said.

'How could you, sir? We've only just got the order. We have to fall back to Zone Grey. The enemy have broken through perimeter Amber. The *Divine Retribution* is going to bombard this area from orbit in twenty-four hours.'

Nipper felt like screaming. Behind them a curtain of fire descended from the sky and the sector they had just left caught fire. From where Nipper stood it seemed as if the whole world was burning.

PESTILENCE

Dan Abnett

'The Archenemy infects this universe. If we do not pause to
fight that infection here, within our own selves,
what purpose is there in taking our fight to the stars?'

– Apothecary Engane,
from his *Treatise on Imperial Medicine*

I

IT IS MY belief that memory is the finest faculty we as a species
own. Through the function of memory, we are able to gather,
hone and transmit all manner of knowledge for the benefit of
mankind, and the endless glory of our God-Emperor, may the
golden throne endure for ever more!

To forget a mistake is to be defeated a second time, so we are
taught in the sermons of Thor. How may a great leader plan his
campaign without memory of those battles won and lost
before? How may his soldiers absorb his teaching and improve
without that gift? How may the Ecclesiarchy disseminate its
enervating message to the universal populace without that
populace holding the teachings in memory? What are scholars,
clerks, historians or chroniclers but agencies of memory?

And what is forgetfulness but the overthrow of memory, the ruination of precious knowledge, and an abhorrence?

I have, in the service of His Exalted Majesty the Emperor of Terra, waged war upon that abhorrence all my life. I strive to locate and recover things forgotten and return them to the custody of memory. I am a scrabbler in dark places, an illuminator of shadows, a turner of long un-turned pages, an asker of questions that have lapsed, forever hunting for answers that would otherwise have remained unvoiced. I am a recollector, prizing lost secrets from the taciturn universe and returning them to the safe fold of memory, where they might again improve our lot amongst the out-flung stars.

My particular discipline is that of materia medica, for human medicine was my original calling. Our understanding of our own vital mechanisms is vast and admirable, but we can never know too much about our own biology and how to protect, repair and improve it. It is our burden as a species to exist in a galaxy riven by war, and where war goes, so flourish its hand-servants injury and disease. It may be said that as each war front advances, so medical knowledge advances too. And where armies fall back in defeat or are destroyed, so medical knowledge retreats or is forgotten. Such are the lapses I seek to redress.

Upon that very purpose, I came to Symbal Iota late in my forty-eighth year, looking for Ebhoe. To provide context, let me say that this would be the third year of the Genovingian campaign in the Obscura Segmentum, and about nine sidereal months after the first outbreak of Uhlren's Pox amongst the Guard legions stationed on Genovingia itself. Also known, colloquially, as blood-froth, Uhlren's Pox was named after the first victim it took, a colour-sergeant called Gustaf Uhlren, of the Fifteenth Mordian, if memory serves me. And I pride myself it does.

And as a student of Imperial history, and materia medica too, you will have Uhlren's Pox in your memory. A canker of body and vitality, virulently contagious, it corrupts from within, thickening circulatory fluids and wasting marrow, while embellishing the victim's skin with foul cysts and buboes. The cycle between infection and death is at most four days. In the later stages, organs rupture, blood emulsifies and bubbles through the pores of the skin, and the victim becomes violently delusional. Some have even conjectured that by this phase, the soul itself has been corroded away. Death is inescapable in almost every case.

It appeared without warning on Genovingia, and within a month, the Medicae Regimentalis were recording twenty death notices a day. No drug or procedure could be found that began to even slow its effects. No origin for the infection could be located. Worst of all, despite increasingly vigorous programs of quarantine and cleansing, no method could be found to prevent wholesale contagion. No plague carriers, or means of transmission, were identifiable.

As an individual man weakens and sickens, so the Imperial Guard forces as a whole began to fail and falter as their best were taken by the pestilence. Within two months, Warmaster Rhyngold's staff were doubting the continued viability of the entire campaign. By the third month, Uhlren's Pox had also broken out (apparently miraculously and spontaneously, given its unknown process of dispersal) on Genovingia Minor, Lorches and Adamanaxer Delta. Four separate centres of infection, right along the leading edge of the Imperial advance through the sector. At that point, the contagion had spread to the civilian population of Genovingia itself, and the Administratum had issued a Proclamation of Pandemic. It was said the skies above the cities of that mighty world were black with carrion flies and the stench of biological pollution permeated every last acre of the planet.

I had a bureaucratic posting on Lorches at that time, and became part of the emergency body charged with researching a solution. It was weary work. I personally spent over a week in the archive without seeing daylight as I oversaw the systematic interrogation of that vast, dusty body of knowledge.

It was my friend and colleague Administrator Medica Lenid Vammel who first called our attention to Pirody and the Torment. It was an admirable piece of work on his part, a feat of study, cross-reference and memory. Vammel always had a good memory.

Under the instruction of Senior Administrator Medica Junas Malter, we diverted over sixty per cent of our staff to further research into the records of Pirody, and requests were sent out to other Genovingian worlds to look to their own archives. Vammel and I compiled the accumulating data ourselves,

increasingly certain we had shone a light into the right shadow
and found a useful truth.

Surviving records of the Torment incident on Pirody were
painfully thin, though consistent. It was, after all, thirty-four
years in the past. Survivors had been few, but we were able to
trace one hundred and ninety-one possibles who might yet be
alive. They were scattered to the four cosmic winds.

Reviewing our findings, Senior Malter authorised personal
recollection, such was the gravity of the situation, and forty of
us, all with rank higher administrator or better, were dis-
patched immediately. Vammel, rest his soul, was sent to
Gandian Saturnalia, and was caught up in a local civil war and
thereafter killed. I do not know if he ever found the man he
was looking for. Memory is unkind there.

And I, I was sent to Symbal Iota.

II

SYMBAL IOTA, WHERE it is not covered in oceans that are the most
profound mauve in colour (a consequence, so I understand, of
algae growth), is a hot, verdant place. Rainforest islands ring
the equatorial region in a wide belt.

I made 'fall at Symbalopolis, a flat-topped volcanic outcrop
around whose slopes hive structures cluster like barnacles, and
there transferred to a trimaran which conveyed me, over a
period of five days, down the length of the local island group
to Saint Bastian.

I cursed the slowness of the craft, though in truth it skated
across the mauve seas at better than thirty knots, and on several
occasions tried to procure an ornithopter or air conveyance.
But the Symbali are a nautical breed who place no faith in air
travel. It was tortuous and I was impatient. It had taken ten
days to cross the empyrean from Lorches to Symbal Iota aboard
a navy frigate. Now it took half that time again to cross a distance infinitesimally smaller.

It was hot, and I spent my time below decks, reading data-
slates. The sun and seawind of Symbal burned my skin, used as
it was to years of lamp-lit libraries. I took to wearing a wide-
brimmed straw hat above my Administratus robes whenever I
ventured out on deck, a detail my servitor Kalibane found
relentlessly humorous.

On the fifth morning, Saint Bastian rose before us out of the violet waters, a pyramidal tower volcanic flue dressed in jungle greenery. Even as we crossed the inlet from the trimaran to the shore by electric launch, turquoise seabirds mobbing over our heads, I could see no discernible sign of habitation. The thick coat of forestation came right down to the shore itself, revealing only a thin line of white beach at its hem.

The launch pulled into a cove where an ancient stone jetty jutted out from under the trees like an unfinished bridge. Kalibane, his bionic limbs whirring, carried my luggage onto the jetty and then helped me over. I stood there, sweating in my robes, leaning against my staff of office, batting away the beetles that circled in the stifling humidity of the cove.

There was no one there to greet me, though I had voxed word of my approach ahead several times en route. I glanced back at the launch pilot, a dour Symbali, but he seemed not to know anything. Kalibane shambled down to the shore-end of the jetty, and called my attention to a copper bell, verdigrised by time and the oceans, that hung from a hook on the end of the pier.

'Ring it,' I told him, and he did, cautiously, rapping his simian fingers against the metal dome. Then he glanced back at me, nervously, his optical implants clicking under his low brow-ridge as they refocused.

Two sisters of the Ecclesiarchy shortly appeared, their pure white robes as stiff and starched as the bicorn wimples they wore on their heads. They seemed to regard me with some amusement, and wordlessly ushered me to follow them.

I fell in step behind them and Kalibane followed, carrying the luggage.

We took a dirt path up through the jungle which rose sharply and eventually became stepped. Sunlight flickered spears of light through the canopy above and the steaming air was full of exotic bird-song and the fidget of insects.

At a turn in the path, the Hospice of Saint Bastian Apostate suddenly stood before me. A great, stone-built edifice typical of the early Imperial naïve, its ancient flying buttresses and lower walls were clogged with vines and creepers. I could discern a main building of five storeys, an adjacent chapel, which looked the oldest part of the place, as well as outbuildings, kitchens and a walled garden. Above the wrought iron lych-gate stood a

weathered statue of our beloved God-Emperor smiting the
Archenemy. Inside the rusty gate, a well-tended path led
through a trimmed lawn punctured by tomb-stones and crypts.
Stone angels and graven images of the Adeptes Astartes regarded
me as I followed the sisters to the main door of the hospice.

I noticed then, fleetingly, that the windows of the two uppermost storeys were rigidly barred with iron grilles.

I left Kalibane outside with my possessions and entered the
door behind the sisters. The main atrium of the hospice was a
dark and deliciously cool oasis of marble, with limestone pil-
lars that rose up into the dim spaces of the high vault. My eyes
lighted on the most marvellous triptych at the altar end,
beneath a stained glass oriole window, which I made obser-
vance to at once. In breadth, it was wider than a man's spread
arms, and showed three aspects of the saint. On the left, he
roamed the wilderness, in apostasy, renouncing the daemons
of the air and fire; on the right, he performed the miracle of the
maimed souls. In the centre panel, his martyred body, draped
in blue cloth, the nine bolter wounds clearly countable on his
pallid flesh, he lay in the arms of a luminous and suitably
mournful Emperor.

I looked up from my devotions to find the sisters gone. I
could feel the subliminal chorus of a psychic choir mind-
singing nearby. The cool air pulsed.

A figure stood behind me. Tall, sculptural, his starched robes
as white as his smooth skin was black, he seemed to regard me
with the same amusement that the sisters had shown.

I realised I was still wearing my straw hat. I removed it
quickly, dropping it onto a pew, and took out the pict-slate of
introduction Senior Malter had given me before I left Lorches.

'I am Baptrice,' he said, his voice low and genial. 'Welcome to
the saint's hospice.'

'Higher Administrator Medica Lemual Sark,' I replied. 'My
dedicated function is as a recollector, posted lately to Lorches,
Genovingia general group 4577 decimal, as part of the campaign auxiliary clerical archive.'

'Welcome, Lemual,' he said. 'A recollector. Indeed. We've not
had one of your breed here before.'

I was uncertain quite what he meant, though in hindsight,
the detail of his misunderstanding still chills me. I said 'You
were expecting me? I voxed messages ahead.'

'We have no vox-caster here at the hospice,' Baptrice replied. 'What is outside does not concern us. Our work is focussed on what is inside... inside this building, inside ourselves. But do not be alarmed. You are not intruding. We welcome all who come here. We do not need notice of an arrival.'

I smiled politely at this enigmatic response and tapped my fingers on my staff. I had hoped they would be ready for me, and have everything in place so that I could begin my work immediately. Once again, the leisurely pace of Symbal Iota was weighing me down.

'I must, Brother Baptrice, proceed with all haste. I wish to begin my efforts at once.'

He nodded. 'Of course. Almost all who come to Saint Bastian are eager to begin. Let me take you through and provide you with food and a place to bathe.'

'I would rather just see Ebhoe. As soon as it is possible.'

He paused, as if mystified.

'Ebhoe?'

'Colonel Fege Ebhoe, late of the Twenty-third Lammark Lancers. Please tell me he is still here! That he is still alive!'

'He... is.' Baptrice faltered, and looked over my pict-slate properly for the first time. Some sort of realisation crossed his noble face.

'My apologies, Higher Sark. I misconstrued your purpose. I see now that you are an *acting* recollector, sent here on official business.'

'Of course!' I snapped. 'What else would I be?'

'A supplicant, coming here to find solace. An inmate. Those that arrive on the jetty and sound the bell are always that. We get no other visitors except those who come to us for help.'

'An... inmate?' I repeated.

'Don't you know where you are?' he asked. 'This is the Hospice of Saint Bastian, a refuge for the insane.'

III

AN ASYLUM! HERE was an inauspicious start to my mission! I had understood, from my research, that the Hospice of Saint Bastian was home to a holy order who offered sanctuary and comfort for those brave warriors of the Emperor's legions who were too gravely wounded or disabled by war to continue in service. I

knew the place took in the damaged and the lost from warzones
all across the sector. But I truly had no notion that the damage
they specialised in was wounds to the psyche and sanity! It was
a hospice for the deranged, individuals who presented themselves at its gates voluntarily in hope of redemption.

And worst of all, Baptrice and the sisters had presumed me
to be a supplicant! That damned straw hat had given me just
the air of madness they were expecting! I was lucky not to have
been unceremoniously strapped into a harness and placed in
isolation.

On reflection, I realised I should have known. Bastian, that
hallowed saint, was a madman who found sanity in the love of
the Emperor, and who later cured, through miracles, the mentally infirm.

Baptrice rang a bell cord, and novitiates appeared. Kalibane
was escorted inside with my luggage. We were left alone in the
atrium as Baptrice went to make preparations. As we waited, a
grizzled man with an old tangle of scar-tissue where his left
arm had been crossed the hall. He was naked save for a weathered, empty ammunition belt strung around his torso. He
looked at us dimly, his head nodding slightly, then he padded
on his way and was lost from view.

Somewhere, distantly, I could hear sobbing, and an urgent
voice repeating something over and over again. Hunched down
at my side, his knuckles resting on the flagstones, Kalibane
glanced up at me anxiously and I put a reassuring hand on his
broad, hairy shoulder.

Figures appeared around us: haggard, tonsured men in long
black Ecclesiarch vestments, more phantom sisters in their ice-
white robes and horned cowls. They grouped in the shadows
on either side of the atrium and watched us silently. One of the
men rehearsed silently from long ribbons of parchment that a
boy-child played out for him from a studded casket. Another
scribbled in a little chapbook with his quill. Another swung a
brass censer around his feet, filling the air with dry, pungent
incense.

Baptrice reappeared. 'Brethren, bid welcome to Higher
Administrator Sark, who has come to us on official business.
You will show him every courtesy and cooperation.'

'What official business?' asked the old priest with the chapbook, looking up with gimlet eyes. Magnifying half-moon

lenses were built into his nasal bone, and rosary beads hung around his dewlapped neck like a floral victory wreath.

'A matter of recollection,' I replied.

'Pertaining to what?' he pressed.

'Brother Jardone is our archivist, Higher Sark. You will forgive his persistence.' I nodded to Baptrice and smiled at the elderly Jardone, though no smile was returned.

'I see we are kindred, Brother Jardone. Both of us devote ourselves to remembrance.'

He half-shrugged.

'I am here to interview one of your... inmates. It may be that he holds within some facts that even now may save the lives of millions in the Genovingian group.'

Jardone closed his book and gazed at me, as if waiting for more. Senior Malter had charged me to say as little as I could of the pandemic, for news of such a calamity may spread unrest. But I felt I had to give them more.

'Warmaster Rhyngold is commanding a major military excursion through the Genovingian group. A sickness, which has been named Uhlren's Pox, is afflicting his garrisons. Study has shown it may bear comparison with a plague known as the Torment, which wasted Pirody some three decades past. One survivor of that epidemic resides here. If he can furnish me with any details of the incident, it may be productive in securing a cure.'

'How bad is it, back on Genovingia?' asked another old priest, the one with the censer.

'It is... contained,' I lied.

Jardone snorted. 'Of course it is contained. That is why a higher administrator has come all this way. You ask the most foolish things, Brother Giraud.'

Another man now spoke. He was older than all, crooked and half-blind, his wrinkled pate dotted with liver spots. A flared ear-trumpet clung to the robes of his left shoulder with delicate mechanical legs. 'I am concerned that questioning and a change to routine may disturb the serenity of the hospice. I do not want our residents upset in any way.'

'Your comment is noted, Brother Niro,' said Baptrice. 'I'm sure Higher Sark will be discreet.'

'Of course,' I assured them.

* * *

IT WAS LATE afternoon when Baptrice finally led me upstairs into the heart of the hospice. Kalibane followed us, lugging a few boxed items from my luggage. Ghostly, bicorned sisters watched us from every arch and shadow.

We proceeded from the stairs into a large chamber on the third floor. The air was close. Dozens of inmates lurked here, though none glanced at us. Some were clad in dingy, loose-fitting overalls, while others still wore ancient fatigues and Imperial Guard dress. All rank pins, insignia and patches had been removed, and no one had belts or bootlaces. Two were intently playing regicide on an old tin board by the window. Another sat on the bare floor planks, rolling dice. Others mumbled to themselves or gazed into the distance blankly. The naked man we had seen in the atrium was crouched in a corner, loading spent shellcases into his ammunition belt. Many of the residents had old war wounds and scars, unsightly and grotesque.

'Are they... safe?' I whispered to Baptrice.

'We allow the most stable freedom to move and use this common area. Of course, their medication is carefully monitored. But all who come here are "safe", as all who come here come voluntarily. Some, of course, come here to escape the episodes that have made regular life impractical.'

None of this reassured me.

On the far side of the chamber, we entered a long corridor flanked by cell rooms. Some doors were shut, bolted from outside. Some had cage-bars locked over them. All had sliding spy-slits. There was a smell of disinfectant and ordure.

Someone, or something, was knocking quietly and repeatedly against one locked door we passed. From another we heard singing.

Some doors were open. I saw two novitiates sponge-bathing an ancient man who was strapped to his metal cot with fabric restraints. The old man was weeping piteously. In another room, where the door was open but the outer cage locked in place, we saw a large, heavily muscled man sitting in a ladder-back chair, gazing out through the bars. He was covered in tattoos: regimental emblems, mottoes, kill-scores. His eyes glowed with the most maniacal light. He had the tusks of some feral animal implanted in his lower jaw, so they hooked up over his upper lip.

As we passed, he leaped up and tried to reach through the bars at us. His powerful arm flexed and clenched. He issued a soft growl.

'Behave, Ioq!' Baptrice told him.

The cell next door to Ioq's was our destination. The door was open, and a sister and a novitiate waited for us. The room beyond them was pitch black.

Baptrice spoke for a moment with the novitiate and the sister. He turned to me. 'Ebhoe is reluctant, but the sister has convinced him it is right that he speaks with you. But you may not go in. Please sit at the door.'

The novitiate brought up a stool, and I sat in the doorway, throwing out my robes over my knees. Kalibane dutifully opened my boxes and set up the transcribing artificer on its tripod stand.

I gazed into the blackness of the room, trying to make out shapes. I could see nothing.

'Why is it dark in there?'

'Ebhoe's malady, his mental condition, is exacerbated by light. He demands darkness.' Baptrice shrugged.

I nodded glumly and cleared my throat. 'By the grace of the God-Emperor of Terra, I come here on His holy work. I identify myself as Lemual Sark, higher administrator medica, assigned to Lorches Administratum.'

I glanced over at the artificer. It chattered quietly and extruded the start of a parchment transcription tape that I hoped would soon be long and informative. 'I seek Fege Ebhoe, once a colonel with the Twenty-Third Lammark Lancers.'

Silence.

'Colonel Ebhoe?'

A voice, thin as a knife, cold as a corpse, whispered out of the dark room. 'I am he. What is your business?'

I leaned forward. 'I wish to discuss Pirody with you. The Torment you endured.'

'I have nothing to say. I won't remember anything.'

'Come now, colonel. I'm sure you will if you try.'

'You misunderstand. I didn't say I "can't". I said I "won't".'

'Deliberately?'

'Just so. I refuse to.'

I wiped my mouth, and realised I was dry-tongued. 'Why not, colonel?'

'Pirody is why I'm here. Thirty-four years, trying to forget. I don't want to start remembering now.'

Baptrice looked at me with a slight helpless gesture. He seemed to be suggesting that it was done, and I should give up.

'Men are dying on Genovingia from a plague we know as Uhlren's Pox. This pestilence bears all the hallmarks of the Torment. Anything you can tell me may help save lives.'

'I couldn't then. Fifty-nine thousand men died on Pirody. I couldn't save them though I tried with every shred of my being. Why should that be different now?'

I gazed at the invisible source of the cold voice. 'I cannot say for sure. But I believe it is worth trying.'

There was a long pause. The artificer whirred on idle. Kalibane coughed, and the machine recorded the sound with a little chatter of keys.

'How many men?'

'I'm sorry, colonel? What did you ask me?'

'How many men are dying?'

I took a deep breath. 'When I left Lorches, nine hundred were dead and another fifteen hundred infected. On Genovingia Minor, six thousand and twice that number ailing. On Adamanaxer Delta, two hundred, but it had barely begun there. On Genovingia itself... two and a half million.'

I heard Baptrice gasp in shock. I trusted he would keep this to himself.

'Colonel?'

Nothing.

'Colonel, please...'

Cold and cutting, the voice came again, sharper than before. 'Pirody was a wasted place...'

IV

PIRODY WAS A wasted place. We didn't want to go there. But the Archenemy had taken the eastern continent and razed the hives, and the northern cities were imperilled.

Warmaster Getus sent us in. Forty thousand Lammark Lancers, virtually the full strength of the Lammark regiments. Twenty thousand Fancho armour men and their machines. And a full company of Astartes, the Doom Eagles, shining grey and red.

The place we were at was Pirody Polar. It was god knows how old. Cyclopean towers and columns of green marble, hewn in antique times by hands I'm not convinced were human. There was a strangeness to the geometry there, the angles never seemed quite right.

It was as cold as a bastard. We had winter dress, thick white flak coats with fur hoods, but the ice got in the lasguns and dulled their charges and the damned Fancho tanks were forever refusing to start. It was day, too. Day all the time. There was no night, it was the wrong season. We were so far north. The darkest it got was dusk, when one of the two suns set briefly and the sky went flesh pink. Then it would be daylight again.

We'd been fighting on and off for two months. Mainly long range artillery duels, pounding the ice-drifts. No one could sleep because of the perpetual daylight. I know two men, one a Lammarkine, I'm not proud to say, who gouged out his eyes. The other was a Fancho.

Then they came. Black dots on the ice-floes, thousands of them, waving banners so obscene, they...

Whatever. We were in no mood to fight. Driven mad by the light, driven to distraction by the lack of sleep, unnerved by the curious geometry of the place we were defending, we were easy meat. The forces of Chaos slaughtered us, and pushed us back into the city itself. The civilians, about two million strong, were worse than useless. They were pallid, idle things, with no drive or appetite. When doom came upon them, they simply gave up.

We were besieged for five months, despite six attempts by the Doom Eagles to break the deadlock. Faith, but they were terrifying! Giants, clashing their bolters together before each fight, screaming at the foe, killing fifty for every one we picked off.

But it was like fighting the tide, and for all their power, there were only sixty of them.

We called for reinforcements. Getus had promised us, but now he was long gone aboard his warship, drawn back behind the fleet picket in case things got nasty.

The first man I saw fall to the Torment was a captain in my seventh platoon. He just collapsed one day, feverish. We took him to the Pirody Polar infirmium, where Subjunctus Valis, the apothecary of the Doom Eagles company, was running the show. An hour later, the captain was dead. His skin had blistered and bubbled. His eyes had burst. He had tried to kill Valis with a piece of the metal cot he had torn from the wall brace. Then he bled out.

You know what that means? His entire body spewed blood from every orifice, every pore. He was a husk by the time it was over.

In the day after the captain's death, sixty fell victim. Another day, two hundred. Another day, a thousand. Most died within two hours. Others lingered... for days, pustular, agonised.

Men I had known all my life turned into gristly sacks of bone before my eyes. Damn you, Sark, for making me remember this!

On the seventh day it spread to the Fancho as well. On the ninth, it reached the civilian population. Valis ordered all measure of quarantine, but it was no good. He worked all hours of the endless day, trying to find a vaccine, trying to alleviate the relentless infection.

On the tenth day, a Doom Eagle fell victim. In his Torment, blood gouting from his visor grilles, he slew two of his comrades and nineteen of my men. The disease had overcome even the Astartes purity seals.

I went to Valis, craving good news. He had set up a laboratory in the infirmium, where blood samples and tissue-scrapes boiled in alembics and separated in oil flasks. He assured me the Torment would be stopped. He explained how unlikely it was for a pestilence to be transmitted in such a cold clime, where there is no heat to incubate and spread decay. And he also believed it would not flourish in light. So he had every stretch of the city wired with lamps so that there would be no darkness.

No darkness. In a place where none came naturally, even the shadows of closed rooms were banished. Everything was bright. Perhaps you can see now why I abhor the light and cling to darkness.

The stench of blood-filth was appalling. Valis did his work, but still we fell. By the twenty-first day, I'd lost thirty-seven per cent of my force. The Fancho were all but gone. Twelve thousand Pirodian citizens were dead or dying. Nineteen Doom Eagles had succumbed.

Here are your facts if you want them. The plague persisted in a climate that should have killed it. It showed no common process of transmission. It brooked no attempt to contain or control it, despite efforts to enforce quarantine and cleanse infected areas with flamers. It was ferociously contagious. Even Marine purity seals were no protection. Its victims died in agony.

Then one of the Doom Eagles deciphered the obscene script of one of the Chaos banners displayed outside the walls.

It said...

It said one word. One filthy word. One damned, abominable word that I have spent my life trying to forget.

V

I CRANED IN at the dark doorway. 'What word? What word was it, colonel?'

With great reluctance, he spoke it. It wasn't a word at all. It was an obscene gurgle dignified by consonants. The glyph-name of the plague-daemon itself, one of the ninety-seven Blasphemies that May Not Be Written Down.

At its utterance, I fell back off my stool, nausea writhing in my belly and throat. Kalibane shrieked. The sister collapsed in a faint and the novitiate fled.

Baptrice took four steps back from the doorway, turned, and vomited spectacularly.

The temperature in the corridor dropped by fifteen degrees.

Unsteady, I attempted to straighten my overturned stool and pick up the artificer that the novitiate had knocked over. Where it had recorded the word, I saw, the machine's parchment tape had begun to smoulder.

Screaming and wailing echoed down the hall from various cells.

And then, Ioq was out.

Just next door, he had heard it all, his scarred head pressed to the cage bars. Now that cage door splintered off its mount and crashed to the corridor floor. Berserk, the huge ex-guardsman thrashed out and turned towards us.

He was going to kill me, I'm certain, but I was slumped and my legs wouldn't work. Then Kalibane, bless his brave heart, flew at him. My devoted servitor rose up on his stunted hind limbs, the bionics augmenting his vast forelimbs throwing them up in a warning display. From splayed foot to reaching hand, Kalibane was eleven feet tall. He peeled back his lips and screeched through bared steel canines.

Froth dribbling from his tusked mouth, Ioq smashed Kalibane aside. My servitor made a considerable dent in the wall.

Ioq was on me.

I swept my staff of office around and thumbed the recessed switch below the head.

Electric crackles blasted from the staff's tip. Ioq convulsed and fell. Twitching, he lay on the floorboards, and evacuated involuntarily. Baptrice was on his feet now. Alarms were ringing and novitiates were rushing frantically into the corridor with harness jackets and clench poles.

I rose and looked back at the dark doorway.

'Colonel Ebhoe?'

The door slammed shut.

VI

THERE WOULD BE no further interview that afternoon, Brother Baptrice made plain, despite my protests. Novitiates escorted me to a guest chamber on the second floor. It was white-washed and plain, with a hard, wooden bed and small scriptorium table. A leaded window looked out onto the grave-yard and the jungles beyond.

I felt a great perturbation of spirit, and paced the room as Kalibane unpacked my belongings. I had come so close, and had begun to draw the reluctant Ebhoe out. Now to be denied the chance to continue when the truly dark secrets were being revealed!

I paused by the window. The glaring, crimson sun was sinking into the mauve oceans, throwing the thick jungles into black, wild relief. Seabirds reeled over the bay in the dying light. Stars were coming out in the dark blue edges of the sky.

Calmer now, I reflected that whatever my internal uproar, the uproar in the place itself was greater.

From the window, I could hear all manner of screams, wails, shouts, banging doors, thundering footsteps, rattled keys. The word of blasphemy that Ebhoe had spoken had thrown all the fragile minds in this house of insanity into disarray, like red-hot metal plunged into quenching cold water. Great efforts were being made to quieten the inmates.

I sat at the teak scriptorium for a while, reviewing the transcripts while Kalibane dozed on a settle by the door. Ebhoe had made particular mention of Subjunctus Valis, the Doom Eagles' apothecary. I looked over copies of the old Pirody debriefings I had brought with me, but Valis's name only appeared in the muster listings. Had he survived? Only a direct request to the Doom Eagles chapter house could provide an answer, and that might take months.

The Astartes are notoriously secretive, sometimes downright blatant in their uncooperative relationship with the Administratum. At best, it might involve a series of formal approaches, delaying tactics, bargaining.

Even so, I wanted to alert my brethren on Lorches to the possible lead. I damned Saint Bastian when I remembered the place had no vox-caster! I couldn't even forward a message to the Astropathic enclave at Symbalopolis for transmission off world.

A sister brought me supper on a tray. Just as I was finishing, and Kalibane was lighting the lamps, Niro and Jardone came to my chamber.

'Brothers?'

Jardone got right to it, staring at me through his half-moon lenses. 'The brotherhood of the hospice have met, and they decided that you must leave. Tomorrow. No further audiences will be granted. We have a vessel that will take you to the fishing port at Math island. You can obtain passage to Symbalopolis from there.'

'I am disappointed, Jardone. I do not wish to leave. My recollection is not complete.'

'It is as complete as it's going to be!' he snapped.

'The hospice has never been so troubled,' Niro said quietly. 'There have been brawls. Two novitiates have been injured. Three inmates have attempted suicide. Years of work have been undone in a few moments.'

I nodded. 'I regret the disturbance, but–'

'No buts!' barked Jardone.

'I'm sorry, higher sark,' said Niro. 'That is how it is.'

I SLEPT BADLY in the cramped cot. My mind, my memory, played games, going over the details of the interview. There was shock and injury in Ebhoe, that was certain, for the event had been traumatic. But there was something else. A secret beyond anything he had told me, some profound memory. I could taste it.

I would not be deterred. Too many lives depended on it.

Kalibane was slumbering heavily when I crept from the chamber. In the darkness, I felt my way to the stairs, and up to the third floor. There was a restlessness in the close air. I moved past locked cells where men moaned in their sleep or muttered in their insomnia.

At intervals, I hugged the shadows as novitiate wardens with lamps made their patrols. It took perhaps three quarters of an hour to reach the cell block where Ebhoe resided. I stalked nervously past the bolted door of Ioq's room.

The spy-slit opened at my touch. 'Ebhoe? Colonel Ebhoe?' I called softly into the darkness.

'Who?' his cold voice replied.

'It is Sark. We weren't finished.'

'Go away.'

'I will not, until you tell me the rest.'

'Go away.'

I thought desperately, and eagerness made me cruel. 'I have a torch, Ebhoe. A powerful lamp. Do you want me to shine it in through the spy-hole?'

When he spoke again, there was terror in his voice. Emperor forgive me for my manipulation.

'What more is there?' he asked. 'The Torment spread. We died by the thousand. I cannot help with your cause, though I pity those men on Genovingia.'

'You never told me how it ended.'

'Did you not read the reports?'

I glanced up and down the dark cell-block to make sure we were still alone. 'I read them. They were... sparse. They said Warmaster Gatus incinerated the enemy from orbit, and ships were sent to relieve you at Pirody Polar. They expressed horror at the extent of the plague-loss. Fifty-nine thousand men dead. No count was made of the civilian losses. They said that by the time the relief ships arrived, the Torment had been expunged. Four hundred men were evacuated. Of them, only one hundred and ninety-one are still alive according to the records.'

'There's your answer then.'

'No, colonel. That's no answer! How was it expunged?'

'We located the source of infection, cleansed it. That was how.'

'How, Ebhoe? How, in the God-Emperor's name?'

'It was the height of the Torment. Thousands dead...'

* * *

VII

IT WAS THE height of the Torment. Thousands dead, corpses everywhere, pus and blood running in those damnably bright halls.

I went to Valis again, begging for news. He was in his infirmium, working still. Another batch of vaccines to try, he told me. The last six had failed, and had even seemed to aggravate the contagion.

The men were fighting themselves by then, killing each other in fear and loathing. I told Valis this, and he was silent, working at a flame burner on the steel workbench. He was huge being, of course... Astartes, a head and a half taller than me, wearing a cowled red robe over his Doom Eagles armour. He lifted specimen bottles from his narthecium, and held them up to the ever-present light.

I was tired, tired like you wouldn't believe. I hadn't slept in days. I put down the flamer I had been using for cleansing work, and sat on a stool.

'Are we all going to perish?' I asked the great apothecary.

'Dear, valiant Ebhoe,' he said with a laugh. 'You poor little man. Of course not. I will not allow it.'

He turned to face me, filling a long syringe from a stoppered bottle. I was in awe of him, even after the time we had spent together.

'You are one of the lucky ones, Ebhoe. Clean so far. I'd hate to see you contract this pestilence. You have been a faithful ally to me through this dark time, helping to distribute my vaccines. I will mention you to your commanders.'

'Thank you, apothecary.'

'Ebhoe,' he said, 'I think it is fair to say we cannot save any who have been infected now. We can only hope to vaccinate the healthy against infection. I have prepared a serum for that purpose, and I will inoculate all healthy men with it. You will help me. And you will be first. So I can be sure not to lose you.'

I hesitated. He came forward with the syringe, and I started to pull up my sleeve.

'Open your jacket and tunic. It must go through the stomach wall.' I reached for my tunic clasps.

And saw it. The tiniest thing. Just a tiny, tiny thing.

A greenish-yellow blister just below Valis's right ear.

* * *

VIII

EBHOE FELL SILENT. The air seemed electrically charged. Inmates in neighbouring cells were thrashing restless, and some were crying out. At any moment, the novitiate wardens would come.

'Ebhoe?' I called through the slit.

His voice had fallen to a terrified whisper, the whisper of a man who simply cannot bear to put the things haunting his mind into words.

'Ebhoe?'

Keys clattered nearby. Lamplight flickered under a hall door. Ioq was banging at his cell door and growling. Someone was crying, someone else was wailing in a made-up language. The air was ripe with the smell of faeces, sweat and agitated fear.

'Ebhoe!'

There was no time left. 'Ebhoe, please!'

'Valis had the Torment! He'd had it all along, right from the start!' Ebhoe's voice was strident and anguished. The words came out of the slit as hard and lethal as las-fire. 'He had spread it! He! Through his work, his vaccines, his treatments! He had spread the plague! His mind had been corrupted by it, he didn't know what he was doing! His many, many vaccines had failed because they weren't vaccines! They were new strains of the Torment bred in his infirmium! He was the carrier: a malevolent, hungry pestilence clothed in the form of a noble man, killing thousands upon thousands upon thousands!'

I went cold. Colder than I'd ever been before. The idea was monstrous. The Torment had been more than a waster of lives, it had been sentient, alive, deliberate... planning and moving through the instrument it had corrupted.

The door of Ioq's cell was bulging and shattering. Screams welled all around, panic and fear in equal measure. The entire hospice was shaking with unleashed psychoses.

Lamps flashed at the end of the block. Novitiates yelled out and ran forward as they saw me. They would have reached me had not Ioq broken out again, rabid and slavering, throwing his hideous bulk into them, ripping at them in a frenzy.

'Ebhoe!' I yelled through the slit. 'What did you do?'

He was crying, his voice ragged with gut-heaving sobs. 'I grabbed my flamer! Emperor have mercy, I snatched it up and bathed Valis with flame! I killed him! I killed him! I slew the pride of the Doom Eagles! I burned him apart! I expunged the source of the Torment!'

A novitiate flew past me, his throat ripped out by animal tusks. His colleagues were locked in desperate struggle with Ioq.

'You burned him.'

'Yes. The flames touched off the chemicals in the infirmium, the sample bottles, the flasks of seething plague water. They exploded. A fireball... Oh gods... brighter than the daylight that had never gone away. Brighter than... fire everywhere... liquid fire... flames around me... all around... oh... oh...'

Bright flashes filled the hall, the loud discharge of a las-weapon.

I stepped back from Ebhoe's cell door, shaking. Ioq lay dead amid the mangled corpses of three novitiates. Several others, wounded, whimpered on the floor.

Brother Jardone, a laspistol in his bony hand, pushed through the orderlies and ecclesiarchs gathering in the hall, and pointed the weapon at me.

'I should kill you for this, Sark. How dare you!'

Baptrice stepped forward and took the gun from Jardone. Niro gazed at me in weary disappointment.

'See to Ebhoe,' Baptrice told the sisters nearby. They unlocked the cell door and went in.

'You will leave tomorrow, Sark,' Baptrice said. 'I will file a complaint to your superiors.'

'Do so,' I said. 'I never wanted this, but I had to reach the truth. It may be, from what Ebhoe has told me, that a way to fight Uhlren's Pox is in our reach.'

'I hope so,' said Baptrice, gazing bitterly at the carnage in the hall. 'It has cost enough.'

The novitiates were escorting me back to my room when the sisters brought Ebhoe out. The ordeal of recollection had killed him. I will never forgive myself for that, no matter how many lives on Genovingia we saved.

And I will never forget the sight of him, revealed at last in the light.

IX

I LEFT THE next day by launch with Kalibane. No one from the hospice saw me off or even spoke to me. From Math Island, I transmitted my report to Symbalopolis, and from there, astro-pathically, it lanced through the warp to Lorches.

Was Uhlren's Pox expunged? Yes, eventually. My work assisted in that. The blood-froth was like the Torment, engineered by the Archenemy, just as sentient. Fifty-two medical officers, sources just like Valis, were executed and incinerated.

I forget how many we lost altogether in the Genovingia group. I forget a lot, these days. My memory is not what it was, and I am thankful for that, at times.

I never forget Ebhoe. I never forget his corpse, wheeled out by the sisters. He had been caught in the infirmium flames on Pirody Polar. Limbless, wizened like a seed-case, he hung in a suspensor chair, kept alive by intravenous drains and sterile sprays. A ragged, revolting remnant of a man.

He had no eyes. I remember that most clearly of all. The flames had scorched them out.

He had no eyes, and yet he was terrified of the light.

I still believe that memory is the finest faculty we as a species own. But by the Golden Throne, there are things I wish I could never remember again.

LACRYMATA

Storm Constantine

HE BREATHED A steam of stars, each mote of light igniting in his lungs bringing a hot, sweet taste to his tongue. Space, time? What are these trifles?

Solonaetz Di Cavagni, navigator of the Imperial trader ship *Dea Brava*, coasted the warp tides of neural ecstasy, oblivious of all save his own blistering responses and the guiding scream-light of the astronomican, the Emperor's own psychic beacon, searing through the heat of Chaos. He and the ship were one; a shining world speeding through the warp, his consciousness the benign god that nourished it.

Real space drop minus fifteen...

Solonaetz realigned consciousness. The warpscreen on the helm just in front of him was pulsing dully, displaying a convulsion of lesser eddies in the immaterium outside; nothing too worrying. He glanced upwards through the translucent plascryst of the navigation blister into an aching tumult of colour and optical noise. This was overlapped by his warp-sight, courtesy of his third eye, a mutation peculiar to navigators, which transmuted the chaotic fluidium of warp space into recognizable symbols. A phantom of his mother's face gaped inches from the translucent blister, evoking the

91

thought response: 'Damn, I forgot the call!' He had meant to send a message back to Terra before the jump into warp space. He knew Laetitia, his mother, fretted during his absence more than she did for any other members of the family. Out of consideration, he always sent brief communications whenever he remembered. Now, some deep shred of guilt within his mind had projected a thought-form into the warp, which was currently scratching disconsolately at the ship itself as if trying to reach him.

Real space drop minus ten...

He felt *Dea Brava* stir around him as the automatic real space navigational functions prepared to relieve him from duty. She was a witch-queen of the heavens, was *Brava*, a sleek little strumpet, one of many owned by the affluent Fiddeus merchant family, who for centuries had enjoyed a lucrative franchise from the Administratum. Solonaetz had been working for clan Fiddeus for some time now, following injuries incurred during military service.

He'd warp-piloted the battlecruiser *Veil of Hecate* (a crueller, less beautiful lady than *Dea Brava*) for three missions before a hideous accident during what should have been a routine purge of mercantile dissidents had decimated the crew and left Solonaetz little more than a disassembled jumble of bones within a leaking bag of flesh. Mercifully, because of his family's prestige, he'd immediately received the best of medical attention, thorough reconsecration and a frozen trip home to recuperate.

The healing had been a long, wearing process, and his body still creaked with frissons of old pain occasionally. He comforted himself with the thought that one day the Administratum would accept his reapplication for duty, deciding, at last, his faculties were once more sharp and steady enough to entrust with the welfare of a battlecruiser. Solonaetz, though still mourning the thrill of such commissions, also suspected his yearnings to return to the Imperial fleet were slightly insane. He had a cosy niche within the Fiddeus fleet and the *Dea Brava* was a dream to work with. Over the three ship's-time years he'd spent in her company, he had come to appreciate her personality. Her totem was one of recklessness and adventure; perhaps, like himself, she fretted impatiently at being confined to the routine function of cargo carrier.

The phantom of Laetitia lost its hold on the slick surface of the blister and was churned into the amorphous boiling that *Dea Brava* left in her wake. Solonaetz became aware of physical pain; his neck was playing up again. That was another thing he'd meant to do before entering warp space: consult the medic about this problem. It had not been an easy trip out this time all round. He would not be sorry to get home. One more drop and then...

Real space drop minus five...

Solonaetz smiled. The warp portal into real space was a stunner this time. *Dea Brava* was dwarfed by an incredible apparition in the void ahead: brazen gates miles high, miles wide, encrusted with elaborate carvings. Giant beasts, their heads invisible in a smoke of stars, blew mammoth horns as if to bid the ship farewell with a star-shattering fanfare.

Solonaetz shook his head. Was it his own influence, he wondered, or the psychic, fluidium-bending whim of another navigator bored after a long stint alone? Perhaps the illusion had been spawned by the creative residue of some dazed eldar poet who'd once coasted the warp tides, coaxing dreams to reality. Whatever. Someone, somewhere liked to leave their own signature upon the warp. Three drops back, he'd cruised the ship through a yawning, fang-toothed mouth, whose gullet delivered him into real space near one of the Ministorum administrative worlds. Someone with a sense of humour, maybe?

The inevitable, and thankfully brief, spasm of nausea vibrated through his flesh as *Dea Brava* left the warp. He couldn't resist glancing over his shoulder as he pulled his bandana back into place over his third eye. There were no mammoth gates closing behind the ship's tail; of course not.

JOURNEY COMPLETED. SOLONAETZ touched a sequence of protective runes above his control helm and then lightly laid his fingers against his brow. 'I thank thee, Lord Emperor, Divine Father of all that lives, for thy endless love that reacheth out to the corners of forever and carries us all, thy children, in safety. Blessings and respect.' He rubbed his eyes when the prayer of thanks was recited and began to unstrap himself from the navigator's pod. His neck was singing in agony now. It would have to be seen to before the next warp shift.

Whatever protections *Dea Brava* might have, Solonaetz was always deeply relieved when they dropped back into real space, even if he never consciously admitted it. Sometimes, the things he saw out there were just too tempting. One sleeptime, he'd had a nightmare about the astronomican suddenly blipping away to nothingness, leaving him alone, without guidance, in a ship screaming blindly into entropy. He'd woken up sweating and pawing the air, his ultimate fear being that his dream self, despite being terrified, had also enjoyed a wild exultation. He had yearned for the final embrace of Chaos. If his subconscious toyed with such sentiments in sleep, Solonaetz was all too aware of how vulnerable he was in the warp.

But then, who wasn't? He'd seen the burn-outs, shielded by their families, newly released from Ministorum retreats, where the priesthood tried to launder the frazzled brains of those who succumbed. It was a risky business he was involved in: his lifeblood.

Solonaetz descended to the walkway leading to the camera recreata, rubbing his neck as he walked. It was always the same, this aftermath: vague depression, insecurity. He knew very well by the time the next warp shift was due he'd be aching to ride the stuff of Chaos once more.

CAPTAIN GRAIAN FIDDEUS was giving in to his usual ritual of inspecting the cargo now they'd dropped back into real space. He was aware that this was slightly neurotic behaviour – *Dea Brava* herself would know if anything was amiss – but could never talk himself out of doing it. Maybe, with time, his concerns would lessen.

He was a young man and the *Brava*, one of his family's smaller vessels, had not long been entrusted into his care. Like Solonaetz, he was eager to return home. There'd been a series of mishaps this trip: an unexpected bout of illness amongst the crew, a near miss with a warp storm near the gate to Hovia Nesta. Problems with the consignment of goods on Phaeton South had caused an irritating delay, thus upsetting the receivers on the following drop. Problems, problems.

Graian was also concerned about the ship's new astropath, Shivania. This was her first trip out with the *Dea Brava*; her first trip aboard any space-faring vessel, in fact. She had been assigned to take over from old Bassos, the previous astropath, who'd been with the Fiddeus family all his working life. Astropaths were essential to communication aboard ship, and Graian felt uneasy about the apparent delicacy of the girl, her strange air of feyness. He had trusted Bassos implicitly, who had been a robust and dependable creature.

Graian mistrusted Shivania's capabilities, despite the impressive references with which she'd been despatched from the Scholastica of Adeptus Astra Telepathica. She seemed little more than a child, although Graian had to admit, however grudgingly, she had a keen mind. If anything, her ability to transmit and receive information surpassed Bassos's considerably. His misgivings were instinctual, but until he could identify some fault or another, he had no proper cause for complaint.

As he walked through the cargo hold, Graian unconsciously ran his fingers fondly over the ribs of the vault. Very quickly, the ship had seemed to become part of his soul. He felt her movements and sighs, each creak and moan, as if he made them himself. Her arched vaults, plated in dull black plasteel, were thickly inscribed with protective runes and totems; she was a virtual fortress. As he'd expected, everything was in order. He knew it was apprehension about the next cargo that was making him jittery. Maybe it was an honour that his father trusted him enough to take the job on, but Graian suspected even the most experienced captain would think twice about stowing a consignment of lacrymata on board. Naturally, most of the legends surrounding it would be exaggerated, but unnerved by the mishaps he'd had to deal with already on this trip, Graian fought a superstitious fear that picking up the lacrymata would only precipitate further dangers.

Taking one last look around, Graian forced himself to leave the hold and make his way to the camera recreata. All Fiddeus ships had a member of the Ministorum on board, so that cleansing rituals could be performed after each warp shift. As well as being effective in cleaning away any psychic debris, it also boosted the morale of the crew.

He met Solonaetz in the passageway two decks up, considering the navigator was looking as fey as Shivania nowadays. Navigators were all inclined to pellucid delicacy but Solonaetz's huge, dark eyes were almost feverish. Graian made a small, formal bow which jerked the navigator's mouth into a smile, not entirely devoid of mockery. 'Hard time, Cavagni?'

'No.'

'You look tired.'

'I am tired!'

SOLONAETZ HAD TO quell resentment of the captain's officious manner occasionally. What did he expect: his navigators to come bursting out from the blister leaping with joy and vitality? Fiddeus looked offended by his tone, however, so Solonaetz smiled to make amends.

'I always look tired after a drop.'

'What's wrong with your neck?'

Solonaetz abruptly dropped his hand. 'Nothing much.'

'Well – get it seen to.' Graian attempted what was clearly supposed to be a fatherly smile, but which Solonaetz meanly interpreted as condescension. 'Well, we mustn't keep Brother Gabreus waiting...'

Solonaetz shook his head wearily at the captain's retreating back and followed him up to the rec. 'Patience, patience,' he told himself.

DEA BRAVA WAS coasting serenely towards a cool, blue gem of a world, which could already be seen through the narrow, arched ports of the rec. Solonaetz could barely concentrate on the words of Brother Gabreus's benedictions, his eyes constantly drifting towards the world they were approaching. He knew Fiddeus was making a pick-up here rather than a delivery and that it was a cargo the Fiddeus clan were especially eager to get their hands on. Because of it, everyone had been promised a bonus when they returned home. Solonaetz presumed this was to over-ride any misgivings the crew might feel about sharing confined space with lacrymata, a potentially destructive material.

Personally, he felt no apprehension. Recorded incidents of fatality had all derived from negligence, which certainly wasn't one of Fiddeus's failings.

Solonaetz never knew whether to respect or be annoyed by the captain's nit-picking. He was not that much older than Fiddeus, yet sometimes Solonaetz noticed a jarring immaturity in the captain, which in bitter moments he felt derived from Graian's lack of hardship in life. The captain tried hard to establish comradeship with his navigator, which Solonaetz was well aware of, but neither of them could ever relax enough for friendship to develop. Solonaetz felt it was something to do with his mutation, ignorant of how adept he was at freezing people off.

Typically, Graian asked Solonaetz if he'd like to accompany him down to the planet's surface. Solonaetz winced inside as the captain made awkward references to the delights to be found below. Salome Nigra was one of those legendary places of the space-lanes, rumoured to be home to a thousand thousand illicit pleasures, all of which were available to discerning travellers for an appropriate fee.

Solonaetz, an unfailing cynic – perhaps a burdensome trait of his kind – knew it was the inhabitants of the planet herself who had engineered and now maintained this reputation. He considered it to be a tourist retreat of the most tawdry kind, and would have preferred to curl into his sleep-cell for a well-earned rest rather than force himself to endure the pantomime of being shocked and delighted by what they might find below. Fiddeus, however, insisted the trip would do Solonaetz good and even in the face of mordant uninterest kept on insisting until the navigator gave in.

'We can visit our contact, Guido Palama, organize delivery of the cargo and then the rest of the drop is ours...' Graian said, with a boyish grin, which Solonaetz had to admit was almost endearing in its innocence.

'If you like – though, as you noticed, I'm in a little pain.'

'Your totems look worn, Sol. Perhaps you should have them renewed. I'm sure Gabreus could do that for you before...'

Solonaetz's hand absently clutched the Navis Nobilite amulets hanging from his throat. 'At the risk of sounding irreverent, it is not a spiritual injury,' he said, stemming any sharpness in his voice. 'An aromatic rub should do the trick. I intended to visit Hermes Foss before the last drop, but it slipped my mind. Relic of old duty, you know.'

Graian nodded gravely. He barely spoke of Solonaetz's previous commission, emitting a restraint that made Solonaetz feel vaguely like a defrocked priest. Often, he wished people would just ask him blatant questions about his past and be humanly curious. Inside, he needed to talk about it, but he suspected old man Fiddeus had charged everybody with the dire command not to upset him in any way by raking up old hurts. Gomery

Fiddeus was a good friend of Solonaetz's own father; the commission had been a favour.

'Well,' Graian said brightly, rubbing his hands together, 'maybe we can find you a sweet young hetaira gifted in the arts of massage. As you know, the city of Assyrion is famed for its therapy shrines. A far more stimulating experience than having old Foss grinding away at your bones, eh, Sol?' He laughed.

Solonaetz smiled thinly and inclined his head. 'As long as we carefully inspect the aromatics before submitting to the treatment, of course.' He felt a weak surge of expectation. Perhaps the planetfall wouldn't be as gruelling as he'd feared.

SEVERAL OTHER CREW members were gathered in the shuttle, intent on visiting Assyrion, Brother Gabreus amongst them, which caused a certain amount of good-natured mockery. Gabreus settled himself fussily into a seat, pretending to be affronted. 'May your tongues be black!' he said grandly. 'All I seek is an assortment of puissant fumes. This you all know, so caw away, as you like! We'll see the grins wiped from your faces when we're back in the warp and only my incenses keep the effluent of Chaos from your sweet, untainted minds!' He wriggled his considerable frame into a comfortable position. 'Come, pilot, let's away! Night spreads her black, feathered fan upon the bosom of Assyrion and I, for one, want to be on the streets before the essence-blenders close shop!'

'Well said, brother!' Graian agreed. 'Pilot, all are aboard. Activate the elementals of the portals!'

The cramped shuttle was filled with the excited atmosphere generated by those who expected to sample exquisite dissipations in the near future. The pilot acknowledged his captain's request with a carefree gesture and made to seal the ports.

A sharp cry stayed his hand. 'Hold!' Someone was scrambling in through the doorway in a flutter of viridian robes. It was the astropath, Shivania.

'Shivania!' Graian said, unable to control his surprise. 'I really don't think Assyrion is the sort of place...'

'Enough, captain. I have eyes in the back of my head, if not the front! I'll be safe enough, especially with all these gallants to protect me!'

None of the party looked especially flattered by that, chaperoning a blind girl not having been on their agenda for the evening. The shuttle fell ominously quiet. Shivania seemed oblivious of the response or else ignored it. She found her way to a seat, as nimbly as any sighted person, turning her head back at Graian. She was wearing an embroidered mask over the upper part of her face. The two thread-woven eyes stared at the captain owlishly. 'You're not going to deny me permission, are you, sir?' she asked sweetly.

'Well, we do have... business,' Graian began, in the voice of someone who was wondering how he could eject the girl without offending her.

'Oh, leave her be!' Solonaetz said. 'I'll be glad to offer you my arm, Shivania.' He smiled at the captain.

'What about your neck?' Graian asked. He looked disappointed, if not mortified.

Solonaetz shrugged. 'It can wait. We've all been cooped up for weeks. I for one would not deny a person the chance to stretch their legs on solid ground if they desire it!'

'I thank you, navigator, for your courtesy!' Shivania said formally, but there was laughter in her voice, mocking laughter. She directed the needle of her attention at the priest. 'Ministorum duties planetside, brother?'

Gabreus shifted uncomfortably. 'Of a kind. Naturally, I would have offered to accompany you but...' he began, but Graian silenced his apologies.

'Come, come, the matter is settled. Let's fly.'

ASSYRION WAS A remarkable confection of a place. Her streets were paved in pearled marble, her towers rose, tier upon tier, aflutter with the pennants advertising which services could be found within. Sulky eyes, painted on silk, gazed through laced fingers, the perfumed breezes causing them to ripple as if alive. Graian had already made up his mind he wanted the navigator with him when he visited the Palama residence, so Shivania ended up joining them. Rather than use public transport, the captain insisted they walk on foot to admire the city sights. Solonaetz was disappointed. The main form of conveyance was provided by elegant open carriages drawn by beasts of burden native to the planet; creatures that seemed to be an absurd blend of camel and wild dog. He would have liked to ride in one. Perhaps later he and the astropath could hire one for a while.

Shivania, extending her heightened senses to encompass all they passed, kept up an awed commentary, which Solonaetz could tell soon began to get on Graian's nerves.

Palama House was situated in the heart of the Aromatics district; a sweeping pale leviathan of a residence, with many low, sprawling workshops to the rear. The air was so filled with the reek of perfume-blending, Solonaetz's and Graian's eyes began to water profusely. Shivania, being blind, did not experience this discomfort.

Presenting themselves at the soaring main entrance, its elegance enhanced by its classical simplicity, Graian and his companions were shown by an imperious servant into an understated yet exquisitely furnished salon near the front of the house. Refreshment was brought: pale, fragranced wine and tender wafers perfumed with local flower essences. Shivania exclaimed that Salome Nigra must be a world created solely for the pleasure of astropaths. 'The stimulus is for the nose, the nose!' she enthused. 'Who needs physical sight in such a place?'

Graian and Solonaetz, still wiping their eyes with kerchiefs, were inclined to agree with her.

GUIDO PALAMA MADE a grand entrance after a suitable time had elapsed. He was a tall, well-built man, his handsome face set in a perpetual smile. After a short, polite enquiry as to his visitors' journey, health and opinions of the city, he settled immediately to business.

'So,' he said, leaning back in his silk-cushioned chair, 'you essay an entreaty to the Dark Lady of Nepenthe!' He helped himself to a biscuit, nibbling thoughtfully. Graian and Solonaetz had both leaned forward expectantly. 'My family have captured the essence of the mystic flower for centuries,' he continued. 'Mysteria Hypno Morta – a prayer, her name, a prayer!' He sighed. 'We call her the lacrymata, the moonskin, the last breath of a favoured concubine. Mysteria – dark maid of the hidden caves. Fragrant, fragile bloom, whose fleeting kiss is spiritual joy, whose bitter juice is oblivion!' He smiled.

The speech was obviously a sales pitch, Solonaetz thought. However, the plain truth would be lacking in romance. The Palamas grew a rare flower in underground catacombs, whose perfume was highly narcotic and whose essential oil was a deadly poison if ingested. It could also be sold for ridiculous amounts throughout this corner of the Imperium. Naturally, such an honest description would not have excited Graian's desire for purchase as much, but then, why bother anyway? The Palamas were rigidly discerning about who they dealt with in the world of commerce. The fact that Graian was here at all indicated the sale had already been finalized with the Fiddeus clan back on Terra. Graian was just a courier. Guido Palama obviously liked to romance his merchandise.

Solonaetz noticed Palama was looking at him keenly. 'Naturally, you wish to see... for yourselves,' their host said, with a wider smile.

THE CATACOMBS WERE accessible via a single door in the heart of the Palama workshops. Violet glowstrips illumined the worn stone steps that led downwards into a damp murk. Shivania slipped her arm through Solonaetz's as they descended. 'Can you smell her?' she whispered. The navigator could feel her trembling.

'Is this what you came down here for?' he asked in an undertone. It was possible. Astropaths, being psychic and therefore mystically inclined, would be bound to be interested in the lacrymata. Shivania squeezed his arm. She did not answer.

'Here the beds of lesser maidens,' Palama intoned when they reached the bottom. Terraces of peaty soil, black as grave-dirt, swept away into the dimness, micred with pale stars; the blooms themselves. 'Mysteria Puella,' Palama said. 'She is destined for the warm throats of ladies of the grand houses of all the worlds. A decoration, merely mimicking the forbidden sensuality of her elder sister.' He plucked a single bloom and presented it to Shivania. 'For you, my dear. Press her well between the pages of your mea libra and she will greet you with a benediction whenever you go to inscribe your meditations.'

'Thank you, sir!' Shivania said. She sniffed the flower cautiously. 'Mmm. Here, Solonaetz!'

He leaned over to sample the perfume. Its first note was bright and fruity, descending for a brief flirtation with the carnal bloom of musk before rising to a final crescendo of riotous spring flowers. 'Excellent! You will look forward to your inscriptions from now on, I think!'

Palama led them further into the breathing dark. Solonaetz's skin prickled with a weird excitement. He felt as if a thousand

sighing creatures of the night were shifting restlessly on black
satin couches around him; vampire beauty concealed from
sight beneath a venomous mat of narcotic flower flesh.

'And here,' Palama whispered reverently ahead of them, 'the
boudoir of the lady herself. Have care, my friends, she sleeps
and dreams.'

Solonaetz heard Graian gasp. He himself was holding his
breath, but not for long. Ahead of them, a gloomy crypt spread
into infinity, its tiers snaking between massive columns and
arches. Each tier was overflowing, indeed gravid, cancerous and
alive with convolutions of shimmering fleshy whorls. Bloom
upon bloom crawled over their sisters, engulfing, tumbling,
sending out whippy suckers festooned with tumescent buds
and the perfume...

Solonaetz had to suppress a groan. The sorcerous elixir of it
seethed and flexed upon the tongue, the throat, reaching down
with limber fingers to the belly and groin. No simple cadence
here, but a hectic symphony of aromatic notes. The first was
fruity too, but this was the over-ripe, giddy eruption of autumn
in full swell, sweeping lustily down to a dark woodland of musk
and sandal spiced with civet and ambergris, rising orgasmically
to the exuberant scream of spring; jasmin, asphodel and creamy
rose. Flowers of the flesh. Solonaetz swallowed thickly, dizzy
with the aroma that was playing havoc with his sense of reality,
never mind his more carnal senses. At his side, Shivania was
motionless. Her touch had become vague upon his arm.

Palama let them all sample the agonizing ecstasy of it for a
few moments before clearing his throat and saying, 'Well, I trust
you are satisfied, Captain Fiddeus. Perhaps we can repair to the
salon once more to arrange delivery of your consignment.'

RATHER OVERCOME, AND silent because of it, Graian, Solonaetz
and Shivania eventually emerged into the streets once more.
Shivania toyed gently with the bloom Palama had given her,
settling it safely behind a talismanic pin on her robes. They
reached the tourist quarter, almost unaware of how they had
got there. Cafes and bars lined streets that radiated out from
quaint squares, discrete alleys limned with globes of deep red
light leading to areas of more lascivious delights. The aroma of
cooking food did something to dispel the enchantment of
Palama's crypt, and Solonaetz suggested the three of them

choose one of the cafes to sample local cuisine. Shivania agreed enthusiastically, but Graian, looking sheepish, mumbled something about going to find the rest of their party. Solonaetz, fighting the urge to poke fun and discomfort the captain, merely smiled and told him he and Shivania would meet him back at the spaceport in three hours, ship's time. Graian gratefully scuttled off down one of the alleys.

'Are you sure you don't want to go with him?' Shivania asked, clearly aware of what Graian was looking for. 'I don't mind. I'll be quite happy sitting here alone. Really.'

'No!' Solonaetz insisted, firmly tucking the girl's hand through his elbow. 'Come along. This looks an interesting place. Glazed fowl hanging everywhere! Take a sniff!'

Shivania laughed delightedly and they went inside.

'I WISH I COULD see you,' Shivania said wistfully as they sat drinking a dessert beverage after the meal. 'I mean, really see you. Your aura is handsome, navigator, and yet...' She shrugged. 'Silly of me. It must be the effect of this little lady here!' She touched the bloom in her robes. 'I suppose I must be ugly to you, blind as a cave bat as I am!'

'Shivania, stop that,' Solonaetz said. 'You are a very pretty girl, as you well know, and I am a rather haggard spectre of a man. Drink your dessert!'

'You haven't seen me without this,' she said mournfully, indicating her mask.

'So show me then!'

'You won't scream?'

Solonaetz laughed. She was joking, of course. 'Only behind my hand. I'm not squeamish, Shivania, really.'

Impulsively, she reached up and untied the strings of her mask, lowering it swiftly, with an air of challenge. Her eyelids drooped over blind milky orbs sunk deep into her skull, as if shrunken. Thin, almost pencil-drawn, brows shadowed the sockets. It was not gruesome, however, which Solonaetz knew the girl must be aware of. A test then? Was she inviting a physical response from him?

'Disgusting,' he said, with a laugh. 'Dress yourself at once!'

She smiled and replaced the mask. 'I could ask you to remove yours, navigator, but there'd be little point. Doesn't it itch having to keep the eye under a band all the time?'

'Not at all.'

'Would you be able to see into the warp now, from here, if you removed it and opened the eye?'

'What I would see is the otherworld of our reality. In a place like this, it might be educational, but rather upsetting, I feel.'

'Strange. I wouldn't have thought you'd be so squeamish.'

'I'm not, just careful. So, tell me, what was your interest in coming down here? You intended to accompany Fiddeus to his client all along, of course.'

'Your warp sight lends you a sharp perception, navigator,' Shivania replied. She was enjoying herself immensely, he could see. She sipped her drink daintily. 'Lacrymata is a legend. I was curious. Also, if the fables surrounding it are true, it possesses innumerable properties which haven't even been guessed at yet.'

'Really. And which of these legends concerns you?'

Shivania laughed. 'You sound like an inquisitor, navigator. Aren't I allowed a girlish curiosity?'

'Allowed it, certainly, but I doubt that is your motivation.'

She shrugged. 'The interest was casual, really. It was only a rumour. I heard the lacrymata stimulates psychic sight – far beyond what a humble astropath can imagine.' She shrugged again, jerkily. 'However, I've smelled the stuff now, and my inner sight has not improved significantly.'

'I should hope not!' Solonaetz exclaimed. 'Whatever properties the perfume has, it is also very dangerous, and possibly attractive to hostile forces.'

'And that, dear navigator, is probably just as much a fable as any other connected with the lacrymata. Palama has to sell the stuff, doesn't he? It was all just talk.'

Solonaetz remembered the effect the lacrymata flowers had had on him and suppressed a shudder. He did not share Shivania's apparent scepticism.

'Anyway, I'm bored with the subject,' she said. 'I'm more interested in you. How old are your injuries?'

'What?!'

Shivania smiled slyly. 'Oh come now, navigator, you should know I see more than others, lacrymata or not. Your aura has scars. How did you get them, and where?'

Solonaetz was impressed. 'It happened what seems a long time ago, and my name is Solonaetz – remember?'

She shrugged. 'Well?'

By the time he'd finished pouring out his life history to the girl, they had scant minutes to return to the rendezvous point with the others from the Brava. Solonaetz felt as giddy as an excited boy as they hurried through the streets; purged and renewed.

He'd been waiting for someone with whom he could exorcise the past to come into his life, someone free from the drippings of cloying pity. Whoever would have thought this young, quirky girl would be the one? So much for the pleasure-vaults of Assyrion. Solonaetz had no doubt that what he'd experienced by simply talking in the dim-lit cafe far superseded any delights of the flesh Graian and the others had experienced.

OF COURSE, SHE came tapping on his cabin door while he lay restless in his sleep cell, weary to the bone, yet unable to rest. Of course, she came with words of reassurance. 'Rest easy, Solonaetz. I ask no more than this of you.' Of course, it was a lie. And she, lithe avatar of release, cast a shawl of tawny hair across his breast and stroked his brow, saying, 'Look upon me, navigator, with the eye that sees my soul!' She removed his bandana and kissed the closed lid, bringing a fragrant memory of the lacrymata to his throat. She was so beautiful and skilled with such dark voluptuousness that, in the midst of their love-making, he did open his eye.

Is this woman, he thought, this that I see?

Pure female, her overlapping currents of spirit rivalling even the chaos of the warp. He had never thought to do such a thing before; no one had requested it. His eye was a danger as well as an intrigue; a glance could kill. Shivania, in her blindness, was immune, but she cried that she saw the light of him unveiled, his forehead shedding radiance which she claimed shared the same brightness as the Emperor's own beacon. Heresy. Maybe.

'If we only had a sample of the cargo,' she said, close to his ear. 'Think, Solonaetz, what ecstasies we could share!'

'Or what pain,' he added. A shiver of presentiment summoned a vision of the next warp drop: he, alone, in his pod, with the dark, moving liquid of the lacrymata, in the vaults below, singing its insidious song to the ever-vigilant powers of Chaos.

'You fear it!' Shivania laughed. 'Ice and passion of the wounded navigator!' She stroked the scars on his chest and belly. 'I envy you your sight,' she said.

AFTERWARDS, SHE CURLED into his arms, humming a strange little tune, running her fingers over his smooth, white skin, reaching up to wind them in his long, fine hair. 'Divine mutant!' she said.

'Hush, don't say that!'

'Well, you are! As I am, in truth. Both of us tolerated for our uses. Blessings upon our Imperial Father that we may find solace with each other.'

'Sometimes, Shivania, I think you say dangerous things.'

She scorned him gently. 'Faithful navigator, always quick to obey, to bend his back before the whip of Imperial doctrine.'

'Shivania!' He tried to ease himself away from her, suddenly feeling she had become a twining, suffocating thing. 'What are you saying? Listen to yourself!'

'I have done that for years!' she said sharply. 'Always listened to myself, from the day the blackship came and took me from my home!'

'You are an astropath. Privileged, honoured! Your very soul is bonded with the Emperor's!'

She sneered. 'Hah! A bonding that burned away my eyes! Bonding is another word for slavery, is it not?'

Solonaetz shook his head in confusion. 'I will not argue with you, but when you say these things, remember what your fate could have been!'

'And you think this is any better?' She sat up, brushing back her hair. Her voice possessed the dry quality of some seasoned, jaded assassin; a woman whose flesh was laced with scars. Solonaetz reflected how you never came within a whisker of knowing someone until they'd shared your bed. 'It is easy for you to be so complacent,' she said bitterly. 'A ship here, a ship there, flitting around, cushioned by the influence of your great family. What am I? In comparison, a mere slave, leased out by the Scholastica. I do not choose my commissions, navigator. Your life is your own. Mine?' She turned her face towards him and the white eyes between their slitted lids looked snake-like. 'I belong to Fiddeus and his clan. My freedom aboard this ship is an illusion.'

'No good can come of this talk, Shivania.'

She shrugged. 'Whatever. I have offended you, shocked you. For that, I am sorry. I like you. Still...' She sighed, her voice taking on a wistful note. 'Perhaps it was a mistake to leave ship. I did not want to come back, you know.'

Solonaetz reached to touch her. 'Forget this. Say nothing else. Come back to me.'

Reluctantly, she curled against his side. 'Sometimes,' she said, 'a great fear comes to me. I feel as if a depthless abyss waits to open at my feet.'

'Not for now,' Solonaetz whispered, and held her tight.

GRAIAN FIDDEUS SUPERVISED the stowing of his cargo, restlessly pacing the cargo vault as members of his crew carefully secured the crates. At Graian's insistence, Brother Gabreus came puffing down the access ramp, clutching a smoking censer of his recently-purchased, potent Assyrion incense and a handful of newly-etched talismans to drape around the cargo.

'We cannot be too careful,' Graian said. 'This stuff, for all its value, is a seductive substance. I am concerned what may occur should warp-leakage steal its way inside the ship. Gabreus, I want the whole of the *Brava* consecrated again; every corner, every duct, every rune re-blessed and anointed. Is this clear?'

'As the bloom of a nebula, captain. Never fear, Gabreus's unparalleled spirit will quell and subdue any effluvia seeking entrance!'

Graian smiled and patted the priest's bulky shoulder. 'I know I can trust you, brother. Now, I must hunt down our little communications system and ask her to transmit a message to my father. I intend to ask him to have a banquet ready for my crew courtesy of Clan Fiddeus!'

Gabreus grinned. 'He could breed whole generations of prime beef by the time we get home!'

IT HAD NOT gone unnoticed by Graian that some kind of carnal transaction was taking place between his navigator and his astropath. For some reason, this caused him deep discomfort. Shivania, he decided, had a streak of insolence inside her. Perhaps it was this that made him distrust her. Sometimes, when he issued a command, he sensed a wry malevolence in her expression; something about the mouth. It worried him she might alter the sense of his messages when she sent them, just out of mischief, to cause him embarrassment and inconvenience. Why should this be? Shivania might be a laser in comparison with Bassos's steady but small candle-flame, but he could not bring himself to have faith in her.

He also feared she might be bad for Solonaetz. After all, who knew what went on in the navigator's head? It was no secret he'd been horrifically wounded and had suffered a serious breakdown afterwards. Gomery had instructed him to treat Solonaetz with care, look out for him. Graian felt his instincts bridle at the thought of the quick, incomprehensible Shivania having him in her clutches. He intended to speak severely with his father on return. There was no way he would have that girl on board again. The crew of a ship were an enclosed community, mostly removed from time and space itself; the universe rolled inexorably on without them. It was, therefore, intrinsic to the ship's well-being that the crew resonated harmoniously with each other. One jarring note and the whole delicate structure could fall apart; entirely the kind of occurrence that foul influences from the warp could get a hook into. This possibility alarmed Graian more than that of engine failure or facing a warp storm. *Dea Brava* was his kingdom and he was sensitive to its ambiences.

WITH THIS IN mind, a few days later, when they were approaching the jump zone into warp space which would lead them finally back to Earth, Graian accompanied Solonaetz as he made his way to the blister, covertly assessing him for signs of strain and fatigue. 'Did you get your neck seen to?'

'Huh? Oh yes. Foss gave me a working over. It's fine now.'

Graian pulled at his lip, standing on the access ramp and watching Solonaetz carefully as he shimmied into the confined space of the blister and eased himself into position.

'Sol, can I speak... plainly with you?'

Solonaetz leaned sideways and peered down the ramp. 'Is that an order?'

'Sol!'

'Sorry, what is it?'

'Shivania...'

'Oh.' Solonaetz began fiddling with the controls to the warp-screen, his face taking on a mulish expression.

Graian fidgeted uncomfortably. 'I have to speak, Sol, as friend and commanding officer. Be careful.'

Solonaetz looked at him again, his expression guarded. He wanted to say: what gives you the right to call yourself my friend, but vented his annoyance with other words. 'I am not an invalid, Graian! I wish you'd stop treating me like some half-fuddled, incapacitated veteran! Quite frankly, much more of this and I'll be forced to resign my position. I am quite over what happened. It has not made me vulnerable. I am an adult and–'

'All right, all right!' Graian raised his hands placatingly. 'I had to speak. Appreciate my position.'

'She knows you don't like her,' Solonaetz said abruptly, once more adjusting his screen. 'Now, that can't help the situation, can it?'

Graian made a non-committal sound. 'At the risk of further tongue-lashing, just how serious is this... business with you and her?'

'As serious as any relationship for people in our positions can be. We live for the day. I can't see it's any of your business, Graian. Have no worry that it will affect my work – or hers. Now, if I could be allowed to get on with the business of warp flight...?'

Graian shrugged, reached up and slapped Solonaetz's thigh in an assuaging gesture, before making his way back to the camera operati, where he would catch up with a little paper-work, leaving the *Dea Brava* in Solonaetz's care. The interview had not progressed exactly as he'd planned.

SOLONAETZ SIGHED, AND settled back in his chair, blinking up through the blister at the streaming stars. If only Graian could know how he too had reservations about Shivania, reservations however that could not compete with the temptation of her body, her sweet soothing of his own. He knew there was an undeniable shred of repulsiveness about her, as compelling as her attractiveness. This, he told himself, was simply because she came out with unwise heretical statements from time to time. She was young, bitter; with guidance she was sure to overcome her grievances. That her quick flashes of temperament could presage anything worse than dissatisfaction was unthinkable; she had been trained by the Adeptus Astra

Telepathica. Their screening processes for removing tainted material was infallible; it had to be.

'It has to be,' he said aloud, as he removed his bandana.

THE WARP WAS quiet beyond the gate. Streams of pure immaterium boiled lazily on either side of the ship, but seemed unlikely to form themselves into maelstrom conditions. The warpscreen showed no inconsistency. Solonaetz dared to hope this would be an easy journey. A few thoughtforms flitted in and out of materiality ahead, but they were minor emissions. Solonaetz recited a prayer to the Emperor to enforce his self-protection and banish all anxieties. It was important to maintain a serene psyche during warp travel. He kissed his totems and fixed his concentration on the journey. A short jump. *Dea Brava* never ventured that far from Terra.

Solonaetz began to hum a mantra, improvising the tune. It lifted his spirits, and he drifted into sublime communication with the ship, becoming one with her body, faster than light, faster than thought, an exultant silver fish upon the the bosom of this arcane sea. He breathed an essence of salt and spume, euphoric, riding the wave of the astronomican as it pulled him homewards. Salt. Sea. Dunes. Dune-flowers. Flowers. Fruit. Musk. Sandal... Sandal? Solonaetz gulped and was pulled into a momentary reality. He inhaled. What? By the Emperor's sweet blood, what was this? Lacrymata? Impossible! He consulted the warpscreen, his head dizzy with the insidious perfume. The blister was full of it! A pulse glowed on the screen, signifying warp activity. But where? Solonaetz wondered frantically. Behind us? Before us? Where? So close. So close!

He fixed his eye towards the warp. Nothing definite and yet, a suggestion of imminence. The immaterium was excited! He scanned for Chaos emanations. Perhaps something had clung to the ship. The screen seemed poised, waiting to bloom with information, denying him the knowledge. He strained his senses to penetrate the cause as the perfume flowed over him in delicious, wicked waves, perverting the purity of his concentration. His skin prickled with sweat. The cargo! A focus! He must ignore it, banish it. The scent was an illusion. He must...

'Solonaetz!' A husky call.

As a lance of pain pierced the muscles of his neck, the navigator's head whipped towards the access ramp. The hatch was open and there, creeping towards him, naked and glowing as a hot flame, was Shivania, her mouth open, red tongue licking her lips, hair flowing like a cloud, her fingers idly stroking her breast. The perfume assaulted him in waves. He tried to speak. Shivania laughed and opened her shrivelled lids. Had he thought those dead eyes milky? No, they were more than that! Opal, fiery, shifting with a hundred colours.

'Solonaetz,' she said, shaking her head, so that her lustrous hair seethed like a nest of furred vipers. 'Come to me. The essence is my flesh. It gives me sight! I have anointed my eyes! I see! I see so much! I see you, Solonaetz!'

'No!' he said, in a strangled voice. He felt as if the very substance of the *Dea Brava* was melting before his eyes. All that existed was the pale, shining form of the astropath, and the hideous seductions of the warp waiting to take him in the final, everlasting embrace.

'No, Solonaetz? What is this no? We are in our place, are we not? Mutants, we! I can hear my sisters calling, vapours upon the warp tides! All those that die, Solonaetz! All those that die! You slide this ship upon a torrent of their blood! Open that great eye of yours and really see! Look at me! Touch me! Open the blister and take me home!'

For a few moments Solonaetz wondered whether he was hallucinating his own desires. Is this what I want, what I've always wanted? Then, Shivania reached out a hand to touch him, her fingers flexing, curdled eyes blinking and leaking sluggish tears. She hissed and smiled. 'I spit your seed into Chaos!' she cried and lunged forward to throw herself into the blister upon him.

Acting reflexively, Solonaetz winced back and then, with an extreme spurt of effort and will, pulled himself from his chair and flicked out his leg to kick the access-way shut. He heard an agonized squeal, and an infinity of violent colours smacked against his warp-sight, bringing peals of agony, pain he could not have imagined in the worst of nightmares. His body writhed and his stomach convulsed. The surface of the blister was aswarm with foul shapes, all grinning, all scratching at the plascryst, telling him with sickening gestures of all they planned to do with his body when they reached it.

Solonaetz tasted salt, knew he was biting his tongue. He slammed his head against the console, screaming, 'Fiddeus! Gabreus! Anyone!' but the communications node seemed a million miles away, beyond his reach. Had the ship left its course? His eye was blind to the route, seeing only a tangle of voluptuous shapes that beckoned and tempted, promising eternal pain, eternal ecstasy. He could hear Shivania scratching at the hatch, her voice a hoarse whisper of desire.

'My Lord Emperor!' Solonaetz screamed. 'Help me! Help me!'

And then a pure strain of unadulterated thought forced its way through the melee. 'Take my hand,' it said. 'I am with you, navigator. Take my hand.'

And he focused on that beam, his consciousness flowing with it, melding with it, following. Although he knew in his heart the Emperor was cocooned within his palace on Earth, his aged, tortured body kept alive by machines, the navigator's spirit saw a figure walking the astronomican's beam as if it was a shining path, leading the *Dea Brava* away from danger, dismissing the effluvia of the warp with the strength and the grief of its soul. A vision of his faith, maybe? But to Solonaetz it was the Emperor himself, spirit-walking in the void.

Some moments later, he came to a kind of reality, and realized the fluidium outside was quiescent, the warpscreen clear of clots. There was no sound beneath the hatch-way and the fume of lacrymata had left the blister. He was *Dea Brava* and they swam the wave of the astronomican, embraced by the spiritual essence of a thousand martyrs, swimming home.

'DID YOU CALL me, Solonaetz?' Back in real space, Graian Fiddeus was at the blister even before Solonaetz had unbuckled his safety harness. 'I thought I heard a call, but the ship's mind told me otherwise. Even so, I thought I'd better check. Are you all right?'

Solonaetz looked terrible, his white face slick with sweat, dark shadows around his eyes. He had not even replaced his bandana; just hanging there in his chair, like a corpse – or someone drugged – the mutant eye staring dully at the warpscreen. Averting his gaze, Graian squeezed into the blister alongside him and gently tied the bandana back in place. 'What happened?' he asked. 'Sol?' He gave the navigator a shake.

Solonaetz shuddered, jerked and then gulped air. Ship's air: faintly metallic, rubbery-sweet and, thankfully, free of perfume.

He sighed and momentarily leaned against the captain. The instant was of silence, suspended heartbeats. Then he pulled away.

'Many die to keep the astronomican alive, don't they?' he said.

'Not unwillingly. You know that.' Fiddeus had a horrible dread Solonaetz had suffered a further breakdown. 'What...?'

Solonaetz shook his head quickly to silence him. 'No. The cargo; it has been tampered with.'

'What?! Impossible! I would have been informed!'

'Nevertheless, what I say is true.'

'It was protected.'

Solonaetz looked at him bleakly. 'Yes, undoubtedly. As I am. Always. Believe me, Graian, I am not mistaken.'

Fiddeus rubbed his face uncomfortably. 'You are ill, Solonaetz. Get yourself out of there. I'll take you to Foss.'

Solonaetz leaned back in his chair and uttered a low, bitter laugh. 'Ill, am I? Take me somewhere where I can talk to you, Graian Fiddeus. Play the part of being the good friend you always profess to be. I have a favour to ask of you.'

SHE WAS IN her cabin, dressed in her finest robes, brushing out her hair. She wore her mask, the eyes unseeing, staring into nothing. 'I thought you would come,' she said, laying down her brush.

Solonaetz didn't comment. 'I have something for you,' he said. 'A gift. It is the best I can give you under the circumstances, Shivania. I know you will understand and use it wisely.'

She accepted the gift, closing her fingers over the small, crystal bottle. Her laugh was shaky. 'Well, Solonaetz, there goes your bonus, I suspect! Such generosity!'

'Not generosity, Shivania. I loved you in a way. It is compassion. Merely that. A report will be made to the Scholastica when we return. You know what the verdict will be, and its consequences. You are tainted; you must know that. You complained before about your lack of freedom. Well, if you reach Terra, your life aboard this ship will seem like paradise. They will send you to feed the Emperor's soul. Because of what we shared, I want to spare you that. Thank me. I grant you your dearest wish: a full draught of the maiden of oblivion. If you are lucky, for a moment, you'll have the sight you craved.'

He left immediately and, for a while, Shivania sat motion-less, the bottle held in her lap. She could not cry, no matter how much she yearned for that release. Her lips shook around the shape of his name. He'd possessed a strength she had not anticipated; to her, a hideous strength.

Then she opened the bottle.

A LANGUOROUS, SENSUOUS aroma flooded her cabin, sweet with desire, poignant with loss. Its crescendo was the last damp fires of autumn, before the winter comes, when all is burnt, the rub-bish from the fields, the dead wood. She smelled dark earth and sensed a welcoming. Somewhere. With shaking hands, she tipped a little of the essence onto a single finger and anointed her throat. Moonskin, lacrymata, lady of tears, dark sister. Not for the weak, oh no.

As the siren scent rose around her in a final, embracing cloud, Shivania tilted back her lovely head on her perfect neck and tipped the contents of the bottle down her throat. For a few, fiery seconds, her body sang a maniac dance of unen-durable beauty and passion, but for a few seconds only.

It was a swift death.

'I KNOW IT IS hard for you,' Gabreus said, 'but you acted in the noblest way, Solonaetz.' The priest fondly patted the navigator's shoulder. They were sitting in his chapel-vault, beneath the light of benediction. It had been a difficult confession. 'Come now, lift your head, young man. Fiddeus is pacing outside like a brooding leopard. Don't give him cause for concern. Be strong!'

'Why, though?' Solonaetz asked helplessly. 'Why her? She was so...'

'Tainted!' Gabreus interrupted sharply. 'Believe it, Solonaetz! The lacrymata was merely a catalyst, and a lucky one in the event. Worse could have occurred if you think about it. You bested the powers of Chaos in your own way. No trivial feat, I assure you. No system is infallible. There will always be mis-takes. The Adeptus Astra are thorough but their dominion is vast. Because of this, it is inevitable the odd blight slips through their screening net. It is true she might never have suc-cumbed, and that the essence itself was the cause, but that is irrelevant really. Live your life, navigator. Forget her! In scant days, we shall be home and your family awaits you.' He smiled. 'And don't forget the feast Fiddeus has promised us!'

Solonaetz nodded, kissed the priest's belt and backed from the vault.

GRAIAN WAS WAITING outside, as Gabreus had told him. 'One thing I have to know,' Solonaetz said. 'The lacrymata: where is it bound? The Adeptus Terra would never allow such a substance to pass hands in the free market, surely. Who commissioned its purchase?'

Graian Fiddeus scratched his neck, wrinkled his nose uncomfortably. 'Well… Guido Palama is indentured to one department back on Terra, just one. The dispersal of the perfume, the true lacrymata, is rigorously controlled.'

'Who bought it, Graian?'

He sighed. 'The Inquisition.'

Solonaetz laughed. 'I should have known! An instrument of torture!'

'Hardly a matter for humour!'

'You think not? We live in a universe of contradictions, my friend, to our continual delight. Now, I suggest we repair to the camera recreata to toast our fair Terra when she reveals herself in the heavens. The Inquisition!' He shook his head.

'You look better, Solonaetz,' Fiddeus said bleakly.

The navigator was already striding away up the passageway. He flung a remark over his shoulder. 'Just a reprieve, my friend. Just a reprieve.'

THE ALIEN BEAST WITHIN

Ian Watson

THE GIANT EXERCISE wheel accelerated yet again while Meh'Lindi raced, caged within it. The machine towered two hundred metres high, under a fan-vaulted roof. Shafts of light, of blood-red and cyanotic blue and bilious green, beamed through tracery windows which themselves revolved kaleidoscopically. Chains of brass amulets dangling from the rotating spokes of the wheel clashed and clanged deafeningly like berserk bells as they whirled around.

Elsewhere in the gymnasium of the Callidus shrine, high-kicking initiate assassins broke plasteel bars, or else their own tarsal or heel bones. Injury was no excuse to discontinue the exercise – now they must master pain instead. Others dislocated their limbs by muscle tension so as to escape from bonds before crawling through constricted, kinking pipes. A pump sucked blood dazingly from two youths prior to their practising unarmed combat, and from another before he would attempt to run the gauntlet along a corridor of spinning knives. Scarred veteran instructors patrolled, ever willing to demonstrate to the unbelieving.

Callisthenics machines shrieked and roared and spun so as to disorient their users.

Meh'Lindi had been running for half an hour, trying to catch a fellow assassin who ran vertically above her, upside-down, wearing an experimental gravity-reverser belt. She ran in a self-induced trance, imagining that she might presently reach such an enlightened state of mind that she could speed up inhumanly and loop the loop, stunning her quarry as she passed by. Whenever she was about to put on such a spurt, the wheel speeded up to frustrate her.

Suddenly, with a thunderous crash of engaging sprockets and a screaming of its gears, the wheel halted.

Meh'Lindi was hurled forward violently. Though the event was entirely unexpected, she was already fully alert, and arching herself into a hoop so as to roll. Uncoiling, she somersaulted backwards. She leapt about-face. The wheel was already beginning to turn in the opposite direction. It was picking up speed. High overhead, her quarry was tumbling. She sprinted, up, up, willing the friction of her bare feet and her sheer renewed momentum to stop her from toppling back down the giant curved track.

Presently a siren wailed, signalling the end of her session – just when she fancied she had a slight chance of succeeding in what was virtually an impossible task.

Dismissing any temptation to feel annoyed, she skipped about, and ran back down the wheel. A filigree gate opened; she stepped out.

'Director secundus invites your presence in an hour,' the wheelmeister told her. The bald old man, one of whose eyes was a ruby lens, forbore to comment on her performance. As a seasoned graduate of the Collegia Assassinorum, Meh'Lindi should be able to assess that for herself. If not, she was less than devout.

'Invites?' she queried. The director secundus was none other than deputy to the supreme director of the Callidus shrine of assassins. Did such a high official invite?

'That was the phrasing.'

IN A DOMED cubicle in the baptisterium, Meh'Lindi peeled off her clingtight black tunic. As hypersound vibrated sweat and grime loose from her, she gazed at her body in a tall speculum framed with brass bones interwoven and knotted. She permitted herself a certain degree of admiration over and above mere physical assessment. For she was trained as a pedigree courtesan as well as a sleek and cunning killer. A courtesan – even one who largely pretended to fulfil the role of a pleasure-bringer – must be conscious of sensuality.

Meh'Lindi was tall, long-limbed, with puissant biceps and calf-muscles, though her sheer height diluted the impression of power. Enticing black tattoos concealed her scars. A giant hirsute spider wrapped around her midriff. A snake, baring fangs, climbed her right leg. Scarablike beetles trod the modest swell of her bosom. Her breasts, which no exercise could mould into weapons, were small and unimpeding, though agreeably firm – dainty little beetle-tipped cones. Her coaly hair was cropped short so that no one could seize it. In her courtesan role she might, or might not, opt to wear a lustrous wig. Her eyes were golden, her ivory face oddly anonymous and unmemorable in repose. But then, she could alter her features to those of an enchantress – or equally, of a hag.

The director secundus did not summon her. He invited her...

She probed at the word just as the tip of one's tongue might tease at a hollow tooth loaded with catalepsin for spitting into a victim's eye to paralyse him.

It was unthinkable that the secundus dreamed of exploiting this wonderful instrument – herself – which his Collegia had crafted from feralworld flesh, for any private aphrodisiac satisfaction of his own. That would be blasphemous. Had Meh'Lindi not been a sham-courtesan as well as an assassin, this thought would hardly have occurred to her at all.

Invite. The word hinted at the protocol of the Mors Voluntaria, the permission to commit exemplary suicide which was granted to an assassin who had failed calamitously, though honourably, in some enterprise. Or whose suicide might be required, so as to erase the principal witness of an error on the part of the Officio Assassinorum...

Meh'Lindi knew that she had in no way failed in her vocation.

Puzzled, she anointed the soles of her feet with consecrated camphor oil, her loins with oil of frankincense, and the crown of her head with rosemary, then performed a devotion to the Emperor before resuming her tunic.

AT THE INVITATION of Tarik Ziz, the secundus, Meh'Lindi seated herself in a double lotus position, facing him.

She bowed her head. The lotus that locked her legs together and the aversion of her gaze were both modes of obeisance towards a superior in his private studium. Thus she signified that she was hampering herself from any assassination bid. True, she could uncoil in an instant and launch herself – nor did a skilled assassin need to be staring at her target. The faint sigh of the man's lungs, his odour, the mere pressure of air in the room located Ziz for her.

But nor would any such traitorous, motiveless attack succeed. Tarik Ziz was reputedly omega-dan.

The black-robed secundus knelt on a brocaded dais, which was also his spartan bed, facing an ancient baroque data-console. His long beringed fingers occasionally tapped a sequence of keys, one side of his mind seemingly involved in other concerns. Tomes bound in skin and data-cubes crowded one wall up to the groin-vaulted ceiling.

A collection of thousands of tiny, burnished archaic knives, many no larger than fingernails, ornamented another wall, resembling a myriad wings torn from metallic moths, shattering the light from an electro-flambeau into quicksilver fragments.

'You may look at me, Meh'Lindi.'

Ziz was swarthy, short, and compact – almost a dwarf, save for his sinuous fingers. The many rune-wrought rings he wore undoubtedly concealed a pharmacy of exotic hallucinogens and paralytic agents, even though the secundus no longer operated in the field. His artificial teeth, alternately of jet and vermilion, were all canines.

'You are one of our finest chameleons,' Ziz said to her softly.

Meh'Lindi nodded, for this was the simple truth. An injection of the shape-changing drug polymorphine would allow any trained assassin of her shrine to alter their appearance by effort of will. This was one of the specialities of the Callidus shrine, the keynote of which was cunning – just as the Vindicare shrine specialized in vengeance, and the Eversor shrine in unstoppable attack.

Under the stimulus of polymorphine, flesh would flow like heated plastic. Bones would soften, reshape themselves, and harden again. Altering her height, her frame, her features, Meh'Lindi had frequently masqueraded as other women – gorgeous and ugly, noble and common. She had mimicked men.

On one occasion she had imitated a tall, hauntingly beautiful alien of the eldar race.

Always, with the purpose of eradicating someone whose activities imperilled the Imperium; with the aim of destroying a foe physically or – more rarely – psychologically...

Yet the drug polymorphine on its own was no miracle elixir. The business of shape-shifting demanded a deep and almost poignant sympathy with the person who was to be copied, killed, and replaced. The trick required empathy – deep identification with the target – and inner discipline.

Inject a non-initiate with polymorphine, and the result would be a protoplasmic chaos of the body, an agonising anarchy of the flesh and bones and organs, an on-going muddled upheaval and meltdown resulting finally in blessed death.

Meh'Lindi was an excellent, disciplined chameleon, exactly as the secondus said. Though she was no psyker, yet inscribed in the cells of her flesh and in the chambers of her brain was assuredly a wild gene-rune for apeing the appearance and traits of strangers – for metamorphosing herself – which the drug allowed her to express to the utmost.

If she had been born on a cultured world she might have been an actress. On her own feral home world she might have become a priestess of some cult of mutability. Recruited willy-nilly when a child from her barbarian tribe, she could now – as a Callidus assassin – become virtually any stranger, which was a fine fulfilment for her.

Ziz leaned forward. 'Because of your talent, our shrine invites you to participate in an epochal experiment.'

'I am but an instrument,' she replied, 'in the service of our shrine.' Her answer was obedient and dutiful, with the merest hint of caution, as one might expect from a Callidus initiate.

'You are a thinking instrument, my daughter. A wise one. One whose mind must be in perfect tune with the changes you will undergo, or else the result could prove fatal.'

'What changes, secundus?'

When Ziz told her, Meh'Lindi gasped once, as if her dwarfish omega-dan superior had punched her in her muscle-stiffened stomach..

WHEN SHE LEFT his studium, she trotted through the labyrinth of shadowy corridors where any but an initiate would soon be hopelessly lost. Reaching the gymnasium, she begged the wheelmeister to evict a novice from the apparatus, and re-admit her. Scrutinising her, the bald old man seemed to appreciate her need.

Soon Meh'Lindi was running, running, as if to race right away from the shrine, away to the very stars, to anywhere else where she might lose herself entirely and never be found again.

As if the worst nightmare in the world was pursuing her, she sprinted. Thus she vented her feelings of appalled anguish without absconding disobediently to anywhere else whatever. Finally, hours later so it seemed, at a point of exhaustion such as Meh'Lindi had never verged on before, she achieved a kind of acceptance of her fate.

Just as the exercise wheel had changed direction of a sudden previously, so had the wheel of her own fortune reversed shockingly.

Out of binding allegiance to her shrine, on account of the solemn and sinister oaths she had sworn, because the Collegia Assassinorum had made her everything that she was, she must comply.

She was invited to do so, but refusal was unthinkable.

The only alternative was exemplary suicide – to volunteer for a mission that was guaranteed to destroy her, after destroying many other foes.

Meh'Lindi was Callidus, not Eversor. Until now, she had never felt suicidal. Till now. Nor, after her passion-purging run in the wheel, did that alternative tempt her. Even if her shrine, in the unrefusable person of Tarik Ziz, seemed bent on ampu-tating her talent. Aye, mutilating it! By way of an epochal experiment..

As THE LASER-SCALPELS hovered over her naked, paralysed body, Meh'Lindi gazed askew at the senior chirurgeon whose robe was embroidered with purity symbols and prophylactic hexes.

She could move her eyeballs fractionally. Her field of view additionally took in the robed, tattooed radiographer-adept mounted and wired into the brass-banded examinator machine. This towered alongside the operating table like a predatory armadillo, scanning the inner strata of her body with multiple snouts. Its lens-eyes projected four infant-sized holo-grams of herself into mid-air, side by side.

One hologram was of her body flayed so that all her muscles were exposed. Another revealed only the rivers, tributaries, and streams of her circulatory system. A third dissected out her nerve network. A fourth stripped her skeleton bare. These homunculi of herself rotated slowly as if afloat in invisible bottles, displaying themselves to her and to the chirurgeon.

The lanky soporifer-adept, who monitored the drips of metacurare that numbed and froze her, sat in a framework resembling a giant spider. Its antennae reached out to sting her insensible, though not unconscious – for her mind must understand the procedure she was about to undergo. An elderly, warty, gnome-like medicus knelt on a rubber cushion to whisper in her ear. Meh'Lindi could hear him but not see him; nor could she see other adepts in the surgical laboratory who superintended the body implants and extra glands awaiting in stasis tureens.

Meh'Lindi felt nothing. Not the clamp that held her mouth, nor the silver nozzle that gargled saliva from it. Nor the grooved operating table underneath her, with its runnels for any spilled blood or other fluids. Unable to shift her head, yet capable of rolling her eyeballs a fraction, she merely saw somewhat. And heard, the murmurings of the warty gnome.

'First we transect your shoulders and your arms. Later, we will of course be heedful of the topography of your tattoos...'

She heard a laser-scalpel descending, buzzing like a busy fly. The process was beginning.

An assassin could block off agony, could largely disconnect her consciousness from the screaming switchboard of pain in the brain. Thus was an assassin trained. Thus was the web of her brain restrung. How, otherwise, could she fulfil her missions if injured? How else could she focus her empathy without distraction during the polymorphine change? However, during a total dissection such as this some muscles might well spasm instinctively, thwarting the chirurgeon's delicate manoeuvres. Consequently she was anaesthetised, awake.

The gnome's words registered. Yet in her heart – in her wounded heart – Meh'Lindi was still hearing Tarik Ziz announce how she would be desecrated.

'Initiates of Callidus can imitate all sorts and conditions of people. Who can do so better than you, Meh'Lindi? You have even mimicked a humanoid eldar, sufficiently well to convince human beings.'

'And well enough to persuade another eldar for a while, secundus,' she reminded him discreetly.

Ziz nodded. 'Yet we cannot adopt the form of other alien creatures whom we might wish to copy. We are constrained by our limbs, by our bones, by the flesh that is available... What do you know about genestealers, Meh'Lindi?'

At that point Meh'Lindi had experienced a chilling, weakening, cavernous pang, as though her entrails had emptied out of her. It took her moments to identify the unfamiliar sensation.

The sensation was terror.

Terror such as she believed had been expunged from her long since, torn out of her by the root during training.

'What do you know?' he repeated.

'Genestealers have four arms,' she recited robotically. 'Two arms equipped with hands, and two with claws that can tear through plasteel armour as if it is tissue. Their heads are long and bulbous, with fangs. Their horny spine bends them into a permanent crouch. They have an armoured carapace and a powerful tail...'

Yet it was not the creatures themselves that appalled her. Oh no. It was the implication behind Ziz's question.

'Polymorphine could never turn us into one of those, secundus.'

'Not polymorphine alone, Meh'Lindi.'

As THE MEDICUS murmured his commentary, interspersed with pious invocations to the Emperor – echoing those of the presiding chirurgeon – she squinted askew at the homunculi of herself being dissected open and knew that the very same was happening to herself. Tiny stasis generators were clipped inside her to stop her blood from spurting and draining away.

She was a snared hare stretched out on a butcher's block.

'WE SHALL USE body implants,' Ziz had continued. 'We will insert extrudable plastiflesh reinforced with carbon fibres into your anatomy. We will introduce flexicartilage which can toughen hard as horn. In repose – in their collapsed state – these implants will lurk within your body imperceptibly. Yet they will remember the monstrous shape and strength programmed into their fabric. When triggered, while polymorphine softens your flesh and bone, those implants will swell into full, active mode.'

The mosaic of tiny, glittering knives on the wall had seemed to take wing, to leap at Meh'Lindi to flay her.

'We will graft extra glands into you to store, and synthesise at speed, growth hormone – somatotrophin – and glands to reverse the process...'

'But,' she had murmured despairingly, 'I still could not become a perfect genestealer, could I?'

'At this stage that is not necessary. You will be able to transform into a convincing genestealer hybrid form. A hybrid with only one pair of arms, and lacking a tail... One closer to the semblance of humanity – yet sufficiently polluted, sufficiently grotesque to persuade those whom you must infiltrate. If this experiment succeeds as we hope, subsequently we shall attempt to implant secondary limbs.'

'Into me?' Did her voice quiver?

Ziz shook his head. 'Into another volunteer. You will be committed to the hybrid form, only able to alternate between that and your own human anatomy.'

Meh'Lindi's horror grew. What Ziz proposed couldn't simply be a gratuitous experiment, could it? One conducted merely out of curiosity?

Meh'Lindi licked her lips. 'I take it, secundus, that there's some specific mission in view?'

Ziz smiled thinly and told her.

To Meh'Lindi, that mission almost seemed to be a pretext, a trial to test whether she would perform to specification and survive.

Yet of course, she was no arbiter of the importance of a mission. The art of the assassin was to apply lethal pressure at one crucial, vulnerable point in society, a point which might not always even seem central, yet which her superiors calculated was so. Often a target was prominent – a corrupt planetary governor, a disloyal high official. Yet dislodging a seemingly humble pebble could in some circumstances start an avalanche. A Callidus assassin wasn't a slaughterer but a cunning surgeon.

Surgery...

'You are one of our most flexible chameleons, Meh'Lindi. Surely our experiment will succeed best with you. This can lead to wondrous things. To the imitating of tyranids, of tau, of lacrymoles, of kroot. How else could we ever infiltrate such alien species, if the need arose?'

'You honour your servant,' she mumbled. 'You say that I will be... committed...'

'Hereafter, when using polymorphine, you will unfortunately only be able to adopt the genestealer hybrid form; none other.'

It was as she had deeply feared. She would lose all other options of metamorphosis. She would be flayed of her proud talent, of what – in her heart – made her Meh'Lindi.

Was it so strange that an outstanding ability to mimic other people could reinforce her sense of her own self? Ah no, not so odd... For Meh'Lindi had been snatched away as a child from home and tribe, from language and customs. After initial stubbornness – insisting on her own sovereign identity – she had yielded and thereafter had found her own firm foundation, in flexibility.

'I'm also trained as a courtesan, secundus,' she reminded Ziz humbly.

A momentary bitter grimace twisted the lips of the swarthy, stunted omega-dan.

'You are... splendid enough to be one exactly as you are. We must be willing to prune our ambitions according to the needs of our shrine, and of the Imperium. Ambition is vanity, in this world of death.'

Had Tarik Ziz sacrificed his own ambitions in the process of rising to the rank of director secundus? Ziz was in line to become supreme director of the Callidus shrine, and thus perhaps grand master of the assassins, a High Lord of Terra.

This experiment, if successful, might play a significant role in his personal advancement...

'I am but an instrument,' Meh'Lindi echoed, hollowly.

And that was why she had fled to the exercise wheel, to run until she felt utterly empty, empty enough to accept.

THE SURGICAL PROCEDURE had already lasted for three painstaking, pious hours. The whispery voice of the warty gnome was growing hoarse.

A sub-skin of compacted, reinforced, 'clever' plastiflesh was now layered subcutaneously within Meh'Lindi's arms and legs and torso. This pseudoflesh was 'clever' in two regards. It was sending invasive neural fibres deeper into her anatomy, fusing physiologically. In this, it was cousin to the black carapace which was grafted into every Space Marine as the crowning act of his transformation into a superhuman. Furthermore, the false flesh could remember the evil contours it was programmed to assume, and would forever override any rebellious impulse of Meh'Lindi to counterfeit a different form.

It was like a map embroidered on supple fabric, which, upon stimulus, would expand, springing into shape stiffly, extruding from its contour lines the mountains of monstrosity.

The anatomical experimentum adepts of Callidus had been ingenious.

Likewise, blades of flexicartilage were inset under her finger and toe nails and sheathed her phalanges, her metatarsal and metacarpal bones. Stubs of the same had been grafted to her vertebrae, to her splint bones and femurs... And elsewhere.

In the phantom holo-dolls hanging above the operating table her new glands glowed as nuggets high inside her chest, not unlike a second set of nipples pointing inward.

Oh, she had been thoroughly, devoutly operated on.

And now the climax was coming, as the laser-scalpels swung down towards her staring face. Instruments came into play around her eyes, her nose, her clamped-open mouth, her cranium.

The medicus murmured huskily, 'By submucous resection we now incise inside the nostrils, to elevate the lining membrane from the septum and insert spurs of flexicartilage; thus to develop the genestealer snout...'

And this was happening to her.

'We drill all the frontal teeth to replace the roots with fang-plasm...'

And this was happening to her, too.

'We sever the frenulum-fold under the tongue, for greater flexibility of that organ. We perform a partial glossectomy – akin to a coring of your tongue, were it a rose-red apple – to insert a similitude of genestealer tongue...'

And this was also happening to her, as she squinted askance at the spinning stems of silver precision tools, while the gurgling pipe sucked away minced and vaporized flesh.

Presently: 'We lift your scalp, so as to trepan the skull. We perform a frontal craniotomy so that islets of skull will spread more easily, to assume the genestealer profile...'

Aye, that profile – and none other!

No eerily elegant alien eldar's silhouette.

No glory-girl's, nor hag's.

No one else's, ever, other than that single bestial shape.

And this was happening to her.

As laser-scalpels sliced her face and skull she screamed within.

Boiling outrage welled in her heart. Grievance, gall, and bitterness mixed their corrosive, acid cocktail in her belly. Her spirit shrieked.

Yet, necessarily, she lay silent as a stone.

She lay silent as a marble woman whom ruthless sculptors were carving into an evil idol.

Aye, silent as the very void that now opened in her tormented soul, swallowing her scream, sucking it away as surely as the silver tube sucked away parts of herself.

And in that terrible silence part of Meh'Lindi still listened to the medicus explaining; for she must understand.

ALONE, ALONE, AND now ever more alone, Meh'Lindi walked towards a huge eroded sandstone temple under a coppery sky inflamed by a giant red sun. That awesome sun filled a quarter of the heavens. Nevertheless, the air was chilly, for such suns yielded only meagre heat.

The temple complex dominated the end of a dusty boulevard lined by arcaded buildings of glazed terracotta with interior courtyards sheltered by domes. The arcades were crowded with vendors of barbecued birds' legs, stuffed mice and hot spiced wine, of holograms of this holy city of Shandabar, of supposed fragments of relics embedded in crystal, and models of relics. Those loggia were thronged with beggars and cripples and conjurors, with fortune tellers and robed pilgrims and gaudy tourists.

Temple concessionaires, some of them retired priests, were selling icons guaranteed as Imperially blessed and, to those who underwent the trivial test of sticking their hand inside a humming hex-box, lurid silken purity tassels, so called. These promised protection from evil in proportion to the size and number and floridity of tassels purchased.

The Oriens temple of Shandabar, built at what had once been the eastern gateway, was in fact the least of the holy city's three major temples. However, it boasted a giant, guarded jar of long, curving, talon-like fingernails. These were undoubtedly clippings from the Emperor's own hands, dating from the mythic days before He had been encased in the golden throne. Due to His immortal power and reach throughout the galaxy, these disembodied nails were understood to continue growing slowly as if still connected to His person. Thus priests could trim and shave off authentic parings for sale to the faithful, who might wear them or grind them to dust so as to drink in potions.

The temple also housed, in a huge silver reliquary, the thigh bones of a Space Marine commander from long ago – and, in a baroque copper cage, what was reputed to be the partial skeleton of a 'daemon.'

Carts, drawn by cameleopards with humps suggestive of huge inflamed boils, with snaking necks and lugubrious, whiskery, stupid faces, creaked to and fro along the boulevard, carrying sightseers and vegetables. Balloon-tyred cars and the occasional armoured police or security vehicle growled by. Even the Oriens temple was notably wealthy.

Meh'Lindi wore the capacious brown robe of a pilgrim, with a cowl that hid her features in shadow. Cinching the waist was her scarlet assassin's sash which concealed garrottes, blades, phials of chemicals, and a digital needle gun. Within her robe were other articles of her primary trade.

And what was hidden within her?

Why, the most evil shape. A vile shape that forever constrained her now; that denied her the option of masquerading as anyone she pleased. That shape, which was indelibly inscribed within her healed anatomy – physically implanted in collapsed form – denied her access to any of the sham physiques and physiognomies that she had thought of as... well, sisters, mothers, cousins to herself.

Thus she was utterly alone. Her only doppelganger was a monster: the alien beast within.

Meh'Lindi grieved as she entered a caravanserai near the temple. Cameleopards were tethered to steel rings set in the flagstones of the vast courtyard. Ropes hobbled their lanky legs, fore and aft, lest they lash out. Flies buzzed around their orange droppings. Guyed to other rings, tents were pitched under the dome. Galleries, reached by curving iron stairways,

housed three upper tiers of semi-private rooms with linked balconies. Smoke from several bonfires of dried dung drifted out
through the open eye at the zenith of the dome. These fires
notwithstanding, the chill of the night would creep in from
outside. The more traditional breed of traveller who shunned
the shivers of the early hours, and who sought privacy, would
rent a tent. Poorer cousins would wrap themselves in bedrolls
on the hard flags.

The hunchbacked, sallow-complexioned proprietor asked, in
the common language of Sabulorb, 'Seeking lodgings?'

Any assassin was already fluent in major dialects of Imperial
Gothic as well a number of human languages which had
drifted far enough from their origins as to bear no resemblance
to their roots. An assassin constantly added new languages to
her repertoire. Meh'Lindi had done likewise, using a hypno-
casque – a knowledge-inducer – on the cargo ship en route to
the sandy world of the giant red sun. The electronic tattoo on
her palm currently declared her to be the daughter of a planetary governor intent on a pilgrimage.

'Preferring lowest room,' she replied. 'Being from cavern
world, surface uninhabitable. Suffering from vertigo and sky-
fear.' She pulled the capacious hood even further forward,
implying that this headgear was her private cave. She paid the
proprietor a week in advance in Sabulorb shekels, exchanged at
the spaceport against Imperial credit programmed into her tattoo, and added a shekel as a modest sweetener.

'Being cellar rooms under your caravanserai?' she asked. A
reasonable question, given her explanation. She allowed a hint
of vulnerability and pleading to colour her voice, though a
harder overtone – of someone accustomed to be indulged and
obeyed – warned that she was not to be taken advantage of.

'Being, indeed… though not habitable.' The hunchback's
palm seemed to itch. 'Being even an old tunnel, perhaps, if this
guest is preferring to visit the Oriens by risking sticky cobwebs,
but avoiding open sky.'

'Oh no,' she demurred. 'Being pilgrim, same as others. But
thanking you for offering favour.' She slipped him an extra half-
shekel.

NEXT MORNING MEH'LINDI took the full-scale guided tour of the
Oriens temple, alert for signs of covert genestealer infestation,

such as any four-armed idol, however small, tucked away in however inconspicuous a niche.

A scrawny, long-nosed priest guided her party. In the Hall of the Holy Fingernails, robed guardian deacons sat hunched on tripod stools around a tall crystal jar of parings, nursing what seemed to be some kind of stun gun of local manufacture. While the guide enthused about the miracle of how the Emperor's nails continued to grow, Meh'Lindi pretended that she was about to make an offering. She contrived to spill some half-shekels far and wide from her purse. Recovering her coins, she stooped to squint inside the hoods of the guards.

Two of those deacons certainly possessed the sharp teeth and glaring mesmeric eyes of hybrids who could hope to pass for true human, at least in shadow.

Massive candles burned, rendering the rune-mosaics of the walls waxy as the inside of a beehive. Bowls of smouldering incense flavoured the honey of the air. She thought of cellars under the caravanserai, and of the tunnel. Under this elderly temple there must be crypts and catacombs, and tunnels extending who knew how far beneath the ancient city...

'Now conducting you to the Hall of Femurs,' announced their guide.

Her journey through the warp to Sabulorb had been brief enough, but some years of local time would have passed since whichever spy of the Imperium had left to report his or her suspicions. The infestation by genestealers had plainly been under way for a number of generations. Genestealers would hide, seeking to maintain a facade of normality for as long as possible. Ultimately the evil brood would hope to control the city through their more presentable offspring, and even the planet, while still maintaining the pretence that life was normal. Long before that stage was reached, the Imperium ought to take utmost measures.

Meanwhile Tarik Ziz judged – cunningly, or rashly? – that there existed leeway for an experiment... Had he consulted with the supreme director of Callidus? Had the supreme director consulted with the grand master? And had the grand master consulted with... whom? The lord commander militant?

An instrument of Callidus should not dream of asking such questions. Nor did Meh'Lindi understand the hierarchy of the Imperium in its complex entirety. She was but an instrument.

Yet she was aware that the rapid and total destruction of gen-estealers, wherever found, was a military priority.

'Please coming this way, pious pilgrims–'

In a crypt beneath the temple, the genestealer patriarch – the first of the evil aliens to pollute a victim – would roost on its throne, attended by its offspring in hybrid or quasi-human form. By the fourth generation, these would each be able to sire or bear new purestrain stealers. Had that stage yet been reached? The nominal leader of the brood, the charismatic, human-seeming magus, would undoubtedly have become high priest of the Oriens temple, which would seem to continue to worship the Emperor of All Mankind.

Humans who had been polluted by stealers were mesmerized. The human-seeming offspring heeded a brood-bond so that they loved their bestial cousins and uncles intensely. Would Meh'Lindi, in her altered body, possess enough chameleon empathy to fool that brood-bond?

She almost ignored the sacred, pitted thigh bones of the Marine poised in their reliquary. At that moment, beneath her feet perhaps lurked the fierce, bloated, armoured, cloven-footed patriarch...

Just as inside herself there lurked an example of its bastard progeny, as if it had kissed her deep with its spatulate, seed-planting tongue...

When presently she saw the partial skeleton of the supposed 'daemon' in that copper cage, filigreed with hexes and a-crackle with blue sparks – energized so that no daemonic claimant could return – she wondered whether the hunched alien bones were actually those of a purestrain stealer, set up sardonically in that place of honour by the patriarch while the real relic languished elsewhere... The tour lasted for two hours, comprising lavishly decaying halls, sacrariums, and lesser shrines. She saw some evidence of on-going embellishment and repair, yet evidently wealth was not being squandered on the Imperial cult.

The donated shekels, and those gleaned from sale of relics, would be sustaining an ever-extending family of unhumans underground.

When Meh'Lindi and her party at last returned to the great courtyard, a liturgical pageant was about to begin.

'Seeing the blessed Emperor defeating the daemon you were witnessing within!' cried a herald.

Daemons and aliens were creatures of a very different stripe; and genestealers certainly fell into the latter category, of natural beings. The less known about the daemons of Chaos, the better! Ironically the herald – knowing no better – blared out something forbidden so as to advertise whatever flummery would be staged...

'A shekel apiece, good pilgrims, so that we may be proceeding!'

A scrofulous dwarf scurried to and fro, collecting coins in a sawn-open skull fitted with silver handles, till he was satisfied with the height of the pile. The herald clapped his hands.

The illusion of a huge and ornate, though melancholy, throne room sprang into being all around, cast by hidden holographic projectors. The sandy ground of the courtyard now seemed to be tessellated marble. A horde of gorgeous, abject lords and ladies grovelled before a leering, green-hued, sag-bellied monster sprawling in a great, spike-backed throne. Mutant guards wearing obscene and blasphemous armour kept vigil, cradling bolt pistols and power axes. The 'daemon' glowed luridly. Jagged threads of lightning flickered between its froggy hands. Meh'Lindi was wryly amused.

At that moment a parody of Space Marines with brutish, bulbous heads burst into the throne room. They fired explosive bolts at the guards, who fired back in turn. Caught up in the illusion, the audience of pilgrims screamed. Rapidly, as if matter met anti-matter, all of the guards and all of the mock Space Marines died and vanished. So did the lords and ladies, leaving the stage clear...

A tall, aura-cloaked figure entered, wearing a flashing golden crown. A mask of wires and tubes hid the 'Emperor's' face. From his outstretched hands sprouted nails which were as long again as his fingers. He gestured challengingly at the daemon – or alien – lord. As Meh'Lindi stared, transfixed, these nails swelled into claws, and an extra set of hands, and arms, burst forth from the sides of the 'Emperor's' rib-cage.

Plainly this pageant was designed to confuse the beliefs of onlookers – already confused – so that they would identify the holy Emperor with the image of a genestealer... who would soon tear the fat green daemon-alien apart and claim that throne...

'Fool!' cried a voice. 'This being the climax, not the prelude!'

Behind the goggling, gasping pilgrims a tall purple-cloaked man was rebuking the herald, whom he was hauling along by the scruff of the neck. Like a ventilator cowl or a radar dish, the newcomer's high stiffened hood cupped a long, menacing, yet enchanting face. His cranium was shaved bald. Knobbly bumps above his brows were tattooed with butterflies unfurling their wings, as if beauteous thoughts were bursting forth from chrysalises there.

It was indeed a magus.

Meh'Lindi slipped closer to him.

'Not noticing our error, exalted one,' babbled the herald. 'Being outside of the holorama. Apologizing. Soon rectifying. Recommencing the performance – '

As Meh'Lindi concentrated all her attention on the magus, the man seemed to sense her scrutiny and gazed towards her piercingly. His nostrils flared like a horse scenting fire on the wind.

His gaze was compelling... but did not compel her.

Shucking her hood further forward, the more to gloom her shadowed face, she withdrew, and walked through the illusory walls of the throne room. She strolled away across the gritty courtyard back towards the boulevard and the caravanserai. The bloated sun of dull blood was sinking.

Let her not be distracted by grief at what she must now do! Let her not betray her shrine – even if her shrine had, in a sense, betrayed her.

She was an instrument.

And now the shape of the tool must change.

THAT EVENING MEH'LINDI crept through a twisting, turning, cob-webbed tunnel, exerting her chameleon instinct. Best that she should be quite close to those whom she copied. The meta-morphosis would proceed more speedily; and she by no means wished to linger over it.

The electrolumen in her hand feebly lit ancient, rune-carved stones matted with dusty spider-silk in which the bones of lit-tle lizards hung.

Presently she reached an appendix to a deserted crypt, in which a solitary nub of candle burned low. Ahead were branch-ing catacombs lit by the occasional oil lamp, leading towards a brighter glow and the moan of a distant choir.

Her robe was loose, and would accommodate the changes, but she dropped it nonetheless. She did not wish to disguise her new form.

She injected polymorphine, and swiftly hid the tiny empty syringe in a crevice where no one should ever find it. She had left her assassin's sash in the caravanserai. With her hands transformed into claws, she could hardly have manipulated garrottes or knives, let alone a miniature jokaero gun that was meant to slip on to a fingertip. She hoped the device she had rigged up in her room to re-inject her and restore her, would penetrate her toughened body. Maybe she would be obliged to inject through her eye.

A wave of agony coursed through her, and she blocked it.

She hunched over. Her body was molten. As she focused her attention, the implants began to express themselves. Bumps thrust up along her bending spine. Her jaw tore open, elongating into a toothy snout. Her eyes bulged. Her arms swelled, and the phalanges of her fingers became long thick claws. Her hips distorted. Now her very skin was hardening into a tough carapace, which she knew would be a livid blue, just as her cordy ligaments were a purple-red in hue.

Fairly soon, she was an extreme specimen of genestealer hybrid, whom no one could surely suspect to be anything else underneath the skin, underneath the carapace.

SHE EXERTED ALL of her empathy as she loped onward through the catacomb... and into a great subterranean chamber, pillared and vaulted, awash with torchlight, alive with brood kin, many of whom were brutish, others of whom might pass muster as human.

The hiss of many throats silenced the unhuman choir that was serenading, or communing with, the patriarch on its horned throne.

Human-seeming guards directed weapons at her. Broodkin rushed towards her, snarling.

Oh, the hunchbacked steward of the caravanserai had dreamed of a pretty prank to play on this high-born pilgrim daughter from another world. He must have been well aware of what he would guide her into.

Hybrids, more human than herself, formed a menacing circle around Meh'Lindi.

On his throne, nostrils flaring, the patriarch bared his fangs.

Through the midst of the deadly cordon, strode the magus, cloak swirling.

'I...,' Meh'Lindi hissed, 'seeeeking sanc-tuary... with my kii-ind.'

Issuing from a distorted larynx, over a twisted tongue, her voice was far from human. Yet the magus must be well accustomed to such voices.

'Where coming from?' he demanded, fixing Meh'Lindi with his mesmeric gaze.

'Hiiiding on starship,' she replied. 'Imperials des-troying my brood, all of my clan but meeee. Craving sanc-tuareee–'

'How finding us here?'

'Wrapping myself in robe... skulking by night... checking temples. Temples being where maybe finding my distant kin.'

The magus scrutinized Meh'Lindi searchingly. 'You being first generation hybrid... Excellent stealer body, mostly...' He locked his gaze with hers, and she felt... swayed; but was trained to resist ordinary mesmeric enchantments.

The magus chuckled. 'Of course we are not compelling one another... We are only compelling the human cattle. Our own bond being one of mutual devotion. Of heeding the calls, which you cannot heed, being not of our brood.' He turned. 'As I am now heeding... our Master. Be coming with me.'

The patriarch was gesturing with a claw.

'Escort her carefully, brothers and sisters,' the magus told the guards with a radiant yet twisted smile.

And so Meh'Lindi approached the monster on the throne: a leering, fang-toothed, armoured hog of a grandsire alien. Its eyes glared at her from under ridged bony brows. One of its lower, humanoid hands, adorned with topaz and sapphire rings, contemplatively stroked a fierce claw-hand that rested on its knee. One of its hooves tapped the floor. Loaves of armour-bone jutted from its curved spine, and it rubbed these against the carved back of its throne grindingly, as if to dispel an itch. Its spatulate tongue stuck out, tasting.

Meh'Lindi bowed lower than her stoop dictated, thrusting from her mind any hint of assassin thoughts, soaking up and re-radiating as best she could the ambience of grotesque, evil worship.

'Craving sanc-tuary, greatest father,' she hissed.

This was the crucial moment.

The patriarch's nostrils flared, sniffing the faintly oily odours of her spurious body. Its violet, vein-webbed eyes, at once odious and alluring, scrutinized her intently. Its gaze caressed her and pried intimately like some dulcet scalpel blade smeared with intoxicating, aphrodisiacal mucus. The grandaddy of evil clicked its claws together contemplatively. One of its hooves drummed the flagstone which was worn, at that spot, into a rut.

No, not evil... That was no way to be thinking of this fine patriarch!

Empathy was the key to impersonation.

Identification.

How Meh'Lindi's yearned to flee from this den of monsters and demi-monsters! – though of course it was far too late to flee.

Flee? Ha! While the very same monstrosity resided within herself?

In such circumstances, fleeing made no sense whatever. For she was monstrous too.

So therefore she must perceive the patriarch as the incarnation of...

Benevolence. Fatherliness. Wisdom. Maturity.

The armoured monster that confronted her personified love. A profound depth of love. Love which quite transcended the passions and affections of mundane men and women – whatever such sentiments might feel like to the possessors.

Meh'Lindi had certainly mimed such emotions in the past. With an assassin's eye she had studied the victims of amorousness, lust, infatuation, and fondness, even if she herself had not been vulnerable...

This genestealer patriarch radiated such a powerful, protective, brooding love – of its true kin, and of itself, of the monster that it could not help but be: the perfect, passionately dedicated, self-sanctified monstrosity.

Yes, love, fierce, twisted love.

And utter, biological loyalty.

And a dream that possessed it, almost like some daemon: an inner vision of its mission.

The mission was to perpetuate its kind. Human beings seemed to manage this same feat almost incidentally and accidentally – all be it that the result was a thousand times a

thousand human worlds, many pulsing to bursting point with
the festering pus of the human species.

Genestealers were compelled to try harder. They couldn't
simply writhe in copulation with their own species and produce a litter of brats.

Genestealers would willingly – nay, compulsively – infiltrate
any species. Human. Ork. It didn't matter which. Eldar. To
bring about, incidentally, the corruption and downfall of those
species.

In a sense, a genestealer almost represented cosmic love. A
love that knew no boundary of species. That heeded no dis-
tinction between male and female. Between human and
abhuman, human and alien.

So this patriarch was love incarnate! Hideous, enslaving love.
Almost…

Its mission also demanded hair-trigger, homicidal fury in
defence of its own destiny.

And, at the same time, cunning restraint – intelligence.

Its intelligence knew naught of machines, of starships or bolt
pistols, of dynamos or windmills. Tools? Our broodkin can use
those things for us! Yet its mind kenned much of glands and
feelings, of hormonal motives, of genetic and hypnotic dictates.

The patriarch's rheumy, violet, magnetic eyes, set in that
hideous magenta countenance, considered Meh'Lindi in her
hybrid guise…

Seeing… true kindred?

Or seeing through her? About to turn down its claw?

Loving you, she thought. Revering you. Admiring you
utmostly.

In the same fashion as she revered Callidus. As she honoured
her omega-dan director…

(No! Not that one. Not Tarik Ziz!)

In the same way as she reverenced… the Emperor on Terra.

This clever, loving patriarch was her Emperor here. Her great
father-of-all.

Did it possess a personal name? Did any genestealer?

The patriarch grunted wordlessly.

Beside her, the magus rocked to and fro, heeding the alien
monster's mental sendings. A hybrid from another star system
need not be similarly attuned to those.

'Granting refuge,' murmured the magus at last. 'Embracing you in our tabernacle, and in our crusade.'

The patriarch closed its eyes, as if to dismiss Meh'Lindi. It folded its humanoid hands across its jutting, carapace-banded belly, and seemed to drift into a reverie. Its claws twitched rhythmically. Perhaps it was numbering its children, grandchildren, and great-grandchildren. Of whom, Meh'Lindi of course was not one. So though it accepted her into the fold, or at least into the fringe of the fold, she was hardly a total communicant, as were all others in this subterranean stronghold.

And how many there were! Brutishly deformed broodkin rubbed shoulders and preened and sang praise. They hissed intimacies to one another. They went about their cult duties. They kept watch and ward. They nurtured the juveniles of the clan, some of whom were marked with the taint, others of whom almost appeared to be sweet, comely children, save perhaps for bumpy brows and the eerie light in their eyes.

As Meh'Lindi gazed at a nursery area, she wondered how many of the deadly, infected children she might need to kill before she could leave this place.

If the patriarch – in the wisdom of its alien glands – had chosen to tolerate her presence, the quasihuman magus retained an edge of scepticism.

'Most welcome refugee from far planet,' he said, 'how being speaking Sabulorbish so readily?' He stroked one of the butterflies – of saffron and turquoise hue – upon his knobbly forehead, as if deep in thought.

'After hiding on ship? After skulking in city? What opportunity of learning? Seeming remarkable to me! Knowing of the plurality of languages in the galaxy. Many worlds; many lingos and dialects, hmm?'

The magus was sufficiently persuaded by her body; that passed muster. How could he disbelieve the evidence of the hybrid body that he saw before him? He could not. Yet he had come up with a question which she had hardly expected from a fanatic posing as high priest of a somewhat dodgy provincial cult devoted to miraculous Imperial fingernails.

His question was cool and logical.

Ought she to have burst in upon the genestealer clan inarticulately, unable to express herself at all? Incoherently? Babbling in some offworld tongue, without explanation?

In that event, she might now be caged behind bars strong enough to hold even a genestealer, while her hosts investigated her at their leisure.

Meh'Lindi's mind raced.

She was Callidus, wasn't she?

'My human mother beeeeing a Psittican,' Meh'Lindi hissed. 'You hearing of planet Psitticusss? Itsss lingo-mimes?'

No such planet as Psitticus, the parrot-world, existed. In an Imperium of a million worlds, no one individual, however well informed, could know much about more than a tiny fraction of planets. Better, by far, to name a world which didn't exist, than one which did, concerning which she might conceivably be faulted...

'Ah,' said the magus. 'You enriching my knowledge. Being a fertile world for our kind, that Psitticus?'

'Inishhhially. Then the killersss coming, in the cursed name of their Emperor... The ruthlessss Marinesss... blasting my famileeee, missssing only meee.'

'Condolences. Have you been seeing inside our temple up above?'

'Only from a dissstance,' lied Meh'Lindi.

'We are using theatrical skills to ensorcel the superstitious pilgrims. We are confusing their image of the God-Emperor with that of... Old Four Arms.' The magus nodded towards the throne, his tone humorously affectionate in that moment. Oh how the magus basked in an embracing, patriarchal love... of the foulest breed. How he relished the monster's wisdom. What a twisted parody of fondness the man exhibited. A fondness that did not make him exactly a fool, however...

The patriarch had nodded off. Its claws and fingers spasmed fitfully as, bathing in adoration, it dreamt... of what? Of mating with human beings gulled here or dragged here by its broodkin? Of the glory and ecstasy of disseminating its genes, carving its own image into the tormented flesh of the galaxy?

'After we are expanding here enough and consolidating our hold enough,' the magus declared, 'we shall be smuggling missionaries out to other worlds to stage religious pageants – to spread the cult of the true, four-armed ruler of existence. We shall be subverting other temples, other pilgrims, other worshippers of that moribund god on Terra – of that brittle stick, that rag-doll locked in his golden commode.'

His eyes glowed. 'How vivid, how alive a four-arm being! How truly superhuman. What other species truly uniting all the strife-torn stars? What other breed of being physically making men and aliens into cousins? And nurturing and preserving the myriad worlds for its breeding ground forevermore? Nor ever casting aside the heritage of men or aliens – those being like nourishing milk to the four-armed ones!'

'You being wisssse,' hissed Meh'Lindi.

'Oh yes, myself studying reports and rumours of other worlds that we might be making our own. But, dear refugee, you being tired and famished. Was I speaking of mere milk? Ha! You be coming this way…'

Meh'Lindi was indeed ravenous. Soon she was feasting on imported grox steaks and offworld truffles and sweetmeats bought with donated shekels. She and the brood tore into the dainties with their fangs. She fed, but took no gourmet satisfaction in the costly foods.

What of the hunchbacked proprietor of the caravanserai? He had to be in league with the stealer clan. Or at the very least he had to be aware of their existence, in relatively friendly fashion. Would he otherwise have mischievously told the lone lady traveller of the tunnel?

If Meh'Lindi remained long amongst the broodkin, and the hunchback noted her absence – then decided to pry into her room, and into her belongings – might he report his puzzlement to the temple guards?

If Meh'Lindi died here, would she care? If she was torn apart by the enraged kin of that vile form which possessed her, would that matter? Would the genestealers, in the act of destroying their own semblance, symbolically annul what desecrated her, as no other death could, thus bringing her a moment's blessed balm before the long dreamless sleep of nullity?

Yes, by Callidus it mattered!

And by Him on Terra it mattered.

Yet had not Callidus… betrayed her?

How long dared she remain here? Alternatively, did she dare to try to leave?

Brooding, Meh'Lindi picked her fangs clean with a claw.

She lay that night in the torch-lit vault among monsters and demi-monsters, a monster herself.

* * *

SHE WOKE EARLY.

She woke into a nightmare – and almost cried out in horror. A convulsive spasm racked her. She flinched from…

…from herself.

For she was the nightmare. She herself. None other.

Oh there were times in the past when she had woken in metamorphosed bodies. In comely bodies. In ugly bodies. Even in an alien, eldar body – ethereally beautiful, that one had been, radiantly lovely…

But she had never woken as a monster.

An assassin was trained to respond instantly, to come wide awake at once and attack instantly, if need be. Yet in that brief instant of awakening Meh'Lindi was almost impelled by the nightmare of reality to attack her own altered person.

She rolled over, rose to a crouch, and stretched… casually, attempting now in alien body language – should any eyes be scrutinizing her – to express relief at finding herself amongst monster kin. Her spasm had merely been the instinctive reflex of the fugitive, the supposed former stowaway amidst hostile human beings. Had it not? Had it not?

A snouty hybrid guard had indeed been eyeing her, she noted. A couple of young whelps of the brood, as well. Another hybrid raised its head, darting a look in her direction. Here was family, hypersensitive to an occult, sticky web of relationships, to hormonal bonds of gossamer that were nevertheless as strong as the steel of a coiled spring.

She was now a fly in that web, permitted to conduct herself as a guest spider. It was a web that would spin outward from here, and from other genestealer lairs – so the magus dreamed – to entrap all sentient creatures of the galaxy in its domineering, adhesive embrace.

As any sensible being – honed to survival – would, in a new environment, she roamed.

The brats and the guard ambled after her as she sauntered, stooped, hooves clicking flagstones, through crypt and vault lit with aromatic oil burning in golden lamps, hung with tapestries depicting abstractly the deserts of Sabulorb, its seas of sand. Here was a librarium full of tomes about worlds, worlds, worlds.

What a hunger for worlds a genestealer must feel. What a blind, frustrated hunger – until a captured species of breeders gave it the means to sate its greed. How appropriate that next to the librarium was a great kitchen and larders piled with extraterrestrial imports.

Here, behind a gaol-like barred door was a treasury, banded chests a-brim with shekels. Behind other bars, an armoury storing different treasure: stun guns, stub guns, bolt pistols, lasrifles.

In a birthing chamber, adjacent to a well-equipped surgery, several hugely pregnant females lay in silk upon the softest feather beds – human-seeming females, bestial females side by side.

Meh'Lindi noted stone stairways leading upward; vaulted tunnels that vanished away darkly. She memorized the subterranean layout, matching it against her recollection of the temple above.

Here, a long stone ramp led up to a great trapdoor that would rise on chains. Garaged below: a long purple limousine with toughened, reflective, curtained windows, its radiator grille a great grin of brass teeth, its armoured panels studded elegantly with chromium-plated rivets. The magus's personal transport, no doubt. Could it be that the patriarch itself ever rode unseen through the dusty streets of Shandabar, leering out at its… pasture of people, its great paddock of prey?

She trotted lithely back from her tour, to the main family chamber. All these tunnels and chambers below the temple were a sewer of alien evil – of an evil compelled by a foul, cunning, imperative joke of nature to be none other than just that; evil that even wore a mask of ultimate community. However, Shandabar City was also plumbed in the sanitary sense. In a privy, Meh'Lindi defecated her transformed supper of the previous night and before flushing that away with a push of her claw wondered whether her excrement had been doubly metamorphosed, the food transformed not only into dung, but into identifiably genestealer dung.

Perhaps her bowels remained her own. Perhaps her dirt was the talisman of her identity.

If so – considering the keen senses of genestealers – thanks be for plumbing. In the Callidus part of her she made a mental note to mention this aspect of her mission. Could an assassin, transformed into an alien, be tripped up… by an all too human stool?

* * *

THE BROOD HAD stirred. The brood fed – she too – and dispersed about their duties, though the throne room was always well visited, as if kin loved to bask regularly in the presence of their patriarch.

That vile eminence, which had snoozed nightlong in its horned throne, stirred at last.

Immediately its violet eyes, rheumy from slumber, sought out Meh'Lindi. It beckoned with a claw.

Its hybrid guards were alert now. The magus hastened to its side as Meh'Lindi approached, sidling deferentially. Not bowing, no. Straightening herself somewhat, indeed. She had decided by now that a frontal stoop might be misconstrued as the attack-crouch.

The magus rocked gently to and fro, heeding.

'We being the dreamers of bodies,' he said to Meh'Lindi. 'We kissing the dream of ourselves into the bodies of human beings, a dream that is enrapturing them. Our grandsire was dreaming of your body, New One.'

Meh'Lindi experienced a brief squirm of courtesanly disgust, of the apprehension felt by a paramour when first confronting a singularly bloated and repulsive debauchee – that virgin instant before professionalism and pretence triumph. But of course, a genestealer was quite without sexual lust as such. A genestealer's loins were blank save for an anal vent protected by a tough flap.

She projected her semblance of love.

'Grandsire's dream was highlighting patterns on your body, which indeed he is perceiving faintly, now that his dream has been showing him those… Dim, distorted images of spider, snake, strange beetles…'

The patriarch could see the trace of her tattoos! Those should have been engulfed, submerged, by the purple-red pigment of her swollen new muscles, by the deep blue of her horny carapace. Certainly they had seemed to vanish utterly when she had first transformed herself, with Tarik Ziz and chirurgeon adepts as audience. No human eyes had spied her eerie – her provocatively sinister – tattoos, which so much spelled out herself, as to be her own private heraldry.

No human eyes.

The mesmeric, veinwebbed orbs of the granddaddy of evil saw somewhat differently.

'Aaah,' she sighed. 'On Psitticusss, being many large poiso-nousss arachnids and serpentsss. Mottled skins of the human lingo-mimes mimicking those... My human mother passing such blemishes on to me. Slight birthmarksss...'

The patriarch grunted several times, ingesting her story like a hog its swill. The magus glared sceptically.

'A variant upon genetic inheritance of acquired characteris-tics,' he said primly, 'being the genestealer glory. That, and the later expression of our own lurking somatotype. Yeah, the pirating of genes – the boarding of the vessel of an alien breed's body – being what is giving us our holy name. But for a human being to be transmitting her personal acquired marks as opposed to a capacity for acquiring such–' Damn his clever mind and his grubbing in that librarium!

'Not undersssstanding,' hissed Meh'Lindi; and truly she didn't.

It was all irrelevant.

All utterly irrelevant.

From the direction of the tunnel by which she had first entered the lair of the brood, bustled the hunchbacked, yellow-faced landlord of the caravanserai.

He held Meh'Lindi's discarded robe and the device she had rigged up in her room that held the syringe of polymorphine. Around his neck he had draped her red sash.

'Being treachery! Bewaring!' he cried.

Guards raised their bolt pistols, staring around for an enemy.

'Seizing that New One!' spat the magus, saliva spraying at Meh'Lindi. Four strong hybrids leapt to pinion her by the arms.

For a moment she stiffened, as if in surprise, both testing their vigour and about to fight, yet then – before they would even have sensed resistance – she relaxed.

She could probably throw them off.

What then?

Could she trigger a salvo of explosive bolts, some of which might strike the patriarch? If she leapt at it? Bolts that would destroy her in the process, too...

No, the brood wouldn't recklessly put their patriarch in such peril. They would surely hold their fire at close quarters.

With her claws and fangs alone she, a hybrid, would never be able to kill a full-blown, mature patriarch. Who might loll. Who might snooze. Yet who was probably the most lethal fighting creature in all the galaxy. Whose claws could rip through a Space Marine's powered combat armour as if that was a mere sheath of thin tin.

She couldn't hope to snatch a boltgun. Her claws were too crude to operate the trigger.

The sash left behind in her lodging... the improvised frame for the little hypodermic... where else could she have left those? And her robe in the tunnel... where else?

Nevertheless, she felt that she had walked into a trap of her own making – marched into it through self-hatred. Or at least through hatred of what Tarik Ziz had done to her.

The patriarch crunched its claws together malevolently. The magus almost jigged with the power of its sendings. That mesmeric, clever leader of the brood was a puppet now, his true role blatantly apparent – that of a lordly, willing slave to the gross granddaddy. For that magus, who boasted of the glory of the genestealers, was not a full genestealer himself. He wasn't a purestrain. He was a sublimely talented, puissant tool of the patriarch and of the genestealer mission. A tool.

Just as Meh'Lindi herself was an instrument.

And thus it would be under the perverted, loving tyranny of genestealers triumphant: a cousinhood of captivated, obedient, cattle-like species, lowing their praise of their predator.

It seemed almost as though genestealers had been, well, consciously devised... to enslave the different races of the galaxy, to prepare the ground, to sow the seed which something else unimaginable might reap...

Meh'Lindi thrust this speculation from her mind, as the hunchback proclaimed slyly: 'A pilgrim woman coming to my caravanserai, from a cavern world saying, seeming an imperious princess in disguise. Then finding her gone, and this sash of many deadly marvels in her room – some enigmatic, some plain in purpose such as a garrotte – and this device for injecting some substance. Discovering her robe in the tunnel I was telling her of, prankfully, so as to be presenting a fine fertile vessel to our lord, His tongue to be kissing deep... A New One being here! And where is that covert princess of the caverns, eh?'

'Cousin,' said the magus, 'we too are having our suspicions of the New One.'

'Oh, are we?' retorted the hunchback.

'Yet that a pilgrim woman should be becoming a mighty hybrid... being contrary to anatomy.'

'Big galaxy, cousin! Full of strange marvels, no doubt!'

'Being well aware.'

'Pedantically aware, at times! Despite charisma of glowing eyes, despite charm of handsome countenance, and splendid limbs!'

'So there we are having it,' said the patriarch's supreme puppet. 'You yourself might be being magus, but for your exaggerated deformity, and because of your lacking sufficient... grace. So our grandsire was not countenancing you, my jealous, loving cousin. Thus you are seeking undermining me, maybe, with this story of a woman.'

Was it possible, thought Meh'Lindi, that the hunchback and the magus might quarrel bitterly enough to allow her some grace, some leeway?

No. For the patriarch arose, exerted its control of kindred.

'Bringing that needle against the New One,' ordered the magus. 'Piercing a part. Testing...' He mused. 'Though which part? Where...? New One, will you be sticking out your tongue?'

'That ssstooped man planning poisssoning this refugee?' Meh'Lindi asked, as if in ignorance. 'This being asssylum in your tabernacle? Yet... willingly, trussstingly, I am obeying my newly adopted lord.'

As she had hoped, at the hunchback's approach, two of the hybrids who had held her moved aside out of the way. The patriarch was watching her fixedly, unblinkingly. She let herself be limp in the grip of her two remaining captors.

Two. Only two.

Yes, she relaxed. However, in her spirit she was back inside the exercise wheel, racing, accelerating. Within her a fly-wheel was accumulating momentum, ready to release it in one great burst, in one transcendental surge of power that would carry her right over the top. A spring was winding up, coiling tight.

She must be utterly lucky too...

Yet luck was often a gift of grace; and who was more graceful than a Callidus assassin? She prayed fervently to the God-Emperor on Terra. Never had she needed his grace more.

The wheel spun wildly. The spring tightened towards that point where it must either snap or be released.

Utterly lucky... if she was to succeed before she died.

For surely she would die.

A suicide song keened through her soul, the harmony of exemplary suicide.

And of course at such a moment an assassin – by bidding farewell to self – could survive and survive, weaving through a host of foes and weapons, killing, killing; as did her cousins of the Eversor shrine.

But she was Callidus.

And Callidus had betrayed her...

So something was missing from her song.

Rage arose in her once more. Utmost fury at her violation. She saw the patriarch before her as a monstrous Tarik Ziz who could blithely implant this vile form within a violated human being.

Alas, she could never vent her scalding vengeance upon the director secundus, on account of her oaths, her loyalties...

But she could aim all of that venom at the patriarch.

Now the wheel was white-hot. Now the spring was razor-edged.

The hunchback held the hypodermic in its framework towards her snout. By a sudden slump, with a twisting spin, with a violent upthrust of her arms, she shucked off her captors. In her claws she seized the framework. She rotated it in a trice. Brushing the hunchback aside, she threw herself at the patriarch, that jutting little needle aimed at its left eye.

The patriarch uttered a squeal – more of surprise than of a pig being impaled. What, impaled by a pinprick, even in the corner of one eye?

Snarling, the patriarch was already batting Meh'Lindi aside. She rolled. She rose, to grip the magus as a shield. Some lurid magenta blood flecked the patriarch's eye. Some violet liquid seemed to leak. It reared its mighty head and roared. This stupid, insignificant injury was as nothing to it. Nothing. A flea-bite. Pure, raw, ravening genestealer now, the patriarch reached out its claw-arms.

Yet it did not attack at once. Perhaps perplexity at the feebleness of her assault caused it to pause. Perhaps, detecting no further threat, it was turning its senses inwards, attempting to diagnose what substance had entered it. A poison? Hardly!

How soon, dear Emperor, how soon?

Abruptly the polymorphine began to work – on an untrained anatomy, on a creature which had no idea of what was happening to it, and hardly enough time to guess by introspection.

The patriarch's body rippled as its carapace softened, as though a coating of worms crawled underneath its previously horny hide. Its head distorted sidelong. Its injured eye solidified into a marble ball. Its teeth fused together – then, as it howled, the joined teeth softened, to stretch like rubber. Its claws began to bud teeth. Its lower, simian hands became floppy pincers.

It was in flux. Nothing could teach it how to hold its form intact. It vented excrement. Its tongue pressed out between the elastic teeth, longer, longer, thinner, thinner. The monster – even more monstrous now – collapsed back across its throne. And now, in its one true eye, Meh'Lindi could see how fiercely, how desperately it was willing itself to keep its shape amidst the anarchy that engulfed it.

Willing itself. Yet failing, since it couldn't perceive the proper shape of its own internal organs… while those swelled or pinched or stretched. And since it was in flux, its broodkin were in confusion. Appalled at its continuing transformation, they were rocked by its now incoherent sendings.

The patriarch's organs and appendages were dissolving and reforming while its tormented will still endured. Suddenly its softened thorax split open. Pulsing mauve and silver coils spilled out, liquefying. The exposed innards of the true master of the Oriens temple melted into protoplasmic jelly.

With her own claws Meh'Lindi crushed the arms of the magus. She drew up her stealer knee to break his spine. Throwing him at the nearest guards, she darted to the hunchback. Seizing him under one arm, she bore him away, the sash still hanging round his neck.

As she raced into a tunnel that would lead to a certain stairway, explosive bolts whined past her inaccurately, detonating against the stonework, spraying splinters. Behind her, broodkin screeched as the patriarch's death agony communicated itself. Confusion, chaos – then an onrush of broodkin in her wake intent on vengeance.

SHE EMERGED IN the Hall of the Holy Fingernails, and sprinted for the great doorway through the reek of candle smoke and incense. Pilgrims scattered. She tossed a hybrid deacon aside, eviscerating him with her free claw, as brutish broodkin boiled up into the hall behind her.

Outside, a morning pageant was in progress. She rushed through the illusory walls of the phantom throne room just as the parody Space Marines were opening fire at the green daemon's guards.

As guards and Marines died and vanished, along with the grovelling lords and ladies, for a moment the gawping audience of pilgrims and tourists must have imagined that the monster Meh'Lindi and her struggling burden were a part of the spectacle.

Then the caricature Emperor entered behind her, gesturing with those extraordinary fingernails. Rushing around him, bursting right through his holographic image, snarling parodies of humanity invaded the throne room.

The brood had temporarily lost all leadership. A salvo of bolts winged into the crowd, blasting bloody craters in flesh. For the spectators were in the way. Their toppling corpses nevertheless served to shield Meh'Lindi. She leapt through the phantom wall into the actual sandy courtyard – and raced. Behind, she heard no more firing; only hideous screams. Nor were the broodkin following her out into the open, under the ballooning red sun.

Perhaps a collective caution prevailed. Perhaps the broodkin were busy slaughtering all witnesses of their wanton exposure prior to withdrawing. Or, insensate, the brood may have decided to wreak their wrath, bare-handed, sharp-clawed, upon any available human victims. Certainly none escaped through the illusory walls – which, in their panic, may have seemed all too real.

Voices cried out around Meh'lindi in disbelief or pious terror about a 'daemon' on the loose.

Sirens of armoured militia vehicles were beginning to shriek, but Meh'lindi was an expert at evasion. Darting down one side alley, then another, she found a sewer hatch and tore it open. She thrust the hunchback down inside the tiled hole to drop to the bottom with a splash, then inserted herself with legs and bony back braced, so as to slide the lid back into place above her. Difficult, with claws instead of fingers!

In part-flooded, stinking darkness, she regained hold of the hunchback. She squeezed him.

'Ssso, would-be magusss,' she wheezed, 'I being helping you, eh? You mussst be waiting for a new puressstrain being born, to whom you shall becoming uncle... then high ssservant and oracle. Who better?'

'What being you?' the hunchback managed to ask, terror and cunning warring in his voice.

'An ally... Would you seeeeing a miracle?'

'Yes. Yes.'

'Tiny electrolumen being in my sssash. You lighting it.'

The hunchback groped for a long while before the tiny light brightened the cramped cloacal tunnel they were crouched in.

'Being needle in my sssash. Hold it out at meee. And I am becoming harmless to you then, as a pilgrim woman, hmm?'

The hunchback nodded. He held the needle firmly. Meh'Lindi bit the tip of her tongue between her fangs. Impaling the injured, softer inner tissue upon the sharp needle point, she pressed her tongue forward to discharge the drug into herself.

Soon her body was molten. Soon her implants were slackening, shrinking. The hunchback stared, goggle-eyed.

SHE SPAT SOME blood from her mouth. Despite the stenchful surroundings, the hunchback now gazed hungrily at the nude tattooed body amazingly revealed to him.

'Safer as a woman,' he agreed, licking his lips. 'Softer to be questioning – about this wondrous liquid that is altering bodies. With such guile we could be disguising our hybrids perfectly.'

He shifted his left hand from behind his back. On one finger he wore the jokaero needle gun. While the convulsive changes had distracted her, while her vision had glazed, the hunchback had filched that miniature weapon from her sash and slipped it on. Or maybe he had already transferred the tiny gun to the pocket of his robe much earlier, recognizing it for what it was, and determined to reserve it for himself.

'Not being fooled into thinking this a ring, princess. My cousin being duped, perhaps. Not I. Ah, how poetically you were bending his spine, making him just like me in death.' He pointed his armed finger at her.

'When I am bending my finger sharply, this gun is discharging, I am supposing?'

Yes. By and large. Yes. The hunchback might well succeed in firing the gun.

'Staying here a while till excitement is dying... Then sneaking to my fine establishment, and into a certain cellar. You ravaged my clan, witch. Softer to question, ah yes.'

He was wrong. Meh'Lindi was herself again, no longer encumbered by clumsy claws and a stoop. Once again, she was a Callidus assassin. If the environs were cramped, what of that? She shuffled ever so slightly.

FIVE MINUTES LATER, during a moment of mild inattention when boots rang on the sewer lid overhead, the hunchback died quickly and silently – throat-punched, nerve-blocked, broken-necked – without even crooking his finger once.

Meh'Lindi was ravenous after the change. She had to feed. She only knew one immediate source of protein. The proprietor of the caravanserai had stared at her hungrily.

Now she repaid the compliment, somewhat reluctantly.

In her famished state, his corpse tasted sweet.

SHE BALLED UP his robe to haul behind her, tied to one ankle. She reasoned that she should crawl for a mile or so to escape from the immediate neighbourhood.

Some pipes were to prove tight and deep in effluent. She needed to dislocate her joints and hold her breath. She did so. She was an instrument. She was Callidus.

WRAPPED IN THE hunchback's sodden robe, cinched with her scarlet sash, she trotted through the city under the cold constellations, heading back towards the spaceport.

Patriarch and magus were both dead. Yet the evil clan remained. Maybe the city militia would react and call in heavy assistance. Or maybe the local forces were themselves infiltrated by hybrids. Meh'Lindi had no intention of discussing matters with any militiamen in Shandabar.

She had infiltrated a genestealer stronghold – for a night and a morning – and had survived. By luck. Through rage. And courtesy of polymorphine, misused as no assassin had misused the drug before. Perhaps that would be a bright enough feather in Tarik Ziz's cap...

The alien beast lurked within her, as it always would: tamed, yet holding her captive too.

How her heart grieved.

SEED OF DOUBT

Neil McIntosh

IT HAD SEEMED an eternity, waiting for the life-raft to crash.

Sitting hunched in the tiny cabin, Danielle had watched the patchwork face of the planet inflating like a balloon as the raft fell towards it. Auras of death glittered, beckoning, in her mind.

The end of the mother-ship had been written in the instant when the warp storm had burst around them. The storm's rage had passed in a moment; time enough to hurl a great fist against the hull and chart the ship a new course, a superheated spiral dive towards the planet Cabellas. There had only been two rafts; one, at least, had made it. She was still alive.

Just for now, Valdez was leaving her alone. The inquisitor was preoccupied with his inventory of equipment: how much salvaged from the ship, how much of that still intact.

Danielle wondered about other survivors, something that would interest Valdez only selectively. Who? How useful? Or how dangerous.

She had watched the launch of the second raft, soon after their escape in the first, but maybe not soon enough. And she remembered her last sight of the *Spirit of Salvation*, a red glow against the black glaze of space, twisting in its final arc towards destruction. Aboard, five hundred souls. Cargo bound for

Terra, final terminus of the Imperium. She had reached into their minds, shared the final moments. Most were stricken with an animal panic, but there had been a few who had already foreseen their fate on Terra. They were calm in the face of early death.

Not for the first time in her life, Danielle was a survivor. And she was alone.

Riders on horseback were approaching the wreck of the life-raft, shabby soldiers decked out in the style of old frontiersmen of the Imperium: greasy denim, leather jerkins overlaid with bandoliers of bullets. The faded badges the soldiers were wearing were for pioneer battles fought and won long before they'd been born.

Inquisitor Mendor Valdez strode out to meet the Cabellans, his brief nod telling Danielle to follow.

A rider with gold insignia splashed over his chest pulled forward and raised a sloppy salute. 'Any more survivors?'

Valdez sized up the reception party. Aside from the troopers there were four spare horses leashed together in a line at the rear. 'We need to be taken to the tithe marshal,' he stated. He turned to Danielle. 'Are you still in contact with the psyker?'

Danielle closed her eyes and searched. 'Yes,' she said at last. 'Not far from here. But her thoughts are weak.'

'Hold on to it,' said Valdez. 'We're going to run the operation as scheduled.'

'Even now?'

Valdez looked around at the wreckage of the raft, massaging his bruised ribs. 'Especially now,' he said. 'What chance, Tchaq?'

A solidly-built figure emerged from the crumpled hull of the raft, las-weld clutched like a weapon in his hand. The Cabellans eyed the bio-enhanced tech-priest mistrustfully.

Valdez spat his pain out in a sour sneer. 'Don't fret, he's staying here. Well, Tchaq? What have we got?'

The tech-priest grimaced, running a hand over his sweaty, bald pate. 'Orks would have better kit than I've got to work with.' He paused and traded stares with the horsemen before continuing. 'Give me a while and I might squeeze a squeak out of the voxcaster.'

Valdez grinned briefly. 'Good.'

Tchaq muttered, 'Just think yourself lucky you dropped out of the sky with two tech-priests.'

A second tech-priest, younger and taller than his comrade, stepped from the cabin, eyes glinting behind slits cut in his metallic face mask. 'We'll fix it, sir,' Golun affirmed. 'Every hour spent on this dung-heap is one too many for me.'

'Then we'll leave it in your capable hands. Now,' Valdez turned to the Cabellans, 'lead the way. And get a move on.'

DANIELLE RODE AT the rear of the procession. Away from the babble of voices she could clearly read what was passing through the minds of the Cabellan troopers. Behind the facades of cheerful banter she found suspicion, mistrust and fear. She looked out through their eyes and saw Valdez, saw herself, as they saw them. Ambassadors from a distant Emperor. Bringers of uncertainty to a sleepy, ordered world. Bad news.

She made no attempt to steal through the aura cast like a halo of ice around Inquisitor Valdez. It would have been easy enough, like lifting trinkets from a blind man's stall. Unlike many of his order, Valdez had no mindsight, no powers beyond other mortal men. He had climbed the Imperial ranks, fuelled by instinct and the primal urge to fight and win. What she had found in Valdez's mind – blinkered refusal to countenance any uncertainty, any deviation from the one path – depressed and confused her. The inquisitor had forged his limitations into a weapon to be used against anyone who saw, who questioned too much. She had long accepted that his mistrust of her bordered on hatred.

The horses climbed out of the valley on to the great plains of Cabellas. Danielle looked down upon fields of wheat grown tall as men that swayed in great, dreaming waves. At the edges of the gold sea, nests of virulent green tangle-fungus competed for space in the rich soil. The tithe domains of Cabellas formed one of the Imperium's great storehouses. Here, as throughout the galaxy, the struggle between order and disintegration continued unabated.

Teams of men worked the fields, purging gouts of choking weed from the path of the harvesters. They stopped to stare at the offworlders as they passed above them. The message on their faces was the same: here are intruders.

Danielle avoided their gaze. Beyond the steel-grey grain spires that ringed the distant settlement a lone, siren voice still called. Although each step brought them closer, the voice was fading.

Hold on, Danielle heard herself saying. But she knew it would be too late.

She looked up. The inquisitor had halted the column and was looking back at her, blue eyes probing, searching. 'Well?' he demanded. 'What is it?'

'Her thoughts are weakening. I thought for a moment I'd lost them.'

Valdez waved her forward impatiently. 'Ride up here with me.'

Danielle obeyed. As she drew level with the inquisitor she noticed he was sitting lopsided in the saddle, hand braced hard against his side. She sensed pain and Valdez's stubborn refusal to weaken.

'Let me help,' she said tentatively. 'I have... powers. I can–'

Valdez tugged at the reins, urging his horse on. 'Don't waste your spells on me,' he snapped. 'Save them for the service of the Imperium. In the Emperor's name, we may need them yet.'

TITHE MARSHAL SHARNEY led his visitors to a portal and waved an arm across the expanse that comprised his kingdom. 'Amazing, isn't it? Anything grows here,' he chuckled, 'and everything tries.'

He handed them glasses of wine. 'You won't taste better than this anywhere.' He took a sip from his own glass and shuffled into the room, watching the inquisitor as he might a barometer. 'If it's the quotas you've come about, there won't be any repeat of what happened last yield-time. You have my word for it.'

Valdez drained his glass without pausing. 'Rot your quotas,' he said. 'The Emperor doesn't send me here as a tax collector.' He leant against the portal rim, gazing down upon the sprawling steel structures below. 'Somewhere in this settlement there's a psyker. That's the cargo we came to collect.'

Sharney looked doubtfully from the inquisitor to Danielle. His mind was insular, protective by instinct. Before he could reply she said: 'We know about her. I was picking up her thoughts before we reached orbit.'

Sharney squinted hard at her and re-filled his glass. 'You're one of them too, aren't you?'

Danielle nodded. 'Like, but stronger. The woman we're seeking may be afflicted by a power she cannot control.'

Sharney shrugged. 'All right, we've got nothing to hide. We can manage our own affairs, that's all.'

'Save the sermons,' Valdez said, patience exhausted. 'Just tell us where the mutant is.'

Sharney drew himself up, puffing out his chest self-importantly. 'I'll take you there myself,' he said, 'but you'll find you've had a wasted journey.'

THE OLD COUPLE sat hunched by a low wooden bed, heads bowed in the attitude of those preparing for mourning. The room was a grey cell lit only by the dusty beams of light that pierced the curtained windows. A single sheet was drawn across the outline of a figure lying on the bed.

As Valdez and Danielle entered, the shape stirred almost imperceptibly.

Danielle stepped forward.

'See?' Sharney muttered, peevishly. 'It's over.'

'Don't get too close,' Valdez warned.

'I know what I'm doing.'

The couple looked up. Without explanation they allowed her to approach the bed.

'She can't hear nor see you,' said the old woman. She looked through Danielle, staring into nothing.

Danielle laid a hand tentatively on the woman's shoulder. 'It's all right,' she said. 'She knows I'm here.'

The head buried deep in the pillow turned towards her. An eye peeled open, a milk-white clouded bead. A voice whispered in Danielle's mind, a butterfly memory: *Sister*.

I hear you, Danielle replied. *Can you still speak to us?*

The girl's face was swollen and dark, as though covered in a massive bruise. Danielle stooped low to hear the word: 'Gestartes.'

She looked up. 'What does that mean?' she asked the old woman. 'Is that a place?'

Unhearing, the woman stared at the wall. Her husband rose slowly and took Danielle aside. 'Gestartes is her brother,' he explained. 'The only one of the family who could stay near once the sickness was on her.'

'When did this sickness start?' Valdez asked, quietly.

'With the storms.' The old man bowed his head. 'We thought it was just a fever. Then she became racked with spasms: violent, terrible. It was as though she'd become–'

Valdez supplied the word. 'Possessed.'

The man looked up, fear mixing with his grief. 'Aye,' he agreed. 'Jula fought for her soul. It's cost her her life.'

Valdez looked pensive. 'And where is Gestartes?'

As if woken from a spell, the old woman spoke. 'Gone,' she said. 'He tended her long into the night, even though he feared the sickness had tainted him. When we woke at dawn he'd gone.' She repeated the word, slowly. 'Gone. Both of them gone.'

Valdez turned quickly to the marshal. 'Find this man,' he commanded. 'I don't care what it takes, just do it. Go now.'

Sharney hesitated for a moment, lips forming round a mumbled protest. He caught the look in the inquisitor's eye, and nodded assent.

Valdez beckoned to Danielle. 'We'll step outside and wait where there's cleaner air.'

She followed the inquisitor out into the daylight.

'The storms they mentioned. And the warp storm–'

Valdez nodded. 'The same. The warp seethed with energy – perhaps with the energy of one of the Dark Powers themselves.'

'Do you think – the Lord of Decay?'

'Yes,' said Valdez, 'and that fool Sharney talks as though a little local quarantine's going to end his problems.' He cast a scornful glance towards the departing figure of the marshal. 'Not this time, my friend. The Emperor alone knows what virulence the warp has set free. Pray that Tchaq gets through to Kar Duniash. Quotas or no quotas, the Imperium may have to dispense with Cabellas.'

'But surely–' dismay tinged her voice– 'surely the infestation has waned. The girl's no harm to anyone now.'

'The girl?' Valdez chewed the word out contemptuously. 'One less psyker worm to blight the Imperium. But whilst she still lived she was an open channel for the poisons of Chaos. Now the infection's running in her brother's veins. Who can say how fast the seed may spread?'

'And when we find Gestartes?'

'Kill him. That'll be a start.'

Danielle had reached into the minds of the grieving family; she knew that they, even Sharney, pumped up with his pompous vanity, were innocent souls. Try as she might she could not approach the cold serenity with which the inquisitor would dispatch them all.

'How can you be sure the infection has spread from the warp?'

Already, she knew the argument was lost. Valdez closed his hand into a white-knuckled fist and held it under her gaze. 'I don't need to be sure,' he thundered. 'Doubt, doubt is all I need. Doubt like a maggot burrowed in the fabric of the universe.' Valdez drew a finger down Danielle's cheek. 'And remember: I have doubt of you, too.'

Danielle flinched away. 'I've been tested,' she countered. 'I've never faltered in the service of the Imperium.' She felt intimidated, and despised herself for it.

Valdez dropped his fist in a gesture of disdain. 'There's always a first time,' he said acidly. 'And I'll tell you something else–'

The vox-comm clipped to the inquisitor's belt started to flash red. Both of them looked down at it in surprise before Valdez found the presence of mind to free the device and activate it.

Tchaq's deep voice was recognisable even over the warbling distortion. 'How's that for service?' he demanded.

Valdez cheered up immediately. 'Thank the Emperor! Have you reached Kar Duniash?'

Tchaq sounded irritated. 'Don't expect the Imperium in a day. We've been working flat out just to patch local channels together.'

'All right. Keep at it. In the meantime see if you can raise the other raft. Grunland's a good soldier; he'll have pulled his boys through if anyone could.'

'Yes, sir. Trouble?'

Valdez snorted and switched off the device abruptly.

MARSHAL SHARNEY WAS back within the hour. The little man's face was flushed with an unaccustomed urgency. 'My stewards have searched everywhere. Everywhere,' he protested. 'Not a corner of the settlement's been overlooked.'

'Don't tell me,' Valdez sighed. 'The bird has flown.'

'Well, he wasn't under arrest you know!' Sharney's indignation was hollow. He began shuffling from foot to foot as though under sentence of execution. He was spared by a cry from the house.

Jula's struggle was ending. Her body writhed in the last throes of battle, blind eyes rolling marble white, searching. As Danielle entered, the young woman grew calmer and sat upright. Clusters of dark tumours were spreading across her face and neck, making her almost unrecognizable. Danielle crouched close by Jula's side to hear the two whispered words: 'Gestartes... Mordessa.'

She died before Danielle could reply.

Valdez doffed his hat and began to fan his face. 'Mordessa,' he murmured. 'What's the significance of that?'

'It's – uh – a ghost town. A derelict,' Sharney replied, discomfited. 'We don't know it by that name any more.'

Jula's father rose, anger stemming the tears. 'We still know it by that name. Tell them what it is.'

Sharney fiddled nervously with his chain of office. The old woman spoke without looking up: 'It's the plague village.'

Valdez took Sharney by the collar and drew him in until the two men were face to face. 'Then this has happened before.'

Sharney was fast getting out of his depth. 'Maybe,' he stammered. 'I don't know. The girl's symptoms are similar.'

'Tell us about Mordessa,' Valdez suggested.

'It was all over long ago. A century at least. There was an outbreak of sickness.'

'Another psyker?'

'Psyker, witch. I don't know. One with so-called powers.' He glared defiantly at his interrogators. 'No, the Imperium never got to hear of it. I told you – we can handle our own affairs on Cabellas.'

Mordessa. The name stirred in Danielle's soul. Sharney had told the truth as he understood it, but there was more. Mordessa. An old name; far older than the pioneers of Cabellas; older, perhaps, than the Imperium itself. The shadow of a struggle, ancient beyond memory, flickered in her mind, then fled.

'So,' she said. 'What was done?'

Sharney sat down and cupped his head in his hands. 'The colony was new; the first habitation of Cabellas since the Age of Strife. Towns and villages were small, easily contained. Guards were posted; no one was allowed in or out of the village.'

Danielle kept probing. 'And then?'

Sharney shrugged.

'And then–' the father's face was puffy, red, 'then they put the village to the flames. A hundred men, women and children died. No one has lived there since.'

'You think Gestartes may have gone there?'

The old man laughed bitterly.

'Where else would a leper go?'

VALDEZ LED SHARNEY, unresisting, back to the marshalry, issuing orders as he thought of them. Far from dismaying him, the news had sharpened his natural instincts of war. For the first time since the crash Danielle saw him invigorated with a sense of purpose.

'I want horses. And you'd better let me have half a dozen of your men, armed. Oh, and one more thing–' He paused, and glanced at the covered bier. 'See to it that body's burned.'

'That's difficult,' Sharney mumbled. 'It's the practice on Cabellas to bury the dead.'

'Burn it.' It was not a request. A brief smile flickered on the inquisitor's face as he walked over to the bier. 'Or would you care to bury this?'

A stench of decay filled the courtyard as the inquisitor lifted the shroud. Danielle glanced once at the body and turned quickly away.

Sharney looked as though he were about to be sick. He summoned guards with an urgent wave of his arm. 'Burn it,' he said. 'Burn it at once!'

THE TONE OF Tchaq's voice deepened. 'That's bad,' he said. 'Could be messy. But there's some better news. At least we'll have company.'

The inquisitor's features lit up in delight. For a moment, Danielle expected him to drop his saddle-bags and hug her. 'How many safe?' he demanded. 'Grunland among them?'

'Grunland, aye. Franca too; Plovitch and Van Meer. Their raft hit the hills about sixty kilometres north. Took it worse than ours. Brody was aboard but didn't make it. Rest of them flamed with the ship.'

Valdez tapped the vox-comm thoughtfully. 'Not bad.' Survival rate had exceeded probability; as much as could be expected.

'Get back to Grunland with my commendation. Explain the position and tell him to get his men to the northern approach to Mordessa, and no further. We'll meet them there. Now, what about Kar Duniash?'

'All the military channels are shot. We'll have to try and pick up one of the freight circuits. Golun's working on it. It'll take time, that's all.'

Valdez made a brief inspection of their Cabellan guides. Six thin youths fidgeted uneasily in the saddle, waiting for the order to move out.

The inquisitor frowned. 'Tech-priest, are you still needed out there?'

Tchaq sounded non-committal. 'I could stay here supervising Golun. Fact is, he can patch in a commnet with his eyes closed.'

'In that case you'll be more use with us. If you set off within the hour we'll rendezvous well before nightfall.'

There was a pause. 'And how am I supposed to get there, with no transport?'

Valdez grinned nastily. 'Then treat yourself to some exercise, tech-priest! Your legs could use stretching. And, Tchaq–'

'Yes, sir?'

'Well done.'

THE METALLED ROAD out of the settlement beat a path through scenes from a well-run war. The land was cut into vast squares, fields of cultivated vegetation stretching to the horizons. Where the man-made plateaux ended, legions of alien plant life erupted like a virus, tracing the lines of demarcation, slicing up the face of the land into chessboard squares.

As the journey wore on, closer to the site of Mordessa, the terms of the battle altered. Men grew sparse in the fields, then disappeared. The hard-fought squares of industry became straggling expanses of thin, untended crops. Even the tangle-weeds had given up. Grey rather than green, they sprouted now in intermittent, limp clusters, as though the land had lost all nourishment.

In time the idle chatter of the Cabellan troopers gave way to an uneasy silence. By late afternoon, new growths were flourishing amidst the wild corn: strange black fungi like mutated rain-spore. They oozed a scent of death.

'Over here!'

A sturdy figure was striding through the field towards them, pushing through the crops and rotting fungus. Tchaq was perspiring under the weight of a disproportionately huge field gun that he'd salvaged from the raft. He was propelling himself towards the riders at a brisk pace, powered in equal measure by determination and bitter curses.

He reached the roadway, keeping a wary eye on the Cabellan troop. 'What's this then? More frightened jackrabbits?'

Valdez laughed. 'A band of heroes to fight for the Imperium. What news?'

Tchaq spat against his sleeve and polished the gun barrel with great deliberation. 'Golun's got it in hand. He'll have Kar Duniash for us, soon enough.'

Valdez nodded, satisfied. 'Ride up here with me. With luck we'll reach the village soon after dusk.'

NIGHT CAME QUICKLY, as though the dark growths thickening in the fields were leeching the light from the sky. The smooth paved roadway had become no more than a rutted, overgrown path. Few travellers had ventured this way.

Danielle reached out with her mind, beyond Tchaq's taciturn fatalism and the inquisitor's sharpening scent for slaughter, into the gathering night. She saw no shadow of living man, but somewhere in the gloom ahead she sensed the first stirrings in a darker well, its epicentre a pool of blackness so deep the universe itself might drown within it.

Somewhere a clock, long stopped, began to mark time again. Old wounds began to re-open.

They had reached their journey's end.

At first sight Mordessa could have been just another small colony village. A crop of low buildings nestled together in a shallow valley, a spire visible above the rooftops. But, off to one side, Danielle saw other structures. The remains of walls, fluted and curved, inlaid with strange, spiral patterns. Something in their line and form suggested an older, pre-human presence, as though the pioneers of the Imperium had built their village beside the remnants of another, long departed race.

Now Mordessa, too, was dead. As they drew closer the village was revealed as a charcoal shell, a skeletal frame of scorched iron and blackened timber. The spire presided over a grave.

The Cabellan captain shook his head ruefully. 'This is an unlucky place.'

Danielle dismounted and followed Valdez down the path to a barricade of rusting razor wire. A signboard, faded and rotten, still clung tenuously to the fence. The legend had been obscured but the crude depiction of a skull was still clear enough. The warning hadn't been heeded. Just beyond the path, the fence had been prised apart.

The sound of feet slithering on stones somewhere in the darkness ahead of them. Cabellan fingers sweated on rifle stocks. A voice called out in greeting: 'Hold your fire. Friend!'

The inquisitor's expression betrayed his astonishment. 'Van Meer?' He spoke softly, seeking corroboration from his companions.

Tchaq shook his head slowly in disbelief. 'He's a better man than I. It should have taken them another hour to reach this place.'

Danielle stayed silent. The voice was van Meer's, she needed no special powers to recognize that. And yet – she bit back a warning word as a tall, powerfully built figure dressed in the night colours of the Third Army of Kar Duniash emerged from the shadows.

Sergeant van Meer strode up the road leading from Mordessa, an unidentifiable load straddling his broad shoulders. The grin on his face was almost as wide.

Inquisitor Valdez returned his salute. 'Greetings, sergeant. The Third Army surpasses itself yet again.'

'Captain Grunland's felicitations, your worship. He sends you this little offering.' He shifted his load over on to one shoulder. 'Rich pickings.'

The body of a man tumbled from the sack on to the ground.

Valdez turned to the Cabellans. 'Gestartes?'

The troop captain, Tolmann, nodded nervously. 'That's him. The Emperor knows, he never did us any harm.'

'Nor will he, now. Van Meer, how did you come by this fortuitous catch?'

'Our paths met as we approached the village from the east. The mutant ran into our arms. He was so ripe with the sickness of evil, he barely knew where he was.'

Van Meer flourished his bolt pistol. 'A few rounds of this was all the medicine he needed.'

Gestartes stared up at the stars, dead eyes fixed in a mask of blistered wax.

Valdez prodded the corpse with booted foot. 'We'll take this and burn it,' he said thoughtfully. 'Are the rest of the men far?'

'Not far at all. Captain Grunland's searching the village as a precautionary measure.'

'Good. Let's hope this one's the last of an unwelcome line.'

'I'm sure of it,' van Meer said. 'I've met these diseased mutants before, on Edmund's World. See this–' He turned Gestartes's face with one heel, exposing a dark crop of subcutaneous welts. 'Until these pretties blossom out, the infection can't take. We caught him just in time.'

Not true. A voice, anonymous but certain, spoke in Danielle's mind.

'Where did your raft crash?' She asked the question even before she was fully aware of it. Van Meer looked perplexed, taken aback. 'What?'

Vexed, Valdez turned to her, but his words were lost. The nebulous darkness which had been bearing down on her suddenly focused. *The raft crashed here. Not in the hills. They never left the village.*

Valdez was striding out to meet van Meer, hand extended. Danielle reached deep into the soldier's mind. The physical outline of van Meer faded out of mindsight. Beneath it–

'Valdez – wait!'

The moment froze. Valdez stood only feet away from the sergeant, surprise turning to anger.

Danielle was taken off-guard by the urgency in her own voice. Then she found the words. 'Don't get near him. That's not van Meer any more. Van Meer's dead.'

The Cabellans slipped the safety catches on their rifles.

Van Meer had stopped in his tracks, astonishment on his face. 'What's this?' he appealed. 'What sort of welcome is this for the Third Army? A mad psyker and a gang of blood-lusty farmhands?'

No one spoke. Valdez looked at Tchaq. The tech-priest's face was unreadable, but his fingers drummed gently against the trigger of his gun.

'Your worship,' van Meer implored. 'We must send word back to sector command.'

The sound of feet pacing carefully on stones behind him. Van Meer's glance flicked briefly rearwards. His eyes were eager, sparkling. 'Kar Duniash,' he insisted. 'They could have a ship here for us in a matter of days.'

'Yes,' Valdez agreed softly. 'They could.'

Further down the path to the village, a second figure stepped from the shadows. 'Trouble, sergeant?'

'A little, sir.' Van Meer fixed his eyes squarely on the horsemen. 'The lord inquisitor's been badly advised.'

'I see.'

Danielle looked from Valdez to Grunland. The squad captain was staying well back by the cover of a ruined outhouse, his face illuminated peach-blonde in a shaft of moonlight.

'Not to worry, your worship,' Grunland shouted to Valdez. 'We'll leave these oafs here to play with their toys. As for the psyker–' his gaze rested on Danielle– 'maybe she'd have been better fitted for the Emperor's table after all.' Grunland smirked contemptuously. 'The village is clean, sir. Time to move off.'

Tchaq nudged his mount forward a few paces. 'Keen to get going, aren't we?'

'Of course. The sooner we–'

One of the horses suddenly reared. Instinctively, van Meer spun round, hand slicing down for his gun. Before he reached it, six rifles blazed. The sergeant was picked off his feet and thrown backwards on to the path.

Utter silence. Even the horses were still.

Van Meer's body twitched, spasmodically at first, then the spasms became co-ordinated movement. Slowly, steadily, the bear-like figure rose to its feet. Even in the darkness there was no doubt most of the bullets had found their mark. The Imperial uniform had been torn open across the chest, twisted shards of bone bursting from the ruptured cavity. The lower part of van Meer's jaw had been blasted away. Remnants of a mouth opened in a cavernous smile, dripping a thick, yellow pus.

Fear ran through the Cabellan troop like bushfire. Valdez snarled.

The creature which had been van Meer turned, but Valdez was faster. The bolt pistol spat four rounds before van Meer had a chance to draw. His features atomized, bone and muscle spewing out in a dark mist. The headless monster toppled, and stayed down.

Another burst of bolt fire; Tchaq was aiming shots at a target further down the path: Grunland.

'Save it,' Valdez commanded. 'We've lost him for the moment.'

He gave the order to dismount. The Cabellan riders circled the remains of the sergeant then dismounted warily.

The inquisitor beckoned Danielle towards the breach in the wire. 'Now's your chance to serve the Imperium. Can you read any trace of them in there?'

Danielle closed her eyes to the night and concentrated on the ebb and flow of aura in the village below. She sensed evil stirring like a slow breeze through the blackened buildings, but only in a general, enveloping swell of unrest. She couldn't focus it.

One thing was sure. However many living men had set foot inside the village, no flicker of a human soul now remained.

'I'm sorry,' she said. 'We'll have to get closer.'

Valdez grunted, a neutral tone that was neither acceptance nor displeasure. 'You,' he said to Tolmann. 'Is there any other way in, except for this path?'

Tolmann hesitated. Like a thief, Danielle lifted a word from his mind. 'Styrus?' she asked. 'Tell us about that.'

The Cabellan's frightened eyes widened further in amazement. 'Who gave you that name?'

'You did,' she said simply. 'Now tell us.'

'Mordessa lies in a valley,' Tolmann explained. 'But for this road, it's cut off by a deep pool. Styrus.'

'But the pool may be crossed?' It was more assertion than question.

The Cabellan looked up at her and rightly guessed it was pointless to deny. 'There's a crossing, of sorts – west of the village. A line of stones. It's said a man with a good eye can leap from each stone from the next.'

'Said?'

Tolmann wrung his hands. 'No one goes across there. The lake stands guard on Mordessa. Styrus is a name from old times.'

Styrus. A name from the old times – from before humanity came to this world. A psychic legacy left for the pioneers. Ancient, alien words took shape like a warning in Danielle's mind. *Stoi Yn Ra*. The One Who Waits. She thought again of the strange, spiral structures lying in the village. For an instant her mind filled with another image, a scene frozen in time, plucked from the forgotten age. She saw battle rage amongst the silver-green facades where Mordessa now stood. She saw alien creatures, half-man, half-amphibian, beset by the forces of eternal darkness. She saw death; the silver structures laid to ruin.

'Old times,' Tolmann repeated. 'Dark times. Legend has it that–'

'I don't want your legends,' Valdez interrupted. 'Times are dark enough now. If there's one small chance of getting into that village without walking naked into the hornets' nest then we're going to take it.'

Tolmann lapsed into gloomy silence, but Danielle read the unspoken words in his mind: the undead.

Emboldened by the same sense of doom, a second trooper approached. 'Sir, wouldn't it be better to return with reinforcements by daylight?'

Tchaq laughed, hoarse and rasping. 'Daylight? None of us'll see daylight again if we turn our backs now.'

'Wise words,' Valdez agreed. 'Whatever abominations are in there, they won't let us go now. We finish them, or they us. Got that?'

'Nine against three.' Tchaq goaded the Cabellans. 'Aren't the odds good enough for you?'

He lifted his gun and peered through the sights. 'What about you?' he asked Danielle. 'Can you weave a spell or two with one of these?'

'I call on other powers.'

Valdez loaded another machine clip into his pistol. 'We'll see about that, won't we? Now, let's move before they cut us down where we stand.'

They turned off the path and skirted through overgrown woodland rising above and away from the village. The forest was dark, air foul with the reek of the grey fungal cancer matted in a canopy over the brittle husks of dead trees, masking off the sky above. Occasional spears of moonlight pierced the gloom, casting pale silver pools amongst the rotting vegetation. Twice the ember glow of watching eyes blinked out on the riders, but there was no sign of pursuit.

At length the path turned downwards again. The forest thinned; the ground grew soft and marshy underfoot. Horse hooves sluiced through shallow, stagnant ponds.

'There. Down below.' Tolmann indicated beyond the edge of the trees where moonlight blistered on a screen of water. 'Styrus.'

On the far side of the lake, the dark outlines of Mordessa. Between them and the village, just visible, a line of smooth stones across the water. The crossing wouldn't be easy, and they would have to leave the horses behind.

Tchaq cursed quietly, distrustful of the slick, black water.

Valdez slapped the tech-priest across the back. 'Don't worry. We'll see if we can't save you a swim.'

'No one swims in there,' muttered Tolmann. Looking like a man condemned, he began to coax his horse down towards the water's edge.

As they passed into the narrow clearing between forest and pool, Danielle felt a white-hot stab of warning. 'Look out!' she shouted. 'They've seen us!'

A metallic whine cut open the night. A Cabellan trooper was catapulted from his horse. The others scrambled for the cover of the trees as the young soldier lay shaking on the earth, life pumping inexorably from a raw fissure in his guts.

Valdez leapt from his horse and dropped to the ground beside Tchaq. 'Foul gods! What was that?'

Tchaq swore and spat a mouthful of dirt. 'Nightfire rifle. If they've salvaged a couple of those they'll pick us off like cattle.'

The Cabellans loosed off a volley of shots across the water. The answering blast struck Tolmann, pulling off an arm like meat ripped from a carcass.

The Cabellan captain lay on the ground, screams drowning the echo of the shot.

'Shut him up in the Emperor's name,' Valdez commanded, 'or they'll have the lot of us.'

Danielle cradled the soldier's head in her hands, dulling lobes of pain until death came. As she lowered Tolmann's body with a silent prayer, a solid form shifted on the fringes of her mindsight.

'There!' she whispered. 'I can sense one of them now. Across the lake. There's a boathouse at the waterfront.'

Valdez raised his head a few inches from cover.

'We'll have to draw him out. No use blasting away at shadows.'

'Seven to three,' Tchaq commented grimly. 'And narrowing.'

Valdez turned at the sound of wood crackling under hooves, just in time to see the Cabellans galloping back into the forest. 'Make that even odds, Tchaq.'

Tchaq clambered to his feet. 'Damn them. I've had enough of wallowing on my belly like some swamp beast,' he declared. 'If

we're going to draw them out, we'll have to give them a tasty
morsel to aim at.'

He began to advance into the open. 'And let's hope you
shoot better than they do, inquisitor.'

The dark outline of an Imperial Guard shimmered in
Danielle's mind. 'He's seen Tchaq. He's moving to the door of
the house. Aim to the left. Further.' The image solidified; she
saw Franca squared within the sights of the inquisitor's pistol.

'Now!'

Bolt fire streamed across the surface of the pool. The
boathouse ignited like tinder. A figure swathed in flame stumbled blindly from the wreckage. Valdez and Tchaq fired again,
in unison. Gobbets of seared flesh sizzled in the waters of
Styrus.

Valdez moved back under cover. He glanced up at the grey
streaking the sky from the east. The short Cabellan night would
soon be ending.

'They'll want to finish it before dawn. They'll take risks; it
could be our best chance.'

Danielle steeled herself against the carnage of death and
searched the distant shoreline afresh. The images were coming
more easily as her senses attuned to the dark power. She saw
Grunland and Plovitch behind the ruined waterfront houses,
moving to opposite ends of the shore.

'They're spreading apart,' she said. 'I can't focus on both of
them.'

'Then concentrate on one. We'll take them as they come.'

She let the mindforce draw her, one image fading as the
other came into sharper focus. 'I see Plovitch now. He – he's
climbing. There must be a tower.'

Tchaq gripped the inquisitor's arm. 'The spire.'

'All right. Hold your fire. We may get a look at him this time.'

The Cabellan moon emerged from a bank of cloud. For an
instant the figure in the spire was clearly illuminated. Tchaq
sprang from cover, dropping on one knee to take aim. In the
same splintered second Danielle sensed a shadow emerging
from the low clump of houses at the other end of the shore.
Her warning shout was lost in the crack of weaponfire, two
shots almost simultaneous.

Plovitch dropped from the spire. His body hammered
against the stones and did not move again. Valdez struggled to

reload his weapon, searching for Grunland. Tchaq remained frozen in a hunter's crouch.

'Get under cover, man, in the Emperor's name!'

The tech-priest turned, slowly. Blood oozed from a wound set like a red medallion in the centre of his forehead. His lips worked round a reply, but only a trickle of blood-flecked saliva emerged. Tchaq's eyes gleamed momentarily, bright with the light of battle, before his head dropped in a warrior's bow.

Valdez slammed a last ammunition clip into the bolt pistol. 'By the Emperor, you'll be avenged,' he vowed. 'Tchaq's gun. See how many rounds are left.'

Gently, Danielle prised the heavy weapon from their dead comrade's grip. She pulled the magazine from the long, rune-carved gunstock and examined it. 'None,' she said, flatly.

Valdez nodded. 'Then we'd better make these count.'

The voxcomm hooked to his belt flashed red. The inquisitor stared at it in quiet disbelief before activating the channel open. The voice, slurred as if underwater, was Grunland's.

'Inquisitor? Inquisitor, are you there?'

'We can hear you,' said Valdez.

'Your ammunition must be running out. I have enough to kill you both several times over. You know you can't win. It would be better to surrender now, I promise you.'

Valdez cut the link. 'Get a fix on the mutant,' he told Danielle. He raised the communicator to his lips. 'And I promise to send you back to hell.'

Danielle watched him turning the pistol slowly in his hands, weighing every shot. Both of them knew Grunland was almost certainly right. A grinning deathmask blossomed in her mind: *Soon, psyker, I'll have your soul.*

She shivered. The phantasm was gone, but so too was the image she had been tracking. 'I've lost him,' she said. 'He – it – must be shielding itself from mindsight.'

'Then it's coming for the kill.' Valdez got to his feet. 'Come on. We'll have to take chances too.'

Before Danielle could follow she was thrown back to the ground as though a great fist had struck her down. Dazed, she tried to sit up, but her strength had vanished. She looked down at the blood streaming across her tunic. She was dimly aware not only that she had been hit, but that the shot had been intended to wound, not kill. Not yet.

She recoiled from the stream of pain and tried to turn her healing powers inwards. The wound was slight; she could close it if only she could calm herself.

She saw Valdez, running as if in slow motion towards the water's edge. The bolt pistol spat, then jammed. As the inquisitor tugged at the ammunition clip, a figure appeared on the far shore and stepped on to the stones.

Smiling serenely, Grunland began to leap across. One. Two. Three. Soon he'd be halfway. The trigger of the bolt pistol locked again in a dull, dead click. Valdez threw the weapon down, desperation in his eyes as Grunland closed on him with smooth, athletic bounds over the stones.

The inquisitor tried his footing on the first white rock jutting like a fist from the pool. Grunland laughed and spread his arms in welcome.

'Come on, mortal man. Pit your puny strength against real power.'

Ice had set in Danielle's limbs. Paralyzed, she lay watching as Valdez jumped to the second stone. Grunland's face was shimmering under the moonlight, contours rippling as though a pupa was about to burst from the human shell. On a plateau of rock no more than six feet across, man and mutant met.

Grunland's first blow nearly crippled Valdez; a vicious hammer punch into the bruised ribs below the inquisitor's chest. Valdez rocked back, fighting to stay up, clawing for a grip on Grunland's throat. Grunland lunged again and missed. For an instant he was off-balance.

Valdez stabbed at the mutant's eyes, fist cracking hard against a socket. Grunland howled in sudden pain but grasped his attacker before Valdez could draw back for another blow, twisting his arm like a rotted branch. The mutant kicked out and knocked the inquisitor's legs from beneath him, spitting savage curses.

Danielle tried to stand; she couldn't even crawl. The mutant was straddling his victim, savouring the moment of victory. Grunland's body was altering now. As the power that had held the chameleon mask was channelled into battle, the mark of the Lord of Decay was revealed. Grunland's face began to blister and crack until the skin ruptured like an over-ripe fruit. Sores opened out over his body, weeping streams of stinking pus into the lake.

Danielle gathered her powers into a single image of light and fled from her body towards the mutant. Her light broke in a flare of incandescence in Grunland's mind. The mutant cried out, blinded for an instant by white sun.

Valdez connected with a final, lunging blow, using his body like a battering ram. Grunland reeled; his feet slipped against the edge of the stone and he fell back into the dark waters of Styrus.

It was no more than a brief respite. Within seconds Grunland had regained his feet, the water barely rising above his thighs. He began to wade back towards the rock, but, as he did so, the waters around him seemed to boil, rising in a sudden tumult around the mutant.

Bewildered, Grunland grabbed at the edge of the rock, but the torrent hauled him back. Then, as Danielle watched, the waters seemed to rise up and take shape, moonlight glinting off the green-tinged flanks of a huge, amphibious warrior. Grunland thrashed out, but his blows passed through the cold glistening body without seeming to touch it.

The mutant slipped back into the raging foam. As he tried to stand, the warrior's scaly arms encircled him, taloned fingers gripping his throat, forcing his body below the waters. The warrior shape collapsed into the turmoil. The waters frothed with heavy waves, then settled. The last thing Danielle saw before unconsciousness took her were the dying ripples on the surface of the lake.

SOMETHING COLD AND hard was pressed beneath her ribs where she lay. The inquisitor's bolt pistol. She must have reached it before she passed out.

Delicately, as though she were made of brittle glass, Danielle coaxed her bruised body until she was sitting upright. She pulled the torn fabric of her tunic apart and inspected the wound. She would keep the scar forever, but the lesion was healed and dry.

She looked up and saw Valdez, wading slowly through the shallows to the shore. He saw her watching him and tried to straighten his beaten body. The inquisitor cursed and hugged his ribs, pain crushing his efforts. It was a while before he would look at her again.

'The mutant?' he asked, finally.

'Gone. There's no doubt of that.' She remembered Tolmann's unspoken fear of what lay below the waters of the lake. The one who waits.

Valdez gazed back across the pool. 'So it's finished. The infection's destroyed.'

Her grip around the pistol tightened. 'Maybe,' she said.

Something was wrong with Valdez, or rather, with her perception of him. She reached out to his mind and realized, with a shock, that her power had gone.

Valdez stepped towards her. 'What is it? Why are you looking at me like that?'

'You fought the mutant. There was contact...'

Valdez made a clumsy grab for the weapon, swearing as she drew back. 'Don't be so foolish. Use your psyker's eyes. You can see plain enough what I am.'

Danielle looked. All she saw was the semblance of a man. Suddenly she understood the universe, the dark sightless universe where only the few were given mindsight. And she understood the ways of the blind men who must guard the gateways of the Imperium.

'Unbutton your tunic,' she said, levelling the pistol.

Valdez stared at her as though she were mad. Finally, he drew back the thick fold of cloth covering his flank. A thick, bloody syrup oozed from lacerations where the mutant's blows had struck.

'How do I know that the infection has been stemmed? How do I know it hasn't reached you?' She forced herself to hold his gaze. 'Tell me,' she demanded. 'What would an inquisitor do?'

'Enough of this rubbish. Let's contact the raft and I might just forget it.' He took another step forward. Danielle raised the pistol until it was aimed squarely at his face.

Valdez halted. A half smile crossed his face. 'That pistol,' he said. 'It's jammed.'

'Was jammed.'

'And how can you suddenly be so sure of that?'

Danielle felt a tightening in her throat. 'I can't.'

Slowly, Valdez extended his one strong arm towards her.

Danielle squeezed the trigger.

THE VOICE ON the voxcomm hesitated, sounding shocked. 'Dead?' Golun repeated. 'Tchaq too?'

Danielle paused, then nodded firmly. 'He gave his life in the service of the Emperor.'

Golun's tone was flat, devoid of emotion. 'Very well,' he said at last. 'It appears you're in charge. I've reached Kar Duniash on the freighter circuit. They'll have a military channel patched back in to us in a few minutes. What's the message going to be?'

A breeze rustled in the trees, freshening the air. Only the faintest shiver now disturbed the calm of the lake. The dead warrior of the ancient lost race had taken its token revenge. The spirit guardian lay again at rest. Waiting. Waiting for the cycle of battle to begin again. A battle without beginning, or without end. She was a part of it.

Danielle looked around at the new world of uncertainties that, for the moment at least, she must walk through. The flower of evil had been cut down. But what of the root, what of the Chaos infection borne on the warp storm to Cabellas? Could she be sure that the seed of evil had been destroyed?

'Well? Can I tell them everything's all right?'

'No. Wait for the military channel to be restored, then put them through to me. I'll tell them what needs to be done. In the meantime, get some help down here.' She looked at the bodies of Valdez and the two soldiers. 'There's work that needs finishing.'

Something glinted in the reeds close to the Valdez's body. Danielle bent down and picked up the tiny silver skull, badge of high office of the Inquisition. She placed it deep within a pocket where she could be sure it would not be lost.

'Thank you,' she said. 'Thank you for testing me. For teaching me the strength which must come from doubt.'

The voxcomm blinked red again. Sector command were ready to receive instructions.

SUFFER NOT
THE UNCLEAN TO LIVE

Gav Thorpe

YAKOV CAUGHT HIMSELF dozing as his chin bowed to his chest, lulled by the soporific effect of the warm sun and the steady clatter of hooves on the cobbled street. Blinking himself awake, he gazed from the open carriage at the buildings going past him. Colonnaded fronts and tiers of balconies stretched above him for several storeys, separated by wide tree-lined streets. Thick-veined marble fascias swept past, followed by dark granite facades whose polished surfaces reflected the mid-afternoon light back at him.

Another mile and the first signs of decay began to show. Crumbling mosaics scattered their stones across the narrowing pavements, creeping plants twined around balustrades and cornices. Empty windows, some no longer glazed, stared back at him. With a yell to the horses, the carriage driver brought them to a stop and sat there waiting for the preacher to climb down to the worn cobbles.

'This is as far as I'm allowed,' the driver said without turning around, sounding half apologetic and half thankful.

Yakov walked around to the driver's seat and fished into the pocket of his robe for coins, but the coachman avoided his gaze and set off once more, turning the carriage down a sidestreet and out of sight. Yakov knew better – no honest man on Karis Cephalon would take payment from a member of the clergy – but he still hadn't broken the habit of paying for services and goods. He had tried to insist once on tipping a travel-rail porter, and the man had nearly broken down into tears, his eyes fearful. Yakov had been here four years now, and yet still he was adjusting to the local customs and beliefs.

Hoisting his embroidered canvas pack further onto his shoulder, Yakov continued his journey on foot. His long legs carried him briskly past the ruins of counting houses and ancient stores, apartments that once belonged to the fabulously wealthy and the old Royal treasury, abandoned now for over seven centuries. He had already walked for half a mile when he topped the gradual rise and looked down upon his parish.

Squat, ugly shacks nestled in the roads and alleys between the once-mighty edifices of the royal quarter. He could smell the effluence of the near-homeless, the stench of unwashed bodies and strangely exotic melange of cooking which swept to him on the smoke of thousands of fires. The sun was beginning to set as he made his way down the long hill, and soon the main boulevard was dropped into cool shadow, chilling after the earlier warmth.

Huts made from corrugated metal, rough planks, sheets of plasthene and other detritus butted up against the cut stones of the old city blocks. The babble of voices could now be heard, the screeching of children and the yapping and barking of dogs adding to the muted racket. The clatter of pans as meals were readied vied with the cries of babes and the clucking of hens. Few of the inhabitants were in sight. Most of them were indoors getting ready to eat, the rest still working out in the fields, or down the mines in the far hills.

A small girl, perhaps twelve Terran years, came running out from behind a flapping sheet of coarsely woven hemp. Her laughter was high-pitched, almost a squeal, as a boy, slightly younger perhaps, chased her down and bundled her to the ground. They both seemed to notice Yakov at the same time, and instantly quelled their high spirits. Dusting themselves down they stood up and waited respectfully, heads slightly bowed.

'Katinia, isn't it?' Yakov asked as he stopped in front of the girl.

'Yes, preacher,' she replied meekly, looking up at him with her one good eye. The other was nothing more than a scabbed, red mass which seemed to spill from the socket and across her face, enveloping her left ear and leaving one half of her scalp bald. She smiled prettily at him, and he smiled back.

'Shouldn't you be helping your mother with the cooking?' he suggested, glancing back towards the ramshackle hovel that served as their home.

'Mam's at church,' the girl's younger brother, Pietor, butted in, earning himself a kick on the shin from his sibling. 'She said we was to wait here for her.'

Yakov looked at the boy. His shrivelled right arm and leg gave his otherwise perfectly human body a lopsided look. It was the children that always affected him the most, ever cheerful despite the bleakness of their future, the ghastliness of their surroundings. If all the Emperor's faithful had the same indomitable spirit, He and mankind would have overcome all evil and adversity millennia ago. Their crippled, mutated bodies may be vile, he thought to himself, but their souls were as human as any.

'Too early for church, isn't it?' he asked them both, wondering why anyone would be there at least two hours before mass was due to begin.

'She says she wants to speak to you, with some other people, Preacher Yakov,' Katinia told him, clasping her hands behind her back as she looked up at the tall clergyman.

'Well, get back inside and make sure everything's tidy for when your mother returns, you two,' he told them gently, hoping the sudden worry he felt hadn't shown.

As he hurried on his way, he tried to think what might be happening. He had heard disturbing rumours that in a few of the other shanties a debilitating plague had begun to spread amongst the mutant population. In those unhygienic close confines such diseases spread rapidly, and as slaves from all over the world congregated in the work teams, could leap from ghetto to ghetto with devastating rapidity.

Taking a right turn, Yakov made his way towards the chapel that was also his home. Raised five years ago by the mutants themselves, it was as ramshackle as the rest of the ghetto. The building leaked and was freezing in the winter, baking hot in the summer. Yet the effort put into its construction was admirable, even if the result was deplorable, if not a little insulting. Yakov suspected that Karis Cephalon's cardinal, Prelate Kodaczka, had felt a perverse sense of satisfaction when he had heard who would be sent to tend the mutant parish. Coming from the Armormants, Yakov strongly believed that the edifices raised to the Emperor should be highly ornamented, splendid and glittering works of art in praise of the Holy Father of Mankind. To be given charge of something he would previously had declared unfit for a privy was most demeaning, and even after all this time the thought still rankled. Of course, Kodaczka, like all the native clergy of Karis Cephalon and the surrounding systems, was of the Lucid tendency, preferring poverty and abstinence to ostentation and excessive decoration. It had been a sore point between the two of them during more than one theological discussion, and Yakov's obstinate refusal to accept the prevailing beliefs of his new world did his future prospects within the Ecclesiarchy no favours. Then again, he mused ruefully to himself, his chances of any kind of elevation within the hierarchy had all but died when he had been assigned the shanty as a parish.

As he walked, he saw the rough steeples of the chapel rising over the squat mutie dwellings. Its battered, twisted roofs were slicked with greying mould, despite the aggressive efforts of the voluntary work teams who maintained the shrine. As he picked his way through a labyrinth of drying lines and filth-strewn gutters, Yakov saw a large crowd gathered outside the chapel, as he expected he would. Nearly five hundred of his parishioners, each mutated to a greater or lesser degree, were stood waiting, an angry buzz emanating from the throng. As he approached, they noticed him and started flocking in his direction, and he held up his hands to halt them before they swept around him. Pious they might be, but kind on the nose they were not. They all started babbling at once, in high-pitched squeaks down to guttural bass tones, and once more he raised his hands, silencing them.

'You speak, Gloran,' he said, pointing towards the large mining overseer whose muscled bulk was covered in a constantly flaking red skin and open sores.

'The plague, preacher, has come here,' Gloran told him, his voice as cracked as his flesh. 'Mather Horok died of it this morning, and a dozen others are falling ill already.'

Yakov groaned inwardly but kept his craggy, hawk-like face free of expression. So his suspicions were correct, the deadly scourge had arrived in the parish.

'And you are all here because…' he asked, casting his dark gaze over the misshapen crowd.

'Come here to ask Emperor, in prayers,' replied Gloran, his large eyes looking expectantly at Yakov.

'I will compose a suitable mass for this evening. Return to your homes and eat; starving will not aid you against this plague,' he said firmly. Some of the assembly moved away but most remained. 'Go!' snapped Yakov waving them away with a thin hand, irritated at their reticence. 'I cannot recall suitable prayers with you taking up all my attention, can I?'

After a few more murmurs the crowd began to dissipate and Yakov turned and strode up the rough plank stairs to the chapel entrance, taking the shallow steps two at a time. He pulled aside the sagging roughspun curtain that served as a barrier to the outside world and stepped inside. The interior of the chapel was as dismal as the outside, with only a few narrow gaps in the planking and crudely bent sheets of metal of the walls to let in light. Motes of dust drifted from the rough-cut ceiling, dancing lightly in the narrow shafts of the ruddy sunlight. Without thought he turned and took a candle from the stand next to the entrance. Picking up a match from next to the pile of tallow lights, one of the few indulgences extracted from the miserly Kodaczka, he struck it on the emery stone and lit the candle. Rather than truly illuminating the chapel the flickering light created a circle of puny light around the preacher, emphasising the gloom beyond its wavering light.

As he walked towards the altar at the far end – an upturned crate covered with an altar spread and a few accoutrements he had brought with him – the candle flame flickered in the draughts wheezing through the ill-built walls, making his shadow dance behind him. Carefully placing the candle in its holder to the left of the altar he knelt, his bony knees protesting at the solidity of the cracked roadway that made up the shrine's floor. Cursing Kodaczka once more – he had taken away Yakov's prayer cushion, saying it was a sign of decadence and weakness – Yakov tried to clear his turbulent thoughts, attempting to find that place of calm that allowed him to bring forth his litanies to the Emperor. He was about to close his eyes when he noticed something on the floor in front of the altar. Looking closer, the preacher saw that it was a dead rat. Yakov sighed, it was not the first time. Despite his oratories against it, some of his parishioners still insisted on their old, barbaric ways, making such offerings to the Emperor in supplication or penance. Pushing these thoughts aside, Yakov closed his eyes, trying to settle himself.

As HE STOOD by the entrance to the shrine, nodding reassuringly to his congregation as they filed out, Yakov felt a hand on his arm and he turned to see a girl. She was young, no older than sixteen standard years by her looks, and her pale face was pretty, framed by dark hair. Taking her hand off his robe, she smiled and it was then that Yakov looked into her eyes. Even in the gloom of the chapel they looked dark and after a moment he realised they were actually jet black, not a trace of iris or white could be seen. She blinked rapidly, meeting his gaze.

'Yes, my child?' Yakov asked softly, bowing slightly so that he could hear her without her needing to raise her voice.

'Thank you for your prayers, Yakov,' she replied and her smile faded. 'But it will take more than prayers to heal your faithful.'

'As the Emperor sees fit,' the preacher murmured in reply, keeping his gaze steady.

'You must ask for medical supplies, from the governor,' she said calmly, not asking him, but stating it as a fact.

'And who are you to tell me what I must and must not do, young lady?' Yakov responded smoothly, keeping the irritation from his voice.

'I am Lathesia,' was her short reply causing Yakov's heart to flutter slightly. The girl was a wanted terrorist. The governor's Special Security Agents had been hunting her for months following attacks on slave pens and the homes of the wealthy landowners. She had already been sentenced to death in absentiaat in a trial several weeks ago. And here she was talking to him!

'Are you threatening me?' he asked, trying to keep his voice level even though a knot of fear had begun to tighten in his stomach. Her blinking rapidly increased for a moment before she gave a short, childish laugh.

'Oh no!' she squealed, stifling another giggle by covering her mouth with a delicate hand, which Yakov noticed had rough skin peeling on each slender knuckle. Taking control of herself, her face became serious. 'You know what you must do for your parish. Your congregation has already started dying, and only treatment can help them. Go to the prelate, go to the governor, ask them for medicine.'

'I can already tell you what their answer will be,' Yakov said heavily, gesturing for her to follow him as he pulled the heavy curtain shut and started up the aisle.

'And what is that?' Lathesia asked, falling into step beside him, walking with quick strides to keep up with his long-legged gait.

'Medicine is in short supply; slaves are not,' he replied matter-of-factly, stopping and facing her. There was no point trying to make it easier. Every one of Karis Cephalon's ruling class could afford to lose a thousand slaves, but medical supplies, bought at great expense from off-world, could cost them half a year's profits.

Lathesia understood this, but had obviously railed against the fate the Emperor had laid down for her.

'You do realise you have put me in a very awkward position, don't you, child?' he added bitterly.

'Why so?' she answered back. 'Because a preacher should not be conversing with a wanted criminal?'

'No, that is easy to deal with,' Yakov replied after a moment's thought. 'Tomorrow when I see the prelate I will inform him that I saw you and he will tell the governor, who will in turn send the SSA to interrogate me. And I will tell them nearly everything.'

'Nearly everything?' she said with a raised eyebrow.

'Nearly,' he replied with a slight smile. 'After all, if I say that it was you who entreated me to ask for medical supplies, there is even less chance that I will be given them.'

'So you will do this for me?' Lathesia said with a bright smile.

'No,' Yakov replied, making her smile disappear as quickly as it came.

He stooped to pick up a strip of rag littering the flagstones of the floor. 'But I will do it for my parishioners, as you say. I have no hope that the request will be granted, none at all. And my poor standing with the prelate will be worsened even more by the confrontation, but that is not to be helped. I must do as my duty dictates.'

'I understand, and you have my thanks,' Lathesia said softly before walking away, disappearing through the curtained doorway without a backward glance. Sighing, Yakov crumpled up the rag in his hand and moved to the altar to finish clearing up.

THE PLEXIGLASS WINDOW of the mono-conveyor was scratched and scuffed, but beyond it Yakov could see the capital, Karis, stretched out beneath him. Under the spring sun the white-washed buildings were stark against the fertile plains surrounding the city. Palaces, counting houses, SSA court-houses and governmental office towers reared from the streets towards him as the conveyor rumbled noisily over its single rail. He could see other conveyor carriages on different tracks, gliding like smoke-belching beetles over the city, their plexi-glass-sided cabs reflecting the sun in brief dazzles as it moved in and out from the clouds overhead.

Turning his gaze ahead, he looked at the Amethyst Palace, seat of the governor and cathedral of Karis Cephalon. Its high walls surrounded the hilltop on which it was built, studded with towers from which fluttered massive pennants showing the symbol of the revolutionary council. Once each tower would have hung the standard of one of the old aristocratic families, but they had been burnt, along with those families, in the bloody coup that had overturned their rule seven hundred and thirty years ago.

The keep, punctured at its centre by the mysterious mile-high black Needle of Sennamis, rose above the walls, a conglomeration of millennia of additional wings, buttresses and towers obscuring its original architecture like successive layers of patina.

Under his feet, the conveyor's gears began to grind and whirr more loudly as the carriage pulled into the palace docking station. Yakov navigated his way through the terminus without thought, his mind directed towards the coming meeting with Prelate Kodaczka. He barely acknowledged the salutes of the guards at the entrance to the cardinal's chambers, only sub-consciously registering that they carried heavy-looking autorifles in addition to their ceremonial spears.

'Ah, Constantine,' Kodaczka murmured as the doors swung closed behind the preacher, looking up at Yakov from behind his high desk. A single laserquill and autotablet adorned its dull black surface, reflecting the sparsity of the rest of the chamber. The walls were plainly whitewashed, like most of the Amethyst palace's interior, with a single Imperial eagle stencilled in black on the wall behind the cardinal. He was a handsome man in his middle ages, maturing with dignity and poise. Dressed in a plain black cassock, his only badge of office the small steel circlet holding back his lustrous blond hair, the cardinal was an elegant, if severe, figure. He wouldn't have looked out of place as a leading actor on the stage at the Revolutionary Theatre; with his active, bright blue eyes, chiselled cheekbones and strong chin he would have enthralled the ladies had he not had another calling.

'Good of you to see me, cardinal,' replied Yakov. At a gestured invitation from Kodaczka the preacher sat in one of the high-backed chairs that were arranged in a semi-circle in front of the desk.

'I must admit to a small amount of surprise at receiving your missive this morning,' Prelate Kodaczka told him, leaning back in his own chair.

'You understand why I felt it necessary to talk to you?' inquired Yakov, waiting for the customary verbal thrust and parry that accompanied all of his conversations with Kodaczka.

'Your parish and the plague? Of course I understand,' Kodaczka nodded as he spoke. He was about to continue when a knock at the door interrupted him. At Kodaczka's call they opened and a servant in the plain livery of an Ecclesiarchal servant entered with a carafe and glass on a small wooden tray.

'I suspect you are thirsty after journeying all this way,' Kodaczka indicated the drink with an open palm. Yakov nodded his thanks, pouring himself a glass of the crisp water and sipping it carefully. The servant left the tray on the desk and retired wordlessly.

'Where was I? Oh yes, the plague. It has struck many of the slave communities badly. Why have you waited until now before requesting aid?' Kodaczka's question was voiced lightly but Yakov suspected he was, as always, being tested somehow. He considered his reply for a moment, sipping more water as an excuse for not answering.

'The other slaves are not my parishioners. They are not my concern,' he said, setting the empty glass back on to the tray and raising his eyes to return the gaze of the cardinal.

'Ah, your parish, of course,' agreed Kodaczka with a smile. 'Your duty to your parishioners. And why do you think I can entreat the governor and the committee to act now, when they have let so many others die already?'

'I am simply performing my duty, as you say,' replied Yakov smoothly, keeping his expression neutral. 'I have made no promises other than to raise this with yourself, and I do not expect any particular success on your part. As you say, there has been an abundance of time to act before now. But still, I must ask. Will you ask the governor and the committee to send medical aid and staff to my parish to help defend the faithful against infection by this epidemic?'

'I will not,' Kodaczka answered curtly. 'They have already made it clear to me that not only is the expense of such resources unjustified, but the lifting of the ban on full citizens entering slave areas may prove a difficult legal wrangle.'

'My congregation is dying!' barked Yakov, though in his heart he felt less vehement. 'Can you not do something to help them?'

'I will offer up prayers for them,' the cardinal responded, showing no sign of being perturbed by Yakov's outburst. Yakov caught himself before he said anything. This was one of Kodaczka's traps. The cardinal was desperate to find some reason to discredit Yakov, to disband his unique parish and send him on his way.

'As I already have,' Yakov said eventually. There was an uncomfortable silence for several seconds, both preacher and cardinal gazing at each other over the desk, weighing up the opposition. It was Kodaczka who broke the quiet.

'It irks you to preach to these slaves?' the cardinal asked suddenly.

'Slaves are entitled to spiritual guidance even by the laws of Karis Cephalon,' the preacher replied.

'That is not an answer,' Kodaczka told him gravely.

'I find the... situation on this world difficult to align with the teachings of my faith,' Yakov admitted finally.

'You find slavery against your religion?'

'Of course not!' Yakov snorted. 'It is these mutants, these creatures that I preach to. This world is built upon the exploitation of something unholy and abhorrent and I believe it denigrates everyone involved in it.'

'Ah, your Armormant upbringing,' the prelate's voice dripped with scorn. 'So harsh and pure in intent, and yet so soft and decadent in execution.'

'We are an accepted and recognised sect within the Ministorum,' Yakov said defensively.

'Accepted? Recognised, I agree, but acceptance... That is another matter entirely,' Kodaczka said bluntly. 'Your founder, Gracius of Armorm, was charged with heresy!'

'And found innocent...' countered Yakov. He couldn't stop himself from adding, 'After a fair trial in front of his peers.'

'Yes,' agreed Kodaczka slowly, his sly smile returning once more.

YAKOV'S AUDIENCE WITH the cardinal had lasted most of the afternoon and once again the sun was beginning to set as he made his way back to the shanty town. As on the previous night there were many of the mutants gathered around the shrine. Rumour of his visit to the cardinal had spread and he was met by a crowd of eager faces. One look at his own expression quelled their anticipation and an angry murmur sprang up. It was Menevon who stepped forward, a troublemaker by nature in Yakov's opinion. He looked down at Menevon's bestial features and not for the first time wondered if he had been sired by unholy union with a dog or bear. Tufts of coarse hair sprung in patches all across his body, and his jaw was elongated and studded with tusk-like teeth stained yellow. Menevon looked back at him with small, beady eyes.

'He does nothing,' the mutant stated. 'We die and they all do nothing!'

'The Emperor's Will be done,' replied Yakov sternly, automatically echoed by some of the gathered mutants.

'The Emperor I trust and adore,' Menevon declared hotly, 'but the governor I wouldn't spit on if he were burning.'

'That is seditious talk, Menevon, and you would do well to curb your tongue,' warned Yakov, stooping to talk quietly to the rabble-rouser.

'I say we make him help us!' shouted Menevon, ignoring Yakov and turning towards the crowd. 'It's time we made ourselves heard!'

There were discontented growls of agreement from the others; some shouted out their approval.

'Too long have they lorded over us, too long we've been ignored!' continued Menevon. 'Enough is enough! No more!'

'No more!' repeated the crowd with a guttural roar.

'Silence!' bellowed Yakov, holding his arms up to silence them. The crowd fell quiet instantly at his commanding tone. 'This discord will serve for nothing. If the governor will not listen to me, your preacher, he will not listen to you. Your masters will not tolerate this outburst lightly. Go back to your homes and pray! Look not to the governor, but to yourselves and the master of us all, the Holy Emperor. Go now!'

Menevon shot the preacher a murderous look as the crowd heeded his words, dispersing with backward glances and muttered curses.

'Go back to your family, Menevon. You can do them no good dead on a scaffold,' Yakov told him quietly. The defiance in the mutant's eyes disappeared and he nodded sadly. He cast a long, despairing glance at the preacher and then he too turned away.

THE TOUCH OF something cold woke Yakov and when he opened his eyes his gaze fell first upon the glittering knife blade held in front of his face. Tearing his eyes away from the sharpened steel, he followed the arm to the knife's wielder and his look was met by the whitened orbs of the mutant he knew to be called Byzanthus. Like Lathesia, he was a renegade, and hunted by the Special Security Agents. His face was solemn, his eyes intent upon the preacher. The ridged and wrinkled grey skin that covered his body was dull in the silvery light which occasionally broke through the curtain swaying in the glassless window of the small chamber.

'I had your promise,' Yakov heard Lathesia speak from the shadows. A moment later she stepped forwards, her hair catching the moonlight as she passed in front of the window.

'I asked. They said no,' Yakov replied, pushing Byzanthus's arm away and sitting up, the thin blanket falling to his waist to reveal the taut muscles of his stomach and chest.

'You keep in good shape,' she commented, noticing his lean physique.

'The daily walk to the capital keeps me fit,' Yakov replied, feeling no discomfort as her penetrating gaze swept over his body. 'I must stay physically as well as spiritually fit to serve the Emperor well.'

A flickering yellow light drew the preacher's attention to the window and he rose from the thin mattress to pace over and look. Lathesia smiled at his nakedness but he ignored her; fleshy matters such as his own nudity were beneath him. Pulling aside the ragged curtain, Yakov saw the light came from dozens of blazing torches and when he listened carefully he could hear voices raised in argument. One of them sounded like Menevon's, and as his eyes adjusted he could see the hairy mutant in the torchlight, gesticulating towards the city.

'Emperor damn him,' cursed Yakov, pushing past Lathesia to grab his robes from a chair behind her. Pulling on his vestments, he rounded on the mutant girl.

'You put him up to this?' he demanded.

'Menevon has been an associate of mine for quite some time,' she admitted, not meeting his gaze.

'Why?' Yakov asked simply. 'The governor will not stand for this discontent.'

'Too long we have allowed this tyranny to continue,' she said with feeling. 'Just as in the revolution, the slaves have tired of the lash. It is time to strike back.'

'The revolutionary council was backed by two-thirds of the old king's army,' spat Yakov, fumbling in the darkness for his boots. 'You will all die.'

'Menevon's brother is dead,' Byzanthus growled from behind Yakov. 'Murdered.'

Yakov rounded on the grey-skinned man. 'You know this? For sure?'

'Unless he slit his own throat, yes!' replied Lathesia. 'The masters did this, and no one will investigate because it is just one of the slaves who has died. Justice must be served.'

'The Emperor judges us all in time,' Yakov replied instinctively. He pointed out of the window. 'And He'll be judging some of them this evening if you let this foolishness continue. Damn your souls to Chaos. Don't you care that they'll die?'

'Better to die fighting,' Lathesia whispered back, 'than on our knees begging for scraps and offal.'

The preacher snarled wordlessly and hurried out through the chapel into the street. As he rounded the corner he was met by the mutant mob, their faces twisted in anger, their raucous, raging cries springing to life as they saw him. Menevon was at their head, holding a burning brand high in the air, the embodiment of the revolutionary ringleader. But he wasn't, Yakov thought bitterly; that honour belonged to the manipulative, headstrong teenage girl back in his room.

'What in the name of the Emperor do you think you are doing?' demanded Yakov, his deep voice rising to a deafening shout over the din of the mob. They ignored him and Menevon pushed him aside as the crowd swept along the street. The preacher recognised many faces in the torchlight as the mob passed by, some of them children. He felt someone step up beside him, and he turned and saw Lathesia watching the mutants marching past, her face triumphant.

'How did one so young become so bloodthirsty?' muttered Yakov, directing a venomous glare at her before setting off after the mutants. They were moving at some speed and Yakov had to force his way through the crowd with long strides, pulling and elbowing aside mutants to get to the front. As they neared the edge of the ghetto the crowd began to slow and he broke through to the front of the mob, where he saw what had stalled their advance. Across the main thoroughfare stood a small detachment of the SSA, their grey and black uniforms dark against the glare of a troop transport's searchlamp behind them. Each cradled a shotgun in their hands, their visored helms reflecting the flames of the torches. Yakov stopped and let the mutants swirl around him, his mouth dry with fear. Next to him the pretty young girl, Katinia, was staring at the SSA officers. She seemed to notice Yakov suddenly and looked up at the preacher with a small, uncertain smile. He didn't smile back, but focussed his attention on the law enforcers ahead.

'Turn back now! You are in violation of the Slave Encampment Laws,' screeched a voice over a loudhailer.

'No more!' shouted Menevon, hurling his torch at the security agents, his cry voiced by others. Stones and torches rattled off the cobbles and walls of the street and one of the officers went down to a thrown bottle which smashed across his darkened helmet.

'You were warned, mutant scum,' snarled the SSA officer's voice over the hailer. At some unheard command the agents raised their shotguns. Yakov hurled himself across Katinia just as gunfire exploded all around him. There were sudden screams and shouts; a wail of agony shrieked from his left as he and the girl rolled to the ground. He felt something pluck at his robes as another salvo roared out. The mutants were fleeing, disorder reigned as they scrabbled and tore at one another to fight their way clear. Bare and booted feet stamped on Yakov's fingers as he held himself over Katinia, who was mewling and sobbing beneath him. Biting back a yell of pain as a heel crushed his left thumb between two cobbles, Yakov forced himself upright. Within moments he and the girl were alone in the street.

The boulevard was littered with dead and wounded mutants. Limbs, bodies and pools of blood were scattered over the cobblestones, a few conscious mutants groaned or sobbed. To his right, a couple he had wed just after arriving were on their knees, hugging each other, wailing over the nearly unrecognisable corpse of their son. Wherever he looked, lifeless eyes stared back at him in the harsh glare of the searchlight. The SSA were picking their way through the mounds of bodies, kicking over corpses and peering at faces.

Yakov heard the girl give a ragged gasp and he looked down. Half her mother's face lay on the road almost within reach. He bent and gathered the girl up in his left arm, and she buried her face in his robes, weeping uncontrollably. It was then he noticed the silver helmet of a sergeant as he clambered down from the turret of the armoured car.

'You!' bellowed Yakov, pointing with his free hand at the SSA man, his anger welling up inside him. 'Come here now!'

The officer gave a start and hurried over. His face was hidden by the visor of his helmet, but he seemed to be trembling.

'Take off your helmet,' Yakov commanded, and he did so, letting it drop from quivering fingers. The man's eyes were wide with fear as he looked up at the tall preacher. Yakov felt himself getting even angrier and he grabbed the man by the throat, his long, strong fingers tightening on the sergeant's windpipe. The man gave a choked cough as Yakov used all of the leverage afforded by his height to push him down to his knees.

'You have fired on a member of the Ministorum, sergeant,' Yakov hissed. The man began to stammer something but a quick tightening of Yakov's grip silenced him. Releasing his hold, Yakov moved his hand to the top of the sergeant's head, forcing him to bow forward.

'Pray for forgiveness,' whispered Yakov, his voice as sharp as razor. The other agents had stopped the search and helmets bobbed left and right as they exchanged glances. He heard someone swearing from the crackling intercom inside the sergeant's helmet on the floor.

'Pray to the Emperor to forgive this most grievous of sins,' Yakov repeated. The sergeant started praying, his voice spilling almost incoherently from his lips, his tears splashing down his cheeks into the blood slicking the cobbles.

'Forgive me, almighty Emperor, forgive me!' pleaded the man, looking up at Yakov as he released his hold, his cheeks streaked with tears, his face a mask of terror.

'One hour's prayer every sunrise for the rest of your life,' Yakov pronounced his judgement. As he looked again at the bloodied remnants of the massacred mutants and felt the tears of Katinia soaking through his tattered priestly robes, he added, 'And one day's physical penance a week for the next five years.'

As he turned away from the horrific scene Yakov heard the sergeant retching and vomiting. Five years of self-flagellation would teach him not to fire on a preacher, Yakov thought grimly as he stepped numbly through the blood and gore.

YAKOV WAS TIRED and even more irritable than normal when the sun rose the next day. He had taken Katinia back to her home, where her brother was in a fitful, nightmare-laden sleep, and then returned to the site of the cold-blooded execution to identify the dead. Some of the mutants he did not recognise from his congregation, and he assumed they were more of Lathesia's misguided freedom fighters.

When he finally returned to the shanty town, the preacher saw several dozen SSA standing guard throughout the ghetto, each carrying a heavy pistol and a charged shock maul. As he dragged himself wearily up the steps to the chapel, a familiar face was waiting for him. Just outside the curtained portal stood Sparcek, the oldest mutant he knew and informal mayor-cum-judge of the ghetto.

Yakov delved into his last reserves of energy as the old mutant met him halfway, his twisted, crippled body making hard work of the shallow steps.

'A grim night, preacher,' said Sparcek in his broken, hoarse voice. Yakov noticed the man's left arm was splinted and bound with bandages and he held it across his chest as much as his deformed shoulder and elbow allowed.

'You were up there?' Yakov asked, pointing limply at Sparcek's broken arm.

'This?' Sparcek glanced down and then shook his head sadly. 'No, the SSA broke into my home just after, accused me of being the leader. I said they couldn't prove that and they did this, saying they needed no proof.'

'Your people need you now, before they...' Yakov's voice trailed off as his befuddled mind tried to tell him something. 'What did you just say?'

'I said they couldn't prove anything...' he started.

'That's it!' snapped Yakov, startling the old mutant.

'What? Talk sense, you're tired,' Sparcek snapped back, obviously annoyed at the preacher's outburst.'

'Nothing for you to worry about,' Yakov tried to calm him with a waved hand. 'Now, I am about to ask you something, and whether you answer me or not, I need your promise that you will never tell another living soul what it is.'

'You can trust me. Did I not help you when you first arrived, did I not tell you about your congregation, their secrets and traits?' Sparcek assured him.

'I need to speak to Lathesia, and quickly,' Yakov said, bending close so that he could whisper.

'The rebel leader?' Sparcek whispered back, clearly amazed. He thought for a moment before continuing. 'I cannot promise anything but I may be able to send her word that you wish to see her.'

'Do it, and do it quickly!' insisted Yakov, laying a gentle hand on the mutant's good arm. 'With all of these trigger happy agents around, she's bound to do something reckless and get more of your people killed. If I can speak to her, I may be able to avoid more bloodshed.'

'I will do as you ask, preacher,' Sparcek nodded as he spoke, almost to himself.

THE DANK SEWERS resounded with running water and constant dripping, punctuated by the odd splash as Yakov placed a booted foot in a puddle or a rat scurried past through the rivulets seeping through the worn brick walls. Ahead, the glowlamp of Byzanthus bobbed and weaved in the mutant's raised hand as he led the way to Lathesia's hidden lair. Though one of the larger drainage systems, the tunnel was still cramped for the tall preacher and his neck was sore from half an hour's constant stooping. His nose had become more accustomed to the noxious smell which had assaulted his nostrils when the grey-skinned mutant had first opened the storm drain cover, and his eyes were now used to the dim, blue glow of the lantern. He was thoroughly lost, he was sure of that, and he half-suspected this was the point of the drawn out journey. They must have been walking in circles, otherwise they would be beyond the boundaries of the mutant encampment in the city proper, or out in the fields.

After several more minutes of back-breaking walking, Byzanthus finally stopped beside an access door in the sewer wall. He banged four times, paused, then banged twice more. Rusted locks squealed and the door opened a moment later on shrieking hinges.

'You should loot some oil,' Yakov couldn't stop himself from saying, earning himself a cheerless smile from Byzanthus, who waved him inside with the lantern.

There was no sign of the doorkeeper, but as Yakov preceded Byzanthus up the wooden steps just inside the door he heard it noisily swinging shut again.

'Shy?' Yakov asked, looking at Byzanthus over his shoulder as he climbed the stairwell.

'Suspicious of you,' the mutant replied bluntly, giving him a hard stare.

The steps led them into a small hallway, decorated with flaking murals on the walls, they were obviously inside one of the abandoned buildings of the royal district.

'Second door on the left,' Byzanthus said curtly, indicating the room with a nod of his head as he extinguished the lamp.

Yakov strode down the corridor quickly, his hard-soled boots clacking on the cracked tiles. Just as he reached the door, it opened to reveal Lathesia, dressed in ill-fitting SSA combat fatigues.

'Come in, make yourself at home,' she said as she stepped back and took in the room with a wide sweep of her arm. The small chamber was bare except for a couple of straw pallets and a rickety table strewn with scatters of parchment and what looked like a schematic of the sewer system. The frescoes had been all but obliterated by crudely daubed black paint, which had puddled on the scuffed wooden floor. The remnants of a fire smouldered in one corner, the smoke drifting lazily out of a cracked window.

'We had to burn the carpet last winter,' Lathesia said apologetically, noting the direction of his gaze.

'And the walls?' Yakov asked, dropping his haversack onto the bare floor.

'Byzanthus in a fit of pique when he heard we'd been found guilty of treason,' she explained hurriedly, moving over to drop down on one of the mattresses.

'You share the same room?' Yakov asked, recoiling from her in disgust. 'Out of wedlock?'

'What of it?' she replied, genuinely perplexed.

'Is there no sin you are not guilty of?' he demanded hotly, regretting his decision to have anything to do with the wayward mutant. He fancied he could feel the fires of Chaos burning his soul as he stood there. It would take many weeks of repentance to atone for even coming here.

'Better that than freezing because we only have enough fuel to heat a few rooms,' she told him plainly before a smile broke over her pretty face. 'You think that Byzanthus and I... Oh, Yakov, please, allow me some standards.'

'I'm sure he doesn't see it that way,' Yakov pointed out to her with a meaningful look. 'I saw the way he looked at you in my bedchamber last night.'

'Enough of this!' Lathesia snapped back petulantly. 'I didn't ask you to come here to preach to me. You wanted to see me!'

'Yes, you are right, I did,' Yakov admitted, collecting his thoughts before continuing. 'Have you any other trouble planned for tonight?'

'What concern is it of yours, preacher?' she asked, her black eyes narrowing with suspicion.

'You must not do anything. The SSA will retaliate with even more brutal force than last time,' he warned her.

'Actually, we were thinking of killing some of them, strutting around with their bludgeons and pistols as if their laws apply here,' she replied venomously, her cracked hands balling into fists.

Yakov went over and sat down beside her slowly, meeting her gaze firmly.

'Do you trust me?' he asked gently.

'No, why should I?' she said, surprised.

'Why did you come to me before, to ask the cardinal for help?' he countered, leaning back on one hand but keeping his eyes on hers.

'Because… It was… I was desperate, it was foolish of me, I shouldn't have,' she mumbled back, turning her gaze away.

'You are nothing more than a child. Let me help you,' Yakov persisted, feeling his soul starting to roast at the edges even as he said it.

'Stop it!' she wailed suddenly, springing to her feet and backing away. 'If I don't do this, no one will help us!'

'Have it your way,' sighed Yakov, sitting upright again. 'There is more to this than the casual murder of Menevon's brother. I do not yet know what, but I need your help to find out.'

'Why do you think so?' she asked, her defiance forgotten as curiosity took over.

'You say his throat was slit?' Yakov asked and she nodded. 'Why? Any court on Karis Cephalon will order a mutant hung on the word of a citizen, so why the murder? It must be because nobody could know who was involved, or why he died. I think he saw something or someone and was murdered so he couldn't talk.'

'But that means, if a master didn't do it…' Lathesia started before her eyes widened in realisation. 'One of us did this? No, I won't believe it!'

'You might not have to,' Yakov countered quickly, raising his hand to calm her. 'In fact it's unlikely. The only way we can find out is to go to where Menevon's brother died, and see what we can find.'

'He worked in one of the cemeteries not far from here, just outside the encampment boundary,' she told the preacher. 'We'll take you there.'

She half-ran, half-skipped to the open door and called through excitedly, 'Byzanthus! Byzanthus, fetch Odrik and Klain. We're going on an expedition tonight!'

THE FUNCTIONAL FERROCRETE tombstones had little grandeur about them, merely rectangular slabs plainly inscribed with the name of the family. The moon was riding high in the sky as Yakov, Lathesia and the other mutants searched the graveyard for any sign of what had happened. Yakov entered the small wooden shack that served as the gravedigger's shelter, finding various picks and shovels stacked neatly in one corner. There was an unmistakable red stain on the unfinished planks of the floor, which to Yakov's untrained eye seemed to have spread from near the doorway. He stood there for a moment, gazing out into the cemetery to see what was in view. It was Byzanthus who caught his attention with a waved arm, and they all gathered on him. He pointed to a grave, which was covered with a tarpaulin weighted with rocks. Lathesia gave Byzanthus a nod and he pulled back the sheeting.

The grave was deep and long, perhaps three metres from end to end and two metres down. Inside was a plain metal casket, wrapped in heavy chains from which hung numerous padlocks.

'Why would anyone want to lock up a coffin?' asked Lathesia, looking at Yakov.

YAKOV STOOD IN one of the rooms just down the hall from where he had met Lathesia, gazing at the strange casket. The mutant leader was beside him looking at it too, a small frown creasing her forehead.

'What do you...' she started to ask before a loud boom reverberated across the building. Shouts and gunshots rang out along the corridor as the two of them dashed from the room. Byzanthus came tearing into view from the doors at the far end, a smoking shotgun grasped in his clawed hands.

'The SSA!' he shouted to them as he ran up the corridor.

'How?' Lathesia asked, but Yakov ignored her and ducked back into the room to snatch up his satchel. More gunfire rattled from nearby, punctuated by a low bellowing of pain. As the preacher returned to the corridor Byzanthus smashed him across the jaw with the butt of the shotgun, sending Yakov sprawling over the tiled floor.

'You betrayed us, governor's lapdog!' the mutant hissed, pushing the shotgun barrel into Yakov's chest.

'Emperor forgive you!' spat the preacher, sweeping a booted foot into one of Byzanthus's knees, which cracked audibly as his legs folded under him. Yakov pounced forward and wrestled the shotgun from his grip, turning it on Lathesia as she stepped towards him.

'Believe me, this was not my doing,' he told her, backing away. 'Save yourselves!'

He took another step back and then threw the shotgun to
Lathesia. Sweeping up his bag, Yakov shouldered his way
through the doorway that led to the sewer stairs as she was distracted. Yakov's heart was hammering as he pounded down the
steps three at a time, almost losing his footing in his haste. At
the bottom someone stepped in front of him and he lashed out
with his fist, feeling it connect with a cheekbone. He spun the
lockwheel on the door and splashed out into the sewers, cursing himself for ever getting involved in this mess. Two hundred
years of penance wouldn't atone for what he had done. As the
sounds of fighting grew closer he hurried off through the drips
and puddles with long strides.

YAKOV SAT ON his plain bed in a grim mood, brooding over the
previous night's and day's events. He had spent the whole day
a hostage to himself in the chapel, not daring to go out into the
light, where some roving SSA man might recognise him from
the raid on the rebels' hideout.

He had prayed for hours on end, tears in his eyes as he asked
the Emperor for guidance. He had allowed himself to get
involved in something beyond him. He was a simple preacher,
he had no right to interfere in such matters. As his guilt-
wracked day passed into evening, Yakov began to calm down.
His dealings with the mutants may have been sinful, but he
had discovered something strange. The chained coffin, and the
murder of the mutant for what he knew about it, was at the
heart of it. But what could he do? He had just decided to confess all to Prelate Yodaczka when footsteps out in the chapel
attracted his attention.

Stepping into the shrine, he saw a figure kneeling before the
altar, head bowed. It was Lathesia, and as he approached she
looked up at him, her eyes red-rimmed from weeping.

'Byzanthus is dead, hung an hour ago,' she said dully, the
black orbs of her eyes catching the light of the candle on the
altar. 'He held off the agents to make sure I escaped. None of
the others got out.'

'I did not betray you,' Yakov told her, kneeling beside her.

'I know,' she said, turning to him and laying a hand on his
knee.

'I want to find out what is in that coffin,' Yakov said after a
few moments of silence between them. 'Will you help me?'

'I watched them; they didn't take it anywhere,' she replied distractedly, wiping at a tear forming in her eye.

'Then will you go back there with me?' he asked, standing up again and reaching a hand down to help her up.

'Yes, I will,' she answered quietly. 'I want to know why they died.'

THEY TOOK THE overground route to the old aristocratic household, Lathesia leading him up a fire escape ladder onto a neighbouring rooftop. From there they could see two SSA stationed at the front entrance and another at the tradesman's entrance to the rear. She showed him the ropeline hung between the buildings, tied there for escape rather than entry, but suitable all the same. Yakov kept his gaze firmly on his hands as he pulled himself along the rope behind the lithe young rebel leader, trying not to think of the ten metre drop to the hard road beneath him. As she helped him onto the rooftop of her one-time lair, a gentle cough from the darkness made them freeze. Out of the shadows strolled a man swathed in a heavy coat, his breath carving mist into the chill evening air.

'A strange pastime for a preacher,' he said as he stepped towards them, hands in the pockets of his trenchcoat.

'Who are you?' demanded Lathesia, her hand straying to the revolver wedged into the waistband of her trousers at the small of her back.

'Please don't try and shoot me,' he replied calmly. 'You'll attract some unwanted attention.'

'Who are you?' Yakov repeated the question, stepping between the stranger and Lathesia.

'An investigator, for the Inquisition,' he told them stopping a couple of paces away.

'An inquisitor?' Lathesia hissed, panic in her eyes.

'Don't worry, your little rebellion doesn't concern me tonight,' he assured her, pulling his hands free from the coat and crossing his arms. 'And I didn't say I was an inquisitor.'

'You are after the casket as well?' Yakov guessed, and the man nodded slightly.

'Shall we go and find it, then?' the investigator invited them, turning and walking away.

* * *

THE SCENE BEFORE Yakov could have been taken straight from a drawing in the Liber Heresius. Twelve robed and masked figures knelt in a circle around the coffin, five braziers set at the points of a star drawn around the casket. The air was filled with acrid smoke and the sonorous chanting of the cultists filled the room. One of them stood and pulled back his hood, and Yakov almost gasped out loud when he recognised the face of the governor. Holding his arms wide, he chanted louder, the words a meaningless jumble of syllables to the preacher.

'I think we've seen enough,' the investigator said, crouched beside Yakov and Lathesia on the patio outside the room. He drew two long laspistols from holsters inside his coat and offered one to Yakov. Yakov shook his head.

'Surely you're not opposed to righteous violence, preacher,' the stranger said with a raised eyebrow.

'No,' Yakov replied. Pulling his rucksack off, the preacher delved inside and a moment later pulled out a black enamelled pistol. With a deftness that betrayed years of practice he slipped home the magazine and cocked the gun. 'I just prefer to use my own weapon.'

Lathesia gasped in astonishment.

'What?' asked Yakov, annoyed. 'You think they call us the Defenders of the Faith just because it sounds good?'

'Shoot to kill!' rasped the stranger as he stood up.

He fired both pistols, shattering the windows and spraying glass shards into the room. A couple of the cultists pulled wicked-looking knives from their rope belts and leapt at them; the governor dived behind the casket shrieking madly.

Yakov's first shot took a charging cultist in the chest, punching him off his feet. His second blew the kneecap off another, his third taking him in the forehead as he collapsed. The investigator's laspistols spat bolts of light into the cultists fleeing for the door, while the boom of Lathesia's heavy pistol echoed off the walls. As Yakov stepped into the room, one of the cultists pushed over a brazier and he jumped to his right to avoid the flaming coals. A las-bolt took the traitor in the eye, vaporising half his face.

In a few moments the one-sided fight was over, all the cultists were dead, their blood soaking into the bare boards. Suddenly, the governor burst from his hiding place and bolted for the door, but Lathesia was quicker, tackling him to the ground. He thrashed for a moment before she smashed him across the temple with the grip of her revolver. She was about to pistol-whip him again but the stranger grabbed her wrist in mid-swing.

'My masters would prefer he survived for interrogation,' he told the girl, letting go of her arm and stepping back.

Lathesia hesitated for a moment before standing. She delivered a sharp kick to the governor's midriff before stalking away, emptying spent casings from her gun.

'I have no idea what is going on here,' Yakov confessed, sliding the safety into place on his own pistol.

'No reason you should,' the man assured him. 'I suppose I do owe you an explanation though.'

Slipping his laspistols back into his coat, the man leant back on the wall.

'The plague has been engineered by the governor and his allies,' the investigator told him. 'He wanted the mutants to rebel, to try to overthrow him. While Karis Cephalon remains relatively peaceful, the Imperial authorities and the Inquisition are content to ignore the more-or-less tolerant attitude to mutants found here. But should they threaten the stability of this world, they would be swift and ruthless in their response.'

The man glanced over his shoulder at Lathesia, who was studying the casket intently, then looked Yakov squarely in the eye before continuing quietly. 'But that's not the whole of it. So the mutants are wiped out, that's really no concern of the Inquisition. But the governor's motives are what concerns us. I, that is we, believe that he has made some kind of pact with a dark force, some kind of unholy elevation. His side of the deal was the delivery of a massive sacrifice, a whole population, genocide of the mutants. But he couldn't just have them culled; the entire economy of Karis Cephalon is based on mutant labour and no one would allow such a direct action to threaten their prosperity. So, he imported a virus which feeds on mutants. It's called Aether Mortandis and costs a lot of money to acquire from the Mechanicus.'

'And the coffin?' Yakov asked. 'Where does that fit in?'

'It doesn't, not at all!' the stranger laughed bitterly. 'I was hiding it when the gravedigger saw me. I killed him, but unfortunately before I had time to finish the burial, his cries brought an SSA patrol and I had to leave. It's just coincidence.'

'So what's so important about it then?' Yakov eyed the casket with suspicion. Lathesia was toying with one of the locks, a thoughtful look on her face.

'I wouldn't open that if I were you,' the stranger spoke up, startling the girl, who dropped the padlock and stepped back. The investigator put an arm around Yakov's shoulders and pulled him close, his voice dropping to a conspiratorial whisper.

'The reason the governor has acted now is because of a convergence of energies on Karis Cephalon,' the man told Yakov slowly. 'Mystical forces, astrological conjunctions are forming, with Karis Cephalon at its centre. For five years, the barrier between our world and the hell of Chaos will grow thinner and thinner. Entities will be able to break through, aliens will be drawn here, and death and disaster will plague this world on an unparalleled scale. It will be hell incarnate. If you wish, for your help today I can arrange a transfer to a parish on another world, get you way from here.'

Yakov looked at the man for a minute, searching his own soul.

'If what you say is true,' he said eventually, 'then I respectfully decline the offer. It seems men of faith will be a commodity in much need over the coming years.'

He looked up at Lathesia, who was looking at them from across the room.

'And,' Yakov finished, 'my parishioners will need me more than ever.'

WARPED STARS

Ian Watson

On Jomi Jabal's sixteenth birthday he watched a witch being broken in the market square of Groxgelt. The time was the cool of the evening. The harsh blue sun had set a while since, however the night with its star-lanterns was a couple of hours away as yet.

The saffron-hued gas-giant still bulged hugely in the wispy sky, shouldering high above the horizon like some mountainous desert dune. Its light gilded the tiled roofs of the town and the dusty, hoof-printed street.

That golden giant in the sky seemed to be such a furnace, such a molten crucible. Yet, unlike the sun, it dispensed no heat. Jomi wondered how that could be, but he knew better than to ask. When he was younger a few whippings had deterred him from excessive curiosity.

His pa's punishments had been well intended. Boys and girls who questioned were perhaps on the road to becoming witches themselves.

A trumpet would sound from the watchtower after the golden giant did finally sink out of sight. That braying screech signalled curfew at the onset of darkness. Thereafter, mutants were said to prowl the black streets.

Did mutants really roam Groxgelt by night, hunting for victims, seeking entry into the homes of the unwise? It struck Jomi as a convenient arrangement that the townsfolk were thus exiled to their houses during the cooler hours. Otherwise the taverns of Groxgelt might well have remained open longer. Workmen might have caroused till late, and thus be tired when dawn came, grumpy and lethargic at their labours during the hot day.

Oh but mutants certainly existed, without a doubt. Witches, hoodooists. Here was yet another one, bound upon the wheel.

Two hours till darkness...

'This witch uses a cunning trick,' Reverend Henrik Farb, the preacher, proclaimed to the crowd from the ebon steps of the headman's residence. 'He can hex time itself. He can stop the flow of the time stream. Though not for very long... so do not run away in fear! Witness his punishment, and mark my words: the witch looks human, but in truth he is distorted. Beware of those who seem human, yet are not!'

Farb was a fat fellow. Beneath his black cloak, leather armour bulged in a manner that, had he been a woman, might have been described as voluptuous. Womanly, too, was the jade perfume phial dangling from one pierced nostril, intercepting the odours of manure and of bodies on which sweat had barely dried. The tattoo of a chained, burning daemon caged within a hex symbol writhed upon one chubby cheek while he spoke, guarding his mouth and porcine eyes from contamination. Usually the preacher wore loose black silks on account of the heat, which was only now draining away. For combat with evil, though, he must needs be suitably protected. A holstered stub gun hung from the amulet-studded belt around his rotund waist.

Horses snickered and stamped. Men patted their long knives for comfort, and the few who owned such, their rune-daubed muskets.

'Destroy the deviant!' shouted one fervent voice.

'Break the unhuman!' cried another.

'Kill the witch!'

Farb eyed the brawny, half-naked executioner who stood beside the wheel gripping a cudgel. As usual, the agent of retribution had been chosen by lot. Most townsfolk might sport wens, carbuncles, and other blemishes of their burnt skin, but few were feeble. Even if so, a puny executioner would only take the longer to perform his task to the tune of jeers and mocking cheers.

'Aye,' declared Farb, 'I warn you that this witch will try to slow down his punishment – stretching it out till nightfall in the vain hope of rescue.'

Spittle flew from the preacher's lips as if he was one of those mutants who could spit poison. Such a mutant had been rooted out a few months earlier, gagged, and broken in this selfsame square. The front ranks of Farb's audience pressed closer to the ebon steps, as if a drop of spray from the preacher's lips might keep their vision clear, their humanity intact.

Farb turned to the standard of the Emperor, which flanked him. The townswomen had painstakingly embroidered in precious wires an image copied from the preacher's missal. When Farb genuflected, his audience hastily bent their knees.

'God-Emperor,' chanted the preacher, 'oh our source of security. Protect us from foul daemons. Guard the wombs of our women that wee mites are not twisted into mutants. Save us from the darkness within darkness. Oh watch over us as we carry out your will. Imperator hominorum, nostra salvatio!' Sacred words, those last, powerful hex-words. Farb snorted through one nostril, spat saliva at the crowd.

Jomi gazed at the standard. That age-old Imperial face was a mask of wires and tubes, which the metallic embroidery persuasively evoked.

'Begin!' shouted Farb.

The wheel, which was powered by a massive, firmly-wound spring, started to turn. It carried the witch around, his limbs bent into a half-hoop. The executioner raised his club.

Nothing happened. The wheel stood still. The stalwart was frozen. Though forewarned, the crowd groaned. The spectators were outside the small zone of hoodooed time cast by the doomed witch; they could still move about – yet hardly a body moved.

'At this very moment,' Farb explained, 'the witch may well be calling out with his mind to some vile daemon – leading it here, showing the way to Groxgelt.'

Jomi wondered whether this was true. If so, why not slay the witch speedily with a knife as soon as they were captured?

Maybe the preacher relished the ceremony for its own sake.
Certainly such a spectacle riveted the crowd and dramatised
their deepest fears. Otherwise, people might grow careless, no?
They might fail to report suspicions of mutants in their midst.
A mother could try to protect a child of hers who only seemed
slightly twisted.

Though wouldn't the permanent presence of the wheel in the
market square put such fear into hoodooists that they would
try their utmost to hide their witching ways, and not betray
themselves? Jomi puzzled about this.

The timeless moment ended. As the delayed cudgel
descended cracklingly, the witch screamed. Time paused once
again in his immediate vicinity. Presently another blow fell,
crushing flesh and snapping bone. Due to his futile evasions the
witch did indeed take much longer to be broken, and would
take longer to hang draped around the wheel, slowly dying in
utter pain. Though what else could the wretch have done?

'Praise the Emperor who protects!' cried the paunchy
preacher. 'Laudate imperatorem!' His leatherclad breasts and
belly quaked. He panted as he sniffed perfume, blood, excrement and sweat.

Each time that a new blow fell, Jomi felt a fierce itch at a different location inside the marrow of his own bones, as if he
was experiencing a hint of that excruciating punishment
through the filter of a pile of pillows. He wriggled and
scratched uselessly...

OVER THE COURSE of the next year a dozen more witches and
muties died in the square of Groxgelt. A few of the more vocal
townsfolk began to ask in their cups whether there could be
some sickness unique to the human seed, which did not plague
beastkind. Mares did not give birth to foals which developed
strange powers as they matured, did they now? Jomi's father,
who was a tanner of lizard hides, discouraged any such speculation under his own roof; and Jomi had long since learned to
hold his tongue. Preacher Farb encouraged the townsfolk as
well as terrifying them. He promised that the Emperor would
not let his people drift into chaos.

On Jomi's seventeenth birthday, he dreamt the first dream.

It seemed that a mouth was shaping itself inside his brain. It
was forming from out of the very substance of the grey matter

within his skull. In his dream he knew that this was so. If only he could turn his dream-eyes backwards, he would see the lips deep within his cranium and, between them, the lolloping tongue that was responsible for the soupsucking sounds he heard in his sleep.

Terror gripped him in the dream. Somehow he couldn't awaken till those internal lips had finished their slobbery mumblings and shut up.

Over the course of the next several nights those interior sounds came more closely to resemble words. As yet these words were too blurred to understand, but they seemed to be coming clearer, almost as if adjusting themselves to the words that Jomi knew.

Jomi shared a poky garret room with his elder brother, Big Ven. Naturally he did not enquire whether Ven dreamed of a similar voice, nor whether Ven ever woke in the wee hours and thought that he heard a whisper coming from within Jomi's brain. Always the wheel stood in the market place as a warning. Jomi sweated as he slumbered. His straw palliasse was damp each morning.

'Am I becoming... unhuman?' he asked himself anxiously.

Maybe he was only experiencing nightmares. He dismissed any notion of consulting Reverend Farb. Instead he prayed fervently to the Emperor to dismiss the mumblings from his mind.

EACH BLUE DAWN, along with a band of fellow labourers, Jomi walked out of town to the grox breeding station and farm. Stripped to his loincloth and charm necklace, he toiled in an annexe of a slaughter shed, sorting offal.

'You're lucky,' his short sturdy mother often told him. 'Such a soft job at your age!'

This was true. The big reptiles were notoriously vicious. If they had not provided meat that was delicious to eat and highly nourishing, and if they had not been so well able to nourish themselves on any rubbish tossed their way, even soil, any sane person would have steered well clear of them. Although the breeding specimens were kept sedated with chemicals, a beast might still go berserk. When penned alongside its fellows, that was the natural inclination of a grox. The meat-stock were lobotomized. When being driven to the slaughter, even these brain-cut brutes could prove fractious. Any grox-herdsman or butcher could lose a finger or an eye, even his life. Virtually all bore disfiguring scars. The rulers in Urpol, the capital city an unimaginable hundred kilometres away, demanded an endless supply of grox meat for their own consumption and for profitable export. Refrigerated robot floaters carried the meat to Urpol.

'You're well-favoured,' Jomi's mother had also told him, more than once. This was true too. Jomi was clean-limbed and clean-featured, unblemished by the cysts and warts which afflicted most of the population.

It was the farmer's wife, tubby Galandra Puschik, who had assigned Jomi his cushy billet. Madame Puschik would often wander through the offal shed to ogle Jomi slicked with blood and sweat. Especially she would loiter by the farm pond to leer at him when he was washing off after a day's work. Oh yes, she had her eye on him. But she was too scared of her bullying husband to do more than look.

Jomi had his own eye set wistfully on the Puschiks' daughter, Gretchi. A slim beauty, Gretchi wore a broad straw hat and carried a parasol to shade herself from the bright blue sunlight. She turned up her pert nose at most of the town's youths, though she favoured Jomi with a smile when her mother wasn't watching; and then his heart would beat fast.

From occasional words he and she exchanged, he knew that Gretchi's sights were set upon becoming mistress to one of the lordly rulers in Urpol. But maybe she might care to practise with him first.

That day, while Jomi sorted grox livers, kidneys, and hearts, the mouth within his brain began to speak to him clearly, caressingly.

'Be calm,' it cooed. 'Don't fear me. I can teach you much you need in order to survive, and to gratify your young desires. Aye, to survive, for you are different, are you not?'

'What are you?' Jomi thought fiercely; and even then he resisted the impulse to speak out loud, and risk being overheard by a fellow worker. Was the languid voice male, or was it female? Perhaps neither…

'What are you, voice?'

'Before you can understand the answer, you need to learn much. Tell me: what shape has your world?'

'Shape? Why, it's all sorts of shapes. It's smooth and rocky. It's up and down–'

'Seen from afar, Jomi, seen from afar so that hills and valleys are as nothing. Seen by a bird flying higher than any bird has ever flown.'

'I guess… like a plate?'

'Oh no… Listen, Jomi, your world is globular like an eyeball. Your world is a big moon that swings around a giant world wholly made of gas, which is an even bigger eyeball. Your blue sun is the hugest eyeball hereabouts.'

'How can that be? The sun's so much smaller than the giant.'

'But hotter, hmm? Have you never wondered why it's hotter?'

'Sure I have.'

'But you thought it wiser not to ask, hmm? Wise, Jomi, wise.' How the voice fondled him.

'You can ask me without fear. Your sun is so vast that its own weight burns it. It's a star; and so far away that it looks like a thumbnail at arm's length. As I myself am far away from you, my Jomi.' The voice seemed to sigh. 'Indeed, much further than your star.'

Jomi continued sorting the slippery, reeking entrails into different trays. 'It can't be a star. The star-lanterns are tiny and cold.'

'Ah, innocent youth. The stars aren't lanterns. Let's take this step by step, shall we? Your moon and your sun and the stars are all spherical in shape.'

'Spherical?' What words this voice knew, such as the lords in Urpol might use.

'Circular. Think loudly of a circle floating in empty space.'

'I'd rather not!' A circle was the shape of a wheel, the terrible taboo wheel. No man must make any wheel, nor use one save for the punishment wheel, or else witches would triumph and rule the world.

'Calm yourself, sweet youth. The wheel is the beginning of knowledge. I will tell you why, if you will concentrate on imagining a circle. That helps me to… focus on you.'

'Focus?'

'To see you, as through a lens.'

'What's a lens?'

'Ah, you have so much to learn, and I will be your secret teacher.'

When Jomi washed himself later, Galandra Puschik stood with hands on giant hips surveying him as if he was the next day's dinner; and to his horror he overheard her thoughts...

She lusted to run her meaty hands all over Jomi. She yearned to kneed him like dough then bake him like bread in her hot embrace. Farmer Puschik would be going on a business trip away from the farm some day soonish. Then she would enjoy the boy...

Jomi could hear thoughts. It was as if the voice in his head was massaging muscles of his brain that had been puny as threads till now; was tickling sensation into nerves of his mind that had previously lain loose, causing them to knot and knit.

He could hear thoughts. Therefore he was a witch.

'Be tranquil,' the voice advised. 'Yet think loudly of the circle. Thus I can find you. Thus I can save you, my bewitching boy.'

For many days the voice told Jomi about the pleasures and beauties of the wider universe beyond his farming moon where there was only toil and sweat and fear.

The delights and glories that the voice described seemed somehow like memories of memories, echoes of echoes, as if the experiences in question had occurred too many years ago to count, and the voice no longer quite understood their nature, yet felt compelled to recount them even so.

IN THE CABIN of the space cruiser *Human Loyalty*, Inquisitor Torq Serpilian brooded about the paradox which had begun to haunt him. He keyed his coded diarium and spoke to it.

'It is a week since we emerged safely from warp space, benedico imperatorem. We are in orbit around the gas-giant Delta Khomeini V.' Beyond the quatrefoil tracery of the viewport the huge orange ball of storming hydrogen and methane held on an invisible leash the crescent of a single large moon that gleamed with atmosphere.

'Propositum: for millennia past, our undying Emperor has defended humanity against psychic attack from the warp, so that – one far-off day – humankind can evolve psychic powers puissant enough to protect itself...'

Battle banners hung from ochreous plasteel walls which were the hue of dried blood. Bleached alien skulls and captured armour were mounted as trophies. For this was a ship of the Legiones Astartes, the Space Marines.

Yet aliens as such rarely worried Serpilian. Even the most devious of aliens were, after all, natural creatures born and bred in the same universe as humankind. Aliens were as nothing compared with the terrible parasites that dwelled in the warp. On Serpilian's home world a certain unpleasant wasp would inject its hooked eggs into the flesh of beasts and men. Warp parasites could lay their equivalent of eggs in human minds. Those 'eggs' would hatch into entities that controlled the body, consuming it and using it to spread contamination. Other warp creatures could seize human souls and drag them back into darkness to feast upon, slowly. And there were far mightier daemonic entities too.

Psyker-witches were beacons shining into the warp. They attracted parasites and daemons that could lay waste a world and make its people unhuman.

'Subpropositum: wild, unguided, wayward psykers must be sought out by our Inquisition and destroyed.

'Counterpropositum: so as to nourish our Emperor, hundreds of fresh young psykers must daily sacrifice their souls – aye, gladly too – to feed his own huge anguished soul.'

Yes indeed, emerging psykers were sought out avidly and sent to Earth by the shipload. Those of high calibre, who could be trained to serve the Imperium, were soul-bound to the Emperor for their own protection, an agonizing ritual which generally left them blind. Exceptional individuals such as Serpilian were allowed to guard themselves mentally. The cream of such free psykers became inquisitors. Yet daily hundreds of those transportees to Earth, duly guided in the blessings of sacrifice, were yielding up their lives in the sucking gullet of the God-Emperor's mind. And elsewhere throughout the galaxy, untamable psykers were being exterminated as witches.

'Paradoxus: we root out as weeds what we cannot harvest. Yet whether we harvest or root out, the new crop is largely crushed, in so far as is within our power. How then can humankind evolve that independent future strength it so desperately needs?'

Serpilian imagined a meadow of grass being trampled repeatedly for millennia. He visualized new green blades struggling up into the light only to be flattened remorselessly lest they feed the malevolent creatures of the warp.

Would the Emperor eventually relax his crushing pressure by permitting himself to die? Thus allowing the grass suddenly to sprout up straight and tall and strong, a crop of superhumans?

Yet until that wonderful epoch, utter repression?

'Let me not become a heretic,' murmured Serpilian. 'I must not.' On reflection, he erased this last entry.

During Serpilian's career he had encountered situations sufficient to persuade him of the Emperor's wisdom. He had been a party to enough acts of harshness; had been the initiator of such deeds of necessary savagery – most recently at Valhall II, where enslavers had been invading from the warp and instigating a fierce insurrection against the Imperium.

'The universe,' he told his diarium, 'is cruel, savage, unforgiving. A battleground. And the darkest enemies hide in the warp, like tigers ever ready to pounce on the human herd. If one of that herd attracts the notice of a tiger, the rest of the herd may be ravaged – or worse, possessed and twisted obscenely into evil.'

Was not Serpilian himself thus forced at times to act like a beast, presiding over atrocities in the service of a tyrant?

Serpilian did not exactly pride himself on his independence of thought. He rather regretted such intrusions of doubt. Still and all, these qualities produced a certain flexibility and ingenuity, thus best serving the cause of the Emperor and of the human race.

His attire reflected that independent demeanour. He wore a long kilt of silver fur, an iridescent cuirass suggestive of the shell of a giant exotic beetle, and a blood-red cloak with a high collar. On both forefingers he wore rare jokaero digital weapons, one of these a miniaturized needler, the other a tiny laspistol. Orthodox guns were always secreted about his person. Amulets jangled round his neck, making exorcistic music as he moved.

Serpilian was tall, dark and lean. His drooping black moustache resembled some insect's mandibles. On his right cheek was the tattoo of an ever-watchful eye.

Long before the cabin door opened to admit Commander Hachard, Serpilian expected his arrival. The inquisitor was a powerful senser of presence, who knew where everyone was within a generous radius. An unusual offshoot of this sense allowed him to anticipate intrusions from the warp. That was why *Human Loyalty* had come to the Delta Khomeini solar system. Shortly after leaving Valhall II, Serpilian had dreamed of a sickly-sweet coaxing voice that was neither man's nor woman's cajoling a bright young mind far far away; and that young mind was... special, in a way that the young Serpilian's had been special, only more so, much more so, it seemed. Thus, even across the light years, and through the immeasurable fluctuating currents of the warp sea, Serpilian heard... something that resonated with his own psyche; that plucked at his instincts, as if threads of dark destiny bound him direly to that mind and to that eerie, seductive voice.

A casting of the runebones by Serpilian in tandem with a Imperial tarot divination performed by the ship's navigator had indicated the blue star that was fourth brightest in the constellation of Khomeini...

'We are in orbit around the parent planet,' Hachard reported respectfully, with only the merest hint of reproach, which he would hardly dare voice. 'I thought it diplomatic not to order our captain to orbit the moon itself till I had presented our compliments by commnet to the governor.' Scar tissue on Hachard's chin stood out whitely as though he had been punched. His cheek-tattoo was of a skull skewered by a dagger. His teeth were painted black as a signal that any smile of his was dark. A vermilion badge of nobility – a stylized power-axe – adorned his right knee-pad modestly so that, whenever bending to the Emperor's image during devotions, he should kneel upon this heraldic honour. His gloved hand strayed to the Imperial eagle emblazoned in purple on his lavender dress cuirass, as if to emphasize his unquestioning loyalty.

Serpilian knew that the commander would far rather have returned to the Grief Bringers' base after the action on Valhall II, to take their dead home and to renew their strength.

Even Grief Bringer Marines had been hard put to quash the enslaver disorder. Losses had been heavy. Only three platoons of the warriors remained. Perhaps the Valhall mission should best have been entrusted to one of the redoubtable Terminator teams, but none had been available. Truly, the resources of the Imperium were stretched thin. En route to Delta Khomeini, during a refuelling stopover at a high-gravity world, Serpilian had commandeered the services of two platoons of ogryn giants as a fighting supplement; also, of a lone tech-priest, for the Grief Bringers had lost their tech-magus on Valhall II. It was an uneasy mixture.

'Yes, that's sensible, commander,' said the inquisitor. 'And have you presented my compliments yet?' Thus did Serpilian emphasize his personal authority, at a time when he nevertheless felt beset by doubts.

'That I have, my lord inquisitor. Governor Vellacott felt obliged to mention that he maintains adequate planetary forces in case of alien attack, and that preachers on that moon root out any psykers fiercely.'

'Would you describe him as an independent-minded governor?'

'Not obstructively so. We are welcome to land and investigate.'

'Just as well for him.'

'He suggested that we wouldn't need too many Space Marines to cope with a moonful of farmers, where there isn't even any obvious threat.'

Serpilian snorted. 'The level of threat is for me to decide. The worst threat is often the threat that hides itself.'

'The governor suggested – most politely, you understand – that it might be beneath our dignity to blow human rabbits to pieces. I wonder whether he has any inkling that our strength is depleted? Perhaps his court astropath somehow eavesdropped on ours; though I rather doubt it. I suspect he has some guilty reason to fear for his dynasty.'

'Such as irregularities in Imperial taxes?'

'The Vellacotts control the finest grox farms in this celestial segment. Much of the meat and other produce goes to Delta Khomeini II. That's a barren mining world, producing rare metals for our Imperium. Perhaps there are secret financial arrangements.'

'Which are none of our concern.'

'I implied as much, without saying so.'

'Ah, a Marine commander needs many skills, does he not?'

'I thank you, my lord inquisitor.'

Serpilian felt obliged to ask, 'How goes morale?' For the Grief Bringers had also lost their chaplain in action on Valhall II.

Hachard hesitated.

'Be frank. I will not be offended.'

'The ogryns... they stink.'

Serpilian attempted an injection of humour. 'They are famous for stinking. If one cannot tolerate some body odour, how can one bear the stench of scorching flesh in combat?'

'My men will fight alongside the abhumans, with honour. But they don't like it much. Having to share a ship with those Stenches. I suppose, my lord inquisitor, you insisted on pressing the ogryns into service because, being abhuman and frankly thuggish, they're more expendable.'

Serpilian winced momentarily. What Hachard implied was perilously close to unthinkable impertinence; yet Serpilian had invited the commander to be outspoken, had he not? The loss of so many brave fighters in the earlier action – however justifiable – was a slight blot on the inquisitor's personal escutcheon of honour. Marines would willingly sacrifice their lives. They were not, however, suicide-berserkers. To replace them with 'expendable' abhumans somewhat smeared the pride of the Grief Bringers, amounting almost to an error of judgement on Serpilian's part.

One did not polish a fine sword with mud, nor repair a broken one with wood.

Muttering a brief prayer, Serpilian unclipped a pouch from his belt. Breathing deeply and slowly to induce a light trance, he cast his rune bones upon a desk of polished black wood. Those finger and toe bones, minutely inscribed with conjurations, had belonged to a rogue psyker mage whom the Inquisition had executed five centuries earlier. Now these relics served Serpilian's psychic sense. They were a useful channel for his talent, a focus.

As he concentrated, the pattern of white bones against black swam until a foggy picture formed, visible to him alone.

'What do you see?' whispered Hachard reverently.

The thought drifted through Serpilian's mind, like some seductive siren song, that it wasn't totally unknown for an inquisitor to sicken of his harsh duties and flee to some lost world, some primitive pastoral planet or other.

Not one such as this moon, certainly! The inquisitor resumed his breathing routine.

'I see a strapping, comely boy. Though his face isn't clear. I see the circle of a portal opening from the warp, and coming through it is… abomination.'

'What species of abomination? Enslavers again?'

A sensible question. The warp entities known as enslavers could open a gateway through the very flesh of a vulnerable psyker and spill out – to do as their name suggested.

Serpilian shook his head. 'The boy's being given an aura of protection now to hide him. He's somewhere within a hundred or so kilometres of the capital city. He's becoming a powerful psychic receiver. Other psychic talents are sprouting in him. I think he's about to be possessed. Unless we reach him first.'

'To capture him, or destroy him?'

'I fear for his potential power. One day perhaps,' and Serpilian sketched a pious obeisance, 'he might be a little like the Emperor himself. Just a little.'

'Not a new Horus, surely?' What loathing crept into the commander's voice as he uttered the name of the corrupted rebel Battlemaster who had betrayed the Imperium, and besmirched the honour of so many Space Marine chapters, long long ago. 'If that's the situation, maybe the relevant quadrant of the moon should be sterilised… though that would include Urpol city and the spaceport, and many grox farms. Delta Khomeini II would starve as a consequence… And the moon has orbital defences as well as its surface troops, who would fight us… They won't have much battle experience. I think we could do it. I think. Perhaps with our last drop of blood…'

'Let us pray it doesn't come to that, Hachard, though your zeal is commendable.'

'What is finer than death in battle to defend the future of mankind?'

'If we are in time, this boy must needs be a gift to our Emperor, for His own divine wisdom to judge. Let us head for that moon as soon as our present orbit permits.'

Serpilian uttered a silent prayer that his inner eyesight might pierce the veil that now partially hid the boy.

'THINK OF THE circle,' crooned the mouth within Jomi's head. 'It grows larger, larger, does it not?'

The boy watched a floater of grox meat depart from Puschik farm. The engine and cargo section were spattered with mystic runes to help hold the vehicle in the air and encourage the robot brain to find its way to the city. Those runes had recently been repainted. If runes faded or flaked off the hull, the floater might stray from its course or its chiller unit might fail.

Clouds of flies buzzed around a couple of sledges on which piles of scaly hides, some barrels of blood, and sacks of bones were setting out for the much shorter journey to Groxgelt, there to be rendered into glue, and sausages, and crude armour. Whips cracked, slicing through the aerial vermin to tickle the draught horses into action. The runners creaked across stones worn smooth by centuries of such local transport.

No, thought Jomi, the floater would only break down if it hadn't been 'serviced' properly. The meat-transporter was only a machine, a thing of metal and wires and crystals, based on ancient science from the Dark Age of Technology.

Courtesy of the voice, Jomi knew now that former ages had existed, unimaginable stretches of time unimaginably long ago. The current age was a time of 'superstition,' so said the voice. An earlier age had been a time of enlightenment. Yet that bygone era was now called dark to the extent that so much had been forgotten about it. So the voice assured him, confusingly. He mustn't worry his pretty mind overmuch about foul daemons such as Preacher Farb prated about. Such things existed, to a certain extent, that was true. But enlightenment was the route to joy. The owner of the voice said that it had been captured by the storms of 'warp space' long ago, doomed to wander in strange domains for aeons until finally it sensed a dawning psyker talent that was peculiarly attuned to it.

'You aren't a witch, dearest boy,' the voice had assured him. 'You're a psyker. Say after me: I'm a psyker, with a glorious mind that deserves to relish all manner of gratifications. Which I, your only true friend will teach you how to attain. Say to yourself: I'm the most lustrous of psykers – and remember to think of the circle, won't you?'

The owner of the voice would come to Jomi. It would save him from the entrail shed. It would save him from the crushing embrace of fat Galandra Puschik and from the terror of the wheel.

'Soooooooon,' cooed the voice, like the coolest of evening breezes. 'Always think of the circle – like a wheel rolling ever closer to you, but not a wheel to fear!'

'Why have we been taught to fear wheels?' An inspiration assaulted Jomi. 'Surely our sledges would run more easily if we used... a wheel on each corner? Four wheels which turn around as the sledge advances!'

'Then it would be called a wagon. You're such a bright lad, Jomi. Bright in so many ways.'

Of a sudden, the voice grew sour and petulant. 'And here comes spurious brightness to cheer you.'

'Gretchi!'

Her slim limbs, mainly hidden by a coarse cotton frock, yet imaginable as fair and smooth... her breasts like two young doves nesting beneath the fabric... her chestnut hair hanging in ringlets, mostly veiling a slender neck... the huge straw hat shading that creamy complexion... the teasing eyes of a blue so much less daunting than the sun: how could such perfection have issued from Galandra Puschik's hips? Gretchi twirled her pink parasol coquettishly.

Did he gawp?

'Whatever are you thinking, Jomi Jabal?' she asked, as if inviting him to flatter her naively – or even vulgarly, to excite her.

He swallowed. He muttered the truth. 'About science...'

Gretchi pouted. 'Would that be the art of sighing for a girl, perhaps? Fine lords will sigh for me in Urpol some day soon, believe me!'

Could he possibly tell her his secret? Surely she wouldn't betray him?

'Gretchi, if it were possible for you to go much further away than Urpol–'

'Where's further than Urpol? Urpol's the centre of everything hereabouts.'

'–would you go?'

'Surely you don't mean to some farm in the furthest hinterland?' She wrinkled up her nose pettishly. 'Surrounded by muties, no doubt!'

He pointed at the sky. 'No, much further away. To the stars, and to other worlds.' She laughed at him, though not entirely with derision. Perhaps this good-looking youth could tickle her fancy in unexpected ways?

Should he whisper in her ear, arranging a rendezvous after work to hear his secret?

'Remember the cruel wheel, Jomi,' warned the voice.

'When you come, voice, can I take Gretchi with me?'

Did he hear a faint, stifled snarl in the depths of his mind?

Gretchi simpered. 'Are you pretending to ignore me now? Are your feelings hurt? What do you know of feelings?'

He stared at the twin soft birds of her bosom, yearning to cup them in his hands. But his hands were soiled with blood and bile. The memory came to him of Gretchi's mother feeling Jomi assiduously in her foetid imagination, exploring and squeezing him, and out of the corner of his eye he noticed Galandra Puschik glaring from the veranda of the farmhouse. Gretchi must have spied her mother too, for she promptly flounced away, turning up her nose as if at some foul reek.

'STRANGE...' GRILL, THE tech-priest, said to himself. 'A world that bans wheels! Strange and many are His worlds!' The priest reached inside his hood to scratch the side of his head, sweat and the coarse material of his cowl were irritating his implant sites.

Grill scanned the cavernous plasteel dormitory through his dark-lensed eyes. Imperial icons gleamed, each lit by a glow-globe, sharing wall space with cruder battle-fetishes of the giants, one of which was draped respectfully with a ram's intestines from the arrival feast the night before. Scraps of meat, hair, broken bones littered the floor, mashed into the semblance of a brown and grey carpet on which assorted insec-toid vermin grazed, or lay crushed themselves.

The dormitory had ceased to reek; it had transcended stench, attaining a new plane of foetor as though the air had trans-muted. Stinks did not usually perturb Grill, but he wore nostril filters.

'Hmm...'

The ogryn, 'Thunderjug' Aggrox, quit sharpening his yellow tusks on a rasp.

'Woz matter?'

Sergeant-Ogryn Aggrox was a BONEhead, who had under-gone Biochemical Ogryn Neural Enhancement. Thus he was capable of a degree of sophisticated conversation. Could be trusted with a ripper gun too.

Grill, hot and uncomfortable in his heavy wool robes, sur-veyed the crudely tattooed megaman in his coarse cloth and chain mail. Several battle badges were riveted to the giant's thick skull.

'I suppose,' said Grill, 'being forced to walk or ride draught horses keeps the peasants in their places, doesn't it?'

'Seems use floaters, though,' objected Thunderjug.

'Oh well, you need to hurry fresh meat to the spaceport and up into orbit to be void-frozen. Banning wheels seems a little harsh... I guess in this neck of the galaxy the wheel represents the beginning of dangerous thoughts...'

These musings were of course too complicated for the BONEhead ogryn to follow.

The giant plucked a thumb-sized louse from his armpit and crunched the grey parasite speculatively between his teeth. Just then, ogryn voices bellowed.

Two warriors had bared their tusks. Seizing mace and axe respectively, they began to hack at one another's chainmail in a bellicose competition. Spectators roared wagers in favour of one combatant or the other, or both, stamping their great feet so that the steel dormitory rocked and groaned.

Thunderjug lowered his head and charged along the dormitory. He butted left, he butted right with his steel-plated skull. The quarrellers resisted, butting back at their sergeant, though not disrespectful enough to raise axe or mace against him. Finally Thunderjug seized the two by the neck and crashed their heads together in the manner of two wrecking balls till the fighters subsided and agreed to behave.

'Shu'rup all!' After issuing that command, Thunderjug ambled back, spat out a broken tooth, and grinned. 'Gorra keep order, don' I?'

Grill removed his fingers from his ears. Would he have been happier billeted with the more than human Grief Bringers? Undoubtedly more comfortable; less liable to be squashed by a reeling heavyweight. On the other hand, he had come to count on Thunderjug as something of a friend, a brainy bull among this herd of buffalos.

Grill hadn't too much experience of Space Marines; there weren't all that many in the galaxy. But they seemed a shade cliquish. Exemplary fellows, needless to say, but so devoutly dedicated to the traditions of their chapters.

From whichever angle, the galaxy was a fairly menacing sprawl of mayhem. Grill decided to strip and clean his boltgun; muttering prayer chants under his breath all the while.

'You were born under warped stars, Jomi,' sighed the voice. 'Once, the warp seemed merely to be a zone through which our ships flew faster than light. Oh we were innocent then in spite of all our science! Naive and callow as lambs, such as your sweet self.'

Jomi shifted uneasily. Of late, a cloying stickiness had begun to creep into the accents of the voice at times. As if his informant realized this, its tone grew crisper.

'But then all over the galaxy that we had guilelessly populated, psykers such as yourself started to be born.'

'So there weren't always psykers around?'

'By no means to such an extent. When the powers and predators of Chaos took heed of those bright beacons, they spilled into reality to ravage and warp the worlds.'

'Those powers are what Preacher Farb calls daemons?'

'As it were.'

'Then he's right in that respect! You said I shouldn't worry my head about daemons.'

'Your sweet head... your puissant mind...'

From the low scrubby hillside Jomi stared towards the huddle of Groxgelt. At this hour the south pole of the gas-giant seemed almost to rest upon the headman's mansion and the Imperial temple as though that golden ball would crush and melt the biggest buildings that Jomi knew. The sun's blue radiance ached. Due to a trick of light and wispy clouds, a bilious greenish miasma – the colour of nausea – seemed to drip from one limb of the hostile parent-world upon the town.

A skrak flew overhead, seeking little lizards to dive upon, and Jomi sat very still until the unpleasant avian discharged a tiny bomb of acidic excrement elsewhere.

'Ah comely youth, guard your skin,' came the voice, which could spy through his eyes.

'Does Chaos make our sun breed wens and carbuncles on our flesh?' Jomi asked.

'Oh no. Your sun is rich in rays beyond violet. You've been fortunate to resist those rays yourself. You'll be even luckier when I reach you.'

'How does Gretchi know to wear a wide hat and carry a parasol?'

'Vanity!'

'Does she have an extra sense to tell her?'

'If so, she needs it. In other respects she appears senselessly empty-headed.'

'How can you say so? She's so beautiful.'

'And presently she will sell what you call beauty, but only as a minion and a toy; only till she withers.'

'Beauty must mean something,' protested Jomi. 'I mean, if I'm fair and I'm a psyker... isn't there any connection, voice?'

From far away Jomi seemed to hear a stifled cackle of laughter. 'So you subscribe to the theory that body and soul reflect one another?' Heavy irony coloured the reply. 'In a dark sense that's often true. Should Chaos seize a victim, that victim's body will twist and warp... if body there be!'

'How can a person not have a body?'

'Maybe one day you'll learn – how the spirit can soar free from the flesh.' Was the voice telling him the truth? And how could that be the road to ecstasy, whatever ecstasy really signified?

As if agitated, the voice began to ramble. 'I was one of the earliest psykers back in the epoch when true science gave way to strife and anarchy... Oh the madness, the madness... I was marooned. Our ship malfunctioned... it died in the warp. All through the dark aeons since, I've heard the whisperings of telepaths from the real universe. I've eavesdropped on the downfall of civilization and on its grim and terrible, ignorant revival... I could never escape. I lacked a beacon that cast a suitable light.'

'How long do aeons last?' Jomi still had very little idea.

For a period there was silence, then the voice answered vaguely, 'Time behaves differently within the warp.'

'Has your body been warped at all?' asked Jomi.

Again, that distant cackle... 'My body,' the voice repeated flatly. 'My body...' It said no more than that.

Phantom gangrene dribbled from the gas-giant.

SERPILIAN PRAYED. 'In nomine imperatoris... guide us to the golden boy that we may 'prison him, or rend him, or render him unto You, as You wish. Imperator, guard our armour and our gaze; lubricate our projectile weapons that they do not jam. Bless and brighten the beams of our lasers; fiat lux in tenebris...'

And cleanse my vision too, he thought. Pierce that aura of protection which cloaks the boy; and tear away any cataract of doubt.

The depleted ranks of Grief Bringers knelt cumbersomely in their bulging, burnished, insignia-blazoned power armour, which was principally a dark pea-green, with engrailed chevrons of headachy purple. Visors raised, they gazed intently at the inquisitor who wore borrowed vestments, of the slain chaplain. Green chasuble; purple apron filigreed with the emblem of the chapter. The long mauve stole dangling from Serpilian's neck to his knees was embroidered with aliens in torments. Amulets and icons chinked and clinked.

'I have decided I shall bless our ogryn warriors too,' Serpilian murmured to Hachard, who knelt beside him. 'Ogryns are men too. After a fashion. A blessing does not depend on the receiver but on the giver. Does a laspistol possess a brain, commander? A spirit, yes! But a thinking brain? Ogryns have spirits.'

Thus, at this sacred moment, did he condone his decision to dilute the strong wine of the Marines with the crude ale of the barbarian giants. Serpilian could guess what the commander might be thinking. 'Not on my ship they don't have spirits. A few bucketsful to drink, and the place would be wrecked.' Or maybe this was only Serpilian's own guilt speaking to him. That he, a survivor, should be wearing the vestments of a chaplain who had fought the enslavers so fiercely.

The assembled Grief Bringers' eyes shone with pious dedication. All this, to hunt for one boy... Serpilian's instinct still told him that this mission mattered deeply. If only his vision was clearer! The very veiling of his insight suggested that he and the Space Marines faced a powerful adversary and might win a great reward.

To Hachard, he whispered, 'Ogryns and Space Marines must be as one body under your command. The former are not simply battering rams. If I do not bless them, we all fail in reverence.'

Would the Grief Bringers' slain chaplain have blessed the loyal, stout Stenches too? Hachard twitched, but of course made no objection.

'Benedictio!' Serpilian called out loudly. 'Benedictiones! Triumphus! Let your watchword for this mission be: Emperor-of-All.'

'Emperor-of-ALL!' the Grief Bringers chorused in response.

As Serpilian quit the assembly area, he vowed to redouble his exertions to sense the ambiguous presence of the boy. His rune bones continued to thwart him almost as if in conspiracy with the power that was aiming itself at the boy; almost as though those bones were enacting a five-hundred-year-delayed vengeance upon the Inquisition which had stripped the flesh from them.

Very well. He must dispense with their aid. He must use sheer mental discipline. He must attempt to put himself into the boy's frame of thought – for there was a link of destiny between himself and his quarry, was there not? He must detect the boy by that ploy.

He must forget all that he himself knew of the Imperium. He must erase all that he knew of the arcane wisdom of the Inquisition, garnered over millennia of terrible experiences and steadfast purity and, in Serpilian's case, some decades of duty.

He must imagine himself born on a farming moon. He must visualize his brain coming into bloom with bizarre petals – unseen by his fellow peasants – petals that served as esoteric psychic radar dishes, with unfurling stamens acting as antennae of the mind; each of these stamens tipped with pollen that would prove tasty to a daemon or a predator.

He mustn't ask himself: where precisely is this flower growing? Instead he must ask: how is this flower feeling right now?

He must identify with what he would pluck and present to the Emperor. He must imitate his prey. By that expedient he might dispel the psychic mist.

Why, if he concentrated sufficiently well on pretending to be such a boy he might even distract whatever malign force was homing in – as though a heat-seeking missile were presented with a glowing decoy.

But first…

Serpilian had paused deep in thought in a corridor braced with mighty ribs and muscled with black power cables. Now he strode onward to the ogryn dormitory.

He ignored the stink, which was really no worse than the odour of many burst bowels; so he told himself. He disregarded the vermin underfoot, which were really akin to diminutive, edible pets.

'Benedico homines gigantes!' he cried out.

'Shu'rup ogryns!' bellowed the BONEhead sergeant, snapping to attention.

As Serpilian rattled through his litany of blessings and invocations all he received from the bulk of his congregation by way of responses were grunts and belches. These noises might, nonetheless, be signs of ogryn piety. The lone tech-priest, head bowed devoutly, smiled sympathetically.

The engines of *Human Loyalty* were beginning to whine and its hull to wail. The cruiser was at last descending through the moon's atmosphere.

Concluding with a final resounding Imperator benedicat, Serpilian fled to his cabin and stripped off those chaplain's vestments.

Activating the viewscreen in its wrought-iron frame of death's heads and scorpions, he stared at the flickering, swelling vista of Urpol city below. The spaceport was a flat grey medal pitted with blast-pads. Spires sprouted like thickly waxed hairs. Suburbs were stubble, roads were wrinkles zig-zagging away into the sallow lumpy skin of the landscape. A snaking blue vein was a river, a lake was a haemorrhage, farms were bruises.

He knelt and thought: I am a strange flower growing somewhere in that land. My lurid, secret petals are ears that hear voices on the psychic winds. My pollen smells luscious to parasites…

He too had once been a strange flower, had he not?

Born into the salubrious upper tiers of the hive city of Magnox on Denebola V, young Torq had been torn between a taste for learning and a sensual nature. Both, of course, were facets of the search for new experiences.

Yet whereas a youth who seeks solely for madder music, stronger wine, stranger drugs, wilder girls, and for the thrill of danger may presently become a poet or a master criminal or some such deviant, he is much more likely to burn out, to run his adolescent course, and to settle thereafter into self-indulging conformity.

Whereas a studious youth may develop into a useful – even a brilliant – drudge.

Put the two together in one skin, though…

Torq's father was chamberlain to one of the noble houses of Magnox. So naturally, soon after puberty, Torq had joined one of the fashionable and privileged brat gangs who rampaged and rousted in the latest glittergarb costumes, sporting black codpieces, grotesque jewellery, and plumed helmets fitted with krashmusik earphones. Who wounded and slew with power-stilettos which would spring a spike of vibrating, searing energy into the guts of a rival.

One night, during a raid on the lower tech levels of Magnox, Torq sensed for the first time the presence of ambush. A glowing, multi-dimensional map of human life-signs swam within his head, distorting, shot through with static, needing tuning...

Subsequently, in that mysterious multivalent map, he was to sense the eerie mauve glow of intrusions from the warp. He led the brat gang against a nest of psykers. These psykers were on the verge of being possessed by daemons. A rival gang were protecting them, and were making a playful erotic cult of them.

Had Torq's gang discovered those psykers first, events might have fallen out otherwise. Avid for thrills, the gilded youths from the upper tier might have made gang mascots of the psykers. Torq might have become a coven leader. Eventually, pursued by fervent witchfinders, he might have been forced to flee and hide among the scum of the undercity.

Yet events did not fall out in this fashion. Furthermore, Torq had studied and he knew the lineaments of the Imperium rather better than his fellow brats. He thought he understood the strength of its muscles and the way those muscles pulled. His gang bested the patrons of those psykers, who had been pampered and abused by turns. Along with those captured playthings he presented himself to the Ecclesiarchy as a would-be inquisitor; whereby he would enjoy the wildest experiences, within a learned framework.

He hadn't by any means relished all of his subsequent experiences; and sometimes he was dogged by doubt that he was betraying kin-of-his-mind, all be it out of a dire necessity that became increasingly clear to him during his years of training. Piety had become his prophylactic against twinges of remorse. Faith was his pain-soothing pill, his vindication. Torq still dressed as a dandy, one devoted to terrible duties; and his superiors had smiled – in their thin, astringent way – at such evidence of honourable excess.

'I am a flower, a flower,' he droned, breathing in trance rhythm.

Torq had been somewhat of an orchid to begin with. Whereas the boy he sought was a wonderful weed infesting some flyblown farm. Could he identify? A mauve glow polluted his inner map every which way, refusing to condense into a single signalling spot. That glow masked the brash young hues of the flower.

A fortified palace stabbed upwards, tilted by the angle of the ship's approach: towers, spiked domes, laser batteries. Other chateaux within walled gardens drifted by. Factories, abattoirs. Then a plain of ferroconcrete loomed.

Human Loyalty settled. The familiar throb of engines faded. A klaxon shrieked twice to signal the shutting down of artificial gravity. As the natural pull of the moon, which was a good twenty per cent weaker, replaced the generated gravity, so the ship creaked. The cruiser was at once relaxing and bearing down.

An inquisitor must bear down firmly without such inner relaxation. The gravity of this mission was, perhaps, extreme.

'I'M R-REALLY DEEPLY honoured,' stammered Reverend Henrik Farb. 'I never set eyes on a Space Marine before, let alone m-met a commander.'

And why should he have? If the Imperium comprised a million worlds, why, there were only a million Marines too.

Musky incense snaked inside the cavernous temple, wreathing icons and writing curlicues upon the air in what might have been the mad script of aliens. Farb, sweating, sucked in tendrils of that smoke like an asthmatic seeking soothing vapours to assuage a panic-stricken attack of suffocation. Candles flickered, contributing their own fainter odour of reptile grease.

This man, who had presumably terrified so many others, was terrified himself.

'Your respect honours our Emperor,' said Hachard. 'So does your dread. But now you must think clearly.'

The inquisitor had finally narrowed the likely area of search to a quadrant north of Urpol City. The Land Raiders that survived after Valhall II had sped forth on their cleated armoured tracks to the various towns in this zone, crushing the primitive roads, carrying Marines and ogryns. And it so happened that Hachard himself had come to this town of Groxgelt. If there was to be action, he wished to be as close as possible, not back at the ship awaiting reconnaissance reports.

How could he put this worthy preacher at his ease? 'Tell me,' he asked lightly, 'does the gelt in Groxgelt refer to cash, or to castration?'

Farb stared at his questioner as if he was being posed a riddle upon which his life depended. Could it be, wondered Hachard, that the preacher didn't understand all of his words? The man spoke decent Imperial Gothic; the dialect used on this moon was quite comprehensible.

'Never mind, preacher. Tell me this: what lad in this community stands out as in any way different?'

Farb's gaze dropped to the Grief Bringer's protruding groin-guard, of a verdigris-smeared skull transfixed by a purple dagger.

'Castration, I think,' he mumbled.

'Concentrate!' snapped Hachard.

'Yes... yes... there's one boy – never caused any bother – prays in the temple here – good worker, so I hear...' Farb licked his fat lips. 'Attends witch-breakings, though they seem to make him squirm... Son of the tanner Jabal. The boy has no visible deformities; that's the odd thing about him. He looks,' and the preacher spat, 'so pure. Lately he has been... going places alone, I hear.'

'How do you come by that information?'

'The wife of the farmer who employs him... I, well, I cherish certain feelings for that woman... between you and me as man to man...'

Hachard forbore to sneer at this attempted comparison.

'Nothing illicit on my part, sir... She's... a woman of substance, if you take my meanings. Perhaps if her husband is ever gored by a grox...'

'What of the boy?'

'Why, Galandra Puschik keeps her eye on him, as a good employer should. The boy speaks differently. His tone seems less... local. He uses the odd word she does not understand...'

As THE GRIEF Bringer strode back to the Land Raider after interrogating the terrified tanner and Goodwife Jabal, who made a better showing, and the hulking stupid son Big Ven, he eyed the ogryn BONEhead and the tech-priest sitting on the uppermost track of the vehicle. Zig-zags of pea-green and purple blotched the plasteel body and the track-walls, mounted with lascannon ball turrets, of the Land Raider, less suggestive of camouflage than of a sickly infestation by some poisonous lichen.

A cowed crowd of townsfolk were eyeing those who perched high upon the massive vehicle. The sprocketed wheels that moved the tracks were hidden from their superstitious gaze by the casings of armour.

For his men to have to mix with these scratching, farting, dumb-witted, sweating peasants. To have to try to tease some sense out of backyard gossip... After the costly victory over the enslavers – a perilous task that had almost proved beyond the Grief Bringers' reach – this present mission almost seemed designed as an insult, a reproof for losing so many comrades, however gloriously.

No, thought Hachard, that way heresy lies. I must trust the instincts of an inquisitor.

At least the fat preacher had understood well enough the power that Hachard and his men deployed, and the seriousness of the threat to humanity that must have brought such warriors here.

Hachard was fairly sure that he had located the prey they sought, while the inquisitor remained unable to pinpoint him. The commander permitted himself a slight, black-toothed smile, not of superiority but of grim satisfaction.

His return to the market square triggered a flurry in the gawping, fearful – and stupidly resentful – crowd. Yet most gazes flickered back quickly to the crudely clad ogryn atop the vehicle. The citizens of Groxgelt could see that the bulky Grief Bringer, with the visor of his helmet raised, was a true man. Did that passive mob of ugly specimens view the BONEhead as more intimidating than an armoured Space Marine? Or, in their squinty eyes, was the grotesque, prognathous ogryn someone to whom they could more easily relate?

Hachard entered the hatch of the personnel den where techcrew and other Marines awaited. The commnet crackled alive as he fingered its rune-knobs, its spirit kindling faithfully.

'Lord inquisitor,' he reported, 'I have identified possible suspect. Name of Jomi Jabal. Curfew approaches but boy has not returned home. Believed to be out by farm four kilometres north-west of Groxgelt town...'

One boy. Against whom: Land Raiders, lascannons, armoured Grief Bringers, and ogryns.

One boy... plus what else?

'I'm within twenty kilometres of you, commander. Am on my way. Don't let the noise of the Land Raiders alert our target. Advance the final four kilometres on foot.'

'Understood.' Hachard switched automatically to battle code to summon the other Land Raiders to rendezvous at speed across country, just outside Groxgelt.

He would have to wait a while, so he stepped outside again. The setting gas-giant peered over rooftops like the disembodied eye of some enormous cosmic parent-creature which was slowly withdrawing its witness from this world so as to allow a cloak of gloom to descend.

'This Land Raider. The armour's cracked. Needs welding.'

'You're a tech-priest. Paint another rune. Utter a charm.'

Grill muttered an unintelligible response from under the voluminous folds of his hood, triggering a brief flare of annoyance in Hachard, at a time when he should be composing himself reverently for combat. He glared at the tech-priest.

'Silence! In any case we shall be advancing on foot to begin with.'

Thunderjug guffawed like distant thunder.

'Sooooon,' the voice soothed Jomi. 'Welcome the circle into your mind.'

The voice had told him where to wait by the biggest grox paddock. Jomi glanced anxiously at the sinking gas-giant. Already the last of the gloaming was upon the countryside. Soon the curfew trumpet would scream out in town, and no one human would be abroad but himself. He would have broken the law.

If the owner of the voice did not come, what could Jomi do? Hide till morning? What, here where mutants might roam? For if muties did not enter the town itself, they might well haunt the open countryside.

Yet he was a mutant too. Why should other mutants be hostile to one of their own kind? Ah, but outcasts would surely be hungry. Jomi's flesh might smell sweet...

Sweet flesh reminded him of Gretchi. If nothing else happened tonight, he could stumble to the farmhouse. He might be able to climb to an upper window, Gretchi's, and tap for admittance.

Surely she would admire his daring in venturing out at night to see her? Surely she would reward him suitably? He ached to cup those white doves in his hands, and to explore her private nest of hidden hair, which itself hid...

'The circle! Think of that! Or I may lose focus.'

He thought of Gretchi's mouth open wide. He thought of another part of her opening to him, a soft ring, of whose exact shape and dimensions he wasn't quite sure.

'Forget that foolish minx! She's worthless. I can let you glimpse such lust-nymphs as will make her seem trite and dowdy. I can conjure lubricious courtesans from memory – ayeeee!' Such a pang of anguish and frustration seemed to afflict the voice.

Glimpsing...? And conjuring? The voice had promised to introduce Jomi to delights, not merely show him, as if spied through a window of thick glass.

'You'll be broken on the wheel if I don't reach you,' the voice threatened.

The wheel... Jomi jerked back to reality. What else was his whole life on this damned moon but wretchedness? Entrails and heat and fear and Galandra Puschik's lusts which she would insist on satisfying one day soon, crushingly and disgustingly. He was about to leave all this vileness behind.

Don't think of Gretchi again until after the owner of the voice arrives!

He forced her image from his mind. Wheel, circle; circle, wheel.

In the last golden light the horned, scaly, toothsome reptiles milled sluggishly in their corral. Each was the size of a small pony. Their claws clicked on the stony ground. Crop-land dipped away towards the river. Boulders, some the size of houses, punctuated the ridged oat-fields. Carried here by sheets of ice long ago, the voice had told him.

Jomi inhaled. He thought he heard whispers on the wind. He sensed minds: disciplined minds, almost completely shielded from him as if a firescreen stood in front of a blaze of grox dung. Yet some of the heat glowed through.

Could witches who were far cleverer than himself be creeping towards this place, attracted by the voice? No witches who had been broken in the square had ever seemed particularly clever. Of course, extreme pain reduced them to imbecility, to shattered bags of white-hot shrieking nerves, and little more than that. Could they ever have been clever to be captured? Compared with those wretches, Jomi had become educated... somewhat.

Maybe really clever witches had escaped and banded together in the furthest hinterlands far from farms and towns. Thus it had taken them months to trek here.

Jomi could also sense other minds nearby that were dull and slow and fierce. Was he hearing the thoughts of the groxen too? Surely not...

'Voice,' he questioned.

'Hush, bonny boy, I must concentrate. Oh it has been so long. Soon I will embrace you. Strive to see the circle in front of you.'

He mustn't fail the voice at the last moment; for thus he would fail himself. Nor must he scare it away by hinting at the presence of those other strange strong minds in the vicinity. Those, and the brutish minds. Obediently he imagined a circle and strained his eyes in the dimming light.

Yes!

A glowing hoop appeared, balanced upon the ground a few hundred metres away. Slowly it swelled in size, though it did not brighten. If anything, it grew dimmer, as though to evade scrutiny from elsewhere. Within the hoop was utter night, a darkness absolute.

THE FACT THAT the portal was coming into existence some distance away from the boy – and slowly – tended to rule out the activity of a warp creature. Warp creatures were usually impetuous in their attack.

Nor could the alien eldar be creating this opening. The eldar were masters of warp gates and such; they hardly needed the type of psychic focus that the boy seemed to be providing. As though anything on this moon could possibly interest the eldar!

This portal was opening almost painfully – if such a thing could be. Almost creakingly, as if its 'hinges' had rusted during long aeons of time. Obviously a warp portal didn't have hinges; but the analogy held.

Grief Bringers in power armour were spreading out under cover of the boulders. A gang of ogryns was lumbering into position in the almost-darkness.

'If we seize the psyker boy now...,' began Hachard, tentatively. 'We may scare whatever is coming. We must wait till the portal-maker steps through. We hunt for knowledge as well as prey.'

'Knowledge...' Did the commander shudder? 'In the Dark Age,' he murmured, 'they sought knowledge for its own sake...'

Serpilian said sharply, 'Only the Emperor knows what really happened during the Dark Age.' How the inquisitor wished that he too knew. Godless science had flourished back then. From time to time remnants were still found: precious, arcane techniques and equipment of utmost value to the Imperium. Long ago the human race had spread throughout the galaxy like a migration of lemmings – heedless of the beings lurking in the warp, for it was heedless of its own psychic potential. Innocents, innocents! Puppies in a daemon's den! Like a sudden storm, insanity and anarchy had erupted till the God-Emperor arose to save and unify, to control the human worlds, to calm the psychic tempest with utmost and essential rigour.

Here was a boy, of the possible future-to-be. Here was... what else? Serpilian extended his sense of presence, but mauve distortions dazed his vision.

A ROBOT HIGHER than any building in Groxgelt, a robot that bristled with what Jomi took to be weapons, lurched through the gate of darkness.

'Here I am, dearest boy,' exulted the voice in Jomi's brain. 'Don't fear this metal body. This is the shell that has sheltered the kernel of myself while I drifted alone for aeons in the warp in a derelict hulk. Now at last I can touch the soil of a world. Now I can hope to be a fleshly body once more. Oh the sweet endearing flesh, the senses that sing, the nerves that twang like harp-strings! And what song did they sing so long ago? Soooooon I shall remember.'

The robot took a tentative step towards Jomi. As if exercising limbs which hadn't encountered the pull of gravity for many millennia, the robot swept an arm around. Energies crackled from the tips of its steel fingers, gusting across the herd of groxen. The reptiles began to snort and hiss and rip at the soil of their compound, and butt their horns against the fence.

What fleshly body was the kernel of this huge machine hoping to be? As the juggernaut took another lurching step in Jomi's direction, he began to sweat. He crouched.

SERPILIAN SHOOK THE bag of rune bones at his waist so that he sounded like an angry rattlesnake, then switched on his energy armour. Beneath his cloak subtle forces wove a cocoon that clad his body, and his cuirass glowed faintly.

He too now heard that voice inside his own head, and shivered at the treachery which the ancient survivor must intend. It was hoping to seize control of the boy's brain and body, dispossessing his spirit, casting it into the limbo of the sea of souls.

The inquisitor stared at the giant gunmetal-grey relic, trying in vain to classify it. It was squatter than a Battle Titan, its limbs less flexibly jointed, nor did any obvious head protrude from the top of its chest in the way that control-heads jutted, turtle-like, from Titans. However, it looked almost as formidable. And what was more, it housed someone who had endured literally for aeons.

Serpilian knew of no mechanical system other than the Emperor's enormous immobile prosthetic throne which could sustain a person's existence for such a long time.

What remnant of flesh and bone could possibly lurk inside that mobile juggernaut? Only the head and spinal column of the castaway? Only the naked brain, bathed in fluids? Or maybe – could such a thing be? – only the mind itself, wrought within some intricate interior talisman by ancient eldritch sorcery?

That robot was treasure.

Its occupant hoped to steal a human brain which housed such great psychic potential, to add to its own psychic powers...

Whosoever controlled such a boy...

Serpilian suppressed within himself a tenuous twinge of traitorous ambition. Was he being corrupted by proximity to this monster from the past?

"Tis ever this way,' Hachard commented grimly. 'A thin line confronts the foulest enemies. Yet, thank Him on Earth, that line is stronger than a diamond forged in a supernova. Permission,' he requested, 'to summon the Land Raiders?'

'Yes. Do so. But only as a reserve. I don't wish the robot destroyed utterly.'

Hachard radioed in battle code.

As the two men stood under a sheaf of stars, a voice called out.

'Sir!' It was the tech-priest, accompanied by the ogryn BONEhead. 'Surely that's a robot from the early Age of Strife!

The portal must lead to a space hulk in the warp. Where else could such a robot have lurked? That hulk could contain a wealth of ancient technology.'

'Yes,' agreed Serpilian. 'I do believe that's so.'

At that moment the curfew trumpet shrieked from afar, as if that tocsin were the signal for battle.

'Commander, disable the robot. Shoot off its legs.'

Hachard rapped out orders. Almost immediately plasma and laser beams stitched the deepening night. Yet the beams glanced away, deflected by some shield – or even by an aura of invulnerability.

For the mind within that machine was potent, was it not? Had it not had mad, lonely aeons during which to examine and hone its powers?

The robot's own inbuilt lasers and plasma cannon fired back, tracking the sources of the energy beams. At the same time a wave of confusion lapped at Serpilian's mind. The creature in the robot possessed psychic weaponry too, so it seemed.

Perhaps something else shared mind-space with the occupant of that plasteel refuge, something that one wouldn't exactly classify as human company...

Serpilian had seen to it that the Grief Bringers wore protective psychic hoods. Still, in that first onslaught two Marines broke cover impetuously, rushing directly towards the robot. Their suits glowed, then incandesced. The overload filter in Hachard's radio stole away their screams. Another brave man took advantage of the diversion to advance at a powered run from a different direction, clutching a melta-bomb. He was obviously hoping to sacrifice himself by detonating this against one of the robot's feet, thus destabilizing it. Plasma engulfed him; the night erupted briefly as the bomb's thermal energy gushed prematurely, liquefying his suit. The Space Marines quickly resumed more disciplined fire.

As Serpilian squinted at the flaring, stroboscopic scene, he could tell that the robot had halted, though it showed precious little sign of disablement. Beams simply slid off it, bouncing away into the sky.

A grim hill hove into view, then another.

'Land Raiders arriving on station,' said Hachard. 'If we aim their lascannons at one leg in concert we should bring it crashing down soon enough.'

'What if the shielding and the aura hold? Even temporarily? Fierce energies will recoil unpredictably. The boy may be evaporated in the backlash. If the lascannon beams do break through, the robot might explode.'

Couldn't Hachard guess at the value of this artefact from elder days? Maybe not. He only saw a present menace to the Imperium. Of all those present, save for Serpilian perhaps only the tech-priest realized...

The inquisitor could hardly confide in him. Indeed, he might need to silence the man.

Once again, Serpilian felt a thread of heretical temptation insinuating itself within his soul, and muttered a prayer. 'Asperge me, God-Emperor. Cleanse me.'

'Permission, sah,' requested the sergeant-ogryn. 'My men... strong. We charge at the robot? Wrestle it on to its side?'

Hachard laughed; and it occurred to Serpilian that the wave of confusion might have affected the minds of the ogryns peculiarly. Unlike the Space Marines, the abhumans had been shielded only by their own dense skulls and by their brutish, if violent, thought processes. The confusion might only now be surfacing in their brainiest representative, the sergeant.

'Why not?' said the commander. 'Listen carefully, sergeant: send all your ogryns round to the north side. Yes, in that direction. Over there. Then you come back to report. As soon as the Marines cease fire, your ogryns must charge. Do you understand?'

'Yus, sah.' Thunderjug stomped over to his troopers and bellowed at them for a while.

'Couldn't one of them scoop up the boy?' suggested Grill.

'They'd probably tear his head off by mistake,' snapped Hachard.

'Um... Commander, sir.'

'What is it now, Grill?'

'Isn't a charge by the ogryns a mite suicidal?'

'Not necessarily,' intervened Serpilian. 'The robot replied to fire with fire. But the ogryn charge might confuse it. I take it that that's the commander's intention, rather than him implying that his hands are being tied.'

'Hmm,' said Grill.

Thunderjug returned and stood to attention.

* * *

JOMI CLUNG TO the ground in terror as the air blistered above him.

'They'll need to change their tactics,' advised the voice. 'A lull must come – and I think I can cause a diversion. When I say run, sprint to me as fast as you can, ducking low. I can take you inside this body. I can transport you back through the portal. Better the warp than death, don't you think?'

The sizzle of lethal beams almost convinced Jomi.

Almost.

'I shall save you, Jomi, save you. I am your safety...'

The voice began to drone hypnotically, bewitchingly. It promised joys, it promised lusts, fulfilments – yet seemed savagely bewildered as to what these might be. Did Jomi hear a background hint of crazed laughter? His body twitched, puppet-like. He threw up his hand reflexively, and a low, stray laser beam seared his wrist superficially. The pain jerked him free from the growing enchantment, plunging him again into a terrain of terrible fear.

'Are you man or woman?' he gasped.

'I hardly remember.'

'How can you not remember such a thing?'

'It became unimportant... Yet a ghost reminds me of the flesh! A goading wraith within. Ah, Jomi, Jomeeee, I know so much, and am so separated from all that I knew. My ghost cries for a body to caress and sculpt to its desire... Come to me soon, Jomeeee, when I call–'

FROM THE VOICE'S moaning words Serpilian gathered ample confirmation that its owner had been a psychic eavesdropper on millennia of war-torn history and even of hidden pre-Imperium history. How the inquisitor thirsted for its knowledge.

But the ancient survivor was also, he strongly suspected, possessed.

Possessed by a daemon of the warp.

This was an unusual species of possession, for the survivor plainly owned no body at all, other than the vast metal body of the robot. The survivor consisted only of mind, wrought within a talisman of crystal wafers or some other occult material, a talisman which strove to maintain the stability of that mind – strove with a fair degree of success, considering the awesome timespan, yet of necessity imperfectly. The daemon had no tangible flesh to twist and warp and stamp its mark upon. It could only lurk impotently, glued to the imprisoned mind, tormenting it spasmodically by stimulating memories and sensuous hallucinations. Maybe the goad of the daemon was what had prevented the survivor from lapsing into sloth...

The voice spoke of science. The truth was corruption. Conclusio: its science was heresy.

Serpilian must not thirst for that!

And now that the castaway's dark scheme to possess Jomi had failed – a cursed, daemon-inspired plan! – the survivor was intent on at least carrying the boy back into exile with it.

At Hachard's command the Grief Bringers ceased fire.

JUST AS THE ogryn squad was commencing its assault, the robot aimed a plasma blast low at the grox compound, crisping several beasts yet also tearing a long gap in the fence. Serpilian sensed the aura of venomous intent which the mind in the robot – daemon-assisted? – directed at the reptiles to stir their blood lust.

Ripping at one another, groxen burst free of their captivity and rapidly were attracted towards the thundering giants. All plasma and laser fire had ceased. The psyker boy staggered erect and stumbled towards the robot; seeing which, Serpilian let out a cry of frustration.

'Catch that lad for the Emperor, Thunderjug!' shouted Grill, as if he was a commander. 'And don't pull his head off unless you have to!'

No appeal could mean more to an ogryn. Tossing his encumbering ripper gun aside, Thunderjug Aggrox bared his tusks and pounded towards the distant youth. The tech-priest stumbled after it, doing his best to keep up, encumbered as he was by his heavy robes.

Careless of his own safety, Serpilian loped after it, blood-red cloak streaming, the very image of avenging angel. The boy must be stopped! A hatch was opening in the lower casing of the robot to welcome the lurching youth.

Just then, the stampeding groxen met the charging ogryns. The insensate animals leapt, clawed, bit, and gouged. They tore chunks of flesh, yet an ogryn hardly heeded such trivia. Ogryn fists smashed grox skulls.

However, the robot noticed the boy's pursuers and swivelled a weapon arm, opening fire with a raking of explosive bolts. Serpilian dived flat. Ahead of him, the ogryn's mighty legs pounded onward for a dozen more strides before the giant crashed to the ground. The tech-priest struggled past; his hood blown back by the wind, implant cabes flapping. Then a blast grenade, launched from a tube in the robot's arm, exploded near him. The shockwave picked the priest up and threw him several metres.

Sprawled on the stony dirt, Serpilian stretched out his right arm, forefinger pointing the jokaero needler. One needle in the boy, and he would be paralyzed. The range was somewhat extreme for such a tiny, lightweight dart. The target was moving. The inquisitor strove to aim.

At that moment, when Jomi was barely twenty metres from the inviting hatch, he halted.

A PSYCHIC MAELSTROM of savagery and pain whirled around Jomi. The death-shrieks of those who had died, the berserker fury of ogryns as they fought the reptiles, the terror of all the energy beams and explosions... these suddenly culminated. A lurid radiance seemed to flare in his mind, as if doors were flying open, behind which fierce furnaces raged, cauldrons of inchoate energy.

'Jomeeee! You've almost reached meee! Run just a little bit more and leap inside meee!'

Looking up at the towering machine, Jomi suddenly perceived it – by that blazing light from within him – not as a mountain of metal in approximately humanoid shape, but as...

...A VAST, NAKED Galandra Puschik looming over him lustfully. Her legs were squat trunks. The hatch was her secret opening. Her enormous torso, thick with fat, writhed with desire to entertain him. Her great muscular arms reached out...

'Jomeeee! My dearest delicious boy, my joy–!'

What confronted him was a robot again. Yet the light from within him did not cease. It changed hue and wavelength, so that he peered appalled into the world of what-might-be...

ASSISTED BY A tentacle, he had leapt into a womb of steel, a metal pod barely large enough to stand up in. The tentacle withdrew, and he was thrown upon the floor as the robot rocked, starting to march back towards the portal, brushing aside the brawling bodies of brutal ogryns and rabid groxen. Its cleated feet crushed deep craters.

The hatch was descending, to close him in.

Through it, while still open, by the resuming, spasming light of energy beams Jomi glimpsed a man in glowing breastplate and blood-red cloak – a thin, tall man with a drooping black moustache and a staring eye tattooed upon his cheek – sprinting frantically towards the decamping robot.

Jomi could hear the man's thumping thoughts. 'Even if I can paralyze him... too late to drag the boy out...! At least cling to some handhold on the robot... Don't lose it entirely, or all has been in vain... Accompany it, willy-nilly, through the doorway of darkness...

'Will there be air on the other side of the portal? Will all atmosphere have long since leaked out of the hulk? Will there be only vacuum, to boil my blood and collapse my lungs like empty paper bags? My energy armour will be no protection from that fate...'

The hatch closed, plunging Jomi into utter obscurity and silence. The body that carried him lurched and swayed.

Presently little lights winked on. Jomi hugged his own body protectively. How could he escape from this pod? Surely he couldn't live inside this miniature chamber even if the machine fed him? He imagined the narrow floor aswill with his urine, in which nuggets of excrement bobbed.

'Welcome to my kingdom,' the voice purred. Bitter mockery tinged the accents Jomi heard in his mind. 'Our kingdom, now–'

('Mine tooo...') A malicious, disappointed echo seemed to haunt the voice, perhaps unheard by it, perhaps all too familiar. ('Failure, feeble failure... But here's a soft body at least...')

The lid of a small porthole slid aside. Jomi pressed his face to the thick plascrystal as floodlight beams lanced from the robot. He stared at a great grotto of metal, from which several steel tunnels ran away into stygian gloom. Strange machines jutted from the plated floor and from the ribbed walls. A debris of loose tools and cargo floated like dead fish in a dank pond.

'There's one other such machine as mine on board,' the voice confided, as if oblivious of the soft, sinister echo that Jomi had heard. 'It has been inactive for millennia, lacking a person's mind to fill it, but I can revive it now. With my science, I'll put you into it. First, of course, I'll need to cut away your body–'

('That'll be an exquisite hour or so…')

Jomi vomited in terror.

'Soon, before you use all the air I sucked in on that moon. Once you're activated we can play games. Hide and seek, for instance… You'll need to rely on the resources of your lovely mind. At least I'll have company now. Oh the madness, the madness. Maybe my imaginary companion will go away. Into you, maybe…'

A figure in a blood-red cloak drifted into view, out in the giant grotto. Its frozen arms stretched out vainly towards a vista which, prior to the flare of illumination, it couldn't possibly have seen.

WHAT-MIGHT-BE – and might still be – vanished.

Jomi still stood before the robot.

'Daemon, daemon, hidden daemon!' he shrieked at it. He spat. Reaching into his memory for an incantation, he recalled Farb's prayers, and howled: 'Imperator hominorum, nostra sal-vatio!'

'Jomeeeee! Do not betray meeeee!'

The white-hot cauldron inside Jomi spilled over. The inner furnaces, so suddenly revealed to him, gushed psychic fire. Hardly knowing how, he sprayed a fountain of defensive men-tal energy, ill-focused yet incandescent, at the voice, which would have betrayed him.

'Nostra salvatio, hominorum imperator!'

'Aiieee!' cried the voice, keening through his head like a scalpel blade attempting to sever the sinews of his new-found psyker ability, raw and unshaped as yet.

Recoiling, his brain in agony, Jomi nevertheless summoned another spout of hot repulsion to hurl at the robot.

THE BOY'S RAW power! And his piety too, albeit born of terror! Bathed in the backwash of inner light from the volcanic upheaval within the boy, with his own senses extended Serpilian had partaken of Jomi's vision of what-might-be.

As if an actor in Jomi's dream, the inquisitor had experienced the death-agony of passing through the portal. Of collapsing lungs. Of utter, absolute chill… He had also known Jomi's claustrophobic, dreadful dismay. Moments later Serpilian found himself still sprawled on the battlefield; and the battlefield was a blessed place by contrast.

Scrambling up, Serpilian signalled back towards Hachard, hoping that the commander could see and would understand his gestures. Then he resumed his reckless run towards the boy who was holding the robot at bay, like a rat defying a bull. He no longer pointed his jokaero needler.

Casting his own aura of protection, Serpilian seized Jomi by the shoulder.

'In the Emperor's name, come with me to safety! Come swiftly, Jomi Jabal!'

HACHARD MUST HAVE understood. As soon as Serpilian had hauled the boy to some reasonable remove, and had ducked with him behind a boulder, the lascannons of the Land Raiders opened fire. Shaft upon shaft of searing energy lanced at the robot. The Space Marines added their contribution. Wounded ogryns scattered, abandoning the remaining groxen which had been preoccupying them.

Had the giants not engaged with the savage reptiles, by now one of those might have attacked Serpilian or the boy.

The robot launched jets of plasma and energy beams. A Land Raider exploded, raining hot shards of plasteel. Several Marines fell victim to beams and jets. The Imperial energies cascaded off the robot's shields, pluming into the sky, rendering the landscape bright as day.

Yet now the robot seemed confused. It backed. It lumbered. Perhaps the mind within was anguished. Perhaps, infected by Jomi's vision, it imagined that it had passed safely back through the portal, though the nightmare evidence was otherwise. Perhaps it was running low on energy.

At last an Imperial energy-beam tore loose a weapon arm. Another beam pierced the vulnerable hatch. Part of the robot's mantle flared and melted. Still firing – but falteringly now, seemingly at random – the great, damaged machine stomped back towards the portal. Land Raider beams focused in unison upon its back, so that it seemed to be propelled in its retreat by a hurricane-torn, white-hot sail woven from the heart of a sun.

As it entered the portal, the robot incandesced blindingly. A detonation as of a dozen simultaneous sonic booms rocked the torn terrain. Glaring fragments of the robot's carapace flew back like angry boomerangs, like scythes. The bulk of its disintegrating body pitched forward, out of existence, vanishing.

SERPILIAN DEACTIVATED HIS energy armour, and Jomi, smeared with dirt and stinking of sweat, wept in his arms.

'I shall,' vowed Serpilian, 'recommend you for the finest training – as an inquisitor yourself.'

The boy cried, 'What? What? I can't hear! Only the awful terrible thunder.'

'Your hearing will return!' Serpilian shouted into the boy's streaked face. 'If not, that can be repaired with an acoustic amulet! One day you will serve the Emperor as I serve him. I came a long way to find you!'

AFTER A WHILE, Jomi listened to Serpilian's thoughts instead and began to understand. This cloaked figure had come a long way to find him. Why, so had the voice; so had the mind, and the daemon, in the robot...

Jomi would be sent far away from the wretched moon, to Terra itself. He thought fleetingly of Gretchi; but as the voice itself had suggested, that kind of yearning seemed to have become extremely insignificant.

GROANING AND RUBBING his head, Grill wandered back to where the BONEhead lay sprawled; but it was undeniable that Thunderjug's whole skull, including the riveted battle honours, was missing. The tech-priest touched the toppled giant reverently on the shoulder.

Bilious-hued power armour loomed. Commander Hachard himself stood over the ogryn.

'I watched him charge,' said Hachard's external speaker. 'The other subhumans remain alive – I think so, by and large – but not their sergeant. The Grief Bringers are... honoured, by his bravery.' Ponderously, the Space Marine commander saluted.

What about me, thought Grill? I nearly got blown to pieces. But he said nothing. It was Thunderjug who was dead.

Bending, assisted by the tech-priest, Hachard dragged the ogryn's corpse into his powered arms.

As Grill gazed up at the indigo sky, the stars stared back down at him blindly. The portal had disappeared a while since, yet a tremor seemed to twist the night air, warping the heavens. Or was the distortion due to moisture in his eyes?

MONASTERY OF DEATH

Charles Stross

TENZIG DIDN'T REALIZE what was going on until he viewed the book in the crypt beneath the library, but when he did it began to come clear. And it didn't make a nice picture.

He was still hunched over the fading screen of the viewer hours later, when the master of the secret arts passed by his booth and touched him on one shoulder with the tip of a finger. Tenzig turned in his seat, then looked up enquiringly. The master beckoned, and Tenzig forced himself to his feet. The world seemed to be spinning around his tired head as he followed the master out of the silence of the scriptorium and into the echoing brightness of the pentagon. The condition of silence was lifted, but even so his lips were too dry for speech. 'Why?' he croaked.

The master spared him a brief, enigmatic glance before turning back to the path. 'White noise,' he said, gravel crunching beneath his sandals. The day was dry and mild, the clouds overhead masking the starglare into a lambent glow that washed all trace of shadows from the scene, so that they seemed to walk through liquid light.

'You will join me in my retreat,' the master said, rubbing his shaven scalp with the heel of one hand, as if the enlightenment

of ages required the polishing of flesh. 'Such things are not...
fit for conversation in public. Perhaps some novice, overhear-
ing these matters, might panic. Perhaps the sky might fall...'

Perhaps, perhaps, Tenzig thought. 'Perhaps' was the holy word
of the order, an admission of doubt in the face of overwhelming
probability. The master might equally well say, perhaps not. The
facts, as Tenzig saw them, were absolutely terrifying.

The Imperium was returning.

THE MASTER'S RETREAT was high in the north tower of the
monastery, one of the oldest buildings in the complex and,
indeed, one of the oldest on the planet. Cold-chiselled blocks
of stone had been placed atop one another without mortar,
their massive weight holding them in position. The clement
weather and lack of quakes in this area had allowed them to
last for a long time; hundreds of generations of monks had
lived, toiled and died beneath the gaze of those high windows.

That was not to say that the retreat was austere. His master
had many rooms, floored and walled in polished parm-wood
that had achieved a dark, glossy finish through centuries of
rubbing. The furniture was of greater antiquity than Tenzig's
ancestry. And it was into this environment that the master of
the secret arts led his postulant and offered him hospitality.

'Please be seated,' said the master as Tenzig slid shut the
screen door behind him and stood, uncertainly, in the portal.
A thin smile flitted across the master's face as he strode over to
the window and looked out. With measured movements his
eyes scanned the horizon; then, as if satisfied, his fingers rested
for a moment on a concealed spot on the window frame.
Tenzig stared with fascination as his silhouette shifted: where
behind him there had been landscape and sky, now there was
only a glowing plane of light.

'A randomizer,' his master said, still with that faintly knowing smile. 'We are safe from eavesdroppers, for the time being.'
He moved to the wooden reading-throne beside the window
and sat in it, hands resting on armrests polished black by generations of his predecessors in office. 'Now, Tenzig. Perhaps you
are ready to report to me what you have seen, so that I can con-
vey the joyful tidings to brother abbot?'

Tenzig shifted in his seat. The cushion beneath him felt unnat-
urally soft after years of meditation on polished wooden floors.

'I fear that there are scant glad tidings for the master of temporal administration,' he said hesitantly. 'As you suggested in your wisdom, I consulted the archives for reference to this ancient body of lore. The old paper archives, the chronicles of the ancients; not the true library. It would appear that at one time the Bodies Secular were visited on a regular basis by an overlord from beyond the sky; while he claimed high office, he claimed that others ranked higher yet than his exalted person. Such taxes as he extracted he took in their name. Insurrectionists were dealt with cruelly, but the last such visit occurred many centuries ago: before the time of the foundation of our order, even before the near stars went out. The texts say little on the matter of the Imperium he claimed to represent, save only what we already know – and that none can stand against such force.'

He fell silent, and the only noise in the retreat was the faint soughing of the north wind outside the walls. The master of the secret arts, those arts upon which the monks had depended for their defence across the centuries, bowed his head in silent contemplation. Tenzig felt fear. If he had caused even the master of the secret arts to despair, a man who possessed such awesome powers that it was whispered that he could cause a leaf to wither by blowing on it, the implications were barely worth considering.

I am a channel, he recited to himself in silence: a stream through which the water of history can flow. I cannot obstruct, I cannot distort, and with the passage of my life I enlarge the channel a little, so that my successors can expand it further. This was the catechism of the Order of the Heavenly Virtues, who defended wisdom in a world so plainly lacking in it – and that branch of the order known as the secret arts, who defended the defenders of wisdom. Tenzig shivered, feeling the roots of his being bend in an unholy tempest of doubt. For if the master could not see a solution, what hope was there for such as he?

The power from beyond the sky would brook no rivals. And, through force of circumstances, the order might almost be one...

The master's head snapped up, and Tenzig froze before his gaze like a small bird before a snake. Eyes of utter blackness seemed to drill right through his soul. His muscles tensed in reflex and he found himself unable to move.

'Never think that we are endangered, Postulant Tenzig,' said the master, mildly. 'There are no absolutes, even for gods. I have much thinking to do, and little time left. Tell me,' he added, his hands fiddling with the bulbous armrests, 'what do we know of the theosophy of those who come from the stars?'

Tenzig blinked. 'They believe in absolutes,' he said. 'Absolute power and absolute evil, and absolute ignorance. They are trapped in the cycle of their own eternal turmoil, and they will subject us to it if they can. They accept only mindless accession to their cant... with which our uncertain dogmas might be–'

'Stop.' The master held up his right hand. 'Your bias is becoming intrusive. Have you learned nothing?'

'No, master.' Humbled, Tenzig bowed his head; rueful self-doubt tugged at him. Have I been colouring them with my own daemons, he wondered?

'The Imperials are undoubtedly inimical to the order,' pronounced the master, 'but to act in haste is worse than not to act at all.' He stood. 'There will be a concillium of the masters, when brother abbot will make his determination. And then we shall see how to deal with the outsiders.' He smiled. 'Perhaps, even with the Imperium, there will be a way.'

JUDIT GLANCED FROM the swirl of stars to the planet through the observation deck window, indescribable thoughts circulating in her head. A billiard-ball of white mist, it was totally feature-less from orbit; it reminded her of her home-world, except that Neuss-Four had been grey rather than creamy white, and every-one on it had died shortly after her departure. Her abduction. Recruitment, rather. She grimaced at the recollection and looked back to the globular cluster, shifting her grip on the free-fall grabrail.

The starswarm was magnificent, a diadem of stars that gleamed across half the sky and drowned the Milky Way with its brilliance; but it was the magnificence of a jewelled cata-comb. During the Age of Strife, entire suns had disappeared into warp space: the frozen husks of a thousand civilizations drifted between the stars. How this world had escaped was beyond understanding, but now that it had been rediscovered, it would be the job of this mission to purge it of deviationists and mutants, and then install puppet rulers to support the Imperial demands.

'Another dirtball, eh?' said Joachim Ahriman, grinning humourlessly at her. He stood behind her, a slim figure clothed entirely in form-fitting blackness, the lightweight armour of a member of the Adeptus Arbites, the order of judges. 'Just another flyblown wasteland full of nomads, I shouldn't wonder.'

'Possibly not,' she murmured. 'When's the report from the preliminary probe due in?'

'Shortly.' Joachim fell silent, also contemplating the world – but from his own perspective of elevated disdain. Joachim considered any world not of the Imperium to be barbaric, its inhabitants barely more than animals. It was a failing, Judit thought. Even barbarians could display sophistication and indirection... which was why they were here. An assassin and a martial priest of the Adeptus Arbites, sent to support the Inquisitor in his reassertion of power over the lost worlds of this cluster, of which Hito was but the seventh in priority.

She pursed her lips as she glanced at him. Why did they have to saddle me with an intolerant fanatic like this? she thought. Surely no one could be this crude? Perhaps it's an attempt to discredit me...

A tone rang out from the annunciator: Joachim answered it. 'Yes?' he said impatiently.

'This is the Holy Office – we have cleared the preliminary probe. Reports are coming in of an indigenous civilization, some techlore, a native government. Would you care to examine them?'

Joachim snorted, but Judit spoke over his shoulder, 'I'll be up shortly.'

'Tell me if they can talk,' he called out after her as she went up the tube into the body of the ship. 'Tell me if they look human!'

She shook her head as she climbed the decks towards the Holy Mission. A government to deal with delicately, and she was going to have to do it saddled with a blunt instrument like Joachim. What kind of bloody mess was he going to make of this one? Then a different thought occurred to her. Perhaps it could be turned to her advantage.

ON LEAVING THE presence of the master, Tenzig returned to his cell. He changed his loose, dark habit for the white woollen surplice of a postulant, then composed himself for meditation.

He was not surprised when, presently, a visitor knocked on his door; moving to open it, he was confronted by a young novice.

'The abbot would see you,' he stammered at Tenzig, eyes wide at the prospect of attracting such attention. 'I am to take you...'

'Then lead.'

Deep in thought, Tenzig followed the boy through the passages of the monastery, out into the open pentagon at the heart of it, and across to the white tower where brother abbot and his staff controlled the day-to-day destiny of the order.

The burden of foreknowledge was heavy on Tenzig as the novice brought him to a halt outside the wide, thick doors of the tower. The boy stopped and looked up at him. 'I am not allowed to go any further,' he said. 'You are to proceed from here alone.'

Tenzig paused, nonplussed. Presently he grinned. Not waiting to see if the boy would go, he turned to the door and rapped hard on the rough surface with his right hand. Invisible eyes stared at him, and presently the door opened.

'Postulant Tenzig,' said the sallow-faced monk behind it, 'you are bidden enter. May your stay bring honour to the order.'

'And may its days be long,' Tenzig replied with an inclination of his head. The door-keeper stepped back, admitting him, and shut the portal. Tenzig looked around, ignoring the strangely fashioned weapon that the monk held loosely. Bare, polished stone and solid black iron: an architecture of war. But of course. The knowledge of the Order of the Heavenly Virtues was its treasure, and during times of trouble the order's reputation was not always an adequate defence.

'You are to come this way,' said the gatekeeper, beckoning Tenzig towards a staircase. They made their way up winding flights of steps and along landings floored in wood that creaked loudly, beneath narrow slots in the ceiling; Tenzig marvelled at how vulnerable the tower was. Presently they arrived in a surprisingly small room, and the gate-keeper took his leave. In all this time, Tenzig had seen not one other person, but now the door slid open and brother abbot himself entered the room.

'Tenzig,' the abbot said, voice grave and totally assured. 'The master of the secret arts has assured me that you aspire to membership of his branch of the order, and all that that entails – to membership, moreover, with mastery. You know that such rank can only be earned?'

'I do,' he replied, throat suddenly dry and tight. The room seemed to be closing in, constricting his chest so that the beat of his heart pressed against the walls themselves.

'Then know this,' said the abbot, 'if you succeed, today, you will achieve just such mastery with glory. But if you fail, far more than this order will revile you. The world will curse your name; legions unborn will suffer for your failure.' He looked away, a half-amused expression on his face. 'I have confidence in you, Tenzig. Your master says that it is justified. Will you accept this burden, at risk of your life?'

Tenzig paused, and the room seemed to focus on him with a thunderous silence. 'I will,' he heard someone say in the near-distance, and realized that it was himself. The abbot smiled grimly.

'Good. Then this is how we shall deal with the dragon...'

THE SCRIBE READ from a text that flopped across his lectern like an expired snake, limp but still fanged and deadly. 'The planet is in a state of intermediate civilization, supported by the presence of records left over from an STC source. Only one continent supports a human population, and there are no nations as such, but a number of warring factions and duchies. A broadly feudal system pertains outside of the religious orders, with homage paid to a ceremonial king by the warlords, who compete for temporal leadership. The tech-records are maintained by a monastery: the Order of the Heavenly Virtues.'

The scribe paused, frowning as if the taste of the words which were to follow were bitter in his mouth. 'The cult of the Emperor is extinct on this world, if indeed it ever existed here. Two religions coexist; one is a superstitious animism based on the sky and the forces of nature, while the other is a broadly philosophical cult which maintains the monasteries – our scouts, to their credit, were unable to understand the basic tenets of the heresy. The cults are both widely respected and the monastic orders in particular are large and almost as powerful as the warlords – perhaps because they control the supply of advanced goods on this world.'

He glanced up from his scroll. 'It would be a mistake to assume because the predominant level of civilization is primitive that these people have no subtlety or machinery. The complexity of their life may hide many details, and I would advise extreme caution in dealing with them, other than from a position of unassailable power.'

He looked down and, presentation at an end, began to roll up his scroll. Judit glanced round at the rest of the audience. Inquisitor Rathman, charged with the responsibility of returning the worlds of this cluster to Imperial rule, looked abstracted; gloved fingers twisted his signet ring from side to side as he waited for the scribe to finish.

'A question,' he said, tapping his fingers on the arm of his chair. 'The STC source – how much do we know about that?'

The scribe shook his head. 'Very little, I'm afraid. The natives refused to talk about it to our agents. But this is a primitive world, by and large. All the libraries of tech-information that we know of were destroyed during the Age of Strife. The odds say that these monks work from records of parchment – but they could contain details of devices long forgotten, bizarre arcana beyond the ken of any – save only the Emperor himself,' he added piously.

Joachim, present as head of the detachment of Adeptus Arbites aboard the fleet, shook his head angrily. 'This whole world is like a can of worms,' he said. 'Little warlord wrigglers waiting to go on the hook one by one. Unless there's a faster way to bag them we could be here forever!'

The inquisitor shook his head. 'That's not acceptable, Joachim. Not at all. We must establish control over this backwater, and swiftly. We need a weak point.'

'There is anarchy down there,' said the clerk. 'The scouts could find no integrated hierarchy – kill one warlord, and another will rise to take their place.'

Judit was staring into space. An opening, she mused; yes, I need an opening. Secret knowledge. A library… The STC library, if there really was one here, would be ideal. Such computerized libraries, relics of the Dark Age of Technology, contained incalculable wisdom vital to the works of the Adeptus Mechanicus – but all the known ones were damaged in some way, and there were so few of them left. If she could find one…

'Our assassin would appear to be lost in a pleasant dream,' Joachim said drily. 'Perhaps our esteemed colleague would be prepared to give us the benefit of her insight?'

Judit turned her eyes on him. For the entire voyage he'd been sniping, little abusive derogations, nasty gibes at the expense of the Assassins' Guild. Relations between the monolithic Adeptus Arbites and their secretive, independent rivals – the Imperial assassins – were far from friendly. She stared at him, pupils narrowing to the semblance of gunsights, until he looked away.

'There is a weakness,' she said determinedly, 'and one which is wide open to action by my team. My team, you understand.' She looked at the inquisitor, who watched her with saturnine interest. 'I can deliver this world to you on a platter,' she said. 'Along with the library, which won't be of use to anyone if we wind up bombing it from orbit!' She glanced at Joachim. 'It should be obvious that we have a perfect lever to bring them into line, of their own accord. Of course it'll take a while, but I believe as few as two kills might be sufficient.'

'I hope you can deliver on that promise,' Joachim said with a smirk. 'If not...'

He left it unsaid, but she knew what he was thinking. There were those amongst the Arbites who would love to adopt the functions of the assassins in addition to their own – and augment the considerable power of the Judges within the priesthood. And Joachim clearly felt that the assassins were not entirely to be trusted; as a secular arm they were a sharp but treacherous blade that might twist in the wielder's hand. Judit had not failed to notice that while she was aboard the flagship Joachim wore his black carapace of armour everywhere.

Inquisitor Rathman nodded at the scribe, who activated a recorder. 'Let it be entered,' he intoned, 'that on this day Assassin Judit Bjarnesdottir did avow that by action under her leadership she could bring the administration of the planet Hito into line with Imperial governance.' He looked at Judit knowingly, a lethal twinkle in his eyes; she suddenly felt a shaft of coldness run through her stomach. Yes, the inquisitor knew how to play off the bureaucracy against itself.

'Let it further be entered that with the power vested in us,' he added, 'that we hold her to her promise and instruct her to work in conjunction with Joachim Ahriman of the Adeptus Arbites to ensure that the rule of this planet passes into our hands within thirty standard days.

'In the name of the Emperor, let it be so.'

WHEN TENZIG RETURNED to his cell after his meeting with the abbot, he spent an unquiet night worrying about the task

which he had been set. Brother abbot had been firm: word of
the proceedings of the meeting must not travel any further.
Secrecy was essential. As the junior member of the order present, execution of the task must devolve on him; it was an
awesome responsibility.

He lay, staring at the ceiling, and remembered the abbot's
words.

As master of the Order of the Heavenly Virtues, the abbot
was wise in the ways of the world, just as the master of the
secret arts was educated in the dark sciences of death.

'They come from far away, but we must not assume that they
are naïve about the sources of power. They will seek us out and
try to manipulate the order, to use us as a tool with which to
control the warriors. They will try to make it look attractive to
us... for they know of our library, do they not?'

How could they not know, Tenzig had thought? The order's
cunning artefacts were everywhere, beyond hiding in the possession of the selfish nobles.

'So,' the abbot had continued inexorably, 'something will be
done. They must be led to believe what they want to – that we
will do as they wish. They will not believe that if they understand our strengths as well as they understand our weakness.
And so–' he smiled wolfishly– 'we must conceal our strength.
It falls to one of us to stem their representatives' investigations
at the source. One of us adept in the secret arts. Tenzig, you will
meet with the Imperials. You will be presented to them as the
most august personage of the abbey. The master of the secret
arts will be with you; the day of his liberation from pain draws
near, and it is better that he should die proudly than by the
wasting sickness. And then you will do what you have been
trained to do.'

Lying sleeplessly on his cot, Tenzig seemed to sense his entire
life at his fingertips. It was a painful feeling, coming to terms
with the embarrassments and grief of a life which had been – if
not harsh – at least full of unasked-for surprises. From the farm
of his father to the monastery, by way of bloody turmoil during
the War of the Marching Sevens, only to find that in this time of
peace there was no call for those who wished to rise.Long life
and prosperity meant that there were no vacancies for the rank
of master, a rank to which he aspired, for it would put his ambition to rest.

But this was not the holy mission for which he had purified his soul, he reminded himself. This was apocalypse; the future status of the world might rest on his shoulders. Too strong a resistance would bring the wrath of the Imperium down on the shoulders of the people, while too easy an acquiescence would invite tyranny. Responsibility for the secrets of his order was a grey curse, weighing down heavily on his soul until he felt as if the very foundations of his mind were creaking with protest.

Eventually he drifted into a troubled sleep, from which he was awakened by the thunder of the morning drums. He opened the shutters over his window to the same pearlescent glow they had closed on, the night before – it was never truly dark on Hito, cloud-shrouded from a million suns. And then he offered prayers for guidance. It was going to be a long day...

THE SHUTTLE CIRCLED the walls of the monastery before it landed, by arrangement, in the valley. Judit watched impassively as Joachim brought it in smoothly, almost contemptuously. The savages – as he insisted on calling them – showed no sign of running in terror; evidently they had been warned, at the very least.

'The list,' Judit told him. Grunting, he powered down the drive unit and released the loading bay door. Unthinkably high above the clouds, the fleet was waiting; but down here there was no sign of it. The isolation was complete.

Followed by the judge, she made her way down to the bay. The crawler was already powered up. She climbed into the driver's compartment, followed by Joachim, and the doors latched behind them.

'You told Sanjit what to do?' she asked, barely expecting confirmation as the engines of the vehicle roared their power behind her.

'I did,' Joachim said amenably enough. 'She agreed. Two of us should be enough.'

'And for your part...?' She paused delicately.

Joachim snorted. 'For my part, I won't sneer at them to their faces, or curse them. So this abbot person–'

'The abbot,' she said with marked self-restraint, 'is possibly the most powerful person on the planet. You know what it is within our power to offer him? Imperial justice is only called for if he defies us.'

Joachim's hands, sheathed in slick black gloves, flexed as if at a throat. Good, she thought. Just as long as your prejudices continue to blind you; just as long as you don't ask any more questions about the ignorant natives...

'So are we agreed? We don't want to kill him arbitrarily. We merely wish to instil an... appropriate attitude among the natives.'

Joachim laughed coarsely. 'You should have been a diplomat,' he said. 'The famous black widow...'

And you, she thought venomously, as she steered the crawler towards the tall walls of the monastery, will make a beautiful corpse!

The gate-captain stared down from the walls of the monastery at the vehicle that was approaching; his eyes narrowed, as if he was ranging it. His smile was not a pleasant one. People who came to the order flaunting their power usually left it in small pieces. The holiest shrine of the most powerful sect on the planet was not to be treated lightly.

Below him, the vast gates slid open on their runners, teams of sweating slaves pushing them out of the path of the crawler. It rolled forwards smoothly, drifting to a halt within the outer wall. Similar meetings were taking place at four other cities around the continent, to conceal the singularity of this particular one. The gate-captain stared down at the metal carapace, then slapped the tympanum beside him; rushing to avoid the lash, the slaves began to slide the doors shut again.

'THE WALLS,' JUDIT murmured, 'they're quite thick. Not just ceremonial. Suppose people hereabouts have a different attitude to the priesthood?'

Joachim snorted. 'From what? Priests are priests. Commoners don't mess with them, whatever. If there's anything I've ever learned, that's it. Why mess around?'

Judit bit back her reply and glanced at him slyly. Yes, but these priests are no servants of the Emperor. They have knowledge that is priceless by the standards of their world. So why are they left alone? If Joachim couldn't figure it out, she wasn't going to help him.

She set the crawler brakes and left the power on standby. Not that they'd have much chance of making a quick getaway; she'd seen the power-bows on the walls, and the automatic rifles.

Symptoms of a tech incursion. Joachim cracked the hatch and lowered the ramp; and out they stepped, onto alien soil.

A party of black-robed men was approaching them, their faces almost chalky-white beneath their cowls. Junior clerics swinging censers preceded them, aromatic smoke falling gently in the still air. It was humid but cool, as if they stood on clouds. Judit waited just ahead of Joachim to greet them, keeping her hands concealed in her cloak. She bit the inside of her cheek, feeling the familiar excitement: the rush of action. Every nerve on fire as her syn-skin sensed her mood and responded to it, interfacing with her nervous system and feeding her amplified senses with data.

The monks stopped just before they reached the crawler and stood there expectantly. 'Greetings,' Judit said in the native tongue, surprised at the ease with which the words came – earlier, she had donned a hypno-casque in order to learn the local language. 'I am the Imperial representative. I have come to speak to your abbot, as agreed with our earlier contact.'

The monks seemed slightly confused by the presence of a female. Presently one of them spoke. 'Where is the one who came to us before?' he asked in a clear, high voice.

'He was a messenger of low importance,' said Judit. 'I am an Imperial diplomat, and it is my honour to talk to your leaders.'

The monk nodded. 'We are in turn honoured by your estimable presence,' he said mellifluously. 'If you would be pleased to come this way...'

Judit moved in the direction indicated. Joachim followed her, his eyes roving contemptuously over the natives. None of the monks were armed – but that meant nothing. She felt her hair twitching at the thought of it. Monks with guns could only mean trouble. Monks without guns could mean anything.

The inner wall, unlike the outer, had no large doors. Instead, a third of the way around the walls from where the crawler had entered, the monks led her to a small portal. As she passed within she noted that it was of hardwood bound in iron, and it was thick, but nothing like as thick as the walls. She glanced up, and her boosted vision noted the narrow slits in the ceiling. Monastery, hell, she thought, this is a fortress!

Joachim was becoming increasingly twitchy. This was the first mission he had gone along on without massive fire support. Good, she thought. Maybe for once you'll see what it's like to do an honest day of work... It gave her a warm glow of triumph to see him discomfited.

They passed out of the inner wall of the monastery and came into a vast open space in the shape of a pentagonal figure. At each corner tall towers reared high into the sky, and yet there was a squat solidity to them that screamed fortification. In the distance, Judit could see monks going about their daily business; the party she was in the midst of seemed to attract no particular attention.

'How much further have we to go?' she asked. The monk with the high-pitched voice looked at her curiously, but censored his reply.

'Not far,' he said. 'The abbot will receive you in the white tower yonder.' He pointed out to her the tallest, most massive tower in the complex; it tapered to a needle-like spire, yet it possessed no windows less than ten metres from the ground.

They proceeded in silence to the foot of the tower. At this point, the censer-bearers stopped; they turned as one to face the east, and raised their voices in a strange chant. Joachim reached out and gripped Judit's arm. 'What's that?' he whispered.

'I don't know.' She shook off his hand in irritation. 'Some ritual. The star rises in that direction on this world, doesn't it? Even if they never see it.' Joachim nodded imperceptibly and stood, listening, while Judit's mind ran in overdrive.

Presently the door at the foot of the tower swung open on a hallway lit by torchlight. 'You may enter now,' said the monk. 'We are forbidden from the tower.' Judit looked at him askance, but no further guidance was coming: his face was a shut book. She stepped forward, and entered the belly of the beast.

Within the tower the evidence of siege readiness was, if anything, greater than without. Even Joachim must be noticing this, she realized. The man who thought that the ideal defence was a strike force of Space Marines and a sterilized planet at the other end, no matter how delicate the prize to be won. Paper and bombs! Which of these narrow steps were mounted on concealed pivots? What of the polished, creaking floor? She felt a creeping admiration for whoever had designed this tower. You could lose an army in a frontal assault on this heap, unless you stood back and bombed it out. The opener of the door beckoned them in silently, then led them up the treacherous steps in perfect safety.

On the landing at the top of the second flight of stairs the monk paused and rapped twice on a sliding door. It slid open with a hiss of well-greased runners, and he bowed deeply before turning to descend the stairs. 'You may enter,' said a voice from within. Joachim caught Judit's eye and nodded imperceptibly. All right. He knows what to do. Contented and ready, she stepped across the threshold.

TENZIG LOOKED UP, breathing in shallow, controlled sips to calm his racing heart. He straightened in his chair. 'You may enter,' he called, as authoritatively as he could. Standing by his side, the master of the secret arts nodded approvingly, then froze into stillness.

Tenzig sweated in the heavy, embroidered robes that had been prepared to impress the ambassadors, trying to look dignified. There were two of them; the minimum requisite number for the display, should it be necessary. And here they came.

The diplomats entered. With a nervous flop of his heart, Tenzig thought: why, one of them is a woman! That was not something to which he was accustomed – not something he worried about unduly however, celibacy being no part of a Hitonian monk's vows. They were both dressed from head to foot in a tight, form-fitting black garment that glistened like oil on water; and above that, a cloak and boots and other accoutrements of an exotic nature. She, the leader, was nondescript, short-haired, instantly forgettable; unlike her companion, who affected a bush of flaming red hair, and a face of brutal demeanour. That one is meant to look like the warrior, Tenzig thought, instantly deciding to concentrate on the woman.

The master opened his lips. 'The brother abbot will receive you now if you should speak your rank and praenomen,' he said stiffly. Tenzig sat attentively, fingers clenched within his deep, long sleeves.

The woman spoke, lightly and intelligibly. 'I am Judit Bjarnesdottir, diplomat of the Adeptus Terra and aide to Inquisitor Rathman, head of the Imperial expedition to this cluster. This is Joachim Ahriman, an Imperial judge. I bring you greetings in the name of the Imperium, and in the name of Inquisitor Rathman who wishes me to express his sincerest wishes for peace and understanding between us.'

Tenzig kept a straight face. Stripped of the diplomatic argot, the meaning was as cold and simple as a naked blade. Imperial expedition. Peace and understanding. There was understanding, all right.

'Thank you kindly for your greetings. May I, too, express my sincere desire for peace and understanding between the Order of the Heavenly Virtues and your Imperium. However, the order being of a purely religious nature, I am filled with some curiosity as to why you might bring greetings from a secular institution to a humble monk such as myself?' And now the confirmation. The fingertips of his left hand fiddled inconspicuously with his sleeve, and he felt the presence of the master beside him, as tense as a coiled spring.

Waiting to unwind in his one, eternal moment of enlightenment.

The female diplomat smiled humourlessly, without showing her teeth.

'There is no need for confusion, I assure you,' she said. 'Shall we dispense with the formalities?'

Very abrupt, Tenzig thought disapprovingly. Is that what we must look forward to in future? No matter. 'Certainly,' he said easily, 'by all means let us be brief. I ask again: why have you come here to trouble us for our attention?'

'You possess a library,' she said flatly. 'We know this. We wish to examine it. Such libraries give the owners great power. You control the supply of certain artefacts to the warlords of this world; you, not they, are important. The Imperium needs such libraries. It will not be desecrated or destroyed – but it will be necessary for Imperial scribes to enter and copy all your records for the archives of Terra.'

Her eyes were calculating, quizzical. If that's the worst she has in store for us, Tenzig thought, may whatever gods there are save us! 'Ah,' he said, extemporising hastily. 'You ask for much, I must warn you. What can we expect of your Imperium in return?'

The Imperial judge stared at him condescendingly. 'Ask not what the Imperium does for you,' he said, 'but what you can do for the Imperium. Do you not know that your very souls depend upon it? That without the divine Emperor the hordes of warp space would be upon you in an instant, bringing savagery and insanity in their wake?'

The master focused on the judge like a living gun. It will be him, thought Tenzig, the hard man, here to play against her diplomacy. Expendable. I wonder if he is aware of it?

The woman spoke up hastily, covering for her companion's outburst. 'Your Holiness, we prefer not to take, but to have given voluntarily. I stand before you unarmed–' at this the master stiffened even more, if that were possible – 'but bearing a warning. We are prepared to be merciful. In return for your cooperation, you shall be made lords of all that you survey; this expedition has other planets to attend to, and Inquisitor Rathman would be more than gratified to leave the maintenance of this world in your caring hands. I beg you, while you have the opportunity, cooperate! We have the power to destroy you in an instant...'

The judge snorted, his eyes narrowing as he focused on the master, searching for some hidden threat.

Tenzig breathed deeply, carefully. That is the dangerous one, he realised. The woman will negotiate, but that one is a fanatic... 'Is that your final word?' he asked, wondering when the master would act. 'Because if, so, I must–'

It seemed to happen in slow motion. As Judit opened her mouth, the master was already moving with the grace of a striking cobra. The disc of shining steel flickered as it left his fingertips, and it was still spinning as he lunged forwards, the rod in his hands a dark promise of pain and death.

The shuriken caught Joachim full in the neck, laying open his aorta in a great gout of blood. He spasmed, the small pistol dropping from his fingers, even as the master altered course towards Judit. That was a mistake.

Her expression never changed as she raised her left index finger – but a pulse of blue light flashed from her ring, and she had merely to step aside from the corpse as it crashed to her feet.

The digital pistol was pointed squarely at Tenzig's abdomen. He stared at it. 'It would be very foolish of you to use that,' he said mildly.

The master lay on the floor; a dark stain was already edging out from beneath Joachim's corpse.

'I know,' said the woman. 'What guarantee of safe conduct can you give me?'

Tenzig felt release at the knowledge that he was not yet destined to die. 'You're no diplomat,' he accused.

'And you,' she smiled, 'are no monk.'

'Oh yes, I am a monk – but perhaps they do things differently in the Imperium.'

They locked eyes squarely. Her gaze was like looking into a mirror. Death in the morning. You must have wanted that one dead quite badly, he thought. You could have saved him!

'An assassin is a kind of diplomat,' Judit said dryly. 'So is a judge. It was up to you to decide which of us you would negotiate with. But I would like to know what kind of monks you are, before I commit myself to anything.'

Tenzig folded his hands in his lap, very slowly. 'Once upon a time,' he said, 'there was a peaceful colony, founded by a breakaway sect from old Terra. It existed in stasis for millennia, a duplicate of a long-dead civilisation. The tech wisdom was given into the hands of the monks for safe keeping… and then came the wars. And the disappearance of the stars, and the coming of madness.'

Judit nodded slowly. 'The STC source was valuable. You had to learn to defend it. You had to fight, use influence, kill those nobles who would–'

'What's an STC source?' Tenzig asked, feigning puzzlement.

Judit chewed her lower lip, watching him intently. After a long time, she said, 'Never mind. Your archives are valuable, then. No?'

'That is correct. Our historical archives are incomplete, but no one else on this world can equal them. There was a sect of old Terra, millennia before our ancestors boarded the starships that brought them here.' The words tripped off his tongue with barely a hint of deception. 'And their descendants, the followers of the heavenly virtues–' and of the secret way. 'What we know, we inherited from them; not just tech, but our ways. And so…' He spread his arms.

Judit nodded again. 'Very good. If we can verify that nothing evil exists in your archives, we may leave you to your works; but first…' She paused.

'Yes?'

'There is still the matter of planetary governance,' she added. 'I was not exceeding my ambit when I offered you the rule of this world. Whatever he may have thought you fit for.' She nudged the corpse by her side with a black-shod toe. 'Your order appears to be able to enforce its desires…'

For a long instant, the world seemed to stand still in reverence. Tenzig heard the hammering of his own heart loud in his ears, a haunting from beyond the past. An offer of supreme power; security for the order, which by serving the Imperium might be ignored by it.

He looked at the slightly-built woman, and seemed to see through her to a time when things had been different; an age when absolutes were not on offer, an age more in keeping with the philosophy of the order, of the holy prophet who had stayed among men and preached of fate and the eternal cycle of being, and who had achieved enlightenment. Finally he nodded.

'On behalf of my order, I am constrained to accept this offer. If you carry the necessary documents, you are free to leave alive. I regret–' his eyes swept the floor– 'the necessity of this show of force.'

'Don't worry,' Judit grinned humourlessly. 'It was a necessary formality. We cannot afford to leave planets in the hands of weaklings.'

Yes, I understand, Tenzig thought. 'You wish to see the library, then?' he asked.

She nodded. 'That was what I came here for,' she said. 'To see it intact. Bombardment can make rather a mess of a planet. Take me there.'

'This way, then.' Tenzig stood, stiffly, and ushered her to the door. Together they descended the stairs, all the way to the basement.

'Here lie records saved in ages past,' said Tenzig, pausing at the great wooden doors. Producing a key, he turned it in the lock and pulled, heart thundering behind his ribs.

'Lights,' said Judit tersely.

'Here,' Tenzig touched a switch, rubbed the dimple in the plastic that was worn smooth by ages of fingers. A warm glow flooded the corridor and the stacks of lovingly-catalogued scrolls that covered the walls. He stepped inside.

'Do you see?' he asked, questioningly. 'Do you see the source of our power?'

Judit nodded. 'Indeed,' she said. For here was wealth indeed, and power beyond the dreams of a barbarian warlord. 'We shall have to arrange for scribes to visit you,' she added, 'but this certainly confirms my offer to you.'

So this is why you came and negotiated, instead of dictating to us from above, he realized. A strange form of taxation, indeed...

He watched as she brought out the creamy parchment of the draft treaty, embossed with the Imperial seal, and held it before him so that he might see.

'And let us hope that this is the start of a great era in the history of your world!'

LATER, AFTER THE assassin had returned to her ship in the sky.

'And the master,' the abbot said thoughtfully. 'Do you believe he misinterpreted their response?'

Tenzig – now Master Tenzig – shook his head. 'Not exactly,' he said. 'More accurately, he understood all too well what their response would be. They are a hard people; some display of force was inevitable, really. A balanced response.'

'Yes,' said the abbot presently, 'then the reverend master fulfilled his duty. And you, Tenzig, have done your part.'

Tenzig bowed his head. 'But they will return. And next time it might be my calling to defend the order with my life. '

'Perhaps,' the abbot said. Then he smiled. 'But their ignorance of us has been increased to a safer level. You left them believing that the paper archives were our only source of wisdom.'

The abbot's words seemed to hang in the air, even after he pressed the button in his pocket to trigger the teleport link to the chamber beneath the scriptorium, where the ancient, unimaginably sophisticated machines of the STC library waited patiently.

UNFORGIVEN

Graham McNeill

THE MIDNIGHT DARK closed on Brother-Sergeant Kaelen of the Dark Angels like a fist. The emission-reduced engines of the rapidly disappearing Thunderhawk were the only points of light he could see. His visor swum into a ghostly green hue and the outlines of the star shaped city below became clear as his auto-senses kicked in.

The altimeter reading on his visor was unravelling like a lunatic countdown, the shapes below him resolving into clearer, oblong forms. The speed of his descent was difficult to judge, the powered armour insulating Kaelen from the sensations of icy rushing air and roaring noise as he plummeted downwards.

With a pulse of thought, Kaelen overlaid the tactical schematics of the city onto his visor, noting with professional pride that the outline of the buildings below almost perfectly matched the image projected before him.

The altimeter rune flashed red and Kaelen pulled out of his drop position, smoothly bringing his legs around so that he was falling feet first. Glancing left and right he saw the same manoeuvre being repeated by his men and slammed the firing mechanism on his chest. He felt the huge deceleration as the powerful rocket motors ignited, slowing his headlong plunge into a controlled descent.

Kaelen's boots slammed into the marble flagged plaza, his jump pack flaring a wash of heated air around him as he landed. Streams of bright light licked up from the city, flak waving like undersea fronds as the rebels sought to down the departing Thunderhawk. But the heretic gunners were too late to prevent the gunship from completing its mission; its deadly cargo had already arrived.

Kaelen whispered a prayer for the transport's crew and transferred his gaze back to the landing zone. Their drop was perfect, the Thunderhawk's jumpmaster had delivered them dead on target. A target that was thronged with screaming, masked cultists.

Kaelen ducked a clumsy swing of a cultist's power maul and punched his power fist through his enemy's chest, the man shrieking and convulsing as the energised gauntlet smashed though his flesh and bone. He kicked the corpse off his fist and smashed his pistol butt into the throat of another. The man fell, clutching his shattered larynx and Kaelen spared a hurried glance to check the rest of his squad had dropped safely with him.

Stuttering blasts of heat and light flared in the darkness as the remaining nine men in Squad Leuctra landed within five metres of him, firing their bolters and making short dashes for cover.

A cultist ran towards him swinging a giant axe, his features twisted in hatred. Kaelen shot him in the head. By the Lion, these fools just didn't stop coming! He ducked behind a giant marble statue of some nameless cardinal as a heavy burst of gunfire stitched its way towards him from the gigantic cathedral at the end the plaza. Muzzle flashes came through smashed stained glass windows, the bullets tearing up the marble in jagged splinters and cutting down cultists indiscriminately. Kaelen knew that advancing into the teeth of those guns would be bloody work indeed.

Another body ducked into cover with him, the dark green of his armour partially obscured by his chaplain's robes. Interrogator Chaplain Bareus raised his bolt pistol. The weapon's barrel was intricately tooled and its muzzle smoked with recent firing.

'Squad form on me!' ordered Kaelen, 'Prepare to assault! Evens advance, odds covering fire!'

A PROPHET HAD risen on the cathedral world of Valedor and with him came the planet's doom. Within a year of his first oration, the temples of the divine Emperor had been cast down and his faithful servants, from the highest cardinal to the lowliest scribes, were cast into the charnel fire-pits. Millions were purged and choking clouds of human ash fell as grotesque snow for months after.

The nearest Imperial Guard regiment, the 43rd Carpathian Rifles, had fought through the temple precincts for nine months since the planet's secession, battling in vicious close combat with the fanatical servants of the Prophet. The pacification had progressed well, but now ground to a halt before the walls of the planet's capital city, Angellicus. The heavily fortified cathedral city had withstood every assault, but now it was the turn of the Adeptus Astartes to bring the rebellion to an end. For the Space Marines of the Dark Angels chapter, more than just Imperial honour and retribution was at stake. Many centuries ago, Valedor had provided a clutch of fresh recruits for the chapter and the planet's heresy was a personal affront to the Dark Angels. Honour must be satisfied. The Prophet must die.

DOZENS OF CULTISTS were pitched backwards by the Space Marines' first volley, blood bright on their robes. More died as the bolters fired again. Kaelen exploded from cover, a laser blast scoring a groove in his shoulder plate. The first cultist to bar his path died without even seeing the blow that killed him. The next saw Kaelen bearing down on him and the Marine sergeant relished the look of terror on his face. His power fist took his head off.

Gunfire sounded, louder than before, as more covering fire raked the robed cultists. Kaelen fought and killed his way towards the temple doors, gore spattering his armour bright red. All around him, Squad Leuctra killed with a grim efficiency. Short dashes for cover combined with deadly accurate bolter fire had brought them to within eighty metres of the temple doors with no casualties. In their wake, more than two hundred cultists lay dead or dying.

Powerful blasts of gunfire spat from the smashed windows. Too heavy to charge through, even for power armour, knew Kaelen. He activated his vox-com.

'Brother Lucius.'

'Yes, brother-sergeant?'

'You have a good throwing arm on you. You think you can get a couple of grenades through those windows?'

Lucius risked a quick glance over the rim of the fountain he was using for cover and nodded curtly. 'Yes, brother-sergeant. I believe I can, the Lion willing.'

'Then do so,' ordered Kaelen. 'The Emperor guide your aim.'

Kaelen shifted position and spoke to the rest of his squad. 'Be ready. We move on the grenade's detonation.'

Each tiny rune on his visor that represented one of his men blinked once as they acknowledged receipt of the order. Kaelen glanced round to check that Chaplain Bareus was ready also. The hulking figure of the chaplain was methodically examining the dead cultists, pulling back their robes like a common looter. Kaelen's lip curled in distaste before he quickly reprimanded himself for such disloyalty. But what was the chaplain doing?

'Brother-chaplain?' called Kaelen.

Bareus looked up, his helmeted face betraying nothing of his intent.

'We are ready,' Kaelen finished.

'Brother-sergeant,' began Bareus, moving to squat beside Kaelen. 'When we find this prophet, we must not kill him. I wish him taken alive.'

'Alive? But our orders are to kill him.'

'Your orders have been changed, sergeant,' hissed the chaplain, his voice like cold flint. 'I want him alive. You understand?'

'Yes, brother-chaplain. I shall relay your orders.'

'We must expect heavy resistance within the temple. I will tell you now that I do not expect many, if any, of your men to survive,' advised Bareus, his voice laden with the promise of death.

'Why did you not brief me on this earlier?' snapped Kaelen. 'If the forces we are to face are so strong then we should hold here for now and call in support.'

'No,' stated Bareus. 'We do this alone or we die in the attempt.' His voice brooked no disagreement and Kaelen suddenly understood that there was more at stake with this mission than simple assassination. Regardless of the chaplain's true agenda, Kaelen was duty bound to obey.

He nodded, 'As you wish, chaplain.' He opened the vox-com to Lucius again. 'Now, Brother Lucius!'

Lucius stood, lithe as a jungle cat and powered a frag grenade through each of the windows either side of the cathedral doors. No sooner had the last grenade left his hand than the heavy blast of a lascannon disintegrated his torso. The heat of the laser blast flashed his super-oxygenated blood to a stinking red steam.

Twin thumps of detonation and screams. Flashing light and smoke poured from the cathedral windows like black tears.

'Now!' yelled Kaelen and the Marines rose from cover and sprinted towards the giant bronze doors. Scattered small arms fire impacted on their armour, but the Space Marines paid it no heed. To get inside was the only imperative.

Kaelen saw Brother Marius falter, a lucky shot blasting a chunk of armour and flesh from his upper thigh, staining the dark green of his armour bright red. Chaplain Bareus grabbed Marius as he staggered and dragged him on. Kaelen's powerful legs covered the distance to the temple in seconds and he flattened his back into the marble of the cathedral wall. Automatically, he snapped off a pair of grenades from his belt and hurled them through the smoking windows. The shockwave of detonation shook the cathedral doors and he vaulted through the shattered window frame, snapping shots left and right from his bolt pistol.

Inside was a blackened hell of smoke, blood and cooked flesh. Bodies lay sprawled, limbs torn off, skeletons pulverised and organs melted. The wounded gunners shrieked horribly.

Kaelen felt no pity for them. They were heretics and had betrayed the Emperor. They deserved a death a hundred times worse. The Dark Angels poured inside, moving into defensive positions, clearing the room and despatching the wounded. The vestibule was secure, but Kaelen's instincts told him that it wouldn't remain that way for long. Marius propped himself up against the walls. The bleeding had already stopped, the wound already sealed. He would fight on, Kaelen knew. It took more than a shattered pelvis to stop a Dark Angel.

'We have to keep moving,' he snapped. Movement meant life.

Chaplain Bareus nodded, reloading his pistol and turned to face Kaelen's squad.

'Brothers,' he began, 'we are now in the fight of our lives. Within this desecrated temple you shall see such sights as you have never witnessed in your darkest nightmares. Degradation and heresy now make their home in our beloved Emperor's vastness and you must shield your souls against it.'

Bareus lifted his chaplain's symbol of office, the crozius arcanum, high. The blood red gem at its centre sparkled like a miniature ruby sun. 'Remember our Primarch and the Lion shall watch over you!'

Kaelen muttered a brief prayer to the Emperor and they pressed on.

'THEY ARE WITHIN your sanctuary, my lord!' said Casta, worry plain in every syllable. 'What would you have us do to destroy them?'

'Nothing more than you are already, Casta.'

'Are you sure, lord? I do not doubt your wisdom, but they are the Adeptus Astartes. They will not give up easily.'

'I know. I am counting on it. Do you trust me, Casta?'

'Absolutely lord. Without question.'

'Then trust me now. I shall permit the Angel of Blades to kill all the Marines, but I want their chaplain.'

'It will be as you say, lord,' replied Casta turning to leave.

The Prophet nodded and rose from his prayers to his full, towering height. He turned quickly, exposing a sliver of dark green beneath his voluminous robes.

'And Casta...' he hissed. 'I want him alive.'

CHAPLAIN BAREUS SWUNG the crozius in a brutal arc, crushing bone and brain. Fighting their way along a reliquary studded cloister, the Marines fought against more followers of the Prophet.

The Dark Angels fought in pairs, each warrior protecting the other's back. Kaelen fought alongside Bareus, chopping and firing. The slide on the bolt pistol racked back empty. He slammed the butt of the pistol across his opponent's neck, shattering his spine.

Bareus slew his foes with a deadly grace, ducking, kicking and stabbing. The true genius of a warrior was to create space, to flow between the blades where skill and instinct merged in lethal harmony. Enemy weapons sailed past him and Kaelen knew that Bareus was a warrior born. Kaelen felt as clumsy as a new recruit next to the exquisite skill of the interrogator chaplain.

Brother Marius fell, a power maul smashing into his injured hip. Hands held him down and an axe split his skull in two. Yet even though his head had been destroyed, he shot his killer dead.

Then it was over. The last heretic fell, his blood spilt across the tiled floor. As Kaelen slammed a new magazine into his pistol, Bareus knelt beside the corpse of Brother Marius and intoned the Prayer for the Fallen.

'You will be avenged, brother. Your sacrifice has brought us closer to expunging the darkness of the past. I thank you for it.'

Kaelen frowned. What did the chaplain mean by that? Bareus stood and pulled out a data slate, displaying the floor plans of the cathedral. While the chaplain confirmed their location, Kaelen surveyed his surroundings in more detail.

The walls were dressed stone, the fine carvings hacked off and replaced with crude etchings depicting worlds destroyed, angels on fire and a recurring motif of a broken sword. And a dying lion. The rendering was crude, but the origins of the imagery was unmistakable.

'What is this place?' he asked aloud. 'This is our chapter's history on these walls. Lion El'Jonson, dead Caliban. The heretics daub their halls with mockeries of our past.'

He turned to Bareus. 'Why?'

Bareus looked up from the data slate. Before he could answer, roaring gunfire hammered through the cloisters. Brother Caiyne and Brother Guias fell, heavy calibre shells tearing through their breastplates and exploding within their chest cavities. Brother Septimus staggered, most of his shoulder torn away by a glancing hit, his arm hanging by gory threads of bone and sinew. He fired back with his good arm until another shot took his head off.

Kaelen snapped off a flurry of shots, diving into the cover of a fluted pillar. The concealed guns were pinning them in position and it would only be a matter of time until more cultists were sent against them. As if in answer to his thoughts, a studded timber door at the end of the cloister burst open and a

mob of screaming warriors charged towards them. Kaelen's jaw
hung open in disgust at the sight of the enemy.

They were clad in dark green mockeries of power armour, an
abominable mirror of the Space Marines' glory. Crude copies of
the Dark Angels' chapter symbol, spread wings with a dagger
through the centre, adorned their shoulder plates and Kaelen
felt a terrible rage build in him at this heresy.

The Marines of Squad Leuctra screamed their battle cry and
surged forward to tear these blasphemers apart and punish
them for such effrontery. To mock the Dark Angels was to invite
savage and terrible retribution. Fuelled by righteous anger,
Squad Leuctra fought with savage skill. Blood, death and
screams filled the air.

As the foes met in the centre of the cloister, the hidden guns
opened fire again.

A storm of bullets and ricochets, cracked armour and smoke
engulfed the combatants, striking Space Marines and their foes
indiscriminately. A shell tore downwards through the side of
Kaelen's helmet. Redness, pain and metallic stink filled his
senses, driving him to his knees. He gasped and hit the release
catch of his ruined helmet, wrenching it clear. The bullet had
torn a bloody furrow in the side of his head and blasted the
back of the helmet clear. But he was alive. The Emperor and the
Lion had spared him.

A booted foot thundered into the side of his head. He rolled,
lashing out with his power fist and a cultist fell screaming, his
leg destroyed below the knee. He pushed himself to his feet
and lashed out again, blood splashing his face as another foe
died. Kaelen sprinted for the cover of the cloister, realising they
had been lured out of cover by the fraudulent Dark Angels. He
cursed his lack of detachment, angrily wiping sticky redness
from his eyes.

The tactical situation was clear, they could not go back the
way they had come. To reach the main vestibule was not an
option; the gunfire would shred them before they got halfway.
The only option was onwards and Kaelen had a gnawing suspicion that their enemies knew this and were channelling them
towards something even more fearsome.

Bareus shouted his name over the stuttering blasts of shoot-
ing, indicating the timber door the armoured cultists had
emerged from.

'I believe we have only one way out of this. Forwards, sergeant!'

Kaelen nodded, his face grim as the icon representing Brother Christos winked out. Another Space Marine dead for this mission. But Kaelen knew that they would all lay down their lives for the mission, no matter what it was. Chaplain Bareus had decided that it was worth all of them dying to achieve it and that was good enough for him.

Under cover of the cloisters, Bareus and the remaining five members of Squad Leuctra sprinted through the studded door that led out of this firetrap. Sergeant Kaelen just hoped that they weren't running into something worse.

'IS THE ANGEL ready to administer the Evisceral Blessing, Casta?' inquired the Prophet.

'It is my lord,' said Casta, his voice trembling with fear. The Prophet smiled, understanding the cause of his underling's unease.

'The Angel of Blades makes you uncomfortable, Casta?'

Casta fidgeted nervously, his bald head beaded with sweat. 'It frightens me, my lord. I fear that we count such a thing as our ally. It slaughtered ten of my acolytes as we released it from the crypts. It was horrible.'

'Horrible, Casta?' soothed the Prophet, placing both hands on the priest's shoulders, his gauntlets large enough to crush Casta's head. 'Was it any more horrible than what we did to take this world? Was it bloodier than the things we did when we stormed this temple? There is already blood on your hands, Casta, what matters a little more? Is what we do here not worthy of some spilt blood?'

'I know, but to actually see it, to taste and smell it... it was terrible!' The priest was shaking now. The memory of the Angel had unmanned him completely.

'I know, Casta, I know,' acknowledged the Prophet. 'But all great things must first wear terrible masks in order that they may inscribe themselves on the mind of the common man.'

The Prophet shook his head sadly, 'It is the way of things.'

Casta nodded slowly, 'Yes, my lord. I understand.'

The Prophet said, 'We bring a new age of reason to this galaxy. The fire we begin here will ignite a thousand others that will engulf the False Emperor's realm in the flames of revolution. We shall be remembered as heroes, Casta. Do not forget that. Your name shall shine amongst men as the brightest star in the firmament.'

Casta smiled, his vanity and ego overcoming his momentary squeamishness. Fresh determination shone in his zealous eyes.

The Prophet turned away.

It was almost too easy.

SERGEANT KAELEN STALKED the darkened corridors of the cathedral like a feral world predator, eyes constantly on the move, hunting his prey. Flickering electro-flambeaux cast a dim glow that threw the carved walls into stark relief and he deliberately averted his gaze from them. Looking too carefully at the images carved into the walls left his eyes stinging and a nauseous rolling sensation in the pit of his stomach.

Since leaving the death trap of the cloisters they had snaked deeper into the cathedral and Kaelen couldn't help but feel that they were in terrible danger. Not the danger of dying, Kaelen had stared death in the face too many times to fear extinction.

But the dangers of temptation and blasphemy... that was another matter entirely. The paths to damnation were many and varied, and Kaelen knew that evil did not always wear horns and breathe fire. For if it did, all men would surely turn from it in disgust. No, evil came subtly in the night, as pride, as lust, as envy.

In his youth, Kaelen had known such feelings, had fought against all the whispered seductions that flesh and the dark could offer in the dead of night, but he had prayed and fasted, secure in his faith in the Divine Emperor of Mankind. He had achieved a balance in his soul, a tempering of the beast within him.

He understood that there were those who gave into their base desires and turned their faces from the Emperor's light. For them there could be no mercy. They were deviants of the worst kind. They were an infection, spreading their lies and abomination to others, whose weakened faith was an open doorway to them. If such forces were at work within these walls, then Kaelen would fight till the last drop of blood had been squeezed from his body to root it out and destroy it.

Bareus led the way, his strides long and sure. The passageway they followed dipped slightly and Kaelen could feel a cool breath of night air caress his skin. The stone walls gave way to a smooth, blackened glass, opaque and blemish free, widening to nearly ten metres across. The walls curved up into a rounded arch above them and were totally non-reflective. Doors constructed of the same material barred the way forward, the susurration of air coming from where the glass had been cracked near the top of the frame. An ominous stain dripped down the inside face of the door from where a torn fragment of white cloth was caught, flapping in the breeze on a jagged shard of broken glass.

'Blood,' said Bareus.

Kaelen nodded. He had smelt it before seeing it. An odd whickering mechanical sound came from the other side of the doors and Kaelen felt an instinctive dread send a hot jolt of fear into his system. Bareus stepped forwards and thundered his boot into the door, smashing it completely from the frame. Black glass flew outwards and Kaelen swept through the portal, bolter and power fist at the ready.

Kaelen entered a domed arena, its stone floor awash with blood and sliced chunks of flesh. The stink of the charnel house filled the air. The same non-reflective black substance that had formed the door enclosed the arena. He pounded down some steps and skidded to a halt, his blood thundering in horror at the sight before him.

A mad screaming echoed around the enclosed arena. A dome of utter darkness rose above them as the horrifying bulk of the creature before the Space Marines turned to face them with giant, slashing strides. Perhaps it had once been a dreadnought. Perhaps it had evolved or mutated in some vile parody of a dreadnought. But whatever it was now, it was clearly a beast of pure evil. Even Bareus, who had fought monstrous abominations before, was shocked at the terrifying appearance of the bio-mechanical killing machine. Fully six metres high, the creature stood on four splayed, spider-like legs of scything blades, that cut the air with a deadly grace. A massive, mechanically muscled torso rose from the centre of the bladed legs and clawed arms, lightning sheathed, swung insanely from its shoulders, upon which was mounted an ornately carved heavy bolter. At its back, a pair of glittering, bladed wings flapped noisily, their lethal edges promising death to any who came near.

The bio-machine's head was a pulped mass of horribly disfigured flesh. Multiple eyes, milky and distended, protruded from enlarged and warped sockets. Its vicious gash of a slobbering mouth was filled with hundreds of serrated, chisel-like teeth and its skin was a grotesque, oily texture – the colour of rotten meat.

It was impossible to tell where the man ended and the machine began.

Its entire body was soaked in blood, gobbets of torn flesh still hanging from its claws and teeth. But the final horror, the most sickening thing of all was that where the metal of the dreadnought's hide was still visible, it was coloured an all too familiar shade of dark green.

And upon its shoulder was the symbol of the Dark Angels.

Whatever this creature was, it had once been a brother Space Marine.

Now it was the Angel of Blades and as the Space Marines recoiled in horror, the monster howled in mad triumph and stamped forwards on its scythe legs.

The speed of the Angel of Blades was astonishing for such a huge creature. Blood burst from its face as the Space Marines overcame their shock and began firing their bolters. Every shell found its mark, detonating wetly within the Angel's dead skin mask, but its lunatic screams continued unabated.

A silver blur lashed from the monster A casual flick of its bladed leg licked out and eviscerated Brother Mellius quicker than the eye could follow. His shorn halves collapsed in a flood of red, but his bellows of pain were drowned by the Angel's hateful shrieks. The baroque heavy bolter mounted on the beast's shoulder roared and blasted the remains of Mellius apart.

Kaelen knew it had to die. Now.

He sprinted across the courtyard as the rest of his squad spread out and leapt in front of the rampaging machine, a brilliant burst of blue-white lightning arcing from his power fist as he struck at the beast's face. A coruscating corona of burning fire enveloped its huge frame as the lethal power of Kaelen's gauntlet smashed home. Its deformed flesh blistered and sloughed from its face, exposing a twisted metallic bone structure beneath. The Angel struck back, unheeding of the terrible hurt done to it.

Kaelen dodged a swipe meant to remove his head and rolled beneath its flailing arms. He powered his crackling fist into its groin and ripped upwards.

The power fist scored deep grooves in the Angel's exterior, but Kaelen's strike failed to penetrate its armoured shell. The beast side-stepped and another leg slashed out at him. He ducked back, not quick enough, and the armoured knee joint thundered into his chest, hurling him backwards.

Kaelen's breastplate cracked wide open, crushing his ribs and shattering the Imperial eagle on his chest into a million fragments. Bright lights exploded before his eyes as he fought for breath and struggled to rise, reeling from the massive impact. Even as he fell, he knew he had been lucky. Had the cutting edge struck him, he would now be as dead as Mellius. Heavy bolter shells spat from the shoulder-mounted gun, hammering into his legs and belly, driving him to his knees.

One shell managed to penetrate the cracks in his armour and he screamed, white hot fire bathing his nerves as the shell blasted a fist-sized hole in his hip, blood washing in a river down his thigh. He fell to the ground as the Angel loomed above him, its bloody claws poised to deliver the death blow and tear Kaelen in two.

With a howling battle cry, Chaplain Bareus and the surviving members of Squad Leuctra rushed to attack the monstrosity from the flanks and rear. Brother Janus died instantly, decapitated by a huge sweep of the creature's claws. Another leg whipped out, impaling his corpse and lifting him high into the air. Brother Temion leapt upon the thing from behind, holding his sword in a reverse grip and driving it into the Angel's back with a yell of triumph. The monster screamed and bucked madly, casting the brave Space Marine from its back. Its wings glittered in the torchlight and powered wide with a ringing clash of metal. A discordant shriek of steel on steel sounded as the Angel's wings slashed the air and a storm of razor edged feathers flew from the beast's back and engulfed Temion as he raised his bolter. He had no time to scream as the whirlwind of blades slashed through him and tore his body to shreds. The bloody chunks of flesh and armour that fell to the ground were no longer recognisable as human.

Bareus smashed his crozius arcanum against the back of one of the Angel's knee joints, ducking a swipe of the beast's razor wings. Brother Urient and Brother Persus hammered the huge machine from the front while Kaelen pushed himself unsteadily to his feet.

Urient died as the Angel caught him with both sets of claws, ripping his body apart and tossing the pieces aside in contempt. The beast staggered as Bareus finally chopped through the silver steel of its leg. It tried to turn and slash at its diminutive assailant, but staggered as the severed leg joint collapsed under its weight. The huge arms spun as it fought for balance. Kaelen and Bareus were quick to press home their advantage.

Kaelen smashed his power fist into the monstrosity's mutated face, the huge gauntlet obliterating its features and tearing through its armoured sarcophagus. Kaelen kept pushing deeper and deeper inside the heart of the monster's body. The stench gusting from the rotted interior was the odour of a week old corpse. His fist closed around something greasy and horribly organic and the Angel shuddered in agony, lifting Kaelen from the ground. He grasped onto the beast's shell with his free hand, still struggling to tear the beast's heart out. Agony coursed through his body as the Angel's limbs spasmed on his wounded hip and chest. Kaelen's grip slid inside the Angel's body, glistening amniotic fluids pouring over his arm and preventing him from slaying the vile creature that lurked within its body. His grip finally found purchase. A writhing, pulsing thing with a grotesque peristaltic motion. He closed his fist on the fleshy substance of the monstrosity's heart and screamed as he released a burst of power within the bio-machine's shell.

The monster convulsed as the deadly energies of the power fist whiplashed inside its shell, blue fire geysering from its exhausts. Its legs wobbled and the massive beast collapsed, sliding slowly to its knees. A stinking black gore gushed from every joint and its daemonic wailing dimmed and at last fell silent. Kaelen wrenched clear his gauntlet, a grimace of pain and revulsion contorting his features as the lifeless Angel of Blades toppled forwards, a mangled heap of foetid meat and metal.

Kaelen slid down the Angel's shell and collapsed next to the foul creature, blood loss, shock and pain robbing him of his prodigious strength. Breathless, Chaplain Bareus grabbed Kaelen's arm and helped him to his feet. Brother Persus joined him, his dark green armour stained black with the monster's death fluids.

The three Dark Angels stood by the rotted corpse and tried to imagine how such a thing could possibly exist. Kaelen limped towards the remains of the beast and stared at the shattered carapace of the Angel's shell. The iconography on the sarcophagus was of a winged figure in a green robe carrying a scythe, its face shrouded in the darkness of its hood. Fluted scrollwork below the image on its chest bore a single word, partially obscured by black, oily blood. Kaelen reached down, wiping his hand across the carapace and felt as though his heart had been plucked from his chest. He sank to his knees as he stared at the word, willing it not to be true. But it remained the same, etched with an awful finality.

Caliban.

The Dark Angels' lost homeworld. Destroyed in the Great Heresy thousands of years ago. How this thing could have come from such a holy place, Kaelen did not know. He rose and turned to Bareus.

'You knew about this, didn't you?' he asked.

The chaplain shook his head. 'About that abomination, no. That we would face one of our brothers turned to the Dark Powers... yes. I did.'

Kaelen's face twisted in a mixture of anger and disbelief, 'The Dark Powers? How can that be possible? It cannot be true!'

A voice from the shadows, silky and seductive said, 'I'm afraid that it is, sergeant.'

Kaelen, Bareus and Persus spun to see a tall, hugely built figure in flowing white robes emerge from the shadows accompanied by a stoop shouldered man with a shaven head. The tall figure wore his black hair short, close cropped into his skull and three gold studs glittered on his forehead. His handsome features were smiling wryly. Bareus swiftly drew his bolt pistol and fired off the entire clip at the robed figure. As each shot struck, a burst of light flared around the man, but he remained unharmed. Kaelen could see the faint outline of a rosarius beneath his robes. The small amulet would protect the Prophet from their weapons and Kaelen knew that such protection would be almost impossible to defeat. All around the arena the opaque glass walls began to sink into the ground and a score of armed men stepped through, their weapons aimed at the three Space Marines. Bareus dropped the empty bolt pistol and reluctantly Kaelen and Persus did likewise.

'How can it be true?' asked Kaelen again. 'And who are you?'

'It is very simple, sergeant. My name was Cephesus and once I was a Dark Angel like you. When your dead husk of an Emperor still walked amongst you, we were betrayed by Lion El'Jonson. He abandoned our chapter's true master, Luther, and left with the Emperor to conquer the galaxy. The Primarch left him to rot on a backwater planet while he vaingloriously took the honour of battle that should have been ours! How could he have expected us not to fight him on his return?'

Bareus stepped forwards and removed his helm, tossing it aside as he stared at the tall figure with undisguised hatred. He raised his crozius arcanum to point at the other's chest.

'I know you, Cephesus. I have read of you and I will add your name to the Book of Salvation. It was necessary for Luther to remain behind on Caliban. His was a position of great responsibility!'

'Necessity, chaplain, is the plea for every act of ignorance your Imperium perpetrates. It is the argument of tyrants and the creed of slaves,' snapped the Prophet. 'Wipe the virtue from your eyes, we were cast aside! Scattered throughout time and space to become the Fallen. And for that I will kill you.'

He nodded towards the dead monstrosity, his earlier composure reasserting itself and said, 'You killed the Angel of Blades. I am impressed.'

The Prophet smiled and parted his robes, allowing them to fall at his feet. Beneath them, he wore a suit of powered armour, ancient and painted unmistakably in the colours and icons of the Dark Angels. The ornate form of a rosarius, similar to the one worn by Bareus, hung on an ornate chain, nestling against the eagle on his breastplate. 'I was Cephesus, but that name no longer has any meaning for me. I foreswore it the day Lion El'Jonson betrayed us.'

'The Primarch saved us!' roared Bareus, his face contorted in fury. 'You dare to blaspheme against his blessed name?'

Cephesus shook his head slowly. 'You are deluded, chaplain. I think that it is time you start looking at yourself and judge the lie you live. You can project it back at me, but I am only what lives inside each and every one of you. I am a reflection of you all.'

Sneering, he descended the steps to stand before the interrogator chaplain, pulling a thin chain from a pouch around his waist. Attached along its length were several small polished blades, each inlaid with a fine tracery of gold wire. Bareus's eyes widened in shock and he reached for his hip scabbard, drawing an identical blade.

'You call these weapons Blades of Reason. Such an irony. It is as much a badge of office to you as your crozius, is it not? I have eleven here, each taken from the corpse of a Dark Angel chaplain. I will take yours and make it an even dozen.'

Without warning he snapped a blade from the chain and spun on his heel, slashing it across Persus's throat. The Space Marine sank to the ground, arterial blood bathing his breast-plate crimson.

Kaelen screamed and launched himself forwards, swinging his power fist at the Prophet's head. Cephesus swayed aside and smashed his bladed fist into Kaelen's ribs.

The neural wires inscribed in the blades shrieked fiery electric agony along Kaelen's nerves, and he howled as raw pain flooded every fibre in his body. His vision swam and he fell to the ground screaming, the blades still lodged in his side.

Bareus howled in fury and slashed with his crozius arcanum. Cephesus ducked and lunged in close, tearing the rosarius from around Bareus's neck. Silver and gold flashed; blood spurted. The chaplain fell to his knees, mouth open in mute horror as he felt his life blood pump from his ruined throat. He fell beside Kaelen and dropped his weapons beside the fallen sergeant.

Cephesus reached down and knelt beside the dying chaplain. He smiled indulgently and scooped up Bareus's intricate blade, threading the thin chain through its hilt.

'An even dozen. Thank you, chaplain,' hissed Cephesus.

Sergeant Kaelen gritted his teeth and fought to open his eyes. The Prophet's blades were lodged deep in his flesh. With a supreme effort of will, each tiny movement bringing a fresh spasm of agony, he reached down and dragged the weapon from his body. His vision cleared in time for him to see the Prophet leaning over Chaplain Bareus. He growled in anger and with strength born of desperation lunged forwards, throwing himself at the heretic.

Both hands outstretched, he slashed with the blades and tried to crush the Prophet's head with his power fist. But Cephesus was too quick and dodged back, but not before

Kaelen's hand closed about an ornate chain around his neck and tore it free. He rolled forwards, falling at the Prophet's feet and gasped in pain.

Cephesus laughed and addressed the men around the arena. 'You see? The might of the Adeptus Astartes lies broken at my feet! What can we not achieve when we can humble their might with such ease?'

Kaelen could feel the pain ebbing from his body and glanced down to see what lay in his hand and smiled viciously. He lifted his gaze to look up into the shining, mad face of the Prophet and with a roar of primal hatred, struck out at the traitor Dark Angel, his power fist crackling with lethal energies.

He felt as though time slowed. He could see everything in exquisite detail. Every face in the arena was trained on him, every gun. But none of that mattered now. All he could focus on was killing his foe. His vision tunnelled until all he could see was Cephesus's face, smugly contemptuous. His power fist connected squarely on the Prophet's chest and Kaelen had a fleeting instant of pure pleasure when he saw the heretic's expression suddenly change as he saw what the sergeant held aloft in his other hand.

Cephesus's chest disintegrated, his armour split wide open by the force of the powerful blow. Kaelen's power fist exploded from his back, shards of bone and blood spraying the arena's floor. Kaelen lifted the impaled Prophet high and shouted to the assembled cultists.

'Such is the fate of those who would defy the will of the immortal Emperor!'

He hurled the body of Cephesus, no more than blood soaked rags, to the ground and bellowed in painful triumph. Kaelen was a terrifying figure, drenched in blood and howling with battle lust. As he stood in the centre of the arena, the black glass walls rapidly began to rise and the armed men vanished from sight, their fragile courage broken by the death of their leader.

Kaelen slumped to the ground and opened his other fist, letting the rosarius he had inadvertently torn from around the Prophet's neck fall to the ground. A hand brushed his shoulder and he turned to see the gasping face of Chaplain Bareus. The man struggled to speak, but could only wheeze breathlessly. His hand scrabbled around his body, searching.

Guessing Bareus's intention, Kaelen picked up the fallen crozius arcanum and placed it gently into the chaplain's hand. Bareus coughed a mouthful of blood and shook his head. He opened Kaelen's fist, pressed the crozius into the sergeant's hand and pointed towards the corpse of the Fallen Dark Angel.

'Deathwing...' hissed Bareus with his last breath and closed his eyes as death claimed him.

Kaelen understood. The burden of responsibility had been passed to him now. He held the symbol of office of a Dark Angels chaplain and though he knew that there was much for him yet to learn, he had taken the first step along a dark path.

NEWS OF THE Prophet's death spread rapidly throughout Angellicus and within the hour, the rebel forces broadcast their unconditional surrender. Kaelen slowly retraced his steps through the cathedral precincts, using the vox-comm to call in the gunship that had delivered their assault. He limped into the main square, squinting against the bright light of the breaking morning. The Thunderhawk sat in the centre of the plaza, engines whining and the forward ramp lowered. As he approached the gunship, a lone Terminator in bone white armour descended the ramp to meet him.

Kaelen stopped before the Terminator and offered him the crozius and a thin chain of twelve blades.

Kaelen said, 'The name of Cephesus can now be added to the Book of Salvation.'

The Terminator took the proffered items and said, 'Who are you?'

Kaelen considered the question for a moment before replying.

'I am Deathwing,' he answered.

More Warhammer 40,000 from the Black Library

The Space Wolf novels
by William King

FROM THE DEATH-WORLD *of Fenris come the Space Wolves, the most savage of the Emperor's Space Marines. Follow the adventures of Ragnar, from his recruitment and training as he matures into a ferocious and deadly fighter, scourge of the enemies of humanity.*

SPACE WOLF

On the planet Fenris, young Ragnar is chosen to be inducted into the noble yet savage Space Wolves chapter. But with his ancient primal instincts unleashed by the implanting of the sacred canis helix, Ragnar must learn to control the beast within and fight for the greater good of the wolf pack.

RAGNAR'S CLAW

As young Blood Claws, Ragnar and his companions go on their first off-world mission – from the jungle hell of Galt to the pulluted hive-cities of hive world Venam, they must travel across the galaxy to face the very heart of evil.

More Warhammer 40,000 from the Black Library

The Gaunt's Ghosts series
by Dan Abnett

*IN THE NIGHTMARE future of Warhammer 40,000, mankind
teeters on the brink of extinction, beset on all sides by
relentless foes. Commissar Ibram Gaunt and his regiment the
Tanith First-and-Only must fight as much against the
inhuman enemies of mankind as survive the bitter internal
rivalries of the Imperial Guard.*

FIRST & ONLY

Gaunt and his men find themselves at the forefront of a fight to win
back control of a vital Imperial forge world from the forces of Chaos,
but find far more than they expected in the heart of the Chaos-infested
manufacturies.

GHOSTMAKER

Nicknamed the Ghosts, Commissar Gaunt's regiment of stealth troops
move from world from world, fighting for their very bodies and souls
against the forces of Chaos.

NECROPOLIS

On the shattered world of Verghast, Gaunt and his Ghosts find
themselves embroiled within an ancient and deadly civil war as a
mighty hive-city is besieged by an unrelenting foe.

HONOUR GUARD

As a mighty Chaos fleet approaches the shrine-world Hagia, a terrible
loss sends Gaunt and his men on a desperate race against time to
safeguard some of the Imperium's most holy relics.

More Warhammer 40,000 from the Black Library

ANTHOLOGIES

**In the far future of the 41st millennium,
the human race must battle for survival
amongst the stars.
Three great collections of tales from the
dark future of Warhammer 40,000.**

INTO THE MAELSTROM

Featuring stories by Barrington J Bayley, Jonathan Green,
Alex hammond, William King, Gav Thorpe and others.

DARK IMPERIUM

Featuring stories by Barrington J Bayley, Andy Chambers,
Ben Counter, William King, Gav Thorpe and others.

STATUS: DEADZONE

Tales from the savage hive-world of Necromunda

Featuring stories by Jonathan Green, Alex Hammond,
Gordon Rennie, Tully Summers and others.

INFERNO! is the indispensable guide to the worlds of Warhammer and Warhammer 40,000 and the cornerstone of the Black Library. Every issue is crammed full of action packed stories, comic strips and artwork from a growing network of awesome writers and artists including:

- William King
- Brian Craig
- Gav Thorpe

- Dan Abnett
- Barrington J. Bayley
- Gordon Rennie

and many more

Presented every two months, Inferno! magazine brings the Warhammer worlds to life in ways you never thought possible.

For subscription details ring:
US: 1-800-394-GAME
UK: (0115) 91 40000

For more information see our website:
http://www.blacklibrary.co.uk